DRAWN IN ONCE MORE...

Chelomeyev returned to his chair. "Rostoff has told me to close the files, but my gut tells me that there is something there. No one believes me, just like they never believe you."

Kazakov closed his eyes. "Your superior officer has told you to close the file."

"You say that now, but listen to the facts."

A rustle of fabric and Kazakov opened his eyes. Chelomeyev had produced two manila envelopes from inside his woolen greatcoat and slid the top envelope across the table to him.

For a moment he almost pushed it away. The lantern light gleamed beckoningly on his tumbler of vodka. Then he tipped the envelope contents onto the table. Police investigation evidence that should be in a police file, not here in his dacha. On top was a photo of a body splayed over strewn documents on a Bokhara carpet. Male. In his fifties, though he looked trim and fit. The body wore an expensive-looking blue suit and white shirt, both covered in blood, but what likely killed him was the gaping second mouth in his neck.

The man was clearly somebody.

"Messy," was all that Kazakov said.

MARESON'S ARROW

A DETECTIVE KAZAKOV MYSTERY BOOK 2

K.L. ABRAHAMSON

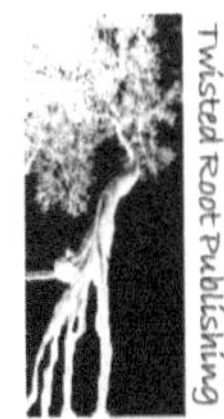

COPYRIGHT

❀ Created with Vellum

MARESON'S ARROW

A DETEKTIV KAZAKOV MYSTERY BOOK 2

K. L. Abrahamson

1

"*Deep in a forest filled with snow, an old couple lived. The snow was so deep that the old man could not hunt on his weak legs and so he and his wife would starve. As a result, the old couple decided to slaughter their mare to have food for the winter.*

"A raven at the window overheard their plan and flew to the stable to warn the mare. "You'd best break down your stall and jump the fence before the deed is done," the raven said.

"And so the mare did, escaping deep into the forest. She wandered for maybe a long time or maybe it was short, for who can say how far was far in those distant times. She came to a cloak thrown across the snow and found upon it a dead man of the east. She took a bite out of his right knee and then of his left and found herself pregnant.

"When the mare gave birth, she named her son Ivan Mareson. He grew into a handsome lad, and when he was old enough to be on his own, she told him to make himself a bow and arrow and every night stick the arrow into the earth. That way she would know that he was alive. If he did not stick the arrow into the earth, she would come looking for his bones."

. . .

Old Mrs. Ryabkov's words seemed to hum in the warm dacha air as she stopped her recitation of the old Russian folktale. She peered at New Moscow Police Detektiv Alexander Kazakov from the tops of her eyes across the worn wooden table her long-dead husband had made. Her bird eyes glittered in the light from the single candle between them and so did the half-empty bottle of vodka and the cracked edges of the old china bowls that had held their supper. Her old cabin's stone walls were lost in shadows. So were the cobwebs amongst the rafters of the low-ceilinged structure and the neatly made up narrow cot against the rear wall. Agafya Ryabkov's dacha was small, built like a part of the earth so that Agafya, her house, and her story seemed to have grown out of the dust and rock of this country. But instead of the usual dusty scent of the herbs drying amongst the rafters, the single, low-ceilinged room smelled of the warm scent of the *kutia* in their bowls. Kazakov had made the traditional Russian Christmas Eve honeyed porridge this afternoon, but the rich poppy seeds, berries, and nuts that he'd included seemed inappropriate to enjoy alone, so he'd brought it through the snow to her house. Oddly, he hadn't wanted to spend this evening alone even though he normally preferred to be on his own.

"Continue, please," he said to her, awaiting her spin on the miraculous tale of the mare's son who had wonderful adventures and who died and was raised from the dead many times. It was a story of resurrection that was near and dear to the hearts of the exiled Russian people in their adopted homeland of Fergana. It was as if they expected Holy Mother Russia to rise the same way. It was *not* something he had expected his ancient Kyrgyz neighbor to choose. But then he had learned to always let the storyteller choose the story and the way of telling. An artist always chose a first story they could tell with confidence. Later, with coaxing, the storyteller would tell the tale that touched her soul. You could always tell by the emotion in their voice. It was the same with witnesses.

Or suspects, for that matter.

Agafya set her spoon down and sat back in her chair. It was one of two that her Russian husband had carved. The chairs, the table, the stone house and his bird-eyed wife, all that he left behind him when he died.

She gave a single, stubborn shake of her head. "It was my husband's tale. Or that of his people—not mine. I thought I could tell it, but…" Agafya's Kyrgyz heritage shone through in more than her diminutive size and her attitude. She still wore the felted embroidered skirts and leggings of her girlhood. What remained of her fine grey hair was wound around her head and her black gaze glittered with old suspicions. "What is it to you? What do you want here?"

Kazakov eased his stiff side and shoulder—the penance he paid for being shot twice and thrown down a set of stairs—and straightened. He nodded at the table. "It's January seventh—Christmas Eve, remember? I brought the kutia to celebrate."

Lips tightening over her teeth, she shook her head. "Pah on your Christmas." She shoved the bowl away. "This is not what I cook."

Kazakov tried a smile. The January 7th date was the Christmas of the Russian Orthodox Christian faith that had not spurned the Julian calendar as most of the world had. Of course, Agafya was not Christian of any stripe, but Muslim.

"But the kutia's good, yes? My mother made it this way. I've spent years trying to recreate her recipe."

Agafya shook her head and took a long drink of the cup of vodka he'd poured her. "I am not your mother." She looked away. "I want to be alone."

Kazakov sighed. Agafya Ryabkov was a fierce woman, perhaps the strongest he'd ever met, save for the one he'd lost most recently. Agafya had always been the perfect neighbor, asking for nothing and barely tolerating when Kazakov came checking that she was safe and well. He knew when her limited tolerance for visitors was surpassed.

He pushed himself up from the table. "All right. I thought it would be good to share Christmas Eve with a friend, but I will leave you to your peace."

As he pulled on his muffling, wool great coat and heavy boots, she stood and shuffled to the old woodstove where he'd put the pot of kutia to keep it warm. He held up his hand. "Keep it and enjoy the kutia. I'll pick up the pot in a few days." For regardless of what she'd said, she'd polished off her bowl in record time. The old woman was made of twigs and skin and he had no idea how she survived. He'd been bringing her groceries for years.

Thankfully, she didn't argue but continued fussing around the cabin. He pulled on his lynx fur hat and tugged up his collar. "Thank you for the hospitality, Agafya. It was good to hear the old tales again."

She only harrumphed, so he grabbed his cane and let himself out, closing the door behind him.

Black night greeted him, and cold. January in Fergana was usually chill, but it was in the mountain foothills like this that winter truly came and this year more than most years. The air was still, except for a few flakes that tumbled down. Even the smoke from Agafya's chimney rose straight up for a hundred feet before swirling into calligraphy against the stars. The new moon was only a sliver and the air carried the scent of wood smoke and pine from the surrounding forest. To the east, a passing cloud picked up the amber glow of New Moscow's streetlights.

This far away he could almost imagine the city slumbering and at peace, but he knew better. Under the white covering of recent snow was the scurrying of rats—both in animal and human form. Rats with guns who had left him minus one kidney and, at forty-five, needing to help himself with a cane like an old man. He hoped it was only temporary.

He limped down Agafya's stairs to the trail his arrival had laboriously cut in the snow. The tip of his cane fought him as he lumbered across the clearing that during the summer would hold Agafya's small garden, and down the treed driveway toward the road. Halfway down the driveway, past where the snow was heavy, waited his trusty Perseus vehicle. He'd parked here for he hadn't been certain whether even the Perseus could navigate through the heavy snow around Agafya's home.

He sank into the driver's seat and realized that he was sweating. Since when had a two-hundred-meter walk stolen all his strength? The answer was simple: since the shooting in late November and the surgery that had left him convalescing. He had done nothing to keep in shape, instead diving deep into reading—folk tales that glossed over the horror of too much killing and that left him trying to determine the stories' purpose; mysteries that left him ready to toss the book across the room; histories that were determined to present the victors in the best light possible and to vilify those on the losing side.

Fictions, all of them.

In response, he'd turned back to the news and nonfiction, but even those he'd come to suspect were not the truth.

He turned the Perseus's ignition and the engine roared. Through the frosted windscreen, a white world was revealed in the headlight beams. Truth, it seemed, was in short supply these days. Even the shooting deaths of two police officers who had been responsible for Kazakov's injuries hadn't been reported accurately. But then, who in the New Moscow police force was going to damn two of their own?

Apparently, no one.

Perseus in gear, he carefully backed out of Agafya's driveway, following the tire tracks in his taillight's glare. At the road, the vehicle bumped over the snowplow's most recent drift and onto the narrow road before starting uphill.

The drive to his dacha was not quite half a mile along from Agafya's. His next nearest neighbor was over a mile farther on and he liked it that way. He guided the Perseus into his drive and under the sheltering dark pines and pale naked poplars, but something about the driveway wasn't right.

The snow clearly showed the tracks of his departure and the half-filled ruts of his comings and goings prior to the most recent snow. But now another set of tire tracks, wider than the Perseus's, followed the upward slope of the driveways and obscured his tracks in places.

He slowed the vehicle and felt his heart beat a little faster. The last time strangers had come to his dacha uninvited had been the first time he'd been shot. The last time a friend had come to the dacha was well back in November just after he'd been released from the hospital. No one had visited in December and that was just fine.

Back up and leave whoever was waiting for him or see who it was? He wasn't in the same situation as he'd been in November, working a case that technically wasn't his and another that he'd clearly been ordered to leave alone. Now he wasn't involved in anything.

Technically.

So. He might as well see who had disturbed his isolation.

He eased his foot off the brake and the Perseus chugged up the slope into the clearing around his dacha. A blocky, black sedan sat waiting, its windows fogged with frost as if whoever waited had chosen to wait in the car.

Interesting. Such a vehicle was the choice of the New Moscow police department.

Jaw clenched, Kazakov drove the Perseus past the unknown sedan. He parked in the shelter behind the dacha and then climbed out. The cold stung his cheeks. The heavy timbers of the dacha's walls were pitch black in the night, but overhead a thin trail of smoke rose from the chimney, so the fire he'd left banked was still burning.

He pulled himself up to his full six foot two and almost set the cane away, but there was too good a chance that, without it, he'd fall. His strength might be better than it was, but he wasn't a young man anymore. He picked his way around the house and the sedan's driver-side door clicked open.

Out stepped a tall, thin, baby-faced blond man who looked as if he should still be living with his mother, but who was, in fact, the youngest member of the New Moscow detective squad. Pavel Chelomeyev was the son of a senior member of the New Moscow police, which was most likely why he had been promoted to detective when most recruits were still taking notes for their training officers. He'd been partnered with one of the hard-case detectives on the squad, though he had worked with Kazakov a time or two in the past. One could argue that Chelomeyev was also responsible for Kazakov being alive today.

"Kazakov!" Chelomeyev's strong baritone was always a surprise, more so when it echoed back from the thick line of trees. He stood swathed in a thick wool coat down over his knees and black fur hat that seemed ungodly large for his scarf-wrapped neck.

Kazakov only nodded and hooked his head at the dacha, then thumped up the four snow-covered stairs to his front door. He stepped inside and Chelomeyev crowded in behind him while he lit a kerosene lamp that lit the interior with a warm golden light. Koshka, Kazakov's rebellious female black cat, twined around his legs. The single-room log cabin was comfortably warm and quite adequate for Kazakov on his own or perhaps with another, smaller, person. The place had no electricity, but it did have running water and had been built by his father when Kazakov was a boy. After his mother died, they had spent many summers here. After his father died and Kazakov's disastrous marriage ended, the dacha was the only thing Kazakov had held on to. He'd moved in then and had no plans to move out again, though he was considering installing a complete bathroom to replace the water closet attached to the kitchen.

At the moment, however, the place did not feel big enough for both Kazakov and Chelomeyev as they removed their coats and hats in the small area between the woodstove that stood against one wall and the table that filled the center of the room. Another narrow table stood against the wall beyond the woodstove and served as Kazakov's desk. A small kitchen filled one corner and a narrow bed sat opposite the desk. A small couch filled the final rear wall. It didn't leave a lot of room for someone whose arms were as long as Chelomeyev's. As usual, Koshka mewed plaintively for food though she had been given her dinner only a few hours before.

"Go on with you." Kazakov used the side of his boot to gently send Koshka on her way as he hung his coat and hat on a peg by the door. In disgust, Koshka leapt up to the shelf above his bed to curl up and hold him in a disapproving glare.

Kazakov turned back to the young detective in his neat grey suit and expensive tie who was trying to figure out what to do with his coat. Kazakov wasn't going to help him. He might have invited the young detective in, but that didn't mean that he'd told the youngster to make himself at home. Chelomeyev settled for folding the garment over the back of one of the two spindle chairs at the table.

"Why are you here?" Kazakov asked, dispensing with any of the niceties. This was home. If he wanted guests, he'd invite them, but Chelomeyev wasn't on the very short list of people Kazakov would consider inviting. No one from the police department was, but at least Chelomeyev was polite enough to wait in the car rather than invade the cabin to wait for him.

Chelomeyev looked back at his coat, perhaps rethinking the garment's removal. "I—I thought I would check up on you. It has been almost two months. Surely you will be coming back to work soon."

Arching a brow at the younger man, Kazakov went to his kitchen and retrieved a bottle of vodka and a single glass, then thought better of it and grabbed a second glass. "You expect me to believe that?"

He thumped the bottle and glasses on the table and studied the younger man. Chelomeyev sidled uneasily where he stood— nervousness—not a good thing in a detective.

"You want something, then." He lifted his chin at the chair. "Sit. Have a Christmas drink with me."

Obedient as a school boy, Chelomeyev sat. Kazakov swallowed a smile. The youngster still had some growing up to do. A shame his father hadn't allowed him to do it the way every other officer matured into the job.

"How long were you waiting?" Kazakov asked as he poured two tumblers and set the bottle down. The sweet glow from his meal with Agafya had worn off, but then Chelomeyev was an unwelcome intrusion of the real world.

"About an hour."

Odd how he felt so resentful when he should be appreciating the youngster's patience in waiting—and waiting in the cold, at that. But Kazakov had been waiting for someone from the police force to come to try to change his mind ever since he'd refused the offer of early retirement from Detektiv Chief Inspector Rostoff. He drained his vodka back and poured himself another as Chelomeyev sipped. The slow, sweet warmth crept from his belly to his heart and then his arms.

"So?" Kazakov asked, leaning back in his chair. "How are you? I won't ask about the department because I know it will be fucked up as usual." He eyed his tumbler, but limited himself to matching Chelomeyev sip for sip, waiting as the youngster found his courage. Clearly it had not been an easy choice to come here. His father would not approve and neither would Rostoff nor the other detectives. "Where is Sherepov?" Sherepov being Chelomeyev's surly partner.

The young detective set down his glass and drew in a deep breath. He shoved back from his chair and stood to pace around in the cramped room. Kazakov watched him and took another gulp of vodka, certain he wasn't going to like anything that caused Chelomeyev such consternation. Chelomeyev's movement stirred the kerosene lamp shadows so the room seemed to expand and contort as if they were inside the old witch Baba Yaga's chicken-legged house with miraculous adventures awaiting beyond its confines. He knew better— unlike Ivan Mareson from Agafya Ryabkov's recent telling, there was no one to put him fully back together again when the bullets came flying. He still ached where his one kidney was missing.

"I've been involved in these investigations," Chelomeyev began. From where he stood in the shadows he looked eternally young, like a tragic figure lost beyond the mythic River Styx who wished to come home.

He shook his head, his bright blond head of hair shifting on his forehead. "I don't know what to do. Sherepov is off on sick leave and one of these is my first murder investigation on my own—like you." He gave Kazakov a proud but hopeful glance. Kazakov was the only detective in the department who worked alone, whether because he distrusted his co-workers or they distrusted him, he no longer cared. Clearly, Chelomeyev had come to him as a last resort. Asking for help would be a sign of weakness. Asking Kazakov for help would damn the young detective in the eyes of the squad.

And just like that, the illusion of safety in the comfortable light and shadow of his dacha disappeared and became only shadows, the outside world intruding.

He shivered. A piercing knife blade cut through his side and he hissed out through his teeth. Did he want any part of this after all that had happened? He took another gulp of vodka, emptying the glass, and poured again.

But this was Chelomeyev and Kazakov owed him.

"What is the problem?"

Chelomeyev returned to his chair and leaned across the table. "Rostoff has told me to close the files. There is not enough evidence, he says. But my gut tells me that there is something there." He shook his head, his expression both pained and hopeful. "No one believes me, just like they never believed you."

Kazakov closed his eyes against that look. He had seen something similar in Maria's gaze before she died. He did not like the guilt. "Your superior officer has told you to close the file. To do anything else is a poor career move. Think about it. Your father would not be happy."

"You say that now, but listen to the cases—the facts as I know them."

A rustle of fabric and Kazakov opened his eyes. Chelomeyev had produced two manila envelopes from inside his woolen greatcoat. From outside the dacha came the sound of the wind stirring in the eaves as if something else was trying to come in—or draw him out. Chelomeyev slid the top envelope across the table to him.

For a moment he almost pushed it away. The lantern light gleamed beckoningly on his tumbler of vodka. Then he tipped the envelope contents onto the table. Police investigation evidence that should be in a police file in the department, not here in his dacha. On top was a photo of a body splayed over strewn documents. Male. In his fifties, though he looked trim and fit. The body wore an expensive-looking blue suit and white shirt, both covered in blood, but what likely killed him was the gaping second mouth in his neck. Blood blackened the edge of a Bokhara carpet and the hardwood floor under him, but through it you could see the expensive haircut, the manicured hands.

The man was clearly somebody.

"Messy," Kazakov said.

"His name is Grigori Ivanov. He runs—or ran—an import-export business in New Moscow specializing in tobacco products, and in particular, expensive American brands. Apparently, he had the Asia-wide franchise, whatever that means. He was found in his home office like this last Monday morning by the housekeeper who comes in three times a week. He was alone in the house," Chelomeyev said.

Kazakov slid the photo aside to look at the M.E.'s report underneath. Numerous bruises on the body, but the M.E. confirmed Kazakov's assessment of the mortal wound. According to the report, the neck wound would have required considerable strength, but the bruising indicated a beating that could have slowed the victim down. The document was signed neatly with the familiar signature of Khalil Khan, the lone Kyrgyz M.E. in the country and possibly its only Kyrgyz doctor.

Kazakov glanced back at the photo. Physical strength, and also a strong stomach.

He closed his eyes again, feeling the old awareness of his country creep back into his soul—something he had been trying to avoid for the past month. Fergana was his people's second chance after the Ottomans drove Yekaterina the Great out of Moscow. After escaping eastward into Siberia, followed by a long diaspora, they had found the tribal Kyrgyz people welcoming and had settled here—only to do to the Kyrgyz what had been done to the Russians by breeding more quickly, taking the land and then simply by excluding the Kyrgyz from the opportunities of modern Ferganese society. The Kyrgyz might still have the ancestral connection to their traditional lands, but they no longer owned it. It made Agafya's bitterness understandable.

He glanced back at the photo. "What about the wife?" he asked. "A bloody death usually speaks of a crime of passion. It would not be so difficult to slit a throat once the victim is down."

"Not this woman. And she was out of town visiting friends." Chelomeyev frowned. "How did you know there was a wife?

Kazakov tapped the photo. "Rings. Not all men wear them, but this man does. It suggests the marriage was important to him—and the wife. You've checked her alibi, of course." He glanced up at Chelomeyev, who nodded and leaned across the table.

His long pale fingers sorted through the documents to a statement. "Hers."

Kazakov's hand itched for his vodka glass. If he was to get involved in a case, it would be a case of his choosing—one that still haunted him.

The statement of Svetlana Ivanova was brief. She was out of town for the weekend with a friend and then her return was delayed for twenty-four hours due to road conditions in the mountains. She last spoke to her husband the day before she left. She had phoned him at work to tell him that she had decided to accompany her friend, Olga Gruenwald, on a ski trip to the mountains. Her husband had complained a little about her going without him, but he was busy dealing with some crisis or another at work and—as usual—had chosen work over her.

He glanced up at Chelomeyev. "Her words?"

The young detective nodded. "As close to verbatim as I could capture."

Kazakov turned thoughtfully back to the papers. The phrasing suggested the wife was less than happy in her marriage. But if the case was that obvious, why was Chelomeyev here? Had someone sent him? Someone intent on ensnaring Kazakov in a case again? But surely Chelomeyev wouldn't do such a thing given how much the young detective had risked to help Kazakov on his last case. On the other hand, perhaps this was his penance to save his career…

Kazakov kept reading. The wife and her friend had left on Thursday afternoon and traveled by automobile for the four-hour trip to her friends' dacha in the small mountain village of Biysk, named after another town long lost to the Ottomans. They went to ski and enjoy the clear air and the natural mineral baths. She returned on Tuesday, the day after the body was discovered, and was shaken and worried that someone might come after her, too. She could think of no one who would want to harm her husband. He was a well-regarded member of the community. He and she were involved in charity work together. It made no sense.

"And does it make no sense?" Kazakov asked.

Chelomeyev shrugged as if it didn't matter—never a good gesture on a detective, and yet he was here.

"Her alibi is strong. Her friend and her friend's employer both confirm her presence at the dacha. It would be impossible for her to get back down the mountain over the weekend, because they truly were snowed in."

Nodding, Kazakov pawed through the papers.

"A mistress?"

"If there was, they were unusually discrete. His office knew of no one."

There had to be something. There was always something. And the death wounds spoke of ferociousness and high emotion that led to the killing.

He read through the wife's friend, Olga Gruenwald's, statement that confirmed Svetlana Ivanova's alibi and stopped dead halfway through, the sudden surge of memories almost overwhelming.

Quickly, he fanned out the other papers across the table and found what he had hoped to find: a photo that likely confirmed Svetlana Ivanova's presence in the mountains. In the photo two women stood arm-in-arm swathed in thick fur coats, their heads encased in matching fur hats that tipped toward each other as fast friends were likely to do. Clearly the wind was blowing for their cheeks were rosy, their furs were blown flat on one side of their bodies, their long hair catching on their faces.

One woman was dark haired and lean featured, but even swathed in the furs, he could tell she had curves in all the right places, though her body was thin. The other woman was blonde with high Slavic cheekbones and bright, intelligent blue eyes. He knew they were intelligent because he knew her—or at least had met her while investigating his previous case. The case that had killed Maria. The case that had resulted in him being shot.

He reached for his glass and drank, holding himself to a sip when he wanted to drain the glass.

"Her." He tapped his finger on the photo. "Let me guess. That is the friend, Olga Gruenwald, yes?"

When Chelomeyev nodded, Kazakov leaned back in his chair and closed his eyes, fighting back the nausea and the vodka burn twisting his gut. He had spent the past month telling himself that he had done all that he could about Maria's death, including identifying the murderers, and yet there was something more. Something that connected her death to a rising star politico named Boris Bure. During the investigation a name had come up, but he had never had the chance to investigate further. The name involved was Olga Gruenwald's employer.

There was something here. He knew there was. Olga Gruenwald's employer was a man named Enver Pasha, an Ottoman businessman—the Pasha being an honorific that was given to Ottoman military of the rank of general. He was also a representative of one of the two most powerful empires in the world and one of the empires that sandwiched in the small Russian country of Fergana. The only reason Fergana hadn't already been swallowed up by the Ottoman Empire was because the Chinese Empire of the Sun was pressed right up against Fergana's eastern border and would take aggression against Fergana as aggression against their empire. Fergana was the gristle buffer grinding between the two massive entities and both China and the Ottomans were apt to meddle in Ferganese affairs.

Enver Pasha had been a person of interest in his previous case, both as a possible instigator of a murder and as a possible target.

Solving the case had killed the woman Kazakov might have loved and left him minus a kidney. He eased his side and looked back at the papers on the table. And now here was Enver Pasha again, like an ill wind.

Chelomeyev's pale face hung like a moon in the shadows of the dacha. Outside, the wind had sent a loose shingle tap-tap-tapping like a mad woman trying to get in.

If he was going back to work, this was a good case to sink his teeth into. If he was returning to active duty, then he could partner with Chelomeyev until Sherepov returned, or until he preferred to work on his own.

If he was going back to work.

The trouble was, he wanted the freedom to conduct an investigation that the police department's senior management would never countenance, not investigate a simple murder even if it might give him grounds to access people he otherwise might not have a right to.

He inhaled and the muscles in his side sent a sharp stab right through his heart. No. He wasn't ready yet to make a decision. His injuries were still healing.

When he could breathe again he shuffled Chelomeyev's papers back into a pile and stood, leaning heavily on his cane to limp over to his bedside.

"I can't help you. I don't want to be dragged into a case like this." He sank down onto his bed and would not meet Chelomeyev's gaze. "I'm sorry. I'm not ready to return to work."

Silently, Chelomeyev shuffled the papers back into the envelope and shoved back from the table. Without a word, he hauled on his coat and hat and, with the envelopes, went to the door. "I just wanted your opinion of where to start. All my leads have led to dead ends so far."

Kazakov chanced a look in Chelomeyev's direction and caught the disappointed gleam in the young man's gaze. Another hero shot to hell. The lad lived in Fergana, he should get used to it.

"It was good to see you, Pavel," Kazakov said and suddenly he didn't want to send the young man empty-handed out into the cold. But it was too late. Chelomeyev opened the door and stepped out onto the porch.

Kazakov lumbered to his feet and across the room to catch the door before it was fully closed. He hurriedly hauled on boots and stepped outside into the wind and swirl of new flakes as Chelomeyev headed down the stairs.

"Pavel."

The young man swung back to him, the light of the kerosene lantern through the dacha window catching on his brow and cheekbone.

"All I can suggest is to look into Enver Pasha. It was the one thing I neglected to do in the Weber-Manas case. There might be something."

Chelomeyev frowned and then nodded before turning back to his vehicle. He opened the door and slid inside.

"And—and for God's sake, be very careful," Kazakov called, but the door thunked shut so Kazakov wasn't sure whether Chelomeyev had even heard.

He stood in the swirl of snow and the wind and watched as the red taillights disappeared down his driveway. Then came the silence of his life—except for the wind off the eastern mountains.

He went inside and poured himself another tumbler of vodka.

2

For some reason, he dreamt of arrows stuck in the earth.

It was a bad dream—one of Yekaterina Weber, again. The young girl who had haunted him since he first saw her body. He had fought long and hard, risked his life, and destroyed his career to find the killer, though whether the actual killer was fully responsible was a judgment call.

In the dream, just as in all the dreams, Yekaterina was running across a field golden with grain, her long pale hair trailing behind her, her navy school uniform skirt hiked around her thighs and her favorite fluffy pink sweater pressed against her heaving breast as if she ran into a headwind. As if the elements themselves conspired to keep her from safety. For she ran like the devil incarnate was in pursuit. In one fist she held a red-shafted arrow.

And in the dream, something tripped her long lithe legs and she tumbled into the grass. She scrambled halfway up and then stumbled again, casting terrified glances over her shoulder. Then she was on her back in the grass as if she'd been pushed and scrambling back and back and back in her final attempt to flee. She dropped the arrow and held her arms up to fend off invisible blows.

Her mouth worked as if nursing for air. Her throat discolored and her pale blue gaze turned skyward for a moment before turning back. Before looking at her killer and seeing deep into Kazakov's soul. Then an invisible hand retrieved her fallen arrow and used it to stab her, leaving it standing in her chest.

Kazakov bolted upright in bed, chest heaving, sending Koshka, squalling, onto the floor. A sour taste filled his mouth as if something had died there. It was one week since Pavel Chelomeyev had visited and the dream had haunted him ever since. Apparently seeing the image of the blonde-haired Olga Gruenwald had knocked something loose in his brain. The woman had had nothing to do with the Weber-Manas case other than advising him that her employer wasn't at home. So why had the sight of her done this to him?

He hauled his legs out of bed and hung his throbbing head as he sat on the side. The night-bound dacha's air was chill, though it still carried the scent of pine smoke. The fire he had banked before bed must be nearly out. Koshka mewed plaintively and he stroked her thick fur. Side twinging, he rose to shuffle across the cool wood floorboards so that he wouldn't stub his toes. He wore only underwear and a t-shirt, warm enough for under his thick covers. Once upon a time there had been a warm woman he had to worry about tripping over because he refused to sleep with her.

The stack of wood beside the fireplace was almost gone and the bunk of wood at the rear of the dacha needed replenishing, but a man with a wound in his side was beyond splitting firewood. He'd been lucky he'd had a good store of wood already set aside against the winter. It hadn't been enough and he'd known it, though he'd felled enough trees in the spring. Soon he'd be forced to get busy cutting the fallen trunks to length and hauling the wood back to the house. He stirred the ashes inside the stove until embers flared, then added a new log to the fire. The flames licked up the side of the wood.

He closed the stove but left the damper open and worked his shoulder. He tried an experimental chop and groaned at the stretched tissue. It was almost time to get back to the wood and his life. But not yet.

He needed to be fully healthy if he was to take on the investigation he planned. At least that was his most recent excuse since Chelomeyev had come. If he was more truthful with himself, he knew that after eight weeks convalescing, inertia had settled on him.

The alarm clock on the small shelf above his bed said it was five thirty in the morning—far too early to be up, but the dream had left him sweating, with a pounding heart, and far too wide awake. After the kerosene lantern was lit, he filled a small dish with canned cat food and the crackle of the fire was joined by the happy cat licks. Then he reached for the vodka bottle he'd been pouring from last night.

Empty. No wonder his head hurt. He stumbled over to the line of eight other soldiers he'd bought on his last foray into town. They were all empty, too. How the hell had that happened?

He scratched his greasy head and when no other possible answer came other than that he had emptied them, he stood there with his hands pressed on the hard wood counter and his head down. What the hell was happening to him?

With shaky hands, he put water on the stove for tea and then settled into a chair. His legs felt weak, his stomach uneasy as if it was trying to tell him something.

There was an itch in his brain that always meant something.

He shook his head—not a good idea with the thudding it provoked. He did not want to get involved again until he was healed and able to do his job—not embarrass himself limping around with a cane like an old man. He wasn't old yet—though on mornings like this, he could feel old age lurking.

It was a slow creeping fog that gradually filled joints and brain, turning one brittle and the other to mush. At times, it seemed like it might be better to just settle back and let it take him. Imagine the ease of simply being a patient—not a person anymore.

That wasn't him—yet.

But the drinking was going to bring it on soon.

What was it about Chelomeyev's case that had caused this uneasiness he felt? This discontent that had him drinking like this? Waiting for the water to boil, he pulled on a flannel shirt, a pair of tattered and mended trousers, and a pair of socks from those strewn on the floor. The water boiled and he made himself a cup of sweet milk tea. Koshka finished her meal and returned to the tangle of his bed to curl up in the place he'd previously warmed.

Nursing the tea, he leaned back in the chair and closed his eyes. Chelomeyev's papers spread across his table once again. The businessman's gruesome body lay splayed amongst his business papers, an Ottoman carpet thick with blood underneath. Definitely a murder committed with passion. The question was whether it was the passion of rage or disgust. Perhaps both. Rage could account for the multiple bruises, disgust for the surgically neat slit of the throat. The knife must have been incredibly sharp. He wondered whether it had been found but guessed not because Chelomeyev would surely have mentioned it.

The dead man's address was not far from the crescent street that edged Yekaterina Park that had been the scene of so much of Kazakov's last dangerous case.

Close enough that the wife could have easily befriended Olga Gruenwald, and yet… Surely the wife of a successful businessman and the self-proclaimed 'housekeeper' of the wealthy foreigner called Enver Pasha didn't circulate within the same social strata. Clearly Olga Gruenwald wasn't the wife's housekeeper because it was the housekeeper who found the body. Was Olga Enver Pasha's lover?

He frowned. Something was off there. He wondered whether Chelomeyev would have thought of it. He wished that he'd read the case file more closely.

The thought made his hands shake and sweat run down his forehead to his eyes.

No. This wasn't his case. It wasn't where he wanted to spend his time.

But he could phone the youngster and provide some advice. Perhaps help from afar. For a moment he wished that he had interviewed Enver Pasha as he'd planned to, but the case had completed before he'd found the chance. If he had, he could provide Chelomeyev with some insights.

As if his insights were worth anything. They got people killed. They got him shot.

His side throbbed. His skin was clammy and his thoughts seemed to claw the inside of his skull. He scrubbed at his face, pinched the bridge of his nose, but it didn't help. He wanted to help Chelomeyev, but his body knew better.

It was all he could do to stagger up from the table. He didn't need to look like anything given he wasn't going to see anyone who knew him. Or at least anyone who could comment. With a week's stubble on his face, he pulled on his great coat, hat, and boots and banked the fire so that there would be something left when he returned.

"Don't worry. I'll be back in time for your dinner," he said to Koshka. The little cat just glared at him, as females seemed keen to do.

The cold slammed into him when he opened the door. He swayed and leaned back against the door for a moment before stiffening against the chill wind that swirled around the dacha's clearing. Overhead the clouds had split open leaving a pale, unleavened blue except on the peaks of the not so distant mountains where more snow brewed.

Collar up and lynx fur earflaps down, he retraced his snow-muffled tracks around the dacha to the Perseus. The workhorse vehicle started on the second try and he turned the Perseus around, tires crunching through the crust of snow, and then trundled down the driveway under the sheltering arch of the trees.

The road into town was clear and soon the land opened up and sloped down to the façade of the city that was New Moscow. Built on the remains of a far older city that had hosted the ancient caravans of the silk and the tea roads, the city sprawled around a lonely mountain that his people had named Yekaterina Mountain after the great tsarina. Yekaterina the Great had lost Holy Mother Russia to the Ottomans and had died as she led her people into the wilds of Siberia. The desperate survivors of starvation and plague had then found their way here and been taken in.

Apparently, the Russian people's memories had died as well, for they continued to revere Yekaterina as a martyr even though she'd brought their devastation, while at the same time reviling the Kyrgyz people who had taken them in. His people had also long forgotten that the original name of the peak in the center of the city was Suleiman's Mountain—after the Muslim saint.

Today, New Moscow was a small city of treed boulevards and modern concrete of no particular design that had laid siege around the old city that had existed long before the original Moscow fell. The old city was made up of narrow streets, many not broad enough for a vehicle like the Perseus, and square, stucco buildings originally made of timbers, horsehair, and mud. There was a certain honest grace to the crumbling homes that once held the gracious courtyards of wealthy tea and silk merchants. It was an honesty he didn't find in the gaudy domes and minarets that topped the façade of the replica of Saint Basil's Cathedral and the faux columns of the front of the Ferganese parliament building that was supposed to look like the long-lost palace of St. Petersburg. Instead of grand, those replicas only looked like they tried too hard—like everyone in the country tried to reclaim past glories that would never come again.

He guided the Perseus down the sloping road into the ravenous subdivisions devouring the open fields. The homes were replica dacha-style houses, except that these sat in miniscule yards with barely a single tree among them. Children played in the grimy snow in the front yard or chased balls, blackened for visibility against the snow, down the street with sticks. Here and there, small signs promoted candidates in Fergana's upcoming spring elections. The sight of the white-toothed false smile of Boris Bure, candidate for the Reformation Party, made him slow the car when he felt like mowing down the sign. Boris Bure —the dead schoolgirl Yekaterina Weber's stepfather. The man who had impregnated her.

A twist of nausea filled his gut and he focused on the road to avoid reading the election signs again. The May election was one of the reasons he'd avoided coming to town very often.

Gradually the quiet suburban streets and houses gave way to the traffic lanes of Suvarov Way. Kazakov's breath quickened and his heart beat faster as he neared the center of town and the police department.

If he turned at the next corner, he would find a large government liquor store. From there he could stock up and return home again.

At the last moment he crossed three lanes of traffic and turned off in a direction away from both the police station and the liquor store. The street took him into a quiet neighborhood and relief flooded through him. His time alone in the dacha had not been good for him.

The street led him around the edge of the old city until a bluff of snow-covered land poked its head up out of the encroaching buildings.

He parked the Perseus not far from a garage that was run by a Kyrgyz man he had met on a previous case and got out. The doors to the garage were open and a small delivery truck was up on a hoist. Someone was banging around underneath, but Kazakov turned away and trudged up the sloped street with his cane and turned through a familiar rusted metal gate.

The Potemkin Cemetery sat on a knoll overlooking the city and Yekaterina Mountain. In the summer, it was a place of green grass and trees that had been allowed to grow almost wild as the middle-class Russians chose different places to bury their dead. At this time of year, the place seemed fitting to his mood, for the snow had been stripped off in some places and deposited over gravestones in wild shapes carved by the wind.

It was hard going and his boots slipped on crusts of ice, but finally he found his way to Maria's grave. It faced west across the waste of snow to distant Constantinople and Maria's more distant homeland in the Anglo-German Empire. Italia, it was called. He inhaled the chill air and felt his heart beating.

The gravestone was of simple gray stone, now carrying a delicate arch of snow across the top like the long, broken neck of a swan. It reminded him of smooth limbs swathed in moonlight, of pink sweaters on schoolgirls, and the running figure of a young man gunned down in a field.

He closed his eyes, fighting back the anger at the useless waste of three young lives.

"Maria, what do I do? The thought of more deaths like yours sickens me. If I help Chelomeyev, is that what will happen? Have I lost my nerve? Am I no longer the man you knew?" And perhaps loved? There *had* been an attraction between them. The lightness of her touch upon his shoulder. The way she spooned against him their one night together. Her faint scent of lavender water, the memory of which still evoked longing in him.

Was Rostoff right that he should retire? To become so entangled with a witness was not proper. To still pine for her said that something was wrong—both with him and his country.

When he opened his eyes again, a wisp of cloud had tattered itself around the five peaks of Yekaterina Mountain. At its base, the carnival grounds that the New Moscow government had approved for a Russian businessman over the protests of the carnival's Kyrgyz neighbors, sat derelict in the snow. On the slope below Kazakov, a lone figure trudged up the snowy hill between the graves toward him.

The figure wore a long black Russian-style greatcoat, but where Kazakov wore a lynx hat, the figure wore mink or ermine, black against the whiteness of the snow. For all the bulk of the winter clothing, the light sway of the fabric told Kazakov all he needed to know. The man was slight of build, more like a dancer or a horseman than someone of the more solid Russians' build.

When the figure neared, Kazakov stepped out to meet him and held out his hand. "Khan. It has been too long."

"I was told by some hopeful soul that you'd likely died in that hidey-hole of yours," Khalil Khan said and shook his hand.

Kazakov arched a brow at him. "By natural causes, of course." Overhead the wind whipped the clouds around Yekaterina Mountain into wisps and streamers that the air licked away like frosting. The fur on his hat tickled his cheek and the wind shoved him with forceful hands.

A faint smile traced its way across Khan's face. He was a small man, dark-haired and -skinned like his people, with slightly slit eyes that spoke of his eastern tribal heritage. His glittering gaze was keenly observant. Kazakov had always been impressed by the M.E., for he was the star in his field regardless of the prejudice against him. He had also surprised Kazakov with his connections to a United States Embassy official who Kazakov would bet was a spy.

On the other hand, for all his greeting, the way Khan's mouth firmed into a line said he wasn't impressed with the Kazakov he saw before him.

"By the look of you, the people who wish you dead need only wait you out."

Kazakov looked down at himself. His long black coat was littered with bits of pine needles and stained with dirt and pine pitch. He wore his usual heavy boots, though he had neglected to buckle them closed and snow had filtered into the tops to melt onto his ankles. "That bad?"

"Old friend, have you eaten a single decent meal since you left the hospital?" Khan asked gently. "Have you had a bath?"

Kazakov thought of the kutia he had made for Christmas eve and sorted through hazy memories. Sausages and bread mostly—easy enough to fix for himself. He shrugged and thought of his critique of Chelomeyev for the same gesture. "Maybe. Maybe not. What is it to you?"

Khan sighed visibly, his breath coming in a cloud. "The man who was one of the best investigators in the New Moscow department has vanished before my eyes. Do you expect to go back to work like this? You'll be just like those detectives that you've always despised."

Kazakov looked away. "They don't need me…. Besides, I have my own investigation."

"Don't they need you?" Khan asked. "And do you really think you can investigate Boris Bure without resources behind you?"

Kazakov watched the cloud form and reform above Yekaterina Mountain. "Did you come just to harangue me?"

"I'm here because a friend told me that you were here again. I've been meaning to visit you, but I thought you needed space. But when I heard that each time you come you look more and more like shit, I realized that I had to stop what I was doing and speak to you." Khan shook his head. "I left a medical exam half-finished because of you. My imbecile assistant will undoubtedly botch the job, but what can you do?"

Kazakov met his gaze then. Khan's source of information about Kazakov was probably the owner of the garage he'd passed down below. "I'm sorry to cause you and your spies so much trouble."

"Quit feeling sorry for yourself," Khan sniffed. "I asked you before why you come here. Why commune with the dead when it's the living who need you and your talents? The dead—they are at peace. There is nothing you can do for them."

Unless, like Ivan Mareson from the old folk tale, their arrow was left unimpaled. Then you could revitalize and rescue them.

"Sherepov is sick. Cancer, I've heard." Khan continued. "The department is shorthanded and now this." He shook his head.

Kazakov frowned. "This?"

Khan seemed to study him and his expression grew serious. "I thought you'd heard. There have been three attacks on Russian gatherings—a church, a market, a winter festival. It has drained detectives from the squad and from departments across Fergana. And now this with Chelomeyev. I thought that was what brought you into town again. After all, he helped you out in the Weber-Manas case."

The wind buffeted Kazakov's shoulders and found its way down his neck. The cold ate down his back and shoulders.

"What are you talking about?"

Khan glanced up at him and then out at the city slowly mobilizing in the morning light. "Chelomeyev, of course. They found him this morning just outside his apartment. He'd been beaten and left for dead. Thankfully the cold slowed his blood so he didn't bleed out, but he might not live. If he does, he might be minus fingers or toes. Or there might be brain damage. It has been all over the news. Haven't you heard?"

3

A shiver ran down Kazakov's back. Before him, the snow-covered hillside seemed to sink away and the blue sky dim. The traffic hum on the greasy streets of New Moscow became the agonizing wail of sirens. From the old city below came the sounds of voices and children laughing as they went off to school. He hadn't noticed that before—how voices carried to the top of the hill like life leaking through a window.

The wind sifted the snow around the headstones so that it glittered like magical dust from one of the old folk tales and the snowy, swan's neck sculpture on Maria di Maria's headstone quivered and collapsed into a nondescript heap. For a moment he held his breath, but the magic had gone away from the scene. He stood on a graying hillside with the dead. Beyond waited the living.

The breath he took hurt his lungs just as much as the sunlight hurt his head. "What happened? Who the hell would go after Chelomeyev? He was harmless enough. So proud of investigating his first case."

Khan's brows rose. "You saw him?"

Feeling like a great bear coming out of hibernation, Kazakov shook his head. He paced away from Khan, then turned back to where his only friend waited.

"He came to me looking for help with the investigation." He told about Chelomeyev's suggestion that Kazakov should come back to work and partner with him. Another blast of wind sent him staggering. "I wouldn't help him."

Except for the one suggestion. Could that have been why Chelomeyev was attacked?

His gut churned. He looked with longing down the hill to the Perseus and the road to the liquor store, but that was a coward's way and he was not a coward. He straightened. "He's in Our Lady Yekaterina Hospital?"

"The critical care ward." Khan nodded.

"Thank you. For coming. For telling me. For waking me up." Apparently, he had not left an arrow in the earth and his old friend Khan had revived him.

The sun was too bright, as if he'd just woken. He shifted the tip of his walking stick in the snow and started down the hill again. Khan came with him.

"How is the side?" Khan asked.

"How is your family?" They had been hostages in the Weber-Manas case and Khan and Kazakov had worked together to free them.

For a moment Khan's face stiffened. "Healing. My wife still has moments of trembling and my boy cries too often at night."

"I'm sorry. I've come to learn that healing takes a long time." If there was even such a thing as being healed. The Russian people were walking wounded and barely even realized they bled away their strength every day.

At the foot of the hill, Kazakov pushed open the rusted metal gate. Across the road the grimy side of a warehouse was plastered with too-bright election signs. Kazakov averted his gaze.

"You still can't stand to see him, can you?" Khan said softly.

"He walked away a free man and barely had the grace to mourn her," Kazakov muttered.

"I suggest that you get used to that fact and to seeing his face. The polls say that he is leading. His party's promise of returning the Russian people to greatness touches a chord with many people. He preaches Russian purity and points to the recent attacks on Russian events and the tribal unrest in the mountains to cause division between Kyrgyz and Russian peoples." There was bitterness in his voice.

Kazakov nodded. "It doesn't surprise me. He does not strike me as a man who understands anything other than getting what he wants." He turned to Khan and grasped his forearm. "Thank you for seeking me out, old friend. As usual, you give me the information I need."

Khan's gaze glittered like obsidian glass as he looked up at Kazakov. Then he nodded in return. "I am a doctor. It is my job. That is what is important, is it not? That we each do what we are best at to help our people?"

"One of your subtle hints?" Kazakov grinned.

"That is for you to decide." Shrugging, Khan turned aside to head across the street and down to a black M.E. van parked at the edge of the moldering buildings of the old city. Presumably he was going back to check his assistant's medical examination.

Kazakov watched him go. Somehow the little M.E. seemed larger.

Returning to the Perseus, he sat in the cold vehicle out of the wind, but he felt like a wind still buffeted him. Chelomeyev attacked. Critical care. That could not be good—at all. Was the squad investigating the attack, or were they responsible for setting the young detective up? Such things had happened before.

He rammed the key into the ignition and the engine roared to life. He had to see Chelomeyev.

It was midmorning when he pulled into the hospital parking lot and squeezed in between other visitors' vehicles. Our Lady Yekaterina Hospital was the major medical center for Fergana. It sat amid its own snow-covered meager lawns with a treed park and fountain across the parking lot. At this time of year, the plows had shoved the filthy snow up over the fountain. In the spring the salt-laden snow would melt to slowly poison the roots of the lovely shade trees. Eventually it would kill them, but not yet. Just as the Ottomans bided their time over Fergana itself. Eventually a tipping point would be reached and the risk of war with the Chinese would be worth the attack. He just hoped it was long after he was dead and gone.

He stepped out onto frozen slush and waded across the treacherous, uneven soup over the parking lot and up to the hospital's front doors. It felt strange to do so. Usually, he took the stairs down to the land of the dead overseen by the Medical Examiners like Khan.

He stopped just inside the broad double doors. The hospital seemed foreign—too much life, too many people hurrying to wherever they were going, their footsteps like thunder on the cold linoleum. With the dead there was no rush. They weren't going anywhere. In fact, it was best if you stood in one place. Only then did you stand a chance of hearing what they were saying.

The gleaming floor and pale yellow walls were disorienting. For a moment he felt disembodied and leaned heavily on his cane. The air though—the air was the same as Khan's domain—carrying the lingering odors of disease, death, and pain. He inhaled deeply, steadying himself. Those things he was familiar with. They were part of his job.

He swung around and realized that people were watching him. Squaring his shoulders, he limped to the admissions desk and leaned down to the girl. She wore a navy-blue sweater set that was pilled down the front and a no-nonsense gaze as she looked up at him.

"Chelomeyev. Where is his room, please?"

The girl's eyes widened. "Are—are you family… sir?"

"I'm his maiden aunt. Do I look like a relative?" He hauled his wallet out of his pocket and flashed his badge. "I need to speak with him. Now. Where is his room?"

He straightened to his full height knowing he towered over her.

"Only family members are allowed to visit, sir."

Apparently, she'd seen through his intimidation.

Gritting his teeth, he leaned down to her again. "Chelomeyev is a friend and co-worker of mine. He was beaten on a case we shared. If you think you can stop me from checking in on him, you'd best think again. Do you understand?"

"Sir. There are rules in this hospital." Her voice was too loud, her eyes deep blue as Chinese pottery. When she was younger she was likely pretty, but something had happened to her to place deep lines beside her mouth. Not a girl, then. A woman who had experienced life's disappointments.

"And I understand rules. I am, after all, a detective. And now I need to find the people responsible for Chelomeyev's condition. Would you be the one to stop justice being served?" A lie, all of it, for when had rules ever been important to him? But the need to see Chelomeyev beat like his heart. He leaned in close. "Now what can I do to make it easier for you to give me the information?"

She met his gaze and seemed to study him. Then her gaze fell to the sheets of names on her desk. "It is against the rules," she said plaintively.

"Then how about you go talk to your friend, there." He nodded at the woman at the next desk. "I will find the room number myself." He tipped his gaze to the sheets of names.

Swallowing, the girl nodded and slid her chair back. "Excuse me a moment," she said in a loud voice. "I must check something." She stood and crossed to the other woman and Kazakov spun the patient list toward him.

Thankfully, Chelomeyev was there on the top page. Room 306a.

He left the admissions desk and limped across the floor to the elevator.

On the third floor, he stepped out into the quiet hum and beep of medical equipment. Across from the elevator, a sign attached to the wall said acute care. It didn't bode well for Chelomeyev and for what Kazakov would find, but he set out down the long hall, with the dim fluorescent lights and the too-shiny floors. Pale green walls pulsed in the flickering light. Open doors gave off the hall from side to side to dimly lit rooms, the humming clearly coming from inside.

He came to a nursing station where three young nurses were talking softly. They stopped when they saw him.

"Sir, you shouldn't be here. This area is not open to the public— only family."

This time Kazakov was ready with his wallet. He flashed his badge. "I've been sent to check on Chelomeyev. Any change in his condition?"

The nurses looked him up and down and then at each other. Finally, a pretty one with one snaggle front tooth marring her smile stepped forward to read his badge.

"Detektiv Chelomeyev is about the same, Detektiv Kazakov."

"And his prognosis?"

She bit her lip. "The doctor says it is wait and see whether he will regain consciousness. There was much trauma to the brain. There—there have been seizures." She looked away to the desk as if she did not like her job much at the moment.

Derr 'mo. Shit. Khan had said Chelomeyev was in critical care, not the extent of his injuries.

"Room 306a?"

She nodded her pretty blonde head down the hall in the direction he'd been going. His footfall sounded heavy—the steps of doom. The pretty nurse followed him like a shadow.

Chelomeyev's room sat in the corner, where the corridor turned to cross the end of the building. On one side was a small lounge with low, well-worn couches, last year's tattered magazines on the side tables, and the ubiquitous scent of uncleaned ashtrays. On the other side was a small alcove with a fridge and kitchen facilities. A break room? A place for visitors? Either way, it did not look well used.

Kazakov motioned the nurse to stay in the hall as he stepped into the room. It was dimly lit from light through a single narrow window that looked out onto what had become a gray day. Snowflakes spiraled down and were tugged away by the wind. In the room were three beds, two made up with bed linens so tightly laid he thought his keys might bounce. The third bed lay occupied and surrounded by monitors beeping out the fact that the patient still lived.

White sheets and a thin white blanket covered the patient. White pillows held his head, and his head was also white from bandages that wrapped his skull and were plastered on a swollen purple face. Tubes ran from his mouth to machines beside his bed. To help him breathe? To feed him? What had happened to him?

Kazakov stood at the foot of the bed trying to assess things clinically as Khan probably would. It just wasn't possible to see blond, eager Chelomeyev in this swathed figure.

Under the bandages, Chelomeyev appeared to be dead, not sleeping. Only the monitors kept on beeping and, when he watched carefully, there was a slow rise and fall of those snowy covers. Life. But life like Ivan Mareson, waiting arrowless for someone to heal him.

The snaggle-toothed nurse still waited at the door. "He has not been awake?" Kazakov asked.

The nurse shook her head. "For a while we thought perhaps he was aware, but there've been no signs of awareness for the past few hours. At least none that the last shift recorded and I've just come on shift myself." She glanced at the swathed figure. "He's young. That gives him a better chance at recovery."

Kazakov followed her gaze back to Chelomeyev's still figure. There were no chairs at his bedside. Had his Deputy Chief of Police father or his socialite mother even been to visit him? Had anyone? Suddenly it was important that Chelomeyev know that he wasn't alone. "I'd like to sit with him a while."

She found him a chair and he settled by the bed amid the faint smell of the urine bag hooked to the bed by Chelomeyev's hip. The nurse excused herself and left him alone. Chelomeyev's long-fingered hands lay still on the white blanket, where once they had pointed out evidence from an envelope.

Why was he doing this? An expiation of his sins? He had given Chelomeyev almost nothing. If he'd given in to Chelomeyev's request and become his partner, this might not have happened.

Sighing, he caught Chelomeyev's cool hand. "I'm sorry. This should not have been like this."

Was it a simple case of being at the wrong place at the wrong time, or had Chelomeyev stumbled onto something that had led to his attack? Such things had happened before. Men had come for Kazakov when he refused to give up his investigation into another murder.

Another murder where Enver Pasha's name had come up.

Derr'mo! Had this happened because Chelomeyev had followed up on Kazakov's last-minute suggestion to investigate an Ottoman national named Enver Pasha?

The hospital room suddenly chilled him and he huddled into his coat. Was he responsible for this?

"What did you do, Pavel? What stone did you turn over?" In the week since Chelomeyev had been at his home, surely it could not have been enough to bring about such retribution. Perhaps it had been something totally unrelated to what Kazakov had told the young detective.

He scrubbed at his face. Who was he kidding? He could tell himself that, but in his gut he knew that he was responsible.

Kazakov bowed his head. He had dragged this young man into this mess simply because Enver Pasha *might* provide a window into the darkness that Kazakov suspected existed. A mess Chelomeyev was ill-prepared to face, as young as he was. The damned honest fool likely rushed right in asking questions.

Kazakov knew better. He might have solved the mystery of the Weber-Manas deaths, but they were only a side issue to something much larger going on in Fergana. He had known it in his investigation, though he had not pursued it. Instead he'd retreated to his dacha and vodka and told himself that he was only waiting to heal.

Perhaps he was just wiser than Chelomeyev—or less honest.

4

He had to know.

Kazakov sat in the Perseus outside the hospital, the clouds streaming overhead, vehicles passing by, their tires hissing and crunching over the frozen slush in the parking lot. The wind shuddered in the empty branches of the trees in the park and sent snowflakes off the trees, whirling like dervishes. Inside the cold vehicle it felt like the wind was inside him, shaking him loose from his inertia. He'd spent too long hiding in his dacha. He'd hidden too long and look what had happened. It should have been him asking the questions, not Pavel Chelomeyev.

He inhaled the musty air of the vehicle. Well, he'd hide no longer. He started the Perseus's engine and a blast of cold air from the heater brought in the scent of diesel and motor oil. He wanted a smoke. He wanted a drink. The cigarette would be less harmful.

Hands shaking, he hauled out his wallet seeking the single cigarette he always carried for emergencies like this—he'd quit smoking years ago. It wasn't there and he remembered a time much like this when he'd smoked his last.

"You're a weak man, Kazakov." In disgust he tossed his wallet on the seat beside him and backed the Perseus out.

With no cigarette and nothing to drink to distract himself, he knew what to do.

There were some things a police officer could not leave unavenged and the injury, perhaps death, of a fellow officer was one of them. He headed back to Suvarov Way. There he glanced back the way he'd come into town, to the road to the liquor mart, before turning toward the center of New Moscow.

The New Moscow Police Department sat near the center of the city facing Yekaterina Square. On a pedestal in the center of the square stood a twice-life-size statue of the great tsarina clad in a long, ornate dress and fur cloak, an extra shawl around her torso. An apparently harsh wind had spun her hair around her shoulders as she held up a lantern and peered eastward on the great diaspora. This was how her people remembered her. The vibrant woman who gave away her shawl to save the life of another. They did not catch the hard glint of her eyes and the hint of cruelty in the determined line of her mouth—the cruelty that had burned out on the long walk eastward after her troika of horses had been eaten.

To one side of the square sat the three-story, bunker-style, *politseyshiyuchastok*, the police headquarters building that was diminished by the steel and concrete towers that had grown ever taller around it. The headquarters had few windows at street level and an uninviting main door that had always seemed designed to keep the people at bay. Glass windows on the floors above were reserved for the officers and their policy geeks. Even the detective squad had none.

Leaning on his cane, he climbed the stairs to the front door and pushed into the cavernous waiting area. It was a large, open space that had always reminded him of a barn. Eight glass stalls that were never all open held duty officers intent on dealing with the citizens who came in. At the moment, one lone junior officer was doggedly dealing with a line of at least fifteen people.

Kazakov limped past toward the locked staff door at the side.

"Here! You!"

Kazakov turned at the voice. The duty officer was on his feet and was looking in Kazakov's direction. Kazakov pulled out his wallet and flashed identification.

The duty officer's eyes widened and he remained standing as Kazakov knocked on the staff door, then flashed his ID through the small window. The door unlocked and he pushed inside—only to be confronted by the officer on guard, a youngster Kazakov didn't recognize and who clearly didn't recognize Kazakov either. He blocked Kazakov's path.

"Identification papers," he demanded.

Kazakov sighed and dug for his wallet again. The changes Khan had noted must be worse than Kazakov had thought. The duty officer inspected the image on the identification and then Kazakov's face. Finally, he handed the identification back but still didn't step aside.

Clearly Kazakov's name and reputation weren't unknown. Shaking his head, Kazakov stepped around him for the elevator and rode up the three floors.

The detective squad room was a windowless box of a room with a litter of desks and an alcove for a break room. The place smelled of stale tea, wet winter wool coats, and the harsh smoke of the detectives' ubiquitous cheap Indian cigarettes. Six detectives were in the room. Two freshly scrubbed faces Kazakov vaguely remembered as being in general duty uniforms now sat at the face-to-face desks Antonov and Alenin had left behind. Surely to God, Rostoff wouldn't pair two newcomers together. But then knowing Rostoff and the department, there was a very good chance that they would. And just who were these two related to, to be promoted so quickly?

Besides the two newcomers, the four others he recognized.

World-weary Detektiv Kuznetzov with the shaggy head of salt-and-pepper hair sat with his hands frozen over the keys of his typewriter. Thirty-year-old Detektiv Popov hauled his feet down off his desk and stood before he realized who had entered.

Detektivs Razin and Pogolin sat frozen at their desks, Razin's bright blue eyes wide. Pogolin scrubbed his hand through his stubble of silver-shot, black hair.

"Kazakov? Is that you?" Pogolin asked.

Kazakov nodded once and crossed to Chelomeyev's desk. "What's happening with the investigation?" he asked as he sank into the young detective's chair.

"Which one?" Razin asked.

Kazakov just looked at him. It was an idiot's question. "You have an officer in hospital after an attack. I would think it must be that one. Is there something more important?" He scanned their faces and reactions. Popov, Kuznetzov, Razin, and Pogolin all met his gaze like rocks in an old stone wall. The two new men just dropped their gazes and avoided his. "So? Who are the suspects?"

Pogolin and Razin glanced at each other. "The evidence points to a robbery gone bad—a chance encounter. Chelomeyev lived in one of those transition neighborhoods—nice enough itself, but too close to the old city to be safe, in my opinion," Razin said.

"In your opinion." Kazakov stood. "In the opinion of a fool, you mean." Contrary to popular bias, the old city had a lower crime rate than many parts of New Moscow. "Did you check whether there was any connection between the attack and Chelomeyev's cases?"

Pogolin stood, his lined, blunt features frozen. "Don't come storming in here after over two months and going off half-cocked like you always do. We worked our asses off on Chelomeyev all day. He was working on nothing. We reviewed his cases but there was clearly nothing there. The files have been sent to Rostoff for his review and direction on whether to proceed." His fists were closed, his posture hunched as a fighter, but threats didn't matter.

"Nothing clearly there? It hasn't even been twenty-four hours. What do you think his father is going to say?" Kazakov's hands shook at his sides. He wanted to lash out at Pogolin's mask of condescension.

"It was good police work. A massive team effort. We all put our own cases on hold." Pogolin said.

"What was he working on?"

Pogolin glanced at the others and continued the tale when no one else offered. "A murder. A theft. A beating. Not much more."

"The murder—the Ivanov case?" Kazakov asked, sitting forward. "What did you find?"

"Find? Haven't I told you? Chelomeyev did a good job of the investigation. He talked to the right people, but there was nothing there. The suspects have strong alibis!"

"And who were the suspects?"

Pogolin sighed. "The wife, of course. His chief executives. There was nothing. Absolutely nothing, and I resent you acting as if we do not know our jobs! Now we have the street officers keeping their ears open. Surely any punk who took out a police officer will eventually start bragging. We will hear of it and we will act!"

Kazakov gritted his teeth and sat back. "What do Chelomeyev's family think?" Kazakov asked. "Where's Rostoff in this? Surely Chelomeyev's father must be demanding better results."

"His father is grieving and supporting his wife." Razin spoke up in support of his partner.

"As for Rostoff, he's where he always is. Out," Kuznetzov said, looking tired without looking up from his typewriter. "If you wanted the case dealt with differently, perhaps you should have been here to help instead of leaving Chelomeyev working alone. But then, even if you'd been here, you probably wouldn't have accepted a partner, because the great Kazakov always works alone. Let it go and retire, why don't you? It will be better for the department. For that matter, you look like you already have."

Scanning their faces brought back to Kazakov all the things he had hated about his job, but most of all it made him hate himself, because what Kuznetzov said was right. These men had been here since word came in of Chelomeyev's beating. By the exhaustion on their faces, they'd put everything behind their investigation during the time they'd had. They'd reached a dead end and were seeking directions from a superior officer. And now here Kazakov came causing—from their perspectives—trouble.

Yes, the squad had been less than stellar in the past with the blind ignoring of facts and evidence and the willful prosecution of the wrong man because the detective refused to look beyond his prime suspect. But this was different. This was the beating of one of their own.

Kazakov had been part of this place. His career had been here—a solitary one, to be sure, because he had refused to work with men he didn't trust. Over the years he had built up a reputation as the detective with the highest conviction rate—and also as a troublesome wild card who did not play by the department's unspoken 'rules'.

Had Chelomeyev broken some of those rules? Certainly he had when he'd helped Kazakov on his previous investigation, but it had seemed that the help had remained anonymous. It made no sense that Chelomeyev's family would accept his injury.

Unless there was interference from even higher up the food chain. Bure's influence?

He pulled Chelomeyev's desk drawers open. As he'd expected, they'd been emptied out during the investigation.

"Fine. If you don't need my help, I've better things to do." He didn't even look at his old desk, standing alone in one corner, just limped back the way he'd come to the elevator, his cane an unwelcome third beat to his steps.

The squad room remained silent save for Kuznetzov's two-fingered typing, but as the elevator dinged and opened and he stepped inside, he heard the two newcomers.

"That's him?" said one.

"*Derr 'mo*. He looks like a homeless person."

The elevator doors closed behind him.

B ack in the Perseus, Kazakov clutched the steering wheel to stop his hands from shaking. Instead the tremors spread from his hands up through his arms to his body. He wanted a drink to calm his fury and guilt but that was a bad idea in and of itself. Outside the vehicle, the wind had torn the clouds loose from the Tian Shan mountains to the east and had dragged them westward to clog the sky overhead. In the dry air, scattered flakes swirled between the concrete towers and stung the faces of pedestrians navigating the snow-covered sidewalks. Only the large department stores shoveled the sidewalks clear. Even the government seemed to expect the population to wade through the snow.

Just like nothing was done properly in this city, this country, things were not going to be done properly to find Chelomeyev's attackers. It was typical, and he, on medical leave, shouldn't meddle, especially when Chelomeyev's family seemed to be content with the department decision. Which made no sense given the strings Chelomeyev's father had pulled to get his son promoted.

He watched an older man navigate the ice and snow of the ten broad steps up to the police station front door and wondered what need he had that the police would not meet. What would stop a father who was committed to his son from demanding a larger, more complete investigation? It was a question he needed an answer to. But then, perhaps Pogolin and the others were right and there was nothing else to follow up.

Kazakov should request to be reinstated, to take over the Chelomeyev case and the young detective's other cases. He went to open the door to do just that, but caught a glimpse of himself in the rearview mirror. He stopped, the cold air rushing into the Perseus like a slap on the face.

His haggard face had not seen soap or a shave for at least a week and quite possibly longer. Greasy brown hair spiked on his head and a map of broken veins had appeared on his nose from his recent overindulgence in vodka. His blue eyes looked faded and watery. He glanced down at his old coat—the one he had kept for chopping wood and outdoor work. Not something he had ever planned to wear into town. He simply hadn't had the heart to buy a new one after his previous good coat was destroyed by bullet holes and blood stains.

Any demand to be returned to active duty would have to wait until he got cleaned up. No wonder the duty officer had almost refused him entry. He'd been a fool to come here.

And perhaps he was a fool even contemplating what he planned.

5

The first bomb exploded at nine o'clock the next morning as Kazakov drove into town from the dacha. Near the base of Yekaterina Mountain, a plume of smoke came up through the sea of rooftops and he stopped the Perseus, wondering what it was. New construction? There were times when developers would raze a building to allow space for their new build, but the location of the plume said it was in or near the old city.

He increased his speed but had to stop at a store on Suvarov Boulevard to purchase a new great coat. He stepped outside bathed, shaved, and wearing his new purchase over his last clean suit just as a second plume rose up from the center of the city. What the hell was going on? He ran to the Perseus and pulled out into traffic, weaving through vehicles that were slowing while vehicles in the oncoming lanes careened past him as if trying to get away. A marked police car came up behind him, its red and white lights flaring, its siren blaring. Swearing under his breath, Kazakov pulled over, but the police vehicle kept going. So did the next one he saw. It careered around a corner and sped up toward the city center. Kazakov tucked in behind him and matched its speed.

The Perseus's engine roared as they entered the snowy canyons between the concrete high rises. Then the canyon ended and the replica Saint Basil's carnival-colored domes came in sight, like a ghostly reminder of what might have been. It floated over the city, swathed in snow and now half-masked by dust and smoke caught up by the wind.

The police vehicle ahead suddenly stopped before it reached the main square he'd visited just the day before. Another police vehicle blocked its way, its driver standing guard with rifle in hand.

Kazakov pulled over and climbed out into a wind that ruffled his fur hat against his skin. The air stank of dust and—cordite. Explosion?

He tugged up the collar of his new coat and trudged across the snow to the police barrier, regretting his cane every step of the way. He needed to be free of the damn thing.

"What's happening?" he asked, producing his badge. It was a good thing that this was today as opposed to yesterday given his improved appearance. His lynx fur hat ruffled against his neck and cheeks.

The few people on the snowy sidewalk were hurrying away, and beyond the police block, people were being helped into the warmth of the buildings. An ambulance came blaring up and was waved through by the uniformed officer from the police vehicle he'd followed.

The first officer glanced at Kazakov's badge and his face. "A second bomb, sir. In the square. Made a hell of a mess."

A second bomb and he wished his new coat had a karakul collar like his old one to keep out the cold wind. The first plume of smoke had been another bomb. His skin chilled from more than the wind and he looked up at the cloudy sky almost expecting the bombers overhead that he had seen as a boy. Then they had been carrying death overhead in skirmishes between the Ottomans and the Chinese. Clearly, the bombs had come this time without the planes. "Where was the first one?"

The officer glanced back at him as he leaned into the driver's window of another vehicle. "The old carnival."

The old carnival built at the base of the mountain. He had looked out over it the day before.

"Casualties?" he asked.

The officer shrugged. "They're still searching the place. Not many people in that part of town, thankfully."

Not many Russians was what the man meant. The Kyrgyz kids from the old city often spent time at the old amusement park when it wasn't in use. Hopefully, at this time of year it would be less so, so there would be less likelihood anyone would be hurt. But why bomb such a place?

He left the police cordon and picked his way through the snow down the road, coming out onto New Moscow's historic square with its statue of the heroic Yekaterina and the unwelcoming front of the main police station. When the city had built the replica of Saint Basil's Cathedral, there has been discussion about locating it here, instead of the police station. Instead the cathedral had been placed in the more picturesque location near the river. Let the square be the domain of Yekaterina.

But the statue of Yekaterina no longer stood in the center of the square.

Instead, a blackened crater filled the spot where her stone pedestal had stood. The huge effigy lay twisted and misshapen, half-embedded in the side of the Ustinov office building across from the police station. Yekaterina's torso had separated from her head and lay caved in on one side, breast-down in a gutter filled with soon-to-be-frozen runoff from the heat of the explosion. In the side of the police building, a metal hand was impaled in the concrete wall. He couldn't spot Yekaterina's head.

Kazakov stood immobile, taking it all in. It was as if the tableau was frozen. Even the clouds ceased to move overhead. Then a gust of wind caught him in the face with the stink of cordite and suddenly the world moved again.

In the buildings around the street, people peered out shattered windows. The main doors of the *politseyshiyuchastok*, the police station, were braced open for the steady stream of officers moving back and forth. Uniformed officers searched for injured—or suspects. The wail of ambulance sirens came from down the side streets feeding into the square. On a corner of the square, a woman was helped up by two young police officers. Miraculously, there did not appear to be many injured in the street, but he would bet that inside the buildings many workers had been caught by flying glass.

Though the square was a main one in the city, the main commerce areas had gradually shifted away over the years. The buildings around the square had been taken over by government, the functionaries of the foreign office inhabiting most of the Ustinov building. The most senior workers, with their privileged views, would be paying a price this morning. He turned to look up at the windows of the police station. Shards of glass filled most of the second-floor window gaps. The third floor had fared little better, though boards were already appearing to block the flow of cold air.

Had someone planned the explosion exactly because so many government offices were here? Who would blow up Fergana's beloved Yekaterina? Not that there weren't numerous other statues of the great queen elsewhere in the city.

But the destruction here was almost like a message to the country and he felt like he stood in a bell, the entire country quivering around him. Fergana was by-and-large a peaceful country. This—this changed everything.

Mulling the possibilities, Kazakov straightened and stepped into the square. He limped toward the police station and up the ten stairs to the open door. An officer stood guard.

Kazakov flashed his identification and today was waved inside without any hesitation. But then he'd spent care on his appearance today—had actually hauled in the old washtub and filled it with water heated on the stove for a bath unlike any he'd had in two months, though he'd used it frequently before his injury. He'd shaved and hacked at his hair until it was almost its old floppy length before dressing in a clean shirt and a suit that he'd bought in the days of Annuschka, his ex-wife. The suit now hung on him as if he'd borrowed it. He'd lost more weight than he'd thought.

Inside, he rode the elevator to the detective squad room. The door slid open and Kazakov stepped out. Instead of the usual quiet, the hallway that led past the squad room to the executive offices was bedlam. Rushing people streamed past him—bloodied, holding bandages to their heads. Medics came to their aid, some carrying stretchers. He saw Rostoff's blonde assistant, Constable Dabria Smirnova, carried past, her bandaged face a pale counterpoint to the bloody tatters of her uniform shirt. Other people yelled orders to workmen carrying boards to block the cold streaming through broken windows.

Kazakov pushed through the people into the squad room. Detektiv Kuznetzov turned a weary eye up from papers on his desk, his shaggy head looking like an old mountain ram whose territory was threatened. The squad room was otherwise empty. Kuznetzov's gaze widened.

"You're back," he said over the noise from the hallway.

Kazakov nodded. "Where are the others?"

Kuznetzov shrugged. "Out at the first explosion site. Pogolin and Razin are on their way back as we speak. I guess you came in for the excitement."

"Rostoff around?" Kazakov looked backed to the madness in the hallway. It was a shock to see the sanctity of those hallowed halls breached. He could imagine the shock the denizens felt—they were all officers and too far above any direct threats. Apparently, someone intended to change all that.

Kuznetzov shrugged again. "Maybe. You know him. He might be out at the explosion if it looked good for his career."

They both knew Rostoff was an opportunist who had advanced by his connections and capitalizing on notable events.

"Any sense of who's responsible?"

"Too early, but we'll catch the bastards."

Kazakov nodded, knowing that even if they didn't get the correct bastards, someone would pay for an event like this. He left the squad room and shoved through the clogged artery of the hallway. Usually closed doors lined the corridor, but today doors were open revealing waiting areas and more doors were open to inner sanctums. Cold air from broken windows flowed into the hall. Drops of fresh blood patterned the floor. A medic station that had been set up in one waiting area was being dismantled, so the wounded must have all been treated and sent on their way.

The overhead fluorescents flickered and flared like the Russian spirit. At a closed nondescript wood door, he pushed inside to the pale tan walls of Rostoff's waiting area complete with the dark wood desk of his secretary.

The place was deserted without the Detektiv Chief Inspektor's pretty secretary. Kazakov couldn't imagine Rostoff functioning well without her able assistance. The detective squad had had their conjectures of a relationship between Rostoff and Smirnova confirmed by innuendos dropped by the great man himself, but Kazakov had never been so certain. Dabria Smirnova had always had the cautious demeanor of an animal used to fending for itself in an unfriendly world.

He crossed to the inner door, knocked once, and went in.

Detektiv Chief Inspektor Valerian Rostoff had been a year ahead of Kazakov in training and even then the impact of his family connections was possible to see. He had been placed in policy and communications positions while Kazakov was working on the street. The two of them had been made detectives at the same time, but while Kazakov had built a reputation as a dogged investigator whose cases gained convictions, Rostoff had quietly become the fixer for Fergana's leading families. When the old Detektiv Chief Inspektor had been moved aside on a special project, it was naturally Rostoff who had been promoted. That had been ten years ago.

Rostoff stood behind his desk, his phone in his hand held six inches from his ear. Even from the doorway, Kazakov could hear the yelling through the phone. The Police Chief Inspektor, unhappy apparently.

Rostoff was a bear of a man, with broad shoulders and barrel chest and the ruddy complexion of the vodka drinker. He was about six feet tall—almost Kazakov's height—and had a thick head of curly hair that Rostoff had always considered one of his best features. After all these years, it was probably too dark a brown to be natural.

He glanced once in Kazakov's direction and turned his back,

making soothing statements into the phone. "Fine. I will call you back."

He turned back to his desk and hung up the phone, then glanced stonily at Kazakov. "What do you want? I thought you'd retired. Or died."

Kazakov smiled from his place by the door. Easier to leave quickly if he needed to. "I am happy to report those rumors are unfounded."

Rostoff shifted through papers on his desk, clearly looking for something. "You were here yesterday. I heard you looked like somebody's half-eaten meal left out for the dogs."

Perhaps it was an apt description. What he'd seen in the mirror hadn't been pretty. "As you can see, another baseless rumor."

Rostoff glanced at the office window. He was one of the fortunate, for though the glass was cracked, the pane hadn't shattered from the explosion. Dabria Smirnova must have been standing too close to someone else's window when the explosion occurred.

"I repeat. What do you want? As you can see, I am busy. The powers that be are…" He looked back at his desk. "They broke her into pieces. Who would do such a thing?"

Kazakov stayed by the door, for surely the question about Yekaterina was rhetorical.

With a sly glance in Kazakov's direction, Rostoff shifted some papers across the top of his desk. "Perhaps you've come of offer your services?"

It was the opening Kazakov needed. He stepped further into the office. The explosion might not have shattered the glass but the concussion had shaken the display of photos on the wall behind Rostoff. They hung in a crooked gallery of images memorializing Rostoff's numerous high-ranking connections.

"I came about Chelomeyev," Kazakov said. "I understand the investigation is over."

Rostoff straightened from searching through another sheaf of papers. "The case has been fully investigated. No suspect was located."

"Based on the belief that his attack was a random robbery. I have reason to believe there may be a connection between the attack and one of Chelomeyev's cases."

Rostoff's harried gaze zeroed in on him. "You think we didn't consider that? Is everyone a fool, save for the great Kazakov?"

Kazakov tensed. It was always like this with Rostoff. The man had no patience for Kazakov's methodical approaches, instead placing more concern on quick case closures because it apparently looked better to his superiors. But this was an attack on the son of one of those superiors and one of their own.

"I know that his cases were looked at, but I have background knowledge that the others did not have." He shook his head. "Besides, I offer fresh eyes." For some reason he didn't want to mention Chelomeyev's visit to his house. Given Rostoff's anger over Kazakov's dogged investigation of the Weber-Manas case against Rostoff's orders, he definitely wasn't going to mention any possible connection there.

"You expect me to waste manpower on a closed case when this has happened?" Rostoff stabbed his finger toward his cracked window and the shattered square beyond. "If I need fresh eyes, it is on this! They destroyed our Yekaterina!"

Recognizing the shocky glaze in Rostoff's gaze, Kazakov sighed and limped to Rostoff's desk. This had been the risk he took by even coming here—being called back to work. "Sir. I will gladly assist, but I would like the freedom to review Chelomeyev's cases and his attack. Surely his family would appreciate that."

The papers went still in Rostoff's hands. His dark gaze caught Kazakov's and held on.

"Are you bargaining with me, Detektiv?" His voice had turned hard. "Or perhaps it is a threat. Let me assure you that before the case was closed, Chelomeyev's father was consulted. He reviewed the file and agreed with the closure."

"I suppose I am making a suggestion. With this cane, I am not yet ready for active duty, but I will gladly help however I can. In return I would like to consider Chelomeyev's files. It would not be good if the department missed something. Surely his family would appreciate such a review."

Rostoff's eyes narrowed. "What are you up to, Kazakov? What is it you know or suspect?"

"I would be no better than a storyteller or a rumormonger if I spoke without evidence. Let me review the files and then I will bring you the facts."

A cagey expression flitted across Rostoff's face. "And you will also provide a second set of eyes on the investigation into this attack on Fergana's heart. After all these years as a detective, surely you have contacts who might help you. I understand that you are friends with a certain medical examiner with questionable connections."

Kazakov went still, guarding his expression. "Just what are you saying?"

Rostoff met Kazakov's gaze directly. "I'm saying that through December there have been threats received by the city. The notes have demanded better access to jobs for the Kyrgyz and Uzbek tribals. Each has been signed Suleiman's Sons—whoever they may be."

Suleiman had been one of the greatest Sultans of the Ottomans during the middle ages and was believed by the Kyrgyz and Uzbeks to have once visited Fergana and to have climbed Yekaterina Mountain to pray—so that the Uzbeks and Kyrgyz citizens of Fergana still called it Suleiman's Mountain. Kazakov bowed his head.

"There is something in what the note says. Young, educated Kyrgyz are not exactly welcomed into Russian businesses." Kazakov sighed. "What was threatened?"

Rostoff's face worked as if he struggled to find an answer. From the square beyond the window came the clamor of emergency personnel. "Is it not enough that they demand from us? I want you to use your connections to find the culprits!"

"But why would the Kyrgyz blow up the carnival? It may not be…"

Rostoff's hands curled to fists, his eyes closed, just as his mind apparently was.

"Just do your job and bring me the culprits. I will expect a report at the end of the week." He turned away to his wall of crooked photographs, his phone clutched in his hand ready to make another call.

Kazakov's audience was over. It was not quite the result that Kazakov had wanted, but it had gone better than he'd expected. And being part of the investigation into the explosions was not a bad thing. If Chelomeyev had not been front and center in his mind, he would have requested the duties Rostoff had assigned. Of course, by providing Rostoff's 'second set of eyes', there was also the potential for Rostoff to blame any lack of arrest on a troublesome detective named Kazakov. It was a chance he would have to take.

Kazakov retreated to the exit. "And the Chelomeyev files?"

Rostoff waved his hand at the door. "Talk to Smirnova."

Kazakov bit back the reminder that the constable-secretary was injured and gone to the hospital. Instead he pulled the door softly closed behind him and turned to Smirnova's desk. The detectives had said yesterday that Chelomeyev's file had been sent to Rostoff for review and direction. Given the furor over the explosions, there was a chance that they might still be here.

Behind her desk was a small stack of boxes—investigation files ready to go to archives. On the front of each box, a flourished signature said that Rostoff had signed off on the archiving. The date was yesterday. He opened the boxes and checked the files. Two contained what he was looking for. Chelomeyev's exuberant script filled the note pages in each file. In addition, included in one file box was a slim file that contained Razin and Pogolin's investigation into Chelomeyev's beating.

Kazakov replaced the lids and carried the two file boxes out of the building and out of the square to the Perseus and locked them inside. Then he returned to the square.

The place was overwhelmed with police: cordoning off the square, escorting people from surrounding buildings, searching the scene. Overhead, the stiff wind blew in clouds so that shadows flowed across the buildings and flickered across the fallen Yekaterina and the dirty snow like ghosts in a wasteland.

He stood watching and then circumnavigated the square before settling into the doorway of a boarded-up coffee shop to watch. A command post had been hurriedly established just outside the doors of the politseyshiyuchastok so that they could surveil the activity, but still easily step inside to warm up. He glimpsed Pogolin and Razin, apparently coordinating the massive task of collecting evidence. They had to move quickly, or at this time of year, the weather would erase their chance. Already stray flakes swirled around in the wind like summer insects seeking something to sting. Kazakov pulled his karakul-less collar up around his neck and studied the scene.

Clearly, the bomb had somehow been set inside the statue—probably in one of the hollow indentations of the tsarina's sweeping skirts. The artist of the statue and its castor had made the statue hollow, with narrow openings up under the sweeping skirts. During the summers, mothers allowed their children to play on the statue and it was a rare Russian family that didn't have a photo of their son or daughter peeking out from under the great tsarina's petticoats. If the bomb had been narrowly shaped and lifted all the way up through one of those openings so that it dropped down into the hollow space inside, the statue's shape would channel most of the force up through Yekaterina's hollow body. That was why the figure had exploded at her shoulders, effectively decapitating the statue. It had also helped channel most of the force skyward. That was clear from the way most of the damage had spared the windows on the ground floor. It was also the only way that the few pedestrians had escaped certain slaughter.

Had the bombmaker planned it that way?

Had they simply wanted to destroy the symbol?

From what he'd read about attacks like this in the places like Constantinople and Bagdad and even Nanjing—though the Chinese were more secretive—most bombers wanted to exact casualties. That was part of their modus operandi—to sow terror amongst those they terrorized.

But the people around him didn't have the same blank stares or film of horror spread on their faces he had seen out of the latest bombing outside the great Constantinople's Ayasofya. They were shocked, of course. He felt the shock himself, for the statue had stood since 1796, only twenty years after the Russian refugees had come here.

No, this was more like a statement to the Ferganese people. *Yekaterina is unwelcome. Yekaterina can be toppled. Yekaterina is dead.*

And you can be, too?

He inhaled the cold air and considered. Yes. That felt right. That made sense. Now who would espouse such sentiments? He had long-ago given up expressing his opinion that his people dwelt too much on their people's historic glories.

And there was the question of how the necessary explosives had been obtained, given that they were restricted and monitored by the government ever since the bombings had begun inside the Ottoman and Chinese Empires. At that time of the Ayasofya attack the Ottomans had suggested that the explosives had come from beyond Ottoman borders. Fergana could not afford to be seen as the source.

In the square, the uniformed searchers collected debris and brought it to the command center. Surely Razin and Pogolin realized that they would need more space if they were going to try to reconstruct the statue to gain a sense of how the bomb was constructed and placed. Of course, they could possibly move everything into the police parking garage.

A young female officer, with cheeks bright red from the cold and the fur flaps of her hat pulled down over her ears, crossed the debris field to Kazakov.

"Sir, we are encouraging all onlookers to move along. There is nothing more to see."

Kazakov nodded and showed his credentials. "Humor me, officer."

The young officer apologized and hurried away. Kazakov straightened. The youngster had been right. There *was* nothing more to see. He left his shelter and limped back to the Perseus. He had important evidence to review.

He turned the Perseus around across traffic and snow piles and headed back through snow-bound New Moscow, considering what he knew. Outside, pedestrians picked their way down unshoveled sidewalks. The wind was picking up. It shuddered the limbs of the trees along Suvarov Way as if they could feel something coming.

An explosion at a vacant carnival and one that destroyed an iconic statue. Clearly, someone was sending a message.

6

―――――――

The snow fell thicker the farther up into the hills he drove until the huge, falling flakes concealed all but the shadowy trees beyond his windows. Usually, at this time of January, there was snow, but not so much. It was as if this year the gods were determined to bury Fergana for dead—or his part of it, at least.

He slowed to a crawl and had to guess when he passed Agafya Ryabkov's driveway. The shape of the trees appeared to be right and so did the appearance of the opening through the trees, but snow transformed everything.

He'd learned that as a boy. New Moscow had never been a city prone to heavy snow. Skiffs of the white stuff would fall and each time they did, he'd see the streets transformed and glistening in the sunlight. Until that same sunlight melted the snow away. It was as if New Moscow was transformed into the city it was supposed to be, but the transformation was only taken halfway and so the city reverted to its dirty, squalling self. For a country as young as Fergana, it was a puzzle why the people clung to the past instead of looking forward to a better future. Even the youngsters seemed born and raised with their gazes turned backward.

Feeling old and alone, he turned into his driveway. It was three o'clock when he arrived back at the dacha and parked behind the building, then struggled through the snow with the two file boxes and his cane. His side ached. Apparently, he was no longer accustomed to extended periods of being up and about. Time to do something about that.

Inside, the wood fire had burned low and Koshka had tunneled under his blankets to get away from the resulting cool. Her little feline face appeared quickly enough when he stomped the snow off his boots before stepping through the open front door. Once he was inside, she leapt down to thread around his legs as he took his coat and hat off and hung them on the peg by the door.

He ran his palm over her small round head as she meowed piteously up at him.

"What? No mice to supplement your dinner, little one? Or was it too cold for you to venture out?" He had built her a small cat door from the far end of the kitchen when she had first decided to move in with him.

He settled onto a chair at the table to toe off his boots, but instead picked her up and set her on his lap. It had become a habit since his injury. He peered down into her yellow-green eyes and noticed for the first time the white flecks on her muzzle. She was getting older, like him, and for a moment a wave of melancholy overcame him.

He shoved the maudlin emotion away and set Koshka on the floor. "Perhaps just a little something to hold you over until dinner, girl."

He washed her plate and put a teaspoonful of canned food out for her. The room filled with the sound of satisfied licking—if only temporarily.

After removing his boots and stirring the fire to life, he carried the file boxes to the desk against the rear wall of the dacha to examine the Chelomeyev investigations. In lantern light, he first went through them quickly, setting aside the investigation into Chelomeyev's beating and another pile of files relating to minor incidents: theft of vehicle from a downtown warehouse; a series of break-and-enters of houses in the eastern suburb of Greenview; an investigation into a break-in at a pawn shop. Then he put a kettle on the woodstove to boil and settled in his old oak desk chair to read.

He started with the investigation into Chelomeyev's beating. It was a slim file.

The young man had been found two days ago, five days after he'd spoken to Kazakov, in the parking lot outside his apartment in the up-and-coming neighborhood of Orlov Park. He'd been found by another tenant leaving for work. His wallet, badge, and gun were gone and his body so brutally beaten that at first the girl who found him didn't know who it was. Thankfully, she had called the police and an ambulance.

The kettle squealed and he got up and put tea, three sugars, and hot water in a cup. He doused it with milk and brought it back to his desk.

The attending detectives, Pogolin and Fedunov—the second a name Kazakov didn't recognize, so it was probably one of the newcomers to the squad—had canvassed the tenants but no one admitted hearing anything. Chelomeyev had gone off duty at five in the afternoon. He hadn't mentioned anything to anyone in the squad about going anywhere after work, but then the young detective had not been in the office as often as he had been when working with Sherepov.

There were notations about unsolved robberies occurring in the neighborhood—a local liquor store and a grocery store both robbed by a knife-wielding robber, and a woman who had her purse snatched. These were cited as reason to conclude that the beating of Chelomeyev was simply a matter of a robbery gone wrong. His wallet was taken, after all.

The chair squealed as Kazakov leaned back and put his feet up on the desk. The dacha had warmed. Koshka had curled up on the bed, her tail in front of her nose, but her yellow-green gaze stayed locked on him. He sipped his now-tepid tea and tasted the rich tannins.

There were so many things he wanted to know. Were occupants of nearby buildings canvassed? Had anyone seen anything suspicious earlier in the day? Had they done anything further to investigate where Chelomeyev had been before he went home? Had he even been alone? There were no notations in the file.

He swore into the silence of the cracking logs on the fire and the hissing of snow across the windows flanking the door. The light outside had faded early, as it usually did in mid-January, and the window was a square of growing darkness except for the flecks of white as flakes hit the glass and the frost forming around the edges. The investigation didn't feel complete to Kazakov. Why had Chelomeyev's father approved it? Would it have been different if Chelomeyev had died?

And that was before everyone in the police force had been drawn into dealing with the two explosions. There were definitely areas that needed following up on.

Sighing, he placed the file to one side and started going through Chelomeyev's investigations, seeking anything that might draw an attack on the investigator.

The first was the beating of a seventeen-year-old prostitute named Mura Stepanova. The woman worked a corner in the warehouse district not too distant from Chelomeyev's home—a possible connection. She had been beaten by a customer and escaped to report it. The file noted that a number of other girls who worked the same area had provided the description of a car cruising their corners. The car was a dark sedan, something expensive and foreign.

Kazakov closed the file, not reading any farther. Bad dates were common for working girls. Chelomeyev had clearly done his job by interviewing the other girls. The file was thick with the numerous interviews and with a multi-page printout of registered foreign sedans. A few had been marked and there were follow-up interviews of a few of the owners on the files. Clearly, Chelomeyev had planned to interview all those that he had marked. With his hospitalization, the file had been closed.

Kazakov took another sip of tepid tea. There were still a number of things he could do to complete the investigation, but that was not why he was here. Still, a Russian with an expensive vehicle could have much to lose in such an investigation…

He set the file aside as well and opened another. Sometime over the last weekend of December there had been a break-in and theft at a construction company down in the new districts being built out of the ruins of ancient caravanserai along the flanks of Yekaterina Mountain. Though there had been security staff on site, the storage shed had been broken into and a variety of tools and supplies taken. The theft had not been discovered until the following Monday because the thief or thieves had been careful to close the door behind them. The security guard claimed to have heard nothing, though Chelomeyev suspected his complicity. Stolen had been new drills and power saws and a crate of explosive that was earmarked to remove a spur of the mountain to allow the building of an apartment building.

Kazakov put down his teacup and straightened. In light of the events in New Moscow this morning, this case had new meaning. This could be the provenance of the bomber or bombers' explosives. He scanned Chelomeyev's notes. The young detective had interviewed all of the construction site staff and the security guard. The latter's statement indicated that they'd had a rash of break-ins into the site. What had begun as spray-painting insults had escalated to vandalism to the earthmoving equipment that had been moved in. As a result, the guard had begun to patrol higher up the slope of Yekaterina Mountain as he believed that was where the "young hoodlums" were getting in. He believed the break-in at the storage building had happened during one of his patrols.

It made sense. In fact, given the explosion this morning, it suggested that the escalating vandalism might have been a ploy to lure the security guard away.

He read further into the file. Chelomeyev had started to call on informers amongst New Moscow's gangs, but so far no one had brought information to him. Unless someone had before Chelomeyev had a chance to enter it into the file. If Chelomeyev was getting too close to solving the thefts, it could explain why he was beaten. Why he wasn't killed outright was the question. Maybe they thought they had...

Kazakov closed the file and set it on the table behind him. He would have to bring this case to Rostoff's attention.

The fourth file was one Chelomeyev had closed himself after a young girl recanted her report of rape. Kazakov set the file amongst the others he planned to file and went back to the last file amongst those to review. He flipped the manila folder open.

The body of Grigori Ivanov splayed on his hardwood floor, his throat cut, his dead gaze staring up at Kazakov. Behind that photo was a series of police shots from various angles and distances around the body.

He lay in an office of book-lined walls, a pair of curtained floor to ceiling windows laying tongues of light across the body. Ivanov lay on the floor between his desk and a couch on the path to the door as if whoever had killed him had caught him as he tried to escape. There were signs of a struggle in shattered glassware, files spilled onto the floor, an overturned chair, and another shoved out of the indentations its clawed feet had left in the carpet.

Kazakov studied the images. The detectives who had closed Chelomeyev's file had suggested the death was a stranger killing—a robbery gone wrong. It could be true.

But there was something… a doubt nibbling at the back of his brain that accorded with Chelomeyev's thinking. Something was wrong with the picture. If Ivanov had been surprised at his desk by a stranger coming through his office door, would he have reacted by running toward the robber? It would be a very unusual man who would run toward that kind of danger—especially if the intruder was armed.

Kazakov shook his head. Perhaps he was simply out of practice at this whole thing.

But if Ivanov hadn't been surprised by a stranger, what would the scenario be then? Taken by surprise by friends, he could be overwhelmed more easily. It would explain why he had come to the couch—to sit with them rather than behind his desk. That worked better to Kazakov's mind. So not a stranger robbery. But that didn't quite fit with the destruction of the scene. Was the scene staged? That suggested premeditation or at least a calculation after the crime had been committed… if the murder had been committed by a friend or family member or at least someone Ivanov felt comfortable with. He set the file down on the desk.

Though he trusted Chelomeyev, he wasn't about to simply fill in the blanks of the young detective's investigation. Instead he would start from scratch as if this was a newly assigned investigation. He flipped through the photos to the image of Svetlana Ivanova and Olga Gruenwald. They hugged each other against the winter chill, as if they were close friends. Close enough to share secrets?

They most likely did, given his previous experience with Olga Gruenwald.

He had first met her at the city home of her employer, Enver Pasha. The attractive young woman in an expensive outfit had claimed to be his housekeeper and assistant, though given her dress, demeanor, and other attributes, he'd had doubts about that being her only role. Enver Pasha, himself, Kazakov had never set eyes on in person, but the man kept turning up in newspaper images with Boris Bure, the stepfather of the dead girl Yekaterina Weber and current candidate for president for the Ferganese Reformation Party. Enver Pasha was also a neighbor of a brothel that had harbored a Chinese spy ring. Kazakov had also seen him in newspaper images of a Chinese spy who had turned out to be a double agent. Any one of these things could be a coincidence, but together they began to form a picture; and then coupled with the fact that Enver Pasha was a wealthy Ottoman, it made little alarm bells go off in Kazakov's brain. Enver Pasha might not be directly involved in any of these cases, but now here he was again, on the periphery of another murder.

Had Chelomeyev found something after Kazakov mentioned Enver Pasha's name?

He flipped through Chelomeyev's file. There was no interview with the mysterious man who Kazakov had only laid eyes on in newspaper photographs. Kazakov couldn't imagine the young detective leaving that bit of work undone, but then he hadn't had much time. Had he been refused an interview? Kazakov turned to the process notes on the other side of the file and scanned the notations of contacts made and attempted.

There.

Chelomeyev had contacted Enver Pasha's office the night of the beating to book an appointment, but whomever he spoke to had taken Chelomeyev's information and indicated that someone would contact him the next day with Enver Pasha's availability. There was no further notation. Since the date of the attack on Chelomeyev, no callback had been received by the office.

Unless Enver Pasha's office had contacted the squad office since the beating had happened and no one had made a note of it.

Kazakov lumbered up. His left leg had fallen asleep and he staggered past the glowing stove to his coat and dug out his phone. For the first time since the Weber-Manas case, he turned it on and dialed.

"Detektiv Pogolin," came the voice from the end of the phone.

By the tone Kazakov could picture his exhaustion, his stubble of gravel-colored hair overgrown on his head, a matching five o'clock stubble of beard.

"Artyom." He called Pogolin by his first name. "It's Kazakov. Rostoff has asked me to look again at Chelomeyev's files. Have there been any messages for Chelomeyev since he was injured?"

Pogolin groaned. "You're asking me to remember something like that after all that has happened?"

Sinking down in a table chair, Kazakov closed his eyes. "I am following up on a person of interest and there was someone who was supposed to contact the office with an interview time. Did anyone call?"

"I'm not a receptionist. You think I have nothing better to do? There was one death and thirty-five injured in the explosions today!" Pogolin snapped.

"Would anyone else know?" Kazakov asked, feeling almost defeated by the other detective's inertia.

There was silence a moment and muffled voices as if Pogolin had his hand over the phone. Then he came back on. "It seems there was. Kuznetzov took a call. Some high-flier's office providing an appointment date. He'd forgotten to put the message in the file, but he's got it now. He'll phone them back and cancel."

Kazakov felt his heart beat a little faster. "Tell him not to. Can I have the details? Please." He'd keep the appointment. He'd finally meet the mysterious Enver Pasha.

"Tell him yourself, Kazakov. I'm not your errand boy." Pogolin disappeared from the phone and then Kuznetzov's rough voice came on.

"Causing trouble again, Kazakov?"

"Trying to do my job."

"And here we were taking a collection for your retirement."

Kazakov sighed. "A tad too early, it seems. When and where was Chelomeyev's appointment?" Please let the time not have already passed. He wasn't certain why he had this sudden sense of urgency. Just why was it so important that he meet Enver Pasha?

Through the phone came the rustling of papers and Kazakov could imagine the usual disarray of Kuznetzov's desk as he dug out the message. No wonder it hadn't gone with Chelomeyev's boxes. He wondered how many messages had gone missing over the years.

"Here it is. Transcontinental Shipping Administration Offices for six o'clock today." He gave the address.

Kazakov looked at his watch. Only forty-five minutes from now. If he left right this moment he might only be a few minutes late.

"Thank you!" he said and clicked off, then scrambled into his coat, hat, and boots, grabbed the file and stuffed it in a briefcase, then stumbled out the door to the Perseus. It was when he reached the Perseus that he realized he'd left his cane behind. He had no time to go back for it.

7

———————

The midwinter darkness obscured the late afternoon as Kazakov made the mad dash down the snow-covered road to the city. The blowing snow and end-of-day traffic had left even Kazakov a little white-knuckled as he pulled into the parking lot in front of Transcontinental Shipping's Administration Office. The wind-blown flakes were orange in the industrial-strength work lights illuminating the large complex of blue-painted warehouses turned brown by the lights. Orange shipping containers sat alongside a fleet of blue long-haul trucks backed against the fence. With their sleek engine housings facing inward, they looked like a pack of wolves held at bay. Perhaps that was fitting given what he knew of Enver Pasha.

Wealthy beyond anything Kazakov could even comprehend, patron of the arts and friend of politicians according to newspaper articles, and yet for all the man graced the society pages of the newspaper, he seemed to generally be a ghost within New Moscow. Transcontinental Shipping? Kazakov wasn't sure he'd ever even heard of it and yet clearly it was a large operation.

The Administration building was a low-slung structure of glass, wood, and steel with an undulating roofline so that it looked like the building was part of the landscape—something far more modern than was found in most of New Moscow. He picked his way across the parking lot. Thankfully, it had been plowed, and though he felt unsteady without his cane, he made it to the front walkway.

Kazakov stomped the snow off his boots outside the door and stepped inside into unbelievable warmth and the sound of trickling water. An artistic grouping of what could only be live palm trees stood in one corner of the reception space, a small pond and waterfall at their feet, their fronds rustling in an unseen warm breeze. His cheeks and ears immediately thawed and he removed his gloves as he crossed to the reception desk. A young woman in a sleeveless tropical-blue dress sat behind the desk, a matching sweater over the back of her chair. Colors like that were rare in New Moscow, and at this time of year, simply not seen. So the outfit was either a uniform or she was paid very well. Or it was gift from someone who could afford to bring such things from elsewhere in the world.

Beyond the receptionist, a security kiosk housed two men whose forearms looked the size of Kazakov's thighs. Their olive skin and dark hair suggested a heritage a long way west of Fergana—say Constantinople for example. He could surmise a similar origin for the dress.

"Detektiv Kazakov to see Enver Pasha," he said, his hat in his hands.

The woman studied her computer screen. "You are not on our list, sir."

"Detektiv. I am not 'sir.' I am detektiv. And you have an appointment scheduled for Detektiv Chelomeyev. He is unable to attend, so I am here in his stead."

The news creased the receptionist's smooth, pretty features. He supposed people did not usually do this sort of thing to Enver Pasha. Then she nodded and made a quick phone call, explaining that he was here in a voice so quiet he could barely hear her. It wasn't long before the click of heels came down a hallway and a woman turned a corner into his view. She wore a sleeveless dress of a similar hue to the receptionist's, also modestly cut just above the knee and around the base of the neck, but the cut perfectly accentuated the curves of her body and the smooth strength of her arms and shoulders. She strode down the hall with a stern expression on a face so pale and perfectly made-up it could be mistaken for porcelain.

She was tall, almost as tall as his six foot two, he realized as she came up to him, with black hair pulled up in a bun behind her head that only accentuated her pallor.

"Detektiv Kazakov." She bowed her head. "Follow me, please."

He did, taking in the broad hallway they followed, the glassed-in boardrooms and glass-walled offices. "Your people work very much in the open," he said.

She nodded. "They can. It brings in natural light. Or they can make them opaque at the touch of a button."

Not dissimilar to suspects who could appear open but still hide dark secrets. "I did not even know this complex existed."

The woman glanced sideways at him. "Transcontinental does not advertise. We do not need to. As you can see, our services are already in demand."

"Your name says you are a shipping company. What do you ship?"

She glanced sideways at him, her brow arched. "Why, everything, of course. Transcontinental ships food, liquor, clothing, appliances, furniture. If you use it or own it, it has likely seen the inside of our warehouse. And our trucks."

Kazakov considered as they came to double doors latticed with black iron strips and decorative nailheads at the end of the hallway. He had never known of a business that did not advertise. Nor had he dealt with one that had touched his life as completely as apparently Transcontinental had.

The woman rapped the amber-colored wood door three times and then opened it.

"Enver Pasha awaits you." The reverence in her voice was more fitting for a religious figure than a businessman.

Thanking her, he stepped past her. He felt the breeze of the door closing silently behind him as a figure stood half-concealed by shadows at the far end of the room.

The office was larger than the detective squad room. It could fit his entire dacha three times over. Dark, hardwood floors were covered with richly colored Persian carpets stacked three deep in places so that he felt like he walked through deep sand. A faint, sweet scent rose from a brazier set on an ebony sideboard along the left wall of glass that gave onto the glowing darkness outside. Through the darkness and falling snow came the orange glow of the lights illuminating the statue of Yekaterina that had been built high on Yekaterina Mountain. In the day the office would have a grand view.

The three other walls were the same tropical-blue as the dresses, but the right wall and the wall with the door were filled with alcoves and niches, their carved edges shaped like arabesques and arches. Each alcove or niche was lit within to showcase glass inlaid vases, statues of misshapen horses, brass lanterns, displays of gold and lapis jewelry. The flash and glitter were almost overwhelming, so Kazakov had to look away. The two things all these items had in common were age—and cost. He imagined that what he was standing among could have bought his dacha—hell, a large swath of Fergana—many, many times over.

A display set to impress.

And overpower.

Interesting.

He focused on the unadorned far wall of the office where a black mahogany desk spread an expansive surface of unblemished, gleaming wood. In front of the desk sat two tropical-blue chairs like small ponds. Behind the desk waited a chair. The owner shifted sideways, stepping from the shadows to stand under the recessed lighting, the master of all he surveilled. With nothing to distract on the wall behind him, he was the centerpiece.

He had graying hair swept back from a high forehead and black eyes that gleamed like onyx pebbles. High cheekbones, a strong jaw, and a luxuriant black moustache all served to frame a hawkish nose with out-swept nostrils so that he seemed to scent the world around him. Perhaps he smelled fear.

Kazakov paced across the carpets, focusing to hide his limp. Enver Pasha did not hold out his hand.

"I am Detektiv Kazakov with the New Moscow police," he introduced himself.

"And I was expecting someone else, I think." Enver Pasha's voice was rich as Ottoman black coffee and more cadenced than expected—as if he was going to break into song—and yet there was a tension to the man. The way he stood with shoulders squared to Kazakov, but with his hips turned slightly askew and stance wide. It was a fighter's stance.

"I am replacing Detektiv Chelomeyev. His is temporarily unavailable." Would he ever be available again? Kazakov watched Enver Pasha closely to gauge his reaction. If there was anything, it might have been the faintest twitch of his right eye.

Then Enver Pasha stirred and came to life. "Most unfortunate. Now how can I help the New Moscow police?"

The tension had disappeared into the faintest of interest as Enver Pasha pulled out his chair and nodded to the chairs facing his desk. He settled facing Kazakov, and Kazakov settled himself and instantly regretted it. The seat was too low, the power clearly held by Enver Pasha, who seemed to hover just beyond and above the massive desk like a behemoth rising above dark waves.

Mind games, all of it, and he wasn't playing. He leaned back in the uncomfortable chair and waited, studying his host.

Finally, Enver Pasha stirred in his chair. "I repeat. What can I help you with?"

Good. The impatience showed a slight breach in Enver Pasha's armor. So the man who controlled all this was not perfectly in control. Kazakov waved his arm vaguely around the room. "Your assistant said you do not advertise and yet you have obviously met with success. How do you do it?" Get the man talking about something unrelated to his enquiry and Kazakov could gain an understanding about the man when he was relaxed.

Pursing his lips, Enver Pasha considered for a moment. Then he shrugged. "You might say that I inherited the business. It was already well known—at least in Constantinople."

"Then you must do a lot of business between the Ottoman Empire and Fergana to bring your headquarters here."

Enver Pasha nodded. "A great deal, but this is not Transcontinental's headquarters. There is no need to advertise because if someone wishes to ship east or west, only Transcontinental provides the complete service."

Kazakov frowned. Perhaps the conversation was not as unrelated as he'd thought…

"So you have no competition."

"Nothing worth noting." Enver Pasha shrugged. "There are small carters for single loads, but if you need a continuous movement of goods, it is Transcontinental that you come to."

"I am investigating the death of Grigori Ivanov. Did you know him?"

Enver Pasha made a show of retrieving a cigarette box from a drawer in his desk. He removed a cigarette from within and slid the box to Kazakov. "Help yourself. I bring them in."

The box gave off the perfumed odor of dark leaf tobacco, the kind the Ottomans preferred. Kazakov's fingers itched to take one, to share this man's lighter and inhale the potent, perfumed smoke.

Instead he denied his old addiction with a shake of the head. Enver Pasha was stalling. "I quit four years ago. So. Did you know Grigori Ivanov?"

Enver Pasha let loose a long trail of smoke and set his cigarette down in a crystal ashtray. "Yes. I knew the man. In a place like New Moscow, it is hard not to meet people who run in the same circles." He smiled, exposing uneven white teeth that reminded Kazakov of the newspaper photos he'd seen of this man posing with people like the now-dead Collin Archer and the far-too-alive Boris Bure. "It was most unfortunate when he was murdered. He left behind his wife and a few siblings, I believe."

Kazakov checked his notes and nodded. He got the feeling Enver Pasha revealed nothing of himself unless he knew it could be checked —like those newspaper photos. But there was something here. Kazakov was sure of it.

"What was he like?"

Enver Pasha looked stonily at him. "What is any man like? Like a Persian carpet, how they appear will depend upon where you are standing."

It was an astute response, but not helpful. Kazakov sighed. "I am trying to get a sense of the man."

Again, that arch of Enver Pasha's brow. "Why? He is dead. What does it matter what manner of man he was?"

"To understand a killer, it is often helpful to understand his victim," Kazakov said. He kept his face impassive.

"He was well-liked. Not a stellar businessman, but sufficiently good to feed his family. He was married, as far as I know. His wife was a friend of my—assistant."

"That would be Olga Gruenwald?"

Enver Pasha nodded. The pause in his previous statement suggested that he wasn't certain what to call the Gruenwald woman, either. Certainly more than assistant, just as she was more than the housekeeper she had claimed to be.

"You speak in generalities. Can you be more specific?"

Enver Pasha's mouth tightened, but his hands remained flat on the top of his desk. "He liked red wine and Parisian food. He was a poor horseman and so rarely rode. He neither beat his wife nor showered her with public affection." His voice was monotone and made clear that was the kind of information he was going to share. Not much help there, but Kazakov *was* getting a sense of the man before him.

"When was the last time you saw him?"

"Just how long is this going to take, Detektiv? I have business to attend to."

Kazakov met his dark gaze and felt cold seep in from the other man's gaze. "As long as it takes, I am afraid. A man was killed."

Sighing, Enver Pasha glanced at a small, antique clock in a wall alcove near his desk. "I can give you another ten minutes."

"Fine. And we will schedule a further follow-up meeting."

The other man's jaw muscles worked under his skin.

"I last saw Grigori at a small dinner party about a week before he died."

Enver Pasha stopped. Kazakov looked up at him, willing him to talk, but Enver Pasha was unlike most men. He answered the question and that was all, instead of filling the silence that Kazakov provided him. It was a special man who did that. Kazakov would need to consider what that meant.

"Tell me about it."

"It was an intimate affair of seven people. Unfortunately, Grigori's wife, Svetlana, could not be there. She was off visiting—her mother, I think. We had a fine wine I had imported from the Rhone River Valley and braised beef cheeks as the main course." The corners of his mouth lifted in a smile as if something in his memory was funny.

"Who attended this intimate party?"

The corners of Enver Pasha's eyes tightened slightly as if he did not like the question. Had he not realized that it was coming, or had he hoped to keep Kazakov off balance long enough that he would not remember to ask? Of course, asking about the dinner party was taking away from time for questions about the day Grigori Ivanov was murdered… Was that what Enver Pasha wanted?

"There was my assistant, Olga. Pieter Vasiliev, the broadcaster, and his wife Nina. Grigori, of course, without partner, and Boris Bure and his wife Natania." Another shrug and another check of the clock. "I am sorry. I must end this. I have another engagement."

Kazakov made notes in his notebook, but his head felt like an echo chamber. Boris Bure front and center again. He could see the man's too-large white teeth smiling like a shark.

"One more question, sir. Svetlana Ivanova claims that she was at your home in the mountains at the time her husband was killed. What can you tell me about that?"

Enver Pasha pushed himself up from his desk, clearly expecting Kazakov to stand as well. Kazakov stayed seated and kept his notebook open, his pen poised for an answer.

Another lift of the shoulder and Kazakov clenched his teeth at the motion. As if the answer, the whole issue, mattered not at all.

"As far as I know, she was. Olga and Svetlana often went to my home in the mountains to ski and to visit with friends. I had planned to join them, but business matters kept me here." He met Kazakov's gaze in a dare. "And before you ask, let me say that the night Grigori was killed, I was at a political function for the Reformation Party. Boris Bure himself and about thirty others can vouch for me."

"So Svetlana Ivanova and Olga Gruenwald were supposedly at your dacha, but you cannot confirm this." Kazakov glanced up and snapped his notebook closed. He slid it into his pocket feeling like an automaton.

"She told me that that was where they were going. I have no reason to disbelieve her. Olga is a very dependable and forthright person. Besides, I had to drive up to get them. I drove both Svetlana and Olga back after the snowstorm that snowed them in."

Olga was forthright to Enver Pasha, perhaps. To anyone who might threaten the great man, she provided an impenetrable wall, or so it had seemed to Kazakov when he met her. Kazakov stood. "I have more questions for you. I will arrange another meeting with your assistant for tomorrow. Thank you for your time today." He didn't wait for Enver Pasha's nod, instead turning and crossing the acre of plush carpet, careful to keep his pace even. Outside the door he found the brunette in the blue dress waiting. To escort him off the premises? Had she been waiting the whole time, or had Enver Pasha somehow called her to him? Or had she known just how much time a detective was to be given?

Most likely the latter.

" A second interview will be necessary," he told his escort as they left the office behind. "I need an hour of his time. I suggest tomorrow and will make myself available at your discretion."

As they reached the reception area, she arched her elegant brow at him again. "I will share your request, but Enver Pasha is a busy man."

Enver Pasha ran his shipping company with a military precision, but then Kazakov had suspected from the beginning that Enver Pasha was more than he seemed. At the imposing glass and timber doors of the Administration building, they stopped.

"And I am a busy detective with a murderer to catch. The longer it takes to see your employer, the colder the killer's tracks become." He bowed his head briefly. "Thank you for your assistance in making this happen."

He stepped outside into the amber streetlight, the blowing snow, and the cold. It cut right through him.

Or perhaps it wasn't the cold wind. Boris Bure seemed to loom like a figure advancing through the gloom.

———

The fire's embers were almost out at the dacha when Kazakov got home. The road had been barely passable in the midst of another unseasonable storm. It was like a new glacial age was coming. Certainly, it felt like the end of the world with the dacha barely visible when the Perseus plowed partway up his driveway. He'd had to leave the vehicle under the trees and limp the rest of the way home. His side ached and all he wanted was his bed, but his mind was whirring.

Boris Bure again. Thoughts of the man had swirled in his head since leaving Enver Pasha's office. Kazakov was fairly certain that it was Bure and his political aspirations that had brought about the premature closure of the investigation into the death of Bure's stepdaughter, Yekaterina Weber. Kazakov had been cut loose from the investigation, the evidence packed away except for the copies Kazakov had kept for himself. It had taken the evidence in an apparently unrelated death to reveal the killer—and something else: Yekaterina Weber had been pregnant, and DNA tests run quietly by Khalil Khan had proven Boris Bure was the father.

It had been tempting to reveal that fact, but both he and Khan had known that evidence like that tended to disappear in Fergana. Not to mention the troublemakers who spread it. So he and Khan had left the matter to fester in Kazakov's mind. Someday he would get the bastard if the chance arose.

And now, to confirm Enver Pasha's story, he had the opportunity to interview Boris Bure again. Stirring the embers to life and adding tinder-dry old leaves and a new log, he waited until the log caught and then put a kettle on to boil. He fed Koshka another meal and dug through his pantry for brown bread and butter and an old wizened apple.

"You're going to get fat, little one," he said, stroking Koshka's black back and tail as she lapped her food up. But then, so was he, without exercise. He watched Koshka happily finish her meal, glance up at him hopefully, and then return to his bed to curl up contentedly, her eyes at half-mast.

Oh, to have so little make him happy. It was a long time since he had felt that way. Sometime back in the early days of his and Annuschka's marriage, perhaps. Surely there had been a time when they had been content together. Perhaps their times on holiday to the mountains. Odd that she loved it there, but hated the dacha. She was probably happy now, with her big house in the city.

While he was in the hospital, he had even heard she might aspire for more—her husband announcing that he, too, would run for office in the upcoming election.

He shook himself free of the specters of the past. He was investigating the murder of Grigori Ivanov. At this point he was still gathering possible motives. Greed and lust were the most common. Ivanov had been in import-export of fine tobacco products, or so Chelomeyev had said. It was likely some of the same product Enver Pasha had been smoking—unless the two men were in competition. Enver Pasha *had* said that what he smoked was a product that he imported.

Kazakov considered. It was an avenue to look into. It could explain the relatively unhelpful responses of Enver Pasha. Or that could just be the man. Even his name was obscure, with Pasha being a titular honorific, though Kazakov had no idea how he came by the title.

Had Ivanov had business issues? Chelomeyev's files included statements from the wife and the company accountant that the business was doing well. That he would need to check. As for the Ivanov marriage, he would need to learn more about the couple's relationship. The fact that Svetlana Ivanova had not attended Enver Pasha's dinner party was suspicious. And as for Boris Bure, he would need to think long and hard before he barged into that man's life again. No, with Boris Bure, it would be better to gather the evidence and have it safely backed up and stowed away before any confrontation.

With that plan in mind, he had a meal of bread and cheese—he really did need to restock his shelves—shed his clothes, and groaning, climbed into bed.

His side ached, but it was good to see that he had survived without his cane this evening. Perhaps he had become too dependent upon it without even realizing.

He fell asleep to dreams of Boris Bure and Enver Pasha, vowing to not use the cane again.

8

T he next morning dawned frosty and white. Bright sunlight poked
around the curtains of his two windows and Kazakov groaned
and rolled over. His sleep had been uneasy, his mind too filled with all
the things he needed to do for this case. Once he got a better sense of
what had happened in the Ivanov case, he could assess whether there
were links to Chelomeyev's assault that he should pursue. He also
needed to canvas the neighborhood where Chelomeyev lived to see
whether there was anyone Pogolin and Fedunov had missed.

He shoved the covers off, disturbing Koshka in the process. The
little black cat complained and went to sit by her empty dish in the
kitchen, looking as disgusted as Kazakov felt at the moment. He used
the toilet in the water closet off the kitchen and came back shivering.
He really needed to complete a proper bathroom. The fire had gone out
overnight and it took more time than it should have to whittle kindling
into wood chips and start the fire. The water in the dacha chugged,
shook, and spat ice from the pipes and he was forced to wash in frigid
water. Still spluttering, he pulled on an old sweater and stained trousers
and boots and went outside to shovel.

Almost a foot of snow had fallen, weighting the tree boughs almost
to the ground. Here and there, a young pine had bent almost double.

The area around the dacha was pristine except for rabbit tracks that ended in the feather pattern of wings. An owl, most likely. The rabbit would not be home tonight.

He was puffing when he finished clearing the path from the door to the rear of the house where the Perseus should park. His side throbbed, but he was almost three months out of hospital. He started on the driveway down to where the Perseus waited, pushing the snow aside of a narrow path. When he was done, he went back to the dacha and made himself a breakfast of the last of his eggs and toast and potatoes and ate them from the frying pan at his kitchen table.

His hands shook with fatigue, but he was done being an invalid. In the past, this shoveling would have only been invigorating. Feeling disgusted at himself, he changed into his suit from the day before and headed back to New Moscow.

The midmorning sun was impossibly bright on the snow and his eyes were watering by the time he had driven down the snow-covered mountain slopes and into the suburbs. The roads were deep with snow until he came within the houses where the plows had reached. It would likely not be until tomorrow that they plowed the road up to his dacha. In the meantime he would need to pick up supplies both for himself and Agafya Ryabkov in case more snow made the roads impassable.

Suvarov Way was busy and he followed the street into town and then along Potemkin Park and the river before turning into the city core. He parked on a side street and closed his eyes a few moments. His side ached like someone twisted a nail deep in his flesh. He waited for the pain to ease a little and then exited the Perseus for the snow-covered sidewalk. Sidewalks were always the last thing cleared because the plows often pushed the snow right back onto them.

Laboring through the churned snow, he reached the city library and pushed inside into a phalanx of eight-year-old children trailing behind a matronly teacher. All of the children wore matching blue uniforms, with down jackets over their navy-blue trousers and skirts.

"I hope we get a real story today—not one of those stupid old fairy stories. They're for babies," one boy said to another. Kazakov waited for the class to filter through the turnstile, remembering Agafya's story of Ivan Mareson. A mother's love of her child, and death and resurrection. Not exactly children's fare.

He pushed through the turnstile, but instead of following the children toward the books, he turned right toward the periodicals section.

It was a great cavernous hall of a room, with low ceilings and none of the arches that gave some grace to the main library. Instead, fluorescent lights illuminated long rows of racks holding yellowing newspaper pages, the tan of the newsprint discoloring darker the farther back into the room you went until, he imagined, they became barely legible tobacco-colored sheaves at the rear.

Close to the door waited a desk and a reading table and a photocopier. There was no one at the desk or the table, though there were papers spread on the desk. He peered down the first and second of the long rows of periodicals. No one. Then shuffling footsteps came toward him. He peered down the middle aisle and a lone figure approached like a mythological creature rising from the dim reaches of time.

The librarian he remembered came toward him, his back still bent, his head almost devoid of hair save for the bouquet from each ear and a ring of fine white around the back and sides of his skull.

His name was Artyom Shepovalov and he claimed to have known Kazakov and his parents when Kazakov was very young, though Kazakov could not place him. He was a wizened man with too many wrinkles that seemed to hold in place his bright pebble eyes and the nose that held his pince-nez glasses. The skin that hugged his features was the same yellow parchment as the old papers he guarded.

The ancient librarian looked him up and down. "Detektiv Kazakov. Again. After what my newspapers said, I thought perhaps you would not be back."

He shuffled past Kazakov to settle with a sigh at his desk. The old man had provided assistance to Kazakov by locating old newspaper articles for a previous case.

"They asked, but I'm not ready for retirement."

Artyom nodded and shuffled through the papers, clearly placing them in an order that was important to him.

"They still haven't computerized everything, I see," Kazakov said, glancing at the rows of newspapers that did not appear in any way diminished even though there had been announcements that periodicals would be placed on microfiche.

"Likely never will in my lifetime. It's the way things work—or don't in this country." The librarian grinned. "But then my lifetime isn't giving them exactly a lot of time. Now what do you want? I feel a nap coming on."

Kazakov considered where to start. "I'd like everything you have on Gregori Ivanov and his wife. Also Transcontinental Shipping and its owner Enver Pasha."

The old man chewed his lip and studied Kazakov. "Picking up where you left off, are you?"

"I'm investigating Ivanov's death and the beating of the first investigator."

The steadiness of the old man's gaze was unnerving. "The young detective. I was most distressed to read of his injuries. Let me see what I can do."

It was painful to watch his slow shuffle back into the paper aisles.

"You do like large mouthfuls, don't you?" The old man's voice floated back to him. "Transcontinental alone could be a good day's reading."

Kazakov groaned. Not what he wanted to hear. "I thought they kept a low profile? I want to know about what they ship and where to and from. I need to know the financials—that the company is solvent. Same about Ivanov's import-export business, too." Hopefully that would narrow things down a little.

Silence reigned in the room and Kazakov imagined the ticking of a clock winding down. For some reason he didn't understand, urgency filled him.

"I'd like to know a little more about Enver Pasha, too," he called. "Who the man is."

The shuffling footfall came toward him and the librarian reappeared with his arms burdened with newspapers. He passed Kazakov and set the papers down with a thump on the reading table. When he turned back to Kazakov, his face was rigid. "You should be careful what you say in here, my friend. Sometimes there are more than my ears listening."

He nodded at the open doorway and the librarian's sorting desk that was just outside. At the moment no one was there, but Kazakov wasn't certain there hadn't been someone there when he arrived. He nodded. It would not be good to have the directions of his investigation get out. Not this early in the game.

"What have you got for me?"

"I have pulled a selection of articles about Transcontinental. Yes, the company is low profile, but there are pieces that speak of the rise of the company and their assets. You might be advised to read a copy of their annual report if you want to know their financials." The old man glanced sideways at him.

Kazakov knew the look. The old librarian knew it wasn't quite what Kazakov wanted—he was just waiting for Kazakov to say it.

"And what about unofficial reports? Rumors? Information without the pretty covers?"

As the librarian shook his head, shadows seemed to follow his movements so that his eyes peered out of a naked skull. "Those are things I don't know, but these articles may give you some help, Detektiv." One hand rested a moment longer on one newspaper and Kazakov nodded and settled himself at the table.

He looked up at the old man. "I have wracked my brain and I still cannot remember you, Artyom. It is a failing that bothers me."

The old librarian's pebble eyes seemed to brighten and then fade away to stone. "It is of no consequence. And call me Dedushka. Everyone else does."

Grandfather. It was a common enough word for men of a certain age, but Kazakov suddenly wanted more. He wanted to know who this helpful man was. All he knew was that the man had known his mother before she died. Well, he was a detective. If the librarian wouldn't tell him, the old man should realize that Kazakov could find out in other ways. He let Dedushka go and turned to the papers.

The scent of old paper and dust rose off the yellow newsprint as Kazakov shifted the papers before him. Old ink stained his fingertips as he flattened the newspaper that Dedushka had indicated. The paper was slightly yellowed and the print a little faded. It was dated February, five years before. He flipped through the news section and didn't find much, but in the culture section he found photographs of an art gallery opening with none other than Enver Pasha center stage congratulating a young female artist who had just returned from studying at the famous Caliph Ali Art School. Behind the two smiling people was a large canvas of intricate floral patterns that used light and shadow to hint at a human shape within them. As if something both was and wasn't there. To his untrained eye, it was most impressive.

He noted the artist's name and read the article that spoke of the contest the young woman had won that had been sponsored by Transcontinental. Flanking Enver Pasha and the artist named Kadija Bogomolova were two other men; Kasimir Krupin was the Chief Financial Officer and Maxim Lagunov was Operations Manager, both of Enver Pasha's company.

Kazakov studied the photo as he noted the names of the people as possible interviewees about the company. The trouble was, interviewing them would undoubtedly get back to Enver Pasha.

The photo itself was typical of the arts and culture section. People smiled unnaturally widely and seemed panicked into being happy. But there was something about the way Enver Pasha held the woman's hand—something genuine. Perhaps they were friends? He noted her name down, as well, and then turned the page.

As was his habit when he read the newspaper, he nearly skipped the financial section but caught himself at the title of a small article in the bottom corner of the first page: "Transcontinental CFO Sacked." The brief article said that Kasimir Krupin had been let go and that there were reports of questionable accounting practices as the reason for the removal.

Kazakov sat back. Krupin could be just the person he needed to understand the Transcontinental Empire even if he might be five years out of date. If the man was around. Krupin was a Russian name, but the man could be one of the numerous ethnic Russians whose ancestors had been slaves of the Ottoman Empire. If so, he could have returned to Constantinople or wherever he called home.

Thumbing through the rest of the financial section, there was nothing more of interest, so he set the newspaper aside and turned to the next paper. This one was more recent, dating back six months. The front page was speculating about the possible contenders for the leader of the Reformation Party. At the top of the list was Boris Bure.

Kazakov stiffened. Boris Bure was the past and he had a new murderer he was seeking. Still, he couldn't help but read the brief biography of the man: of impeccable bloodlines, but tragically orphaned in a mountain accident that had left him moderately well off and raised by foster parents. He had risen above his circumstances to become a contender after an illustrious career as a civil servant. The bio didn't mention what kind of civil servant, but it did mention rumors that Bure's family was related to the original Yekaterina the Great and likened Bure's rise to the top as akin to Yekaterina's.

An interesting metaphor given there were some who said that it was Yekaterina herself who had ordered her husband, the tsar, killed. Of course, that was a less than popular version of ancient events and as for Bure being related to the dearly departed empress, it was a rumor that couldn't be proven either way. A nice bit of political theater if he was any judge.

But then, he was suspicious by nature. To stop his mind roving into areas he had no time to explore, he turned the page and flipped through the news section. Nothing there. The arts and culture section yielded nothing either. Dedushka must have brought this paper for the financial section. He flipped through and must have missed whatever it was he had been meant to see. Another, slower, pass through and he noticed a section called the *Insider.* It was a business rumor section. He scanned through it. Amongst other bits of business news, it mentioned the murder victim Ivanov's tobacco firm as a possible take-over target for larger import-export businesses. The article was written by Kasimir Krupin.

Putting the paper aside to copy the article, he turned back to the stack of papers and kept reading. There were a few photos of Grigori Ivanov and his wife, the lovely Svetlana, at various social functions, but most of the articles were about charity events that Svetlana had organized and even an interesting article about New Moscow's "power couples" that included a mention of them.

Kazakov sat back, feeling like his head was too full of silk designer dresses, artwork, and too many bottles of cheap Fergana wine. He scrubbed at his forelock of bristly hair and turned around to Dedushka's desk. The old man was asleep, his light snoring a white noise that reverberated in the long hall. From the open doorway, the bustle of the main library seemed overloud.

His chair groaned as he shoved it back and stood. His back and side ached from sitting in the uncomfortable old chair for too long. He would pay for it tomorrow. But there were more articles for him to read given the stack of papers that Dedushka had stacked waiting on his desk. Kazakov crossed to him and, against his better judgment, cleared his throat.

Dedushka spluttered awake, his thin eyelids opening like shutters on his bright eyes. "So. You have finished the reading? Find anything interesting?"

Kazakov nodded. "The fact that an ex Chief Financial Officer now writes rumors for the newspaper is interesting."

Dedushka smiled, exposing gaps in his yellowed teeth. "You caught that, did you? I wondered if you would."

As if this was a game they were playing. Kazakov leaned heavily on Dedushka's desk. "I am investigating the beating of a promising young police officer who may not recover from his injuries. Part of that investigation is reviewing cases that he was investigating and that leads me to the death of Gregori Ivanov. You seem to be a well-read man. I believe you told me your memory is photographic. Perhaps you can save me some time and tell me what is in these newspapers that might be relevant?"

Kazakov leaned in so close that he inhaled the beet borscht scent of the old man's lunch. "Please. I sense this is a game to you, but people have been hurt. People have died. Now what do you know that you're not saying? What is in here?" Kazakov stabbed his finger on the stack of newspapers.

"I don't know." The old librarian shook his head and the light caught in the wisps of hair that haloed his head and the layers of wrinkles around his eyes. He was even more ancient than Kazakov had supposed, perhaps in his eighties or nineties. "I see—I suppose you could say I see patterns, things swirling around us that most people don't notice. I hope that when I bring you the papers maybe you will notice the currents pulling us under and do something about it?"

"Currents pulling us under?" What was the old man on about? Who is "us"? What currents?

Dedushka looked up at him with bright, patient eyes as if he was talking to a child. "Was it nonsense to see the connections between Boris Bure and Collin Archer when no one else could see them? Was it wrong to think that there is something wrong with Bure's past?"

He shook his head as Kazakov considered.

The old librarian had brought him newspapers in the Collin Archer case that had gotten Kazakov thinking and exploring avenues that he otherwise might not have. It had helped hint at connections. As for Boris Bure's past, information Kazakov had found had suggested Bure's preference for young girls had not started with his stepdaughter. It was that information that had made it possible to believe that Bure had made his sixteen-year-old stepdaughter pregnant. It was only when those possibilities had been raised that he'd been able to close the case.

The old librarian raised a single caterpillar brow. "You see, neh? There are currents swirling in this country and they threaten to swirl the country away."

The air in the cavernous room turned a little colder.

"Are you suggesting that Grigori Ivanov was killed for a larger reason?"

"I suggest nothing. I just say that there are things happening. Darkness growing. You read it in the newspapers. You hear it in our election politics." He shook his head. "People are scared, Detektiv. There are rumblings over the borders. And then there are these explosions in the city. The people want someone to pay for Yekaterina's destruction. They want someone to keep them safe."

Kazakov considered what the old man was saying. Perhaps it was motive, but it was far beyond his pay scale. Most murders occurred for far more mundane reasons: Love/lust, greed/money, and revenge. There were suggestions in the newspaper articles that kept him pursuing those directions—at least for now.

"And where does Enver Pasha sit within this secret web of yours?" Kazakov asked.

"A spider, of course. Or a puppet master. There is just no telling which strings he is pulling. If you investigate him, you must be very careful." The old librarian nodded. "Things happen to those who are not. But then you know about such things." His gaze shifted down to Kazakov's side.

"A hard lesson, but one well-learned," Kazakov said and held out his few articles to be copied. "What can you tell me of the man? What is his history?"

Dedushka's paper-thin lids slid over his eyes and he inhaled and then sighed in a motion that reminded Kazakov of how, when posed with a query, the police data machine paused for a moment and seemed to think before returning any relevant information.

"He was the child of a public prosecutor and an Albanian peasant. His parents named him Ismail Enver, but he will forever be known as Enver Pasha because of his role addressing the Cairo crisis. Pasha is an honorific given to a military officer who rises to the rank of *mirliva*—what we would call a major general. At the time he was a junior officer posted in Cairo, and when the uprising threatened to inflame the Nile River delta in rebellion, he led the attack on the rebellion leaders' headquarters deep in the Sahara, beyond the Dakhla Oasis. The rebel leaders were wiped out and the rebellion collapsed. Enver was rewarded. He is married to a granddaughter of the Ottoman Sultan Abdulmejid."

"Are you telling me that a granddaughter of the sultan lives here in

Fergana?" For some reason the possibility filled him with alarm. It was as if Fergana was simply a bedroom to the powers of the Ottoman and he had only just realized it.

But Dedushka shook his head. "She remains in their home in Constantinople. One wonders how good their relationship can be, given the distance between them."

So Enver Pasha was here alone in that big house across from Yekaterina Park. "Are you suggesting that he has abandoned his wife? That he has someone else?" Olga Gruenwald came to mind.

Dedushka shrugged his boney shoulders. "Who can say? But there are others who might share rumors better than I."

So the old librarian was not going to say more. Kazakov thought a moment.

"Is there anything in these news articles to link Svetlana Ivanova to a lover? Anything you have heard or seen?"

"The most important articles were those you read. These simply give a sense of the people you told me to research. Svetlana is a fashionable woman who wears the best. She drives a Turin sports car and openly displays her wealth, but she also uses it for charity. There are those who say her charity is only an excuse to buy the clothes, that she has no heart for it, but those could just be her detractors."

The old man shoved himself up from his seat and faced Kazakov. "Grigori Ivanov was a self-made man and still had strong links to his old neighborhood friends. As for Enver Pasha, he is a man's man. Women come to him willingly, yet he uses a certain brothel to avoid the intimacy of something more. He is a skilled polo player and downhill skier. He admires gardens, the arts, and is a collector of rare orchids—and other things. And people." He looked over his glasses at Kazakov. "Will that do, Detektiv?" His tone had changed from friendly to frost, but then he glanced down at the papers on his desk. He gathered them up and swiftly made copies. "I need to return these to their proper racks." Ignoring Kazakov, he gathered the papers and shuffled off amongst the newspapers like the last of the dinosaurs.

Guilt was an emotion Kazakov was too familiar with. He had pushed the old man harder than he should have, but he needed to make sense out of this investigation. Finding Chelomeyev's attacker depended on it. The trouble was it was a tangle of investigations. Chelomeyev's beating, Ivanov's death, the mysterious Enver Pasha all needed to be looked into.

"Thank you for your help, Dedushka," he called.

There was only a soft sound like feathers on stone that might be an old man's shuffle. Kazakov had no time to apologize. He had people to talk to. He decided where to start as he left the hall.

9
___

The *New Moscow Now* newspaper headquarters sat on Suvarov Way before it reached the center of the city where the police station stood. The offices faced Potemkin Park where, at this time of year, the park lined the river with naked, twisted trees. In the summer the trees would be green, and couples would promenade along the shady river walkway. Across the river sat Yekaterina Park so that Yekaterina and her lover were forever close.

The newspaper's building was old-fashioned by the standards of the glass and steel of the new construction overtaking the center of the city but had a certain venerable grace hanging on by a thread in its gray stone face and the pillars of its front portico. It had been built at a time when the faux front that emulated Tsarina Yekaterina's great palace had been completed for Fergana's parliament building. Many other buildings had copied the old splendor. There had been an effort in that brief period to make New Moscow beautiful by copying what they had had before.

Unfortunately, all that old splendor was gone now and Fergana had developed nothing new to fill the void. Most of the old buildings of that style had been razed for more modern structures that emulated those of other world capitals, leaving nothing Ferganese behind, but the old *New Moscow Now* building held on. The soot from vehicle exhaust and the dirty snow placed a gritty edge over the grace of the building. Its tall, narrow windows blindly reflected the blue sky and the distant mountains. If buildings had memories, he got the sense that perhaps the sheer weight of all the news that had passed through these doors had led to a dotage.

He parked the Perseus on the street and waded through the heavy slush and, thankfully, up shoveled stairs to the door. His side throbbed and he wanted to rest, but he had to get used to working long hours again.

The heavy wooden doors moved surprisingly easily at his touch and swung inward into a marble-floored hall. Years of foot traffic had worn a channel into the marble toward the elevator. Highly polished wood ceilings and a chandelier over an open foyer gave a sense of faded grandeur. A round table set under the chandelier held a huge oriental vase filled with hothouse lilies that oozed potent perfume but still could not dispel the scent of ink and newsprint that seemed to stain the wood-panelled, wainscoted walls.

Limping, Kazakov followed the shallow groove in the floor to a reception desk set before the bank of elevators.

"Kasimir Krupin, please." He flashed his credentials at the young receptionist.

Her gaze widened slightly, but she picked up her phone and turned slightly away from him. A whispered conversation ensued. Then she nodded and set down the phone.

"Mr. Krupin will see you, but he has very limited time. He asked me to warn you."

"Did he now?" At least the man could fit him in. So why did Kazakov feel disinclined to either trust or like the man he was about to meet for the first time?

The answer was simple: he was an associate of Enver Pasha.

The receptionist gave him directions and he limped past her onto an elevator and up three flights. The doors dinged and opened onto a room filled with back-to-back desks, much like the detective squad room except this room was the entire floor of the building. The tall narrow windows laid long bars of light across the twenty or thirty people who bustled down aisles and bent over typewriters. Just what did it say about a society when its reporters outnumbered its detectives? Most likely something positive, but he could not think what.

Along the rear of the building, glass walls of offices lined the outer walls of the huge room. The drill of phones and the buzz of voices filled the air—along with that ubiquitous ink and newsprint scent. It must be part of these people's skins after working here a few years. Did they dream in news headlines? His main contact at the newspaper, an old crime beat reporter named Demetri Popov had certainly talked that way.

A man at the doorway of an office at the far side of the room waved to catch Kazakov's eye and Kazakov waded into the sea of desks mounded with paper and laden with behemoth electric typewriters.

Kazakov recognized the waiting man from the newspaper image, but the years had not been kind. He was slightly shorter than Kazakov's six foot two, with a wild head of graying hair that stopped short at his earlobes. His face was creased as if he'd spent his years scowling even though now he held out his hand with a welcome smile. He wore a graying white shirt with rolled up sleeves, thick woolen trousers, and a sweater vest unbuttoned down the front to expose a flat belly that was unusual in a man of about sixty. He hadn't looked so trim in the art contest photo, but then perhaps he'd lost weight since leaving Transcontinental.

Kazakov shook his hand. "Kasimir Krupin? I'm Detektiv Kazakov, New Moscow police. Thank you for finding the time to speak with me. I'd like to ask you about an investigation I'm involved in."

Krupin inclined his head like a gentleman and ushered Kazakov through a glass door into one of the glassed-in offices. It was small, and the first thing Kazakov noticed was the cold radiating through the window as if the privilege of having your own office also came with a curse. He eyed Krupin's sweater vest—certainly not enough to keep a normal person warm. A statement perhaps? *You don't know who you are dealing with.*

The fact the man had worked with Enver Pasha gave Kazakov an inkling.

With Krupin's nondescript clothes and the lack of anything ornamental on the glass walls, both the office and the man were ciphers. There was nothing to provide a clue as to who Kazakov was dealing with, except a childish looking lump of glazed clay that sat on the corner of his desk. It was round like a disc that a child's hands had flattened with what looked like a stick poking out of the top. A boat, perhaps.

"A gift from my son when he was much younger," Krupin said. "It's not a boat, like most people think. It's an arrow stuck in the earth. He was fascinated with the old folktale of Ivan Mareson that his nanny told him. At the time I was traveling a great deal. He made it as a symbol that no matter where I was, or what happened, he would come for me. Sadly, it was him who died first. Childhood leukemia." He smiled softly and shook his head. Kazakov was taken back briefly to old Agafya Ryabkov's cottage. What would move a child to think his father needed an arrow to bring him back from death?

"Please. Sit." Krupin motioned to a plain wooden chair that sat before an immaculate desk. A typewriter with a half-typed page in the roller sat on a side spur of the desk, a neat stack of handwritten notes beside it. Krupin settled into his web-backed desk chair and placed his hands on the desk. "What can I do for you, Detektiv?"

Kazakov sat. "As I said. I am conducting an investigation. A young detective who was investigating Grigori Ivanov's murder has been badly beaten so I have taken over the case. I come to you seeking background information on the man, his family, and his business dealings."

Krupin momentarily studied his desktop and his outspread hands. "Yes. I see. You come to me as a man familiar with finance and rumors —given I have been both a victim of some and the starter of others." He smiled, and for a moment Kazakov caught a glimmer of something in Krupin's gaze—something dark, lurking.

Instead of responding, Kazakov opened his notebook and readied his pen. "How well did you know Grigori Ivanov?"

"I met him about twenty years ago when we were all much younger men with dreams we labored to bring to fruition. We spent time together. Played polo together when we'd come up far enough in the world to afford the game and the horses. We traveled in the same circles. My wife and I had dinner at Grigori and Svetlana's home a few times and we reciprocated. We weren't close but we knew each other." He stopped talking and waited, a small smile on his lips that said he was aware of the detective's trick of waiting. Reporters apparently used the same tactic.

"So you knew Grigori and Svetlana as a couple. Tell me more about them."

Grigori shook his head. "They were a couple and like all couples, over the years the relationship changed. They were happy, then less happy, then happy again, then not. Grigori loved his business and Svetlana had her charity work."

An interesting phrasing. "What can you tell me of Svetlana?"

Krupin pursed his lips. They were too red, like a vicious rosebud. "Not a lot. She was more my wife's friend than mine. Pretty woman. Smart, too. She went to school in Constantinople, could speak about six languages, and had been friends with the Sultan's family. Good conversationalist if you wanted to keep a party going."

Interesting. Kazakov filed away the information about Constantinople, given his dealings with Enver Pasha. "And her friends? Who was she close to?"

Krupin closed his eyes a moment, then looked piercingly at Kazakov. "I never got the sense that she was particularly close to anyone. She had friends involved in her charity work. She mentioned friends from her past—mostly with regret."

Kazakov frowned. "Tell me more about that."

Krupin shook his head. "I don't remember the details—just that she had once been close to someone and something had happened to end it. There were times when the best word I can find to describe Svetlana would be lonely."

Interesting. "So she had nobody other than her husband. Would you describe them as close?"

Krupin removed his hands from the desk and gripped the arms of his chair before leaning back. "Let's quit beating around the bush, shall we? You're wondering whether there were other men in her life, and all I can say is I don't know."

Kazakov kept his gambling face on and looked from his notes to Krupin. "Actually, I was just looking for information and wondered who I should talk to."

Hesitating a moment, Krupin eyed him. Then he nodded. "You could talk to my wife, Margarete, or there is Luba Markov, the clothing designer. Luba might be able to provide more names. I think I heard that Svetlana and Luba had planned events together a few times."

He checked a small clock on his desk. "I'm sorry. Those are all the questions that I have time for at the moment."

Kazakov stayed where he was. "I have other questions about Grigori Ivanov and his business. What can you tell me about it—the facts and the rumors."

Krupin's gaze flitted to the window that gave onto a snow-filled parking lot. "I really don't have time…"

"Don't have time, or does talking about Grigori Ivanov make you uncomfortable?"

Gaze narrowed, Krupin looked back at him. Then he smiled. "You picked up on that, did you?" He shook his head. "And here I thought I had become inscrutable with age."

"So what can you tell me about Ivanov and his business?"

The buzz of voices came from the outer office as Krupin considered. "Grigori started it from the ground up. He hadn't an inherited fortune or anything. He worked for what he had. As a young man he made contact with an American tobacco grower—I don't know how, but they stayed in touch and Grigori borrowed the money to import his first product. It sold well through elite Ferganese circles and for years he kept his business small, gradually building up a following and demand. As far as I know, he was happy doing a niche business and had no plans to broaden the market."

It was interesting information, but what it meant as far as the murder, Kazakov couldn't fathom. "Had he made enemies in his business?"

Krupin's bark of laughter seemed overloud for the small glassed-in room. "He was a businessman, Detektiv. A successful one. Every businessman makes enemies or he will not have a business."

The wooden chair was uncomfortable and Kazakov shifted to ease his side, certain that the wooden chair was doing exactly what it was intended to do.

"And who had Grigori Ivanov made enemies of?"

"There are other importers who would have liked a piece of Grigori's very exclusive pie."

"Can you name them, please?" Kazakov readied his pen over his notepad.

"Who are the other tobacco firms in town? Ottoman Tobacco. Ri Tobacco from China. Impact Tobacco. Smooth. They all have market share and would like to expand. There were those who accused him of undermining any attempts by other firms to gain access to American tobacco. There were even stories of thugs attacking envoys to American producers."

Beyond the glass walls, the bustle and hum had become indistinct —a white noise to Kazakov's ears. He supposed that to Kasimir Krupin it didn't exist at all. "That would be a good way to make enemies," Kazakov said.

Krupin snorted. "Welcome to business. Such things are done everywhere. Hell, these men even marry off daughters into other corporations to consolidate allies, just like royal houses."

"Are there any of these corporations that had particular animosity toward Ivanov or particular designs on the business?"

The newspaperman thought a moment and then shook his head. "I really couldn't say. I am sorry. It makes a lot of work for you, I suppose. Is that it, then? May I go?"

Kazakov considered his notes. "Just how well was Ivanov doing?"

"On paper, I would say well, but lately I have heard rumors that someone else has started importing American brands and selling them cheaply on the black market. The rumors suggested that it undercut

Ivanov's business and that he was experiencing financial challenges. Other rumors suggested that Ivanov Tobacco was ripe for takeover as Ivanov might be forced to sell to avoid bankruptcy. I suppose it is costly to maintain all the bribes that keep the distribution rights to himself."

More interesting. Money was often the heart of motives for murder. "And who in particular did Ivanov owe money to?"

Kazakov pursed his rosebud lips again and tapped long, spider fingers on his desk. Kazakov quelled his revulsion. There was something about Krupin he could not abide.

"There were trucking firms, I suppose. In the past there were those who wanted his business, but Grigori Ivanov was a rebel. He liked to arrange the shipments himself and often contracted with some of the smaller, local trucking companies. I suppose that he could have hurt people that way. And his suppliers, of course. Though why a supplier would hurt Ivanov, I couldn't fathom. Surely they would simply shift their business and sell to someone else."

Pushing back from his desk, Krupin stood up. "I really must excuse myself. I am already late for an appointment."

Kazakov looked up at him, but still kept his notebook open.

"What happened between you and Enver Pasha, Kasimir? There you were, the second in command at a company like Transcontinental, and then you are here, a meager reporter, almost no more than a rumormonger."

Krupin seemed to freeze. Then he sank slowly back down into his chair. "What does this have to do with Grigori Ivanov's death? What happened to me is all ancient history."

Kazakov ignored his comment. "What happened to you, Mr. Krupin? A fall that far—well, it can destroy a life. A marriage."

Krupin simply looked at him.

"What happened?"

Krupin closed his eyes and sighed. "Money is what happened. Some went missing from Transcontinental and even though I was the one who brought the matter to Enver's attention, I had the finger pointed at me." He shook his head. "Rather than risk the ruin that would come if there was a full investigation, I left the company."

Kazakov let his pen scratch across the paper and then looked up at Krupin. He wasn't looking quite so in command of the situation as he had at the start the interview. Instead he seemed to have collapsed back in his chair as if a weight pressed him there.

"Most innocent men would fight for their reputation," Kazakov said quietly.

A flush flooded up Krupin's neck as if he would explode. The cords of his neck and jaw stood out whitely.

"But then most innocent men aren't dealing with Enver Pasha, are they?" continued Kazakov. "Did he pay you to go, or threaten to harm you?"

A tremor ran up through Krupin's body and culminated in a shake of his head. "What is this?"

Clearly Krupin did not like where this was going.

"Transcontinental is a very large company. I understand it is diversified in many areas and operates in many parts of the world."

Nodding, Krupin laced his pale hands together on his desk as if he was once more a company executive. "There are five divisions. The main one is shipping. It recently acquired the Perseus Auto company, and has expanded into large truck and heavy equipment manufacturing, and the aerospace industry—plane engines actually."

"And is it successful in all these areas?"

Krupin looked at his watch and then sighed and picked up the phone. "Sarah, please contact my appointment and advise them I will be on my way shortly." Then he turned back to Kazakov. "Before you ask, there were dealings between Ivanov Tobacco and Transcontinental. Transcontinental wanted Ivanov's shipping business, but Ivanov wasn't interested in signing a long-term contract. It led to hard feelings between Ivanov and Enver, but no more than businessmen feel when a deal falls through."

Krupin spread his hands palm up on his desk like open pages, but Kazakov had the feeling they could just as quickly snap shut like a trap. Considering what he'd learned, Kazakov closed his notebook and slid it and his pen back into his jacket pocket.

He stood up, swallowing back a sharp intake of breath from the stab of pain in his side. He held out his hand. "I thank you for your time. I'll let you get on to your appointment. I may have further questions, but I will try to phone for an appointment in future."

Kazakov left Krupin and crossed the crowded room of desks and reporters. At the bank of elevators, he turned and glanced back. Krupin hadn't yet pulled on his coat and showed no sign of rushing off to a meeting. Instead, he was back at his desk, his phone in his hand.

Now just who was he calling?

10

The lunchtime rush to restaurants had faded by the time Kazakov exited the *New Moscow Now* newspaper building. At this hour, most of the workers would have returned to work and be peering out of windows wishing for the end of their shift. He stood on the stairs at the front of the building's colonnades and peered up at the old stone, pondering what Kasimir Krupin had told him and wondering just who it had been so important for Krupin to phone as soon as Kazakov had left the room.

Did Krupin still have allegiances to Enver Pasha? Or was there someone else who he reported to? Was the fact that a detective had been asking questions newsworthy?

Standing out of the wind by a column to one side of the door, Kazakov hunched into his heavy wool coat with his hands deep in his pockets and wished for a cigarette. Just how long would it take for Krupin to leave? He'd been mightily anxious to leave throughout the entire interview, so what held him up now?

Fifteen minutes later, swathed in a heavy winter coat and mink fur hat, Krupin shoved out the heavy wood main door and hurried down the stairs to the traffic-filled streets. He didn't enter a car, instead turning left to pick his way down the snowbound sidewalk.

Interesting. No one who was anyone walked New Moscow's poorly maintained sidewalks. There were limousines for the wealthy, and taxis and personal vehicles—or buses—for the middle class. Was Krupin going to his original appointment?

Kazakov eased himself away from the column and set out at an easy pace, keeping his distance as Krupin hunched along the sidewalk. At the first corner he turned left and crossed the street to Potemkin Park that in this location was a narrow strip along the ice-bound river. Kazakov held back following, waiting until Krupin reached the summer promenade and turned right along the water. He set off briskly. Kazakov paralleled him along the street.

Even with the trees between them, Krupin was easy to track for there were few people following the unplowed river path except for a few doughty runners in cleated shoes, sweating steam as they outran the cold. Along the river promenade, the paved path widened occasionally to provide a seating area overlooking the river and Yekaterina Park, beyond. Today the view was of ice on the river and snow in the park. On a clear day the encircling ring of white-crowned mountains would stand above the rooftops, but today the clouds had swallowed them up.

Looking eastward, Kazakov could almost feel the maw of the Chinese Empire opening wide to swallow Fergana. Behind him, westward, the Ottomans did the same as if two massive serpents battled for the same unlucky mouse.

Krupin stepped off his path to settle onto one of the frozen seats.

Kazakov waited, stomping his feet on the sidewalk to stay warm. The noontime rush had subsided enough that his position would soon be noticeable. Five minutes later a figure approached from the direction opposite from the *New Moscow Now.* The lone male was tall and swathed in a Russian great coat but his hip-slung gait was distinctive. No Russian had ever moved like that. Kazakov straightened.

He knew the man the gait belonged to, even though his usual attire was as far from Russian as his homeland. The American, Eric Clinton, usually wore a broad brimmed hat with a gently curling brim, and his knee-length leather coat was usually lined and trimmed in shearling. His surefooted stride suggested that he had traded in his pointed leather boots with the opulent tooling for something more practical in the snow and his hat for a fur Russian cap. He settled himself beside Krupin.

Well. Well. Well.

Kazakov had met Eric Clinton through the Medical Examiner, Khalil Khan. Clinton was a man of unusual skills, including the ability to access data on a unique Chinese data machine Kazakov had found. Accessing the data had helped solve Kazakov's last case and Clinton's intervention had actually brought about action against a Chinese spy ring. It had been too little, too late, but at least it had been action while Kazakov was recovering in the hospital.

And now here he was again. But then there were plenty of reasons for a rumor monger reporter and someone who was likely an American spy to meet together. Not the least of which could be reporting Kazakov's visit to Krupin's office.

Filing the information away, Kazakov returned to the Perseus and climbed inside. He turned the engine on and then scraped away the frost on the inside of the windshield. It was two o'clock, still too early to call on Chelomeyev's neighbors. Instead, he turned the vehicle out into the steady flow of traffic and headed to the old town. He had established himself as, if not a friend, at least a neutral ally of the Kyrgyz people through his solving of the murder involving a favored Kyrgyz son. Perhaps he could use that relationship to gather a little information about the protests and explosions that had rocked the city.

The streets narrowed as he wound away from the core of New Moscow to the heart of the city that had stood at the base of Yekaterina's Mountain when it was still known as Suleiman's Mountain. But then, to the Kyrgyz and Uzbeks who lived in these parts, it still was. The name Yekaterina was like a puff of smoke that would eventually be blown away on the wind.

The old city's yellow-gray mud and stucco walls grew up out of the snow like they were part of the earth. He turned down the narrow streets until he knew he risked trapping the vehicle between the encroaching walls and left it there to proceed on foot. His destination was a small copy and print shop and the owner who had been involved in Kazakov's previous case. The small establishment sat on what passed for a corner in the old city. Here, two buildings met at an odd thirty degrees and a narrow, green door gave onto the shop's interior. He pushed inside into warmth and the dusty scent of ink and paper as a small silver bell over the door tinkled his entrance.

The poorly-lit shop was filled floor to ceiling along one wall with small shelves that held various colors of paper. On the opposite wall, more shelves held shadows and completed orders with information on folded tags. Three-foot-tall cardboard rolls leaned in dark corners, and boxes suitable for shipping cluttered the base of the wall. More reams of paper stood in precarious stacks on the floor like broken soldiers. Even in the quiet, the place radiated a pensive readiness Kazakov could inhale. The little hairs on the back of his neck stood on end.

The sound of shuffled footsteps came from beyond the curtain behind the small counter that occupied the center of the room. The curtain guarded a storeroom occupied by more paper and the copier machines.

When the curtain pushed aside, it set free a stream of light and a current of air that set the shop's lone, bare lightbulb swaying. Shadows swirled across the shelves like specters gathering as Kazakov stepped up to the counter.

The proprietor was a small, thin man named Kadet uulu Semir, his first name being Semir. He wore a long-sleeved, white shirt with black-stained cuffs and black trousers that dragged on the floor. At the sight of Kazakov, the man's dark, slanted gaze widened.

"You. Again." He glanced behind him as if he might withdraw beyond the curtain.

Kazakov nodded. "I don't think I had the chance to thank you before now. Neither Khan nor I would be alive if not for you and your friends." He did not want to think about the number of old city men who had not survived while aiding them.

The shopkeeper just stood there and then finally sighed. "You found our boy's killer and he will not kill again. That was what mattered."

A very tactful reply when the tribal traditions of the Kyrgyz led to vengeful skirmishes.

The little man met Kazakov's gaze. "You are well? There were some who said it was doubtful you would live."

"As well as might be expected. Still tender, but I'll live."

A slow nod from the shopkeeper. "At least Adilet gave his life for something."

Kazakov had to look away. Adilet Sultanbek had been all of seventeen when his actions saved Kazakov's life and cost his own. He shook his head. "It should never have happened. I mourned when I heard."

"You did not come here simply to thank me—or apologize." The little man's gaze was hard on Kazakov's face.

Guilt overfilled the hollow place in Kazakov's chest. Adilet had had no arrow and no time to pull one from the earth to call for rescue.

Finally, Kazakov nodded. "No. I did not. Once more I come to seek your help. There have been protests of Kyrgyz youth. There have been explosions in the city. Some say that the two are linked. I thought that if this was true you would know."

Semir's unwavering regard was unnerving. He stood with his hands flattened on the counter, so still Kazakov could imagine that he was a statue, a figure of wax. "Why would I help you?"

The little man's voice was brittle as the shifting ice floes on the river. Why, indeed.

"Because actions like these injure innocents. Because I want to understand what is happening and stop those responsible. The killing must stop." He said it softly, not a rebuff of Semir's question, but a reasoned answer that Kazakov prayed he would believe. "There is an old Russian folktale of Ivan Mareson, who was brought back to life by his mother every time he died. But none of us are Ivan Mareson. We have no magic arrow to plunge into the ground to tell our mother we are safe, and no arrow to pull from the earth to draw our mother to us when we die. We are simply dead and gone, leaving grieving families behind."

Unless, like Kazakov, you had no one. Koshka, alone, might miss him.

"I thought I might do some good to stop tensions from rising."

Semir shook his head. "You are too late. Your friends in the police were here earlier today. They arrested many of our young men and some family men, too. They were taken away and we don't know where. If you want to help, help them gain their release."

Kazakov closed his eyes and swore. It had to be this time that Razin and Pogolin and the others acted swiftly.

"I had no idea. When did this happen?"

Semir's black gaze still studied him as if trying to decide whether to believe that Kazakov didn't know. Finally, he nodded. "It was late this morning. There were many officers and they came in from all sides of the old city so that there was little our young men could do. A few chose to fight, but mostly they went quietly. They are family men and sons and daughters—not violent at all. They were dragged away as if they were."

"And—and was there a reason for the police to believe that young men and women from the city might be involved?"

The black gaze became obsidian-hard. "Would it be difficult to believe that our youth might have reason to harbor resentment?"

Kazakov had heard the reasons before: lack of job opportunities. Systemic discrimination. Disenfranchisement in a country that their people had occupied far longer than Holy Mother Russia had even existed. He shook his head. "There is always a reason. It still does not provide a license to kill and maim innocents. Surely you can agree with that?"

But Semir's gaze had become opaque. He shook his head. "I am sorry, for you have done our community a service, but I cannot help you."

He glanced behind Kazakov at the door and Kazakov nodded.

"Thank you for your help. I pray for a time when circumstances allow us to be friends." Heavily, he turned and crossed to the door. He stepped into the fading light of late afternoon, feeling Semir's gaze on him. There was only simmering animosity there.

———

He stopped at a small hole-in-the-wall café because his stomach growled so loud that it would be a detriment to any further interviews. He ordered a bowl of noodles and broth from the Chinese proprietor and was pleased when it came without the usual oily scum he found most Russian restaurants served. A few carrots and sautéed greens swam in the broth along with fatty chunks of meat. He gulped it down, listening to the radio that blared the local news. The lead story was the arrest of the Kyrgyz youth, but the story told held a different slant than that Semir had told him. The story emphasized the bravery of the police, entering the dangerous lairs of rebels. He shook his head. This was no way to maintain peace in Fergana. Instead it could incite ill-conceived reprisals. Had Rostoff sanctioned this kind of reporting?

The news report soon quelled that question with a report of the election candidate reaction to the recent events. Leonid Nikolaev, the incumbent prime minister, expressed his condolences to those injured in the explosions and their families and pledged aid in addressing medical costs. He urged whoever was responsible to think of the innocents they had injured and to give themselves up. The Ferganese government would not stand by and allow such things to continue.

It was a reasonable, reasoned response to the recent events. It did not target the Kyrgyz.

That task was taken up by the other two candidates: Mikhailov, the leader of the traditional opposition party, called on all citizens to report suspicious activity to the police and particularly called on Kyrgyz citizens to think of the safety of their countrymen.

Boris Bure, the Reformation Party candidate, presented stronger opinions. "It is long past time for Fergana to tolerate intolerable actions. This is our homeland. We cannot and will not tolerate malcontents. I call on our government to require all citizens, including the Kyrgyz, to swear their allegiance to Fergana or be stripped of citizenship. To those who love Fergana, this is no hardship. All citizens must feel safe on the streets and in their homes. If I am elected, my government commits to permanently addressing such dangers."

His voice rang out in a sonorous tone, filling the small coffee shop. The voices of the patrons cut off and the staff and customers paused to listen. When the recording ended, the voices started again. Kazakov considered the people he shared the space with. There were too many considered looks and nodding.

Bure had scored points with these listeners, but then Kazakov supposed Bure knew exactly what he was doing with his words. In a country that had lived under the shadow of war for so many years, the fear of it finally exploding inside Fergana's boundaries was coming to a boil.

Kazakov shook his head. These people clearly hadn't met Bure.

He finished his meal and the waitress came over. She smiled down at him. "I hope they catch whoever destroyed Yekaterina and lock him away for the rest of his life. That or kick him out of the country altogether—that way we don't have to pay for his upkeep."

Kazakov dug out correct change and a tip. "You have strong feelings."

"I do." She gave an emphatic nod. "Lots of other people do, too. If people don't like Fergana, they should leave."

Kazakov met her gaze. "And if they have been here longer than we have?"

His money in her pocket, her expression changed. She shook her head. "They need to get with the times, don't they? At least try to fit in."

She walked away, leaving Kazakov to pull on his jacket and head for the door. Regardless of his tip, the waitress didn't smile when he passed her.

Outside, the afternoon had darkened and traffic streamed past with their headlights catching in a light falling snow. Across the city, spotlights illuminated the domes of the false Saint Basil's Cathedral like a specter. He shifted his collar higher and hunched back to his car before heading over to Chelomeyev's neighborhood.

The bright lights of the central city fell behind as he passed through an area of squat, one-and two-story warehouses. Here and there, scaffolding and for sale signs spoke of the gentrification of the area. A few blocks to the east stood the old city. It would be next to feel the pressure of development. But for now, the warehouses of New Moscow were being relocated outside the city and the old buildings were being refurbished into trendy apartments for Fergana's younger set—like Chelomeyev.

The young detective's address was a three-story building of brick built at a corner where one street became the main road that led directly into the heart of the old city. The cross street circumnavigated the city toward Yekaterina's Mountain. In the snowy night, the remaining statue of the tsarina gleamed down on them from the highest peak. If the news reports were correct in their presentation of the Kyrgyz as responsible for the explosions, he wondered how much longer the mountain statue would stand.

The Perseus cruised into the curb and he turned the engine off. The fat snowflakes made soft patting sounds on the windshield before melting from the engine heat as a low-slung vehicle cruised down the street past him. Taillights flashed red as it turned a corner and disappeared.

Collar up and lynx fur hat pulled down, and fighting back a sudden wave of pain from his side, he climbed out and stood in the almost silence. Nights like this had always been his favorite because the falling snow isolated you from the rest of the world. He considered the neighborhood. There were still a number of older buildings toward the old city that had not been developed. He'd need to check the neighborhood, for often there were prostitutes who worked in such areas. They might also have seen something.

His breath smoked in the cold as he headed for Chelomeyev's building. His side continued to burn so that it was clear that this wasn't simply the result of a sudden movement. No—he'd overdone his activities today. At the door, he buzzed the emergency contact and identified himself to the designated owner. He was buzzed inside to a lobby of cold white marble floor and with a low, faux leather black couch and chairs that were meant to provide comfort under the fluorescent light glare. A thirty-something woman met him wearing a plush robe and slippers. Her tangled dark hair and the smudges of darkness under her eyes suggested she had just gotten out of bed.

"I'm Nat Volkov. Sorry about my attire. I've spent the past few days sick with the flu. Today's the first day that I've been up at all." Her pale skin said that it had been a difficult illness.

Kazakov produced his badge and explained that he was investigating the attack on Chelomeyev. Nat Volkov shook her head. "I was appalled when I heard. Pavel is such a nice young man."

"So no one has asked you any questions?" he asked.

She shook her head. "Perhaps they tried, but I was likely asleep."

"Chelomeyev was found beaten in the parking lot in the morning three days ago. I'm interested in what you might have seen or heard during the night four days ago. It would have been after seven o'clock, for he was seen at about that time in the office. If he'd worked a while longer and had then come home, that would put him here at about eight." Unless, of course, he tried to make contact with Enver Pasha. "Were you here?"

She nodded and pulled her robe collar tighter around her neck. If anything, her face had turned paler. "I came home about that time. I'd been out with friends but started to feel ill, so I left and came home."

He thought a moment and then ushered her to one of the faux leather chairs. "Think back. When you arrived home, what did you see?"

The woman sat, clutching her robe about her, though the lobby was warm with a scent like hot wool. "Not a lot. It was snowing fairly heavily. I remember thinking how it hid so much. There must have been two inches on the vehicles. There was a little traffic, but not much. This time of night it's usually pretty quiet except for the bar down the street. Sometimes there are fights." She brushed her hair back from her face, looked up at him, and shook her head. "I'm sorry. I don't think I'm a very good witness."

"Think back on that snowy night. Did you see anyone else? Someone from the building, maybe. Or someone who didn't belong?"

She shook her head, but then frowned. "Maybe there was someone. There was a woman on the other side of the street. I remember, because it looked like one of the whores that we'd had trouble with before. We and a couple of the other new buildings hired security to warn them away. I was going to talk to the other buildings when I was feeling better."

"Do you recall what she looked like?"

Another shake of her head. "It was dark and it was snowy. All I saw was a shadowy figure, but she was dressed in a short skirt and short jacket. I suppose she must have worn boots." She wore disapproval like a shield, but then she was like so many Russians who did not know how life and circumstance forced ill choices on others. At least her description gave him something to go on. If such a woman had been there, she might have seen something. A street whore's lifestyle bred vigilance and attention to detail.

He thought a moment. "You mentioned the vehicles in the parking lot. I take it that residents have assigned spaces?"

She nodded.

"Do you happen to know where Detektiv Chelomeyev's space is?"

A pink flush flattered the woman's cheeks as she nodded once more, so perhaps she'd been an admirer.

"Then I'd like you to think back to that night. Close your eyes."

She obeyed.

"It's snowing and cold. You've just arrived home and you're not feeling well. Tell me what you see around you."

She was silent a moment, her eyelids twitching, her lashes dark crescents on her pale cheeks.

"The snow is very heavy. It keeps catching on my lashes and stinging my nose. I just want to get home and to bed. I leave my Lenka in my spot and start across the parking lot. There are a lot of vehicles already parked and covered with snow. People are home having dinner and I don't have a thing in my fridge at the moment." She stirred uneasily in her chair.

"Now look around the parking lot to where Pavel Chelomeyev parks his vehicle. Can you see it there?"

He waited as her head craned around as if she truly was there again. Then her eyes flashed open. "It wasn't there. He wasn't home yet!" She heaved a huge sigh. "I was so worried that he had been lying in the snow and I had walked right past him!" Her eyes were huge, her gaze thankful.

Which meant that it was highly likely that Chelomeyev had pursued some other line of enquiry before returning home. Like trying to contact Enver Pasha?

"That's very helpful, Ms. Volkov. From what you know of Detektiv Chelomeyev, had he any enemies?"

"No. No. Pavel was a charming young man. Everyone liked him," she said.

"Did he have any particular friends in the building that I might talk to, or had you seen him with anyone? A buddy? A girl?"

Nat Volkov thought a moment, but then shook her head. "He was relatively new to the building so I don't think he'd made any friends. I never saw him with anyone either, except maybe once. I think it was his parents. He was saying goodbye in the foyer. They seemed unhappy he was here and he seemed happy to be rid of them. Pavel always impressed me as a quiet thinker, if you know what I mean. Someone who preferred his stories far more than time out with friends." Her lips did a slight downturn as if that fact had been a disappointment.

Pavel's associates were something to follow up on with Chelomeyev's parents.

"You mentioned that there had been issues that caused your building and others to hire a security firm. Was it only the prostitutes you were worried about?"

"No. Definitely not. There had been graffiti painted on our walls, too. And there are always the people from the old city passing by. Who knows what they might do." She shivered a little and tugged the robe closer to her chin, her glance going to the window as if there were hordes of such people about to break in.

"Do you still employ the security firm?"

"They are employed to do nightly sweeps of the area. They provide a report once a month."

"And the name of the firm?"

"Transcontinental Security."

11

The overheated apartment lobby was dry enough that Kazakov's skin tingled. His breath quickened and so did his pulse as Nat Volkov looked up at him with a still-fevered dark gaze. He might not be ill as she was, but his stomach clenched.

The name Transcontinental could not be a coincidence. Krupin had said the company had many fingers in many pies. This could easily be one of them.

"Can you suggest residents that I should speak to? People who come home later than you? Perhaps the residents who have the parking spots around Pavel Chelomeyev's?"

She provided the information and he jotted it down, but she asked that he not contact anyone until she could notify the residents that the police would likely be calling. The community was shaken enough by Chelomeyev's beating.

His side throbbed painfully and it was becoming harder to think. He had been up and working since early this morning—something he was no longer used to after over a month convalescing. Normally, he would conduct the other interviews now, but it was too likely that he would miss something. Given Nat Volkov's request, he agreed to come back tomorrow and get it right the first time. He thanked her for her help and gave her his card in case she recalled anything else. Then he left her and stepped outside into the cold.

The Perseus still held the last vestiges of warmth from the drive to Chelomeyev's building, but he turned the engine on and the heater up to roaring, trying to dispel the chill eating through him. Just what had he sent Chelomeyev into? The young detective would have stumbled into it totally unprepared, all because Kazakov had wanted to wallow a bit longer in his vodka and memories of Maria.

He'd been an irresponsible fool. Now he needed to determine just what he had sent Chelomeyev into.

He scrubbed the fatigue out of his eyes and straightened, groaning at the knife blade pain in his side. After almost two months he knew the rhythms of his wound and this wasn't a good one. It meant he'd done too much and needed his rest. But still… he looked back at the building. He should complete the interviews while he was here.

He was about to climb back out of the Perseus when a shifting shadow down a side street stopped him. Two women in jackets and shorter skirts danced from foot to foot trying to avoid freezing.

With a glance at the building, he settled back in his seat. The building and its tenants would be here tomorrow. He used the key in the ignition and headed the Perseus out of the parking lot and toward the women. Whores. They seemed central to these cases—at least they had been for the last one. From a distance, the two women had looked much the same, with long hair straggled by the snow and sodden fur jackets with tiny skirts, black stockings, and knee-high boots that would give little protection from the snow and cold. As he neared he could make out their differences. One woman had red hair cut shoulder length. The other was a bottle blonde.

When he slowed to a stop in front of them and rolled down the passenger window, the two women leaned in—until they saw him.

"Police!" the blonde spat and withdrew. She was obviously the older of the two, with lines beginning to form at the edges of her muddy brown eyes. She pulled the young redhead after her. The youngster was a pretty girl Kazakov would put in her teens, but a thin scar down her right cheek marred the perfection of her pale skin.

"I'm not here for trouble. I just have some questions. A man was beaten and left for dead a few days ago. I was hoping you might have seen something." He looked at the two shivering women and caught the quick glance of the redhead to her elder. "Why don't you climb in and at least warm up for a moment. It's a hell of a night to be out."

The little redhead's glance turned hopeful, but the blonde shook her head and straightened on the curb. "Sitting nice and warm in a cop car is no way to make a living."

"Okay." Kazakov sighed and turned off the Perseus to climb out and stand with them, though the pain sawed at his focus. The temperature had dropped and it was hellishly cold. Far too cold to be out dressed as they were. "Three nights ago a working girl was seen down the street across from that building at about eight o'clock in the evening." He pointed out Chelomeyev's apartment. "The next morning a man was found badly beaten in the parking lot. I'm hoping the woman might have seen something."

He looked expectantly between the two women. The blonde was stone-faced and kept her gaze beyond him. The little redhead looked scared and like she would like to be anywhere but here.

"You are cold," he said.

She nodded.

He caught her by the arm, opened the Perseus's rear door, and urged her inside into warmth.

"Hey! You can't do that!" the blonde protested.

"Out here she's freezing to death and she entered willingly. Now you can get in with her and we can talk together or I can take her to the station." A lie, but she didn't know it.

"Bastard!" She flounced past him and climbed into the car.

Kazakov climbed in the front seat and started the car and turned the heater up to high. Then he craned around to them, ignoring the pain radiating from his side to his brain. "To be clear, I do not want to arrest you; I just need information." He turned to the shivering redhead. With the snow melting down her hair and face, she looked younger than he'd first thought, perhaps only fourteen or fifteen, and by the nervous way she worked her mittened hands in her lap, still a novice in the business.

The blonde woman was likely her handler and protector until she was more seasoned.

"The witness saw you, didn't they?" he said to the girl.

She gave a single nod.

He could ask her for her name, but neither would tell him the truth. They would likely share only their street names. Better to get to the point. "Tell me about that evening?"

"We have no time for your questions. We have money to make," said the blonde.

"Difficult to do without customers. I do not see a single car out in this snow." He lifted his chin at the window. Though an occasional vehicle passed down the street that fronted Chelomeyev's apartment building, no one turned off onto this side street.

"We—we are waiting for someone. A regular appointment," the blonde said. She was a sharp featured creature with a pointy nose and high cheekbones and very little flesh on her body. The girl, though, she still had the plump beauty of a girl transitioning to a woman.

He turned back to the girl. "Tell me about it. Please."

The girl glanced at her companion and back at Kazakov. Her shivers were gradually subsiding. Finally, she nodded.

"It was cold and there were no customers coming by so when Raisa went to find a washroom, I shifted up to the main street. I was hoping I could make some money before she returned." She sniffed, pulled a slim hand out of a mitten, and wiped water off her face.

"But no one stopped. Vehicles went past and some pulled into the parking lot." Her gaze flickered away from him. Clearly there were things she wasn't telling him.

"How long were you there?"

She shook her head. "An hour or so. Raisa took longer to get back." She glanced at the blonde.

"I met someone along the way." The blonde's voice dared him to ask about it. "And now we should go, yes? You're done with your questions?"

"Tell me about the people you saw arrive at the apartment building."

"I didn't see anyone." The girl huddled into her sodden jacket looking forlorn.

Kazakov smiled gently at her. At least he hoped it came off gentle. "But that cannot be the case, can it, because someone saw you."

Looking even more miserable, the girl picked at a small hole in her stocking. Her flesh underneath was as white as the snow she had stood in. He'd put her in a difficult position because she didn't know who had reported seeing her. Anyone she reported could be the wrong person.

"I saw a woman arrive alone and go into the building. I saw a couple arrive and go into the building. The woman was carrying a child. I saw a man arrive alone, go into the building and then come out again."

"Did they arrive in that order?"

She gave a curt nod and he considered. The woman might have been Nat Volkov.

"And how long after the woman arrived and went inside did the couple arrive?"

"It was a long time. At least an hour. Maybe more."

It was something he could check. There couldn't be that many couples with young children in the apartment block.

"And the man? When did you see him?"

The girl's gaze was black in the dimness of the car. Streetlights barely reached this far down the block.

"It wasn't long after the couple arrived. He got out and strode into the building as if he was in a hurry."

"And how long before he came out?"

She thought a moment. "Not long, I think. Raisa had called me back down the street. I had started toward her, but glanced back and saw him."

But her gaze wavered a moment, still guarding her secrets.

"Can you describe him?"

She shook her head. "He was far away across the street. But I would say he was tall and slim. I thought he might be young."

Headlights panned across the Perseus as a vehicle turned onto the street. It lit up the inside of the Perseus and the jolt of fear on the blonde's face.

"That is all. We have to leave. Mura, out! Now!"

The redhead jerked and obediently opened the door. The other vehicle cruised toward them between the rows of warehouses. The blonde scrambled out the other door, then leaned in to Kazakov.

"Leave," she hissed. "You've already given her a little more hell tonight. She cannot miss this appointment."

The rear doors slammed shut and he dropped the Perseus in gear and eased away from the curb, watching in the rearview mirror as the other vehicle slid to a stop before the two women. A door opened and a large man stepped out. He waved in Kazakov's direction, clearly agitated, and the blonde responded. A single backhand sent the blonde staggering backward and the tableau froze.

Then the man climbed back in the vehicle and the two women joined him.

Sighing for all the ills of the world he could not heal, Kazakov turned the Perseus around a corner in the sifting snow.

———

Even back on Suvarov Way the traffic had dwindled. The rush was over from January's Orthodox Christmas holiday and shopping blitz and people settled into their houses early in weather like this. Slow-moving vehicles chugged through the mess of squeaking snow on the road. Kazakov headed east toward home, yearning for a drink and his bed to quell the pain and mulling what he'd learned.

The man the redhead had described going into and out of the building could have been Chelomeyev. Her description and even the timing worked. So where was he going in such a rush? Had he received a phone call? Made an appointment? Or was he simply meeting friends or a girl somewhere? That was something he needed to check with Chelomeyev's family. Either way, it could mean that his beating had taken place a good deal later than he'd thought.

And it meant that he was back to square one in trying to find someone who had seen something related to the beating. If the redhead was telling the truth.

He sighed. Well, there was still a lot to do in the Ivanov investigation that might bear fruit.

He had a few questions about Eric Clinton and why the American man might be meeting with businessman-turned-reporter Kasimir Krupin. There was one man he knew who might help him.

Kazakov groaned and slowed the vehicle. He checked his watch—just past seven o'clock. Khalil Khan might still be in his office. The little M.E. was known for his late hours. And there were a few other things Kazakov might ask as well—if he was careful.

He pulled back out onto the street and headed to Our Lady Yekaterina Hospital.

The new snow covered a multitude of sins and flocked the naked trees in the park into beauty again. But when Kazakov parked the Perseus and climbed out, the hospital's lights stained the snow piss-yellow. He trudged through the ankle-high snow and wondered how Chelomeyev was doing. He should check, but maybe Khan knew.

The M.E.'s office sat in the basement at the end of one wing of the large hospital building. Turning away from the well-lit main doors, Kazakov carefully climbed down the steep concrete stairs to the basement morgue level. The door was locked and he banged on it until a faint voice inside called "I'm coming! I'm coming."

The locks clicked over and the door pulled open four inches, exposing the impatient glare of Khalil Khan. His dark eyes widened. "You! I should have known. I'm of half a mind to shove the door closed again, but that wouldn't do any good, would it."

Kazakov grinned. "You know me too well. I can guard a door forever. It's part of police training."

"I could just sneak out through the hospital. I was just on my way home."

And it looked the truth, for the little M.E. had on his long black coat with his collar turned up in preparation for the cold.

"You wouldn't leave me to catch my death." Kazakov looked up to the patch of sky above the stairwell and a fat snowflake caught him full in the eye. Blinking, he looked back at Khan. "Well? Are you going to let me in?"

With a shake of his head, Khan pulled the door open and stepped aside. Kazakov stomped his boots clear of snow and stepped into the formaldehyde-scented warmth of the M.E.'s front reception office. As expected, there was no one else there, which made his meeting with Khan far easier. Khan suspected his new receptionist had been brought in to watch him and report his movements and visitors. Given the mood in the city, it could be true.

"Thanks for letting me in. Any updates on Chelomeyev's condition?" Kazakov asked as he followed the M.E. back to his office.

Khan glanced over his shoulder as he ushered Kazakov into his small, book-laden office. It had a battered desk and chair backed by shelves with one guest chair facing it.

"Did you not read the sign?" Khan asked, deadpan. He sat at his desk. "This is the medical examiner's office, not a hospital ward." Then he shook his head. "No change. He remains unresponsive."

Kazakov settled in the guest chair and sighed. "Like sleeping beauty. And I've gotten exactly nowhere in the investigation. I've been interviewing people in his neighborhood. Apparently, a man fitting his description was seen coming home and then leaving again soon after. I haven't had any luck finding someone who might have seen when he returned home again, or had time to discover where he was going."

He stretched his legs out in front of him. "I've been pursuing some of Chelomeyev's cases. The Ivanov case put me in touch with a reporter named Kasimir Krupin. Do you know him?"

Khan shook his head.

"He writes a rumor column in the paper's finance section. The man didn't seem pleased to see me or to answer my questions. When I left he was on the phone immediately and I followed him to what looked like a clandestine meeting."

Khan shrugged. "Why tell me?"

"Because he was meeting with your friend Eric Clinton, and for the life of me I can't figure out why. Given Clinton is a friend of yours, I thought perhaps you could enlighten me."

The soft hush of the air circulation system filled the room as Khan met his gaze. This time there were shutters on Khan's usually open gaze.

"Just who is Eric Clinton, Khan? American, you said. Technologically advanced beyond you or me. I can't help thinking that Krupin was reporting on me and for the life of me, I can't figure out why. Why would Eric Clinton be interested in me?"

Khan's brows rose, but his hands found a stack of papers and began to fidget. "A comment like that reeks of narcissism, my friend. Not everything in the world is about you."

"And now you play games with me, old friend. I asked you a question. Will you answer it?"

Setting the papers aside, Khan sighed and shook his head. "It is not my place."

Kazakov jerked upright. "Damn it, Khan. This is serious. If you know something, tell me."

Khan met his gaze. The straight set of his mouth said he had made up his mind. "There are some things that are not mine to tell. If you want to know about Eric Clinton, then I will ask him to meet with you and you can ask him yourself."

Kazakov slumped back in his chair. "All right. Arrange it. At least you should be able to tell me about how you met him."

The hush of the air filled the room again. Kazakov shifted and the chair groaned under him. Khan remained immobile and silent.

"You told me that you met him at a conference."

"Yes. Yes, that is where we met. You see? There is nothing new to tell you."

Climbing out of his chair, Kazakov's side throbbed painfully. He winced as he leaned on Khan's desk and looked Khan in the eye. "What's happened to you, my friend? I thought we helped each other. I thought we worked together to solve these cases."

It was Khan who looked away first. "We still do, but there are sometimes things told in confidence that only the original teller should divulge."

Kazakov jerked upright and paced away from the desk to study the notices tacked on Khan's corkboard. A vacancy in hospital administration. A flyer for a symposium. A policy directive that smoking was no longer allowed in the hospital patient wards. "You sound like a politician, Khan. What's happened to you?"

The little M.E. remained silent. "I'm sorry," he finally said. "It is the way it has to be."

There was an undercurrent in the room—something that placed a barrier between them. Khan looked sad as he sat at his oversized desk, and perhaps a little lost as if the world had overtaken him.

"Fergana is in trouble, Khan. You've seen the news. The authorities are blaming the Kyrgyz and Uzbeks for the explosions in the city. It's going to divide the country even more than it is."

Khan's troubled expression showed that he was well aware.

"Is it true?"

Khan's gaze jerked up to Kazakov, so it was as Kazakov feared— something was happening in the Kyrgyz community that made the rumors more troubling.

"Surely you have influence in the community. Surely it can stop young hotheads."

"Hotheads?" Khan's voice was soft. "Hotheads?" A little louder. "Do you think your Russian youths would be any different if they were stopped from obtaining the good things in life? If every time they applied for a job, they were turned away even though they were well-qualified? If the best schools would not accept their applications? If those who were employed earned only a percentage of their Russian co-worker's wages? Would those Russian youths be considered hotheads?" He had pushed himself up out of his chair, a fury on his face that Kazakov hadn't seen before.

Kazakov held up his hands to placate his friend, though Khan did not look as if he was going to be placated. "Is this what Fergana has done to us? We used to be able to discuss anything."

"Did we? The way I recall it, it was mostly about you and your cases."

Now that Khan pointed it out, Kazakov realized that it was unfortunately true. He crossed back to the desk and slumped back in the chair. "And for that I am sorry. You see what Fergana does? It takes good-hearted men and pits them against each other."

"And that is politics, old friend. My people have been second-class citizens for too long. We've been told we were equal, but it has not been like that and now our youths are tired of waiting. Did you know that my people have more children than the Russians? We are a steadily growing part of Fergana's population, but do you see us represented in Fergana's government in more than a token way? Do you see us being able to buy houses in the best neighborhoods, or represented in jobs like policing or the judiciary—or—medicine?"

Kazakov shook his head.

"There have been grumblings amongst my people for a long time, but something has changed. Something or someone has called them to action. And that is all I can and will say." Khan folded his hands before him.

It was more than Kazakov had known before. A call to action by an unknown party. That could explain so much. He stood up from his chair. "Thank you, my friend. No matter what happens, I will always count you as one. And now I will leave you to go home to your lovely wife and family."

Lynx hat clutched in his hand, he turned to go.

"And so the great Detektiv Kazakov had returned. Perhaps that is why Eric Clinton is interested in you. A man like Eric Clinton likes to know about men who can do the impossible."

Kazakov glanced back, suspecting sarcasm, but Khan's face held only a smile—and a hint of sadness. Kazakov nodded farewell and left the office.

It was late. Kazakov's side throbbed violently and a sense of hopelessness seemed as pervasive as the formaldehyde scent. It was time to go home and to his bed.

12

———————

The morning came with the sound of trickling water and sun streaming through the dacha's plaid curtains. Kazakov groaned and rolled away from the light, succeeding in disturbing Koshka, who hissed and shifted to fit his new position. The little cat was pushy and knew what she wanted. He was tired from a night of ill dreams and tossing and turning. Off and on all night he had dreamt that he was dead and though Khan came to help him, the M.E. could not because Kazakov had forgotten to pull his arrows from the earth before he died. He pulled the covers up to his chin and tried to fall back to sleep, but the sound of trickling water wouldn't let him. He lay there, wondering where it was coming from. It sounded like water running down the eavestroughs, but there had been only layers of snow on the roof when he had gotten home last night.

But snow could melt and dream arrows meant nothing in life.

Curiosity finally got the better of him and he rolled out of bed, making Koshka squall.

"Come, little one. Breakfast will make it all better."

The dacha was cool, but he couldn't see his breath. That was different from some of the colder mornings over the past few months. He stirred the fire into wakefulness and added new wood before feeding Koshka. The dacha filled with the sound of Koshka's happy licking as Kazakov went into the water closet to relieve himself and then used the kitchen sink to splash himself awake and clean. He filled the kettle and put it on the heated wood-burner, then sliced thick slabs of stale rye bread to toast and crumbled old cheese on top. A meager breakfast, but it would have to do until he refilled his larder.

When the water boiled, he made tea and settled at his desk, still stacked with Chelomeyev's files. He had spent a full day interviewing yesterday and all he had were more questions. He pulled a pad of paper to him and pulled out a pen to draw a line to create two columns, one for each area of his investigations. At the top of column one he put "Chelomeyev Assault." At the top of the second column he wrote "Grigori Ivanov Murder." He sat looking at the paper for a moment and then added a third narrow column at the edge of the paper purely because of Rostoff's request. At the top he squeezed in the header "Explosions."

Then he started making notes in the Chelomeyev assault column. The young detective had been involved with a number of cases, not the least of which was the Ivanov murder. From what Kazakov had seen, Chelomeyev had been proceeding carefully in all of the cases. He wrote down what he'd learned at Chelomeyev's apartment and that he needed to interview other residents and learn more about the young detective's social relationships. He needed to get inside Chelomeyev's apartment and see what the young detective had at home. Not that such things had revealed much to him so far. *If* the man who had been seen coming home had been Chelomeyev, and *if* he was also the man seen leaving, what had led to him leaving in such a rush? Where was he going and why? Had he arranged to meet with someone pertinent to the case? What had happened in the parking lot upon his return?

It was a lot to learn, but the people who lived there could help. He needed to get on with it. Contact Chelomeyev's family to identify his friends. There might also be evidence in Chelomeyev's apartment. Both were something to do today.

With regards to the Ivanov murder, he had the wife and her friend to interview and also Eric Clinton, though what he might say to the

American, he wasn't sure. He flipped back to his notebook and transcribed what he'd learned the previous day into his column sheet: the difficulty Ivanov's business was rumored to be in, the black market inroads into Ivanov's exclusive territory, the little redhead's description of the man she had seen, Khan's information about the Kyrgyz people.

Khan.

Kazakov slumped back in his chair. He didn't like how whatever was going on in the Kyrgyz community had the potential to seriously impact their friendship. Not the potential. It *was* impacting it. He'd seen it in the M.E.'s eyes and heard it in his voice. It was off-limits to discussion, just as it had been with the print shop owner. He'd thought —no, hoped—it might be different with Khan.

What was the saying about blood? Thicker than water? Blood was the whole basis of tribal ways—he'd just never thought of Khan as tribal.

So what could he do to further that investigation? He'd used his contacts and met a brick wall. But he couldn't imagine Rostoff accepting any excuse. The powers that be wanted someone to hang high for the explosion.

Khan wouldn't want him sniffing around, but there might not be anything Kazakov could do about it. Better him than Pogolin and Razin or any other of the detective squad. At least Kazakov was a known entity to the old city residents.

His tea and breakfast finished, he decided to place one call. He dialed his mobile and the phone drilled into his ear.

"New Moscow politseyshiyuchastok," said the female voice at the end of the phone. "How may I direct your call?"

Did he really want to do this? Rostoff would be furious if he knew what Kazakov was doing, but standard investigative procedure said he should speak to Chelomeyev's family.

"Chief Inspector Chelomeyev, please. I am calling about his son."

There was a pause as if the operator could not believe that someone had the temerity to call such a rarified number. Then the line went momentarily dead before ringing at the other end of the line.

"Chief Inspector Chelomeyev's office," said a cool feminine voice that left no doubt as to its competence. It made him wonder about the constables like Dabria Smirnova who were kept from real police work because some officer wanted the service of that competence. How many excellent female officers were being denied policing because the police hierarchy held them prisoner in reception duties? But that was not why he was calling.

"Chief Inspector Chelomeyev, please. It is Detektiv Kazakov calling. I am investigating the beating of the Chief Inspector's son."

"One moment, Detektiv." The phone clicked to hold and Kazakov tapped his fingers on his desktop and then flipped open his notebook to the next fresh page.

The phone clicked and then, "Kazakov. This is unexpected. I had understood the case was closed."

The voice boomed through the phone and Kazakov could picture the older Chelomeyev, about six foot four, with his son's white-blond hair and broad shoulders. But where the younger Chelomeyev moved with the grace of a runner and was built like one, the older carried too many good years of eating around his waist and as opposed to Pavel's too-open face, his father held the jaded look of someone too accustomed to getting what he wanted.

"Not closed, sir," Kazakov said. "The beating of a fellow detective is something that must be looked into fully and that has not been done. That is why I am calling. Your son. When was the last time you saw him?"

A harrumph came across the phone. "I don't know. A month or two, I suppose. When he moved into that ridiculous apartment of his. His mother and I visited."

Confirmation of what Nat Volkov, Chelomeyev's building emergency contact, had told him. He noted it down. Ask about family relationships? If the tension he was sensing was true, then he doubted Chief Inspector Chelomeyev would give him any answer. It was more likely that the call would be ended.

"I would like to speak to Detektiv Chelomeyev's friends and girlfriends about Pavel's movements the night he was beaten. I hoped you could provide me with names."

There was silence on the phone.

"Are you there, sir?"

"Detektiv Kazakov, I appreciate your phone call and your interest in finding my son's attackers, but Pavel had no girlfriends and no friends I knew of, either. He had a problem, my son. He preferred to live his life like one of his damned fairy tales. Did you know he studied the damned things? A wasted six years at University for a dissertation on some damned thing to do with pig skins. Now I tell you—the best thing his mother and I ever did for our son was to demand that he become a police officer. We hoped it would make a man of him."

There was a break in his tirade and his voice before silence. Pain radiated across the phone line.

"And that is all I have to say, Detektiv. My boy was at the wrong place at the wrong time and now he is in the hospital."

The line clicked dead before Kazakov could say anything. He closed his phone and set it down.

It was more than he had ever known about Detektiv Pavel Chelomeyev. Fairy tales and loneliness and apparently his family had little use for either. The young man had reached out to him, not once but twice, and Kazakov had turned him down both times.

Feeling subdued, he once more dressed in his suit, this time including his gun in a holster under his jacket. It felt heavy and cold against his side. Then, great coat, gloves, hat, and boots on, he headed out to the Perseus. The air was balmy after the past few months of frigid weather. The wind carried warmth that had originated over the Mediterranean and had raised the temperature overnight to above freezing. He picked his way down the stairs where the melting snow had turned to ice on the treads. Snow melt trickled off the roof and had created a small stream down the driveway that would be treacherous when the cold came again.

Careful of ice, he made his way through the sodden snow to the Perseus and headed toward town. The sun was bright on the steppes that led up into the mountains and on the melted snow on the road. Through the city, he followed the salt-darkened pavement and wound through the streets back to Chelomeyev's apartment building. There was no sign of blonde Raisa or the little redhead this morning, but then it was barely ten o'clock. He parked amid the cars remaining in the apartment's lot and climbed out. Down there were the narrow streets and steep, seemingly impenetrable walls of the old city. What was brewing there? Had Chelomeyev stumbled on to something that had spilled out and bombed the city?

There were so many questions. Seeking answers, he headed for the apartment building's front door and once more buzzed Nat Volkov.

"Yes?" her voice came on the intercom sounding stronger than it had the day before.

"It is Detektiv Kazakov of the New Moscow police again. I am sorry to disturb you, but I was hoping to come inside and inspect Detektiv Chelomeyev's apartment."

There was silence at the end of the phone, then, "Give me a moment to get dressed."

He stood in the sunshine, his boots getting wet in the pooling meltwater. Finally Nat Volkov appeared inside, this time dressed in navy trousers and a heavy cream-colored shirt with a robe pulled over the top. She still looked pale and wan, her eyes huge and dark against her skin. She unlocked the glass door and he stepped inside.

"You are lucky. Chelomeyev left emergency keys for the apartment council. Many residents have not." She dangled a key ring before him. "He is in apartment 336."

He took the keys and left Nat Volkov with a promise to return them to her. There was no elevator in the building, so Kazakov trudged up the two flights to the correct floor and found the apartment. The door clicked open easily and swung inside.

The place was nothing fancy—a single large loft room with living and dining space defined by low couch and chair and small dining table, and a small, rudimentary kitchen in the corner. The ceiling was tall—almost two stories—and the walls were of old brick, with an iron staircase to a second floor along one wall. Windows set too high to see out of comfortably allowed streamers of light to fill the floorspace.

Not the kind of place he would enjoy, but he could imagine it held some appeal for others.

He did a circuit around the room, taking it all in. A pile of books by the lone chair suggested Chelomeyev's choice for seating. Kazakov examined the reading material. Textbooks on investigation processes that had been written in the Anglo-German empire. A well-worn copy of Russian fairy tales folded open to the story of Pig Skin, that the Anglo-German's called Cinderella. A popular mystery novel. A copy of an annual report from Transcontinental Corporation. A variety of academic books on folktales and a coffee table book with images of Kyrgyz people. Idly, he flipped the coffee table book open. An image of a Kyrgyz grandmother in her traditional scarves and heavy felted red skirts and leggings peered out at him. Like Agafya Ryabkov, Kazakov's neighbor, her face was lined and weathered like old leather as she gazed out at him, but her eyes were clear and seemed to see right down to his soul.

He flipped the page and noticed a slip of yellow paper tucked between the pages like a book mark. Settling onto the couch, he flipped to the spread. It held two facing images. One was a black-and-white image of streets of warehouses caught in the early morning with smoky air swirling around them and the sunrise-lit crags of Yekaterina Mountain in the background, the statue of Yekaterina glinting at the summit.

The opposing page might have been taken from almost the same spot. Also black-and-white, it showed the night-darkened streets with barely a streetlight. Far down the empty street, backlit by a streetlight beyond them, a lone woman in short skirts and high boots had her arms slung around a much taller man. Her rescuer? Her client? There was no question but that the woman was a street whore. It could be blonde Raisa or the redhead, for all he could tell. But it struck a chord within him and seemed to set his insides chiming.

It was a striking image of desolation, longing, and hope.

Maria. She had carried just such emotions in her eyes when she'd looked at him.

He closed the book sharply, set it away, and climbed to his feet. He didn't need those memories. Maria was gone.

And all this nostalgia in a young man's apartment—it was vaguely reminiscent of Kazakov's dacha. He could almost understand why Chelomeyev's parents were upset. Their son was not living the life they expected.

Sighing, he took the wrought-iron staircase to the second floor and found a sleeping loft with a small desk pushed against the railing to the floor below and a washroom along the rear wall.

The washroom was likely typical of today's young men—hair product, shaving equipment, aspirin, a single toothbrush. A box of prophylactics, except Chelomeyev's were unopened. Still, the fact that they were there gave Kazakov hope that there was a woman in the young detective's life. A spice-scented soap sat by the sink.

Nothing useful there.

He left the bathroom for the bedroom and looked around. The bed was unmade, the covers simply pulled up; a small pile of clothes lay in the corner. He picked them up. Black trousers with empty pockets looked like the kind Chelomeyev wore to work every day. A dress shirt beneath it confirmed his thoughts. He picked it up, but there was nothing in the breast pockets. He went to toss it back in the pile but a small mark on the collar stopped him. Lipstick, pale pink.

Well, well, well. Contrary to his parent's beliefs, young Chelomeyev had a secret life and right now there was probably a young woman growing frantic because her boyfriend had disappeared. Had there been phone calls to the police station? To the hospital to find out how he was?

Something else to check, if the hospital switchboard could help him…

He dug through the bedside table drawers, but there were only paperback novels and bottles of cough medicine. He stood up to ease his back and aching side and headed for the desk that he'd saved for last.

The top of the desk was empty except for a reading light. Damn kid was neater than he'd expect given the clothing on the floor. Kazakov flipped the light on.

The top drawer held pens, pencils, and paper clips, but the drawer to the side held a neat stack of well-worn slim journals. He pulled out the top one and flipped it open. Chelomeyev's cramped writing filled the lined pages from top to bottom.

Kazakov held the ledger up to the light. It *was* a journal that started about six months back. Chelomeyev had laid bare his thoughts and feelings about his life and each of his investigations. Kazakov flipped through the pages, scanning the young detective's reflections on his job. He was less than flattering about his partner, Sherepov, calling him a dinosaur who liked to brute his way through investigations and lord it over others. Kazakov's own name turned up halfway through with a tone of cautious admiration at another arrest and conviction. Underlined on the page was *and he works alone!*

Kazakov flipped the page and read more as the idea of either working alone or partnering with Kazakov took hold in Chelomeyev's imagination. Then abruptly those ruminations stopped and there were comments about Kazakov's lone-wolf investigations and how the squad disapproved. Chelomeyev made allowances because Kazakov was a good detective.

Sitting back in the chair, Kazakov shook his head. Both the squad and Chelomeyev were probably right. Working alone might be preferable to Kazakov, but it came at a price, both in terms of the amount of work to be carried by one person and the fact that there was no one on whom to bounce off ideas.

On another page, one paragraph was set out with a space before and after.

"I saw M again today. I brought her a coffee and we talked for a while, but she would not come home with me. Every time I look at her it's as if I can see right down to her soul and she can see mine. I wonder if she feels it, too."

Kazakov smiled. So, Chelomeyev did have a girlfriend, or at least a woman he was infatuated about. That would explain the rapid departure to go out again after work. Perhaps he was rushing to meet her.

He flipped back through the pages seeking more information that might tell him who she was, but nothing jumped out at him, just mentions of investigations—robberies, thefts, public lewdness, assaults. He flipped forward through more of the same and found the Ivanov murder. Chelomeyev had started a clean page as he wrote about feeling overwhelmed at this, his first murder investigation alone. He wondered why Rostoff had given it to him given its seriousness, but then everyone had expected Sherepov would be returning to work soon.

From the emotive language he'd used before, Chelomeyev's language changed to more factual as he attempted to sort through his reactions to the crime scene and what he had learned as he conducted his investigation. He wrote about sensing that there was more to the case than met the eye, and how although Svetlana Ivanova had an alibi in Olga Gruenwald, he was not sure he trusted it. Something simply did not feel right to him.

Kazakov sighed. Chelomeyev had good instincts. He flipped through the next journal down, but didn't find any mention of M or of anything else that might relate to the current investigations. Finally, he stood and looked around the room once more. There was nothing else to see. Carrying the journal of interest, he stumped down the stairs into the pools of dusty sunlight and let himself out. Three stories down, he returned the keys to Nat Volkov.

"Thanks," he said. She walked him to the door of the apartment building. "Are there any women in the apartment block whose name begins with *M*?"

Frowning, Nat stopped at the glass door. "There's Mina Alexeev. She and her husband live in 204."

A married woman. He couldn't rule it out, but it did not seem like something Chelomeyev would do. "What can you tell me about them?"

"They have been here since the building opened." Nat shrugged. "I was surprised they liked it given the place was intended to attract a younger population of residents."

"How are old are they?"

"Well…," Nat hugged herself as if she could feel a chill off the glass door even though the weather was warmer. "I'm no judge of age, but I'd guess close to forty at least. So old, I guess."

Older than he would have thought Chelomeyev would be attracted to, but that was not necessarily the case.

"Are there any other women in the building whose name begins with an *M*?"

Still hugging herself, she thought for a minute before shaking her head. "Sorry. No. Why? Is it important?"

"Do you recall Detective Chelomeyev having company at home? A woman, perhaps?"

She shook her head again. "Sorry. Like I told you before, I never saw him with anybody. But then, we are all very private people. We don't check up on each other."

So no help there.

He thanked her for her time and stepped out of the door. To the east, the mountains stood in a white crown of glory that barricaded Fergana away from China. Once, the tribesmen of the mountains and the people of the city were related with many marriages between them. Now there was less intercourse between them. He had heard that people who spent the summers guarding mountain herds had not returned home for the winter as they usually did, and that it was becoming more difficult for the tribespeople to follow their old trading routes. There were even stories that the young people who went to China to work were having difficulty with the Chinese authorities when they wanted to come home again.

It made sense given the saber rattling going on both east and west of Fergana. The Chinese Empire was stirring as if something had ruffled its scales the wrong way.

At this time of day, with most people at work, there was little more that he could do here. He would come back this evening to canvass the other residents. That meant that he could turn his attention to the Ivanov murder.

Back inside the Perseus, he pulled out his notebook to find Ivanov's home address, but noticed something else. The construction company that had had explosives stolen a few nights before the explosion in the city's main square was located not far from here. He decided to have a look.

He pulled out onto the street and turned toward the crags of Yekaterina Mountain. The street swept him around the side of the old city and beneath the shadow of the graveyard where Maria lay. There was little traffic—a few large trucks, a battered flatbed stacked with timber. The buildings around him changed from the gentrified apartment buildings back into the warehouses and small garage and shipping businesses owned by the residents of the old city. He passed another narrow street that arrowed into the old city. By its angle it would run close to Khalil Khan's clinic. He wondered how Khan and his family were doing, rebuilding after the destruction of Kazakov's last case.

That was another reason to investigate alone and to be alone. He looked in the rearview mirror at the graveyard behind him. There was no one else to be killed if you turned over the wrong stone.

Three blocks back, a lone vehicle trailed him. It was a sedan, built low to the ground, black in color and had the sleek styling made popular by the Ziln. This was no Ziln, though. It had too little chrome on the front end and the silhouette wasn't quite right. A Torrento, perhaps?

Hadn't such a vehicle cruised past last night when he was at Chelomeyev's apartment?

But that could mean exactly nothing. There were surely more than one vehicle like this in New Moscow and a lot of people lived near Chelomeyev. And yet...

He guided the Perseus almost to the base of Yekaterina's Mountain and then turned aside, following the road that had been built around the mountain and then widened to carry people to the carnival grounds that had been the scene of the first explosion. The brightly painted red and yellow striped concrete walls of the carnival had been built to honor the circuses that had once come to Fergana. Inside the walls, roofs of concrete and timber tried to mimic the tents and awnings that had once covered merry-go-rounds and circus performers. Now a yellow police barricade stood at the tall gateway.

He slowed the Perseus and then pulled over to the side of the road.

He'd seen the mayhem at the city's central square. Let him see what had been done here, too.

The sunlight was warm on his face when he climbed out of the Perseus, but the freshening wind was cold. Melting snow glittered on either side of the road and on top of the carnival walls. The sign over the gate said New Moscow Carnival. Surprisingly, the venture had never been a huge success, though people still flocked to the traveling shows that occasionally found their way across the Ottoman borders. When it came to their entertainment, the crowds seemed drawn to the foreign rather than the predictable tried-and-true they seemed to prefer in the rest of their lives. He picked his way over the rivulets of meltwater running down either side of the road and crunched over the snow-covered gravel at the carnival entrance. Easing around the barricade, he stepped inside the carnival grounds.

Sunlight played across bright rainbows of paint, but here and there the weather and years of neglect had allowed the grey concrete to shine through like shoulders through a worn t-shirt. A huge concrete structure shaped like a big top tent filled the center of the walled area. Around it, various carnival rides sat derelict, dead insect carapaces in the snow. The big top structure had a fire-blackened hole in its roof. The explosion site, no doubt.

He crossed the snow toward the entrance that had broken doors hanging open. The blackened snow at the entrance was trodden down into hardpack that was now slick as ice in the melt. At the door, he stopped and peered inside. As he remembered from his one visit with his wife, broad corridors went left and right, but this time instead of happy crowds, there was only darkness around the building's circular exterior walls. He stepped inside, past the corridor to where, illuminated by dusty light through the hole in the roof, lines of seats around the sides of the building looked down on a central arena. Across the building, a portion of the seats had collapsed into a blackened heap, while high overhead in the gloom of the ceiling, lines and wires hung like a torn spiderweb. There'd been spectacles here, including a bullfight imported at great expense from Anglo-German Iberia. Such shows had been popular, as had no-holds-barred troika races. Other spectacles hadn't caught on. Not Russian enough, he'd heard some citizens complaining, although what was Russian about bullfights or maiming horses and drivers? Though the people still came for the carnival rides like the carousel that had been invented based on the battle preparation exercises of Ottoman horsemen and Anglo-German knights, without the spectacle revenue there hadn't been enough regular customers to sustain the business. Now the place was known mostly as a hangout for youth from the old city, though the carnival rides opened for the summer.

Or they had.

Walking to the arena, his footfall crunched in debris and the sound echoed around the building's circular walls. An answering slight sound brought his gaze up in time to see three slim figures slinking into the shadows from seats high in the stands. He stayed where he was, listening, and caught the slight tremor of footsteps to his right, so he ducked back to the corridor and waited. With the collapse of the seats on the other side of the arena, it was highly unlikely that there was another way out. Just who was here if Pogolin, Razin, and the others had arrested the old city's youth?

He loosened his gun in its holster and ventured down the corridor, careful to step on bare ground. The building ticked around him. Dust filtered down. The scurry of rats came from the boarded-up interior of a food kiosk that had sold hamburgers and sausage on a bun. He listened a moment but then stepped past, following the curved corridor illuminated in columns of light from small windows placed sporadically high up on the wall.

When he reached the collapsed section of seats, he knew he'd lost whoever had been here. They were either holed up somewhere inside or they had another way out. They obviously knew the place better than he did. They could have stuck to the shadows high in the seats to get behind him and exit. At least that's what he would have done. He went back the way he'd come and stepped outside into sunshine.

Sure enough, three new sets of tracks cut away from the door and back around the building's curve toward Yekaterina Mountain. He hesitated, for it had not been how he planned to spend the day, but then set out after them. If they were simply kids, they might have seen something. If they were something more—well—that was another thing.

He followed the tracks to the rear wall of the carnival grounds and found where old crates and rotting bales of hay had been stacked against the wall. The tracks led straight up onto the stepped bales and the top of the wall showed where the broken glass and blade wire placed by the carnival owner to stop just such incursions had been cut and peeled away. He clambered up and leapt-scrambled to the top of the wall.

His side blazed with pain, but he was just in time to see three figures disappearing across the snowy slope. The speed with which they were moving meant that it would be almost impossible for him to catch up. The scarf on the head of one of the three said it was a female, but unlike most women in the old city, this one wore trousers. Such clothing had been taken up by a few of the more progressive young women, but not many. He would have thought most of such women would have been picked up with their men in the scouring of the old city.

The woman's companions moved with a much heavier gait. Not youth. Older? Not grandfathers, certainly, but not men in the first flush of youth, either. He thought of the print shop owner and Khan's refusal to talk with him and a shiver ran through him.

Something much more than youthful frustration was happening.

The three figures disappeared amid the boulders and folds of the base of Yekaterina's mountain and Kazakov checked the snow outside the wall where he stood. Amid a bevy of older prints, three sets of new ones led off toward the mountain. They, or those like them, apparently came here often.

He turned and eased himself back onto the hay bales. The earth was peppered with tracks suggesting that the threesome or others came here often. Most of the tracks indicated smooth-soled footwear, though there were a few that held the ornate swirls of popular summer sneakers. The tracks he'd followed from the arena held such marks. He followed the tracks back to the covered arena and then made his way back to the Perseus.

The construction company that had reported the stolen explosive sat only two short blocks away from the carnival entrance. He stopped the Perseus at the company's gate and studied the place. Barbed wire-topped chain-link fence surrounded the place, even on the side that backed onto Yekaterina Mountain. Construction equipment was parked at the rear of a small office building built of yellow stone that might have actually come from the mountain. Another smaller shed was just visible behind it. A security hut sat by the gate with a lone guard inside it. The man was studying him.

Kazakov climbed out of the Perseus and approached the security hut.

He identified himself. "I'm investigating the recent explosions and wondered whether the company has had any further problems since the theft of explosives a few weeks back?"

The guard shook his head. He was balding and had the exploded capillaries under his skin that spoke of a drinker. "The break-ins have stopped. At least the vandalism has and we've placed double the security on the explosives. You don't think our explosives took out Yekaterina, do you?"

Kazakov gave a sober nod. "There's a possibility. Only so many places people can get explosives."

The guard crossed himself. "Well, it won't happen again."

At least they could hope.

"Mind if I have a look around?"

After the guard called his boss, he waved Kazakov inside. Kazakov walked the perimeter fence and finally spotted what he'd expected in a corner behind a fuel tank. There, the fence had been neatly cut and just as neatly wired back in place in a manner that would allow access to the place with only a few twists of wire. Footprints in the snow beyond the fence weren't recent enough to punch holes in the melted snow crust, but the indentations suggested a large man and showed that someone had been here after last evening's snowfall.

He went back to the guard, reported his find, and asked to see the site manager.

The manager was a tall, thin man of about Kazakov's height, with three days' worth of black beard that dragged down his face. Kazakov introduced himself and led the manager and security guard to the hidden corner to show them what he'd found.

"Shit!" the manager exploded and turned on the guard. "How did we miss this?"

The guard stuttered, seeking an answer.

"I think it was designed not to be spotted," Kazakov offered. "The bigger question is whether they got any farther. We need to check your explosives."

The manager set off through the snow, with Kazakov and the guard trailing behind. The manager led them down past the low stone office building and around the side to a shed built of the same yellow stone. A heavy-looking red metal door was set into the doorframe and a metal roof covered the ceiling. Secure enough looking.

A padlock hung from a closed hasp and a key hole waited beside a door handle.

The manager pulled out a ring of keys, but when he touched the padlock, it fell off the hasp into the snow at his feet.

"What the hell!" The manager grabbed the door handle and the door swung open under his hand. He shoved the door open and would have plunged inside, but Kazakov caught his shoulder. The interior floor was half-frozen earth covered with a tracery of work boot tracks that probably came from the company employees. But there might still be something that could be picked up by forensics.

"Step inside, but stay to the side, and don't touch anything," Kazakov said to the manager. "You wait out here," he instructed the guard. Then he followed the manager, cautiously keeping his footsteps close by the wall and studying the floor as he went. The heavy tracks of work boots remained consistent.

The interior of the building was a single stone room lined with shelves stacked with wooden crates. An acrid scent filled the inside.

"We have the explosives here. The blasting caps are elsewhere. We learned that from the last break-in." The manager scanned the shelves and shook his head. "Shit. There're three crates missing." He turned wide, dark eyes on Kazakov. "They took a complete box of blasting caps last time."

"How much explosive is that?" Kazakov asked. The manager's expression suggested a lot.

"Each of the crates contain enough to level a good-sized apartment building. A single box of blasting caps could serve five boxes of explosives."

Three crates of explosives. With the caps, it was enough to do serious damage. Kazakov eased the manager back outside.

"Secure the building, either with locks or a guard. I'll arrange for forensics to examine the shed and the cut in the fence. They might be able to find something."

The security guard was left at the shed and the manager and Kazakov went back to the stone administration building. Kazakov gave the man his card and went back to the Perseus. There, he used his mobile to call Rostoff.

"Rostoff." The man's voice was gruff, as if he'd just been interrupted.

"It's Kazakov. I'm at Mountain Construction. There's been a development."

Rostoff was silent for three heartbeats. "A development in what?"

Clearly, something had him distracted.

"The explosions. Chelomeyev was investigating the theft of explosives from the company last week. This morning it looks like there's been another break-in. Three more crates of explosive are missing and the break-in last week got the blasting caps to ignite what was taken last week and this new load."

Rostoff swore. "You're saying that we'd better brace ourselves for more attacks."

"I'm saying that three more crates of explosives are missing and that we'd better be on our guard."

Another oath from Rostoff.

"How's Constable Smirnova?" he asked after Rostoff's pretty secretary.

"Not good. The shattered glass cut through her like knives." A heavy sigh followed. "I am praying for her recovery." Clearly, the curmudgeonly Rostoff had a softer side for his comely secretary.

"I need a forensics team at the construction firm. There may be trace evidence. I'd like them to check the tracks around the old carnival, too, and then look for matches. It looks like the young Turks of the old city have been using the old arena."

"I'll see to it," Rostoff growled. "When are you coming back to regular duties? There are too few detectives at the moment."

Kazakov looked out the window where the sun lit the crags and ragged sides of Yekaterina Mountain. The wind blew shreds of cloud around the peaks, obscuring and revealing them like tantalizing secrets. He felt the same about the Chelomeyev investigation. He felt like the investigation kept revealing tantalizing glimpses of what might have occurred, but so far the full scope of the case was beyond him.

"It will be a while, yet. There is something in these cases. I am sure of it."

"You and your bloody certainty." Rostoff swore. The line went dead.

Sighing, Kazakov started the Perseus and made a quick phone call to the number given for Svetlana Ivanov. Time to concentrate on the Ivanov case.

"Hello?" The voice was cool and husky for a woman, but also melodious.

"Svetlana Ivanova?" he asked.

"Ye-es," the voice turned cautious.

He introduced himself as the new investigator into her husband's death. "I would like to speak with you. I am headed to your house."

"But I'm not staying there. It is—too difficult. I am staying at a friend's place."

"The address, please. I will interview you there."

There was a pause that went on too long, as if the woman scrambled to come up with an excuse. Then she gave him an address.

Kazakov immediately knew where it was.

"I will be there in ten minutes," he said and hung up, then pulled the Perseus back into traffic, noticing a low-slung black sedan appear a block behind him. Almost as if it had been waiting.

He looked back at the address and shook his head.

Enver Pasha, again. This time his residence.

13

In the summer, Enver Pasha's home sat across the street from the green lawns, wide paths, and graceful trees of Yekaterina Park. In the winter, the house faced a wilderness of unbroken white and skeletal trees that had yielded up at least two bodies this year. Kazakov shuddered.

He did not want to remember the case again, but every twinge in his side was a reminder. So was the ache in his heart that he did not like to acknowledge.

The house was four stories tall, including the aboveground basement intended as the servants' quarters. The main part of the house was built of pale gray stone, fashioned into large bricks. Dormer windows filled the third-floor roofline of the main residence, and the windows below held white-framed windows curtained with lace. A set of steep, shoveled stairs led up to the white-columned portico that shielded the slick, black front door. The ground floor was built of dark kiln-baked brick and blended into the low bushes in the yard.

Kazakov parked and climbed out of the Perseus. A scent of burning and wet debris filled the air as if the smoke from one of New Moscow's factories had been blown back over the city. The sound of traffic on the sloppy streets came from across the river and beyond

Potemkin Park. On the quiet crescent that wound past Enver Pasha's house, the air was filled with the hush of the breeze in naked branches and the trickle of water off the house eaves. To one side of the house, the brothel known as the Red Veil was primed and ready to greet its well-heeled, noonday customers.

Kazakov turned away from that brothel and focused on Enver Pasha's house. A lower floor curtain twitched, suggesting they were watching for him.

He lumbered up the steep stairs, feeling the ache in his side. The door opened before he could knock and he found himself once more facing the blonde-haired woman he had come to know was Olga Gruenwald. Once before he had stood here and questioned her. That time it had been about a dead body found in the park and she had denied him access to her employer's house.

This time she stepped aside and ushered him in.

She wore a simple black skirt, crisp white blouse, and white sweater thrown over her broad shoulders. White pearls glistened at her throat and earlobes and she carried a faint scent of something spicy. She exuded far more elegance and athletic grace than one would expect for a woman who had claimed to be no more than Enver Pasha's housekeeper.

The foyer of the house was a grand reminder that he did not belong in a place like this. A haunting hint of incense sweetened the air, too similar to that which had been used by the now dead Yekaterina Weber. A gleaming, broad wooden staircase wound up one side of the circular, wood-paneled room and immaculate, thick Persian carpets lay underfoot. He was surprised that paintings of Byzantine figures adorned the walls, each lit by individual spotlights recessed in the ceiling, for he'd always been taught that the human form was not found in Ottoman art. So much for what he'd been told. Or so much for its relevance when it came to men like Enver Pasha.

He turned to Olga Gruenwald. "You perform your duties well."

Her brow twitched as if she was confused.

"You told me you are the housekeeper. The place is very clean," he clarified.

"Of course," she said, nodding as if she'd known all along. "Come in, Detektiv. Svetlana is waiting." She graciously motioned him to a double-doored room to one side of the foyer.

It was a small parlor with ivory and mint green floral wallpaper and delicate, carved furniture, as if this was a room for women only. It held a pale green settee with floral cushions and three spindle-legged chairs gathered together around a low coffee table to face a white marble fireplace that looked as if it had never been lit. On the mantle were a grouping of three pale green candles in silver candlesticks and a six-by-eight-inch gold-embellished box that had a patina of age. The whole room was painted in light and shadows from a single narrow window at the front of the house that left him feeling as if the room's pale colors were a mask for darkness elsewhere in the house.

Or he was imagining things.

He shook himself.

On the settee, facing the empty fireplace, sat a slim, dark-haired woman who sprang up to face him when he stepped through the door.

"Svetlana Ivanova? I am Detektiv Alexander Kazakov. I am very sorry for your loss," he said as he shook her hand.

She was prettier than Chelomeyev's evidence folder had shown. While Olga Gruenwald was blonde and had an openly sensual form under her suits and sweaters, Svetlana Ivanova had a dark refinement with smoldering dark eyes and a square jaw that set off her full mouth. She wore a simple black dress with long sleeves and no makeup other than an orangey-red lipstick that belonged on her, though on other women it might look severe.

She held out her hand, gesturing him to a chair and then gracefully settling herself back on the settee.

"I'll bring the tea," Olga Gruenwald said after taking Kazakov's coat and exiting the room. The air carried a chill that threatened to cut to the bone and yet Svetlana Ivanova appeared not to feel it.

"What can I do for you, Detektiv?"

And there it was: that husky voice that seemed to settle right down in Kazakov's groin. Did she use the same voice on all men? It was a weapon, he was sure. Just as Olga's curves were.

"Detective Chelomeyev has had to step back from your husband's case. I am here to complete the investigation. Familiarizing myself with all the parties is part of that process."

She met his gaze squarely, as if she dared him to find fault in her. Finally, she nodded. "You have questions?"

He nodded. Too many of them. "Tell me about your husband."

Shaking her head, her fingers plucked at the hem of her dress. "You can read it all in the newspapers. Businessman, philanthropist, husband, with the third aspect coming a distant third." Her accent of the western border towns came through and was charming.

"The newspapers said he was a sportsman, too."

"Yes. Yes, he liked his horses. His polo."

"Oh? What club did he play for?"

She rolled her eyes. "I don't know. AngloTec or something, I believe. What of it?"

What of it, indeed. AngloTec had been the team that a Chinese spy had played for, and also Enver Pasha. The Chinese spy had been suspected of double-crossing his Chinese masters and had ended up dead in the snow in Yekaterina Park just outside this mansion's doors.

"Tell me about the man you knew."

She sighed and studied her hands. They were long fingered with many rings.

"Grigori was a dedicated man—to his business, to his friends, to me. He loved me as much as he could love anyone. It is unthinkable that someone would kill him." Her gaze was shiny with unshed tears.

An act, or the truth? She seemed genuinely sorry that he was gone.

Olga Gruenwald appeared in the doorway carrying a tray with an ornate Ottoman teapot covered in blue and terra cotta abstract mosaic. Three delicate blue china cups and saucers surrounded the pot along with a small pitcher of milk and a bowl of cubed sugar. She set the large copper tray on the table and stepped back. "Shall I pour, or would you rather I not stay?" Her gaze tracked to Svetlana almost like a warning.

"Stay, please," Svetlana said. "I feel better when you are around."

Was it just feminine friendship or something more? "Tell me about your husband's business," he asked as Olga Gruenwald poured black tea from high above the cups to aerate the liquid. Then she added two sugars and milk to two cups and paused. He held up three fingers and she quickly put three sugars and milk into the third cup, then passed him the cup and a spoon for stirring.

"He focused on importing American tobacco. It had been very lucrative, but his competitors did not like him for it. Lately it had been not so good. Not so much money for my charities. It was…not to my liking…or his. Grigori was a generous man."

"So there had been problems at work."

"Yes. Yes. Problems. He was there all the time, trying to deal with the situation. There were others circling like sharks, you know? Poor Grigori would come home for dinner and be gone again immediately back to the office. Always the office." Her shoulders sagged as she shook her head as if the memory of it exhausted her.

"How did that make you feel?" He asked quietly and felt his words swallowed up by the shadows.

"Helpless," she said immediately. "Frustrated. Angry that they would do this to Grigori." The light through the window caught her face at unflattering angles.

"And to you," he offered to see her reaction.

"Yes, to me." She sipped her tea. "I lost my husband as he fought to save his business. He was not able to be in both places and the business won." She shook her head. "The damned business won. And then they killed him so that he would never be mine again!"

She set her teacup down, spilling the pale liquid over the side so it pooled in the saucer on the copper tray. Her hands fisted in her lap. "I have lost my husband and my home, you know. How can I ever return to that place knowing Grigori died there in his office?"

He didn't bother to answer. Instead he pulled out his notebook and flipped back to his notes about the Grigori file.

"I understand that you were both in the mountains at the time of Grigori's death."

The two women looked at each other.

"We told the other detective," Olga Gruenwald said.

"Yes. You did. What took you up to the mountains?" He sipped his tea as if he was only half-interested. The two women looked at each other again.

"Friendship," Svetlana said.

"A need to get away," Olga murmured.

He looked at her enquiringly hoping she would elaborate.

"Svetlana was feeling so neglected that I thought she needed a change of scenery. Something to take her mind off Grigori—and his problems—for a while. I spoke to Enver and he said that we could use his mountain house for a while so I spirited Svetlana away." Seated on the couch beside Svetlana, Olga's fingers lightly grazed Svetlana's knee. Her smooth features spread in a smile. "I am lucky to have such an employer."

"Indeed," he said and looked at his notes. "Where is this mountain house?"

"In Biysk, near the ski hill. The house has a lovely view of the slopes."

Biysk lay high in the mountains not far from Guicho that was, in turn, not that far from the Chinese border. There had been times when the border area was contested—until the Ottoman Empire stated that it saw such incursions as threats to its borders, too.

Interesting that an Ottoman Pasha would have a home so close to what had been a troubled border. Was he there to keep watch?

"When did you depart New Moscow?" he asked.

"The day before Grigori died. I can't help but think that if I'd stayed home, perhaps it would never have happened." Svetlana's hands were shaking. She was either a consummate actress or she was truly troubled.

"You mustn't say that!" Olga reached for and gripped Svetlana's hands. "Whoever did this could have killed you, too. If there is something good out of this, it is that you were safe."

Svetlana lifted her lustrous gaze. "For what? Safe for what? With Grigori gone, what life is there for me?" Her voice hiccoughed.

"This is hard for her," Olga said as if Svetlana was some hothouse flower to be shielded.

"When did you last see Grigori?" he asked Svetlana.

"It was the day before we left—no, two days before because I spent the night before with Olga so that we could make a good start the next day. It was at home. I was there, planning dinner, when he came home."

She looked up from her and Olga's interlinked hands. "He was clearly preoccupied and had his briefcase with him. I asked if he would like to join me for tea, but he only shook his head and went into his office." Her gaze turned liquid. "That was the last time that I saw my husband alive, Detektiv. With a door closing between us again." She gave a shaky sigh.

"I'm sorry to ask you these questions in this time of grief, but can you recall what time this was?"

Svetlana wiped her eyes. "Around three o'clock, I think. That's why I was so surprised that he was home. I put it down to a business meeting. Sometimes he took them at home."

"Had he mentioned meeting with any particular business associates?"

She shook her head.

"Were there any he was having particular difficulties with?"

Another shake of the head. "They were all just tobacco men. Importers who were jealous of Grigori's foresight in arranging a monopoly."

"One would think that such a monopoly wouldn't amount to much. Fergana isn't that large a country, and how many people can afford to pay your husband's premium price for their addiction?"

The grief cleared from her gaze for a moment and he momentarily saw the high level of her intelligence. "Then you would be mistaken, Detektiv. My husband was no fool. When he obtained the monopoly, it was for all of Asia. The Chinese and Ottomans were hungry for his product." Then her gaze clouded again and she was a new widow consumed with grief.

The information changed things. Ivanov might had had competition in Fergana, but to compete with the large companies that came out of the two great empires—that took nerves of steel and the guts of the

Potemkins and Suvarovs of the world. Grigori Ivanov had been a modern warrior. The news also broadened the suspects to beyond Fergana's borders. Why had the reporter, Kasimir Krupin, left out this piece of information?

"Were there any of his competitors that your husband was more worried about? Think back to any conversations you might have had or anything you might have overheard."

She shook her head. "I'm so sorry. I've wracked my brain trying to think of anyone who would want to kill him. There was no one—at least no one in particular that I can identify."

"Who should I speak to at his company to learn more about his competitors?" He sat with his notebook open, pen poised to write.

Svetlana glanced down at her hands again. "I suppose that would be Arthur—Arthur Blackstone. Arthur is an American who came over to support Grigori's start-up and stayed on. You can find him at the company. The man works almost as long hours as Grigori did." Her lips turned down in a feminine frown.

Kazakov noted the name and decided to take the interview back to its original direction now that he'd had a chance to read Svetlana's mood. He looked up at the two women.

"Tell me about your weekend."

The two women gushed about the lovely weather they'd had their first day and how they'd bundled up and rented a sleigh to explore the town and had stopped for a meal at a restaurant. He got the name. Then Svetlana talked about skiing and meeting up with friends, and, regardless of the snowstorm that closed the roads, how busy she'd been once the invitations started pouring in. It had totally taken Svetlana's mind off her problems.

Until they received the news of Grigori's demise.

Unfortunately, the snowstorm had closed the roads and they couldn't get home until road crews opened the road to the bravest of drivers and Enver Pasha drove up to rescue them. He had an employee bring down Olga's vehicle afterward.

He listened to their story, the two of them embellishing each other's contribution until he finally held up a hand to stop them. "You mentioned all the friends you were in contact with. Can I have their names and contact information?"

Olga Gruenwald frowned. "I thought the fact that we could confirm each other's story was enough."

Kazakov shook his head. "The names?"

The two women looked at each other. "Well, there is Tasia Aristov. And then there is Polina Poverov," Olga said.

"What about Annuschka Yevseyev? She went for lunch with us the first day and hosted the party the next evening. There were many times we saw each other skiing."

The world telescoped for a moment and Kazakov froze. The two women's lips moved, but he could not hear. Did they know that they had just named his ex-wife, the one woman in the world that he did not wish to see? The woman who had left him dead inside until Maria had briefly brought him back to life again. That was it, wasn't it—why he kept going back to Maria's grave. She had replanted his arrow to give him life again.

"I'll get you their contact information," Olga Gruenwald was saying as she stood up and smoothed her skirt over her thighs. Gracefully, she left the room, leaving Svetlana studying him.

He wondered how long he had been distracted. What had been said that he had missed. His insides felt rattled as he lurched to his feet. "Thank you for your time, Mrs. Ivanova. If you think of anyone who might have wanted to harm your husband, please give me a call." He provided her with his card and stepped out of the room into the foyer to heave in a deep breath as he pulled on his coat and hat.

It was as if the two women had sucked all the air out of the room. Or perhaps it was mention of his ex-wife, Annuschka. His stomach knotted at the thought of interviewing her, but that seemed to be the way of these cases, from dealing with the owner of the Red Veil brothel to navigating interviews with the Kyrgyz people to dealing with foreigners, nothing in the past case had been easy and somehow this case simply felt like an extension of everything that had come before.

Olga Gruenwald glided out of a room at the rear of the house and came to him carrying a folded piece of paper. "These are the people we mentioned and their contact numbers. Would you like me to call them and tell them you'll be calling?"

He shook his head. "I would rather you didn't. I'll contact those I think necessary."

But the look in her eyes suggested that she would be contacting them anyway. He thanked her and stepped out the door into the failing mid afternoon sunshine. A brisk wind had picked up, bringing the chill of the mountains; and the trickle of meltwater was already failing.

He looked down at the list he held in his hands and felt the full impact of winter's freezing.

14

─────────

The interior of the Perseus felt like a safe haven in the lengthening shadows of the Red Veil and Enver Pasha's mansion. He'd never noticed it before, but it was as if the two buildings were somehow counterpoints to each other. The Red Veil's gingerbread facings, narrow base, and height made it seem as if it stood on chicken legs ready to mock the city with a dance. The mansion beside it hunkered, wide base to the ground as if it had impaled itself in the earth. For all its pale gray stone and white columns, at the moment the residence reminded him of nothing so much as a half-buried bomb waiting to go off.

He pulled his collar up against the chill, even though he'd turned the vehicle on and heat chugged out of the vents. Something didn't feel right about this investigation and now his ex-wife was involved.

He peered out at the park through the frosted windshield. While he had been inside, a thin veil of clouds had rolled over the sun, and eastward, heavier cloud hung over the mountains. The wind had changed direction, shifting from the disarming illusion of Ottoman warmth to the frozen cold that blew out of the Chinese east. The Chinese claimed that the great Genghis Khan had subdued the

Ferganese area and brought Chinese settlers to Ferganese lands. Thus, they claimed, Fergana rightly belonged to the Empire of the Sun.

The only thing saving Fergana from the Chinese fulfilling their claim was the Ottoman Empire, which laid an equal claim that Ottoman forbearers had once ruled here. Both countries lusted after the Ferganese patch of land, but neither wished to be the one to start the final war. If Fergana's government made a choice between the two superpowers, what would the other superpower do?

That was a question far beyond the scope of his investigation and nothing to do with the death of Grigori Ivanov—or Chelomeyev's beating.

He hoped.

He needed to contact Enver Pasha's office to confirm his follow-up appointment and also to arrange an interview with Arthur Blackstone at Grigori Ivanov's company. He needed to speak to the Transcontinental Security guards who had patrolled Chelomeyev's area and to interview Chelomeyev's neighbors. He wanted to visit the young detective again, too. And he needed to speak to the American, Eric Clinton. And Annuschka.

He used his mobile to call Enver Pasha's office and was told that they were still trying to find time in Mr. Enver's schedule. He left them with the message that he expected to hear from them today. Then he tried to contact Arthur Blackstone, but was told by his receptionist that the man was out of the country. Feeling stymied, he dropped the Perseus in gear and guided the vehicle along the curve of the street around the park. A low-slung dark vehicle appeared a block or two behind him. Limousine? There would be plenty of those vehicles in this neighborhood. Spotting a vehicle like that behind him once or twice might be nothing, but this was unusual. No, he was being followed. And not well.

At the end of the park he turned toward the river and crossed the low, stone bridge that had been one of the first that the Russian refugees had built—something rugged enough to withstand spring runoff from the mountains. A newer steel bridge now stood upriver and took most of the traffic across at the other end of the park, but this was

Fergana's history. Something solid, something theirs beyond the make-believe facades of Yekaterina's palace and Saint Basil's Cathedral. The Perseus's tires rumbled over the cobbles that still covered the bridge, but then he was across and into the city proper. He turned left, away from the direction most traffic was flowing and kept his eye on the rearview mirror.

The dark Ziln-type vehicle turned left after him. He sped up, weaving through traffic and turned right into the city core toward the police station. Then he pulled into the curb and watched behind him. The dark vehicle slid across the intersection without following. Was he paranoid?

He pulled into traffic again and made his way across the city to a new business park that held Transcontinental's security division. The business park was made up of long rows of brick and stucco buildings built to resemble an updated version of the mud-daub structures that had once formed the Silk Road caravanserai. When Kazakov was a child, there had been such a building of mud, straw, and horsehair over timbers set at the base of Yekaterina's Mountain next to the old city. He had gone there once on a dare as a teenager and had thought it a sad place. Its dark rooms had still carried the scent of spice as an undertone to animal dung. The people of the old city had used the place to house their goats from time to time. But the whole structure and its history had been torn down to make way for the carnival.

And now it, too, was decrepit and falling down.

He parked in a parking spot in front of the unit that had a small Transcontinental Security sign in an alcove over the plain door. There were no windows in the fronts of any of the units and all of them looked the same except for the signs above the doors. This was what Fergana was coming to. Statues of a long dead monarch and monotonous buildings. He climbed out, knocked once on the closed unit door, and pushed inside.

A small reception room greeted him with a scent of floral potpourri that didn't fit with the scarred wooden desk facing the door, nor the bruiser of a man seated behind the cluttered desk in a desert-khaki-colored uniform with Transcontinental Security flashes on his shoulders in navy-and-orange. Kazakov recalled similarly attired men at Enver Pasha's office. Keeping the profits all in-house.

The room had sand-brown wallpaper and bench seats built along the outer walls with orange cushions on the tops. The benches reminded him of the traditional houses of the old city. So whoever had built the complex had tried to include selective parts of the traditional construction.

The big man looked up at him. He had startling blue eyes that didn't quite fit the mop of earlobe-length black hair and swarthy skin that suggested tribal heritage somewhere back in his bloodline. His long-sleeved shirt was pulled tight over bulging shoulders and biceps, and he wore his name embroidered above his left breast pocket. Radulov.

Security Officer Radulov met Kazakov's study with his own assessing gaze.

"May I help you?" he asked in a voice that was a surprisingly cultured tenor.

Kazakov produced his badge. "Detektiv Alexander Kazakov, New Moscow police. I'm investigating an assault and hoped you might help."

Radulov arched a single thick eyebrow. "What do you need? We at Transcontinental Security are here to serve." The words came out well-rehearsed.

"You have a contract with a cadre of apartment blocks in the old warehouse district near the old city. I believe you were contracted to conduct patrols and keep the locals away."

Radulov's gaze flickered. His shoulders stiffened. "We hold a contract to protect the residences from property damage and theft."

"In speaking with building residents, their impression was that your officers help to keep them safe." Kazakov nodded in encouragement.

Radulov's stiff shoulders seemed to ease.

"How long have you held the contract?"

"About a year. We were contracted to keep the local indigents, drug addicts, and whores away." He shook his head. "Those poor apartment owners move into their shiny new apartments and then find that they're living next door to the worst New Moscow has to offer. We offered them security when they first opened, but they thought that they wouldn't need it. Then too many of the apartment blocks had damage and they called us in." He shrugged as if it had been inevitable.

Perhaps it had been. All it would have taken was a slight push of the working girls toward the apartment blocks and a few nighttime ventures to paint a few walls or break a few windows.

Kazakov met Radulov's gaze and realized that he was being paranoid again. Suspicion of everyone around him was not a good sign.

"Tell me about your patrol schedule through the area."

Radulov stirred the clutter on the top of his desk and produced a file. He smiled. "I was just doing our monthly billing so I have it handy." He flipped it open. "We're contracted to provide three sweeps of the area each night. We usually have five patrol vehicles out in the city each night so one of them is assigned responsibility to swing through the neighborhood three times."

"And who was assigned to swing through last Monday night?"

"Monday? Let me see." Radulov turned to another page of the file and ran his finger down a list. "That would be Constantine Elderov and Sergei Izotov. Good men, both of them."

"Do they file reports of what they saw on their patrols?"

"Of course." He flipped to another section of the file and turned the whole thing to Kazakov. "There." He tapped his finger on a notation in a cramped, messy hand. "Izotov completed the end of shift report that day."

Kazakov bent over the desk to read. *Regular patrols spaced two hours apart. First pass at 7:30 p.m. Area dark. Little foot traffic. Undesirable noted and told to move along. No issues. Second pass at 10 p.m. Undesirable not evident. Some street traffic due to bar closing. Third pass 1:30 a.m. Delayed due to broken window at New Moscow museum. No foot traffic or street traffic. All appeared quiet.*

Two sets of initials sat to the side of the entry as indication that they both concurred with the report. There was no mention of street conditions, nor of checks of premises other than the drive-bys.

"I'd like to interview these two men," he said and slid the file back to Radulov. "I'd also like a copy of that report." It provided a good touchstone for future interviews.

"Elderov and Izotov come back on shift this evening. I could hold them here so that you could interview them before they go out on patrol."

"That would be helpful," Kazakov nodded and stood. "What time should I return?"

"About seven p.m. They'll be here for shift change."

Kazakov considered. "Tell me something: If your men saw someone lying in the snow who looked like he'd been beaten, what would they do?"

"Call the police, of course."

"And if they saw something in a parking lot that they couldn't quite identify because it was dark, would they investigate?" Kazakov sighed. It was many hours since he'd stopped for a meal and many more since he'd rested. His side ached and so did the shoulder he'd injured.

"Yes," Radulov said. "At least, I like to think so."

Kazakov thanked him and said he'd return at seven. Outside, the late afternoon air had turned chill once again. He huddled in his coat, feeling heavy and tired and every one of his forty-five years. His watch said it was five thirty and the light had faded to almost black. The streetlights around the business park had flickered on and now the orange light pooled on the slushy roadsides. Too late to go home and too early to simply wait. Return to the office or...?

The streets were busy with vehicles headed toward home. Kazakov sent the Perseus among then along Suvarov Boulevard and then turned off into the quiet that led toward the old city and Yekaterina Mountain.

The streetlights ran fewer here, and so did the traffic. He pulled into the curb and parked, then climbed out into the cold. Overhead, a thin layer of clouds placed a nacreous caul over the sky and a rainbow of ice crystals formed a halo around the moon. Westward, the city hummed with traffic, but here there was only the shuffle of the wind in snow.

He made his way to the graveyard gate and slowly climbed the hill.

The wind from behind him whipped around the graveyard headstones and pressed his greatcoat around him as if it was in a hurry to find its way to Yekaterina Mountain. The moon gleamed like a malformed embryo through its membrane of clouds, and the diesel and old oil smell of New Moscow cut through the donkey dung and spice scent of the old city. The amber lights of New Moscow glittered in the cold but, from his spot at the top of the graveyard hill, the old city sat dark and warm like a favored dog curled at the base of Yekaterina Mountain. Why did he feel this affinity for the old tribes, the old ways, and yet yearn for a country that looked to the future? Why did he mourn a woman he had barely known? Why did he return to her when life and his job in New Moscow threatened to overwhelm him?

Somehow Maria was more real to him than Annuschka had ever been, though he and Annuschka had been married for seven years.

"What is it about you that haunts me, Maria? That brings me back to you?" he said into the wind.

"I was a lost soul, just like you, Alexander," came an almost indistinct voice on the wind.

He spun around.

The graveyard spread around him over the top and sides of the hill, the headstones standing in erratic rows like children playing at soldiers. These were the dead of the old city and early New Moscow, when there was more or less equality between the Russians and tribal residents and still an air of looking forward to the future instead of focusing on the past. At least that was what he liked to think—that his people had not always been lost in mourning past greatness.

Nothing moved in the graveyard except the wind. Newly fallen dead leaves shuffled across the snow. His breath steamed around him and the faint light of the city and the fickle moon cast fitful shadows.

"Who's there?" he called, but there was no answer. He didn't expect one. Why would anyone but him be standing in this graveyard at this hour? Why would—how could—anyone answer him in Maria's soft voice?

So… he was going mad now. Hearing voices when none existed, though her sentiment might be truer than he liked to think.

And why was he here at all? He sighed, knowing it was partially because Annuschka's name brought up so many memories, none of them good. The memories had soured just as their marriage had, though it had taken his brief knowing of Maria to point it out to him.

But there was something more than Annuschka coming into his life again. Something about Radulov's information caused a slight tingle in the back of his mind, but he couldn't put his finger on what it was. He needed to talk to those security guards. As for the Ivanov murder, it was time that he began looking more seriously at the corporate competition angle. After all, wasn't the motive for murder usually connected to money?

Or love/lust. But Svetlana Ivanova appeared to have a strong alibi.

He looked down at Maria's grave, shadowy in the dark. Snow had drifted around the headstone base as if it was needed to help prop the headstone up.

Like his own aversion to seeing Annuschka made him want to believe Svetlana Ivanova's story. He really only had the support of Olga Gruenwald and Enver Pasha's story that he had brought the two women into town when the roads were bad. The women could be in it together…

And that was based on no evidence and a bias that he held toward Enver Pasha and those involved with him. Time to be objective and put old feelings aside. He'd see Annuschka tomorrow.

The cold had eaten its way through the collar of his coat and his boots and gloves. He stomped to keep the blood circulating and checked his watch. Time to go. He'd spent enough time with Maria for tonight. Khan would shake his head and tell him that he was just as consumed with the past as other Russians. His "past" just happened to be more recent.

"'Til we meet again," he said and touched the top of the concrete headstone before heading down the trail he'd left in the snow. He knew full well that the voice he'd heard hadn't really been there.

The path was slippery from where his past footprints had melted in the sun during the day and now had frozen with the onslaught of night. He picked his way, concentrating on his footing and grasping at headstones for balance. The last thing his side needed was the torque of a fall.

He was almost at the gate to the street when two shadows detached themselves from the trees that guarded the entrance. Kazakov barely had time to register when one lunged and slammed into him. He stumbled and went down, his shoulder slamming against a headstone. Then the stranger was on him.

Kazakov drove a fist into the attacker's face and felt the cartilage give. The man oomphed and swore and blood sprayed Kazakov's face. Kazakov bucked him off and scrambled to his knees, seeking the gun under his coat.

The man's fist found Kazakov's ear. Searing pain slowed him long enough that the attacker scrambled up. He kicked Kazakov's side, and the pain of his injury exploded. He collapsed to the ground. Another kick to his lower back and he lay, panting against the pain.

A pair of shiny black boots appeared in his view. "Detektiv Kazakov, my employer suggests that you give up your investigation. You frequent places like this with such icy paths and you live so far from civilization—far from any help. Who knows what ills could befall you. Surely you do not want that to happen."

Kazakov blinked trying to clear his eyes to see who made these threats. He shook his head and managed a futile, "What's he so afraid of?"

The unseen stranger reached down and patted Kazakov's shoulder. "It is you who should have fear. Fear enough to ensure you do what is right."

Then he was gone, those shiny black boots crossing the crunching snow, joined by the more burly man who had led the attack. Vision gradually clearing, Kazakov struggled up to sitting. A vehicle engine started down the street. He got to his knees and almost threw up at the pain in his side. He should probably have it checked. He used a headstone for support and stood swaying in the wind.

He limped to the gate and looked into the street. A set of taillights

—likely his attackers'—was disappearing around a curve in the road toward town. His Perseus stood alone and the streets were empty except for a low-slung dark vehicle parked two blocks down.

Damn it all to hell! What was going on? Stop his investigation? Just which investigation were they referring to? Who were they? And the low-slung car? It looked like the vehicle he'd been seeing far too frequently over the past few days. Was the driver connected to the attack on him? Was something similar to this what had happened to Chelomeyev?

He started to the Perseus and climbed in, feeling something shift painfully in his side and lower back. Perfect. He'd be pissing red again.

He started the Perseus's engine and sat there a moment. Damn them, whoever they were. Enver Pasha—if he was somehow involved in the Ivanov murder or was trying to protect his friends, he could have sent this little warning. He swung the Perseus into the street in a ragged U-turn and started toward the low-slung vehicle. If this was the vehicle he'd seen and if there was anyone inside, they were about to get the surprise of their lives.

Pedal to the metal, he roared down the street, only to slam on the brakes and slide to a stop beside the unknown vehicle. Kazakov slammed open the Perseus's door and scrambled out, ignoring the knife-blade of pain. The low-slung vehicle's engine turned over and its headlight flared on, but Kazakov had the driver-side door handle and yanked the door open.

Eric Clinton blinked up at him.

15

The six thirty air stung Kazakov's nose and ears. The air reeked of the Perseus's engine exhaust swirling between him and the open door as he stood shocked and looking down at the man he had least expected. Eric Clinton sat caught in the dashboard lights of his car and the edge of the streetlights that painted his flesh amber.

From standing to one side to present a smaller target in case of weapons, Kazakov straightened to face the man he knew.

Eric Clinton was a tall, lanky American from the American capital of Charleston, whom Kazakov had last seen meeting clandestinely with Kasimir Krupin. Clinton favored wide-brimmed hats and pointy-toed, leaf-scrolled boots. He had a ruddy complexion and sun-bleached brown hair that said he was an outdoorsman and piercing blue eyes that now gazed up at Kazakov in consternation. Then he relaxed back into the seat of his vehicle and smiled.

"How the hell are you, Kazakov?"

"How the hell—what the hell are you doing, following me?" Kazakov recovered from his momentary shock and scanned the vehicle's interior. Clinton was alone.

"Who said I was following you?"

"How about the fact that this is at least the fourth time I've seen this vehicle since I spotted you with Kasimir Krupin."

The revelation had its effect. Clinton looked away, no longer able to play innocent. "You saw that, did you?"

"The man virtually shoved me out of his office and was on the phone so fast it didn't take a genius to know something was going on. I waited outside and, sure enough, he bolted out the door, so I followed him."

"How'd you know he wasn't just going for lunch?"

"I didn't. But I took a chance and, wonder of wonders, saw the newspaper's star financial reporter meeting with a certain American. Now I wonder why that could be."

The heat from Clinton's vehicle dissipated in the night. Kazakov shifted from frozen foot to frozen foot and the pain in his side made him want to sit for a very long time. A tall glass of vodka would be good, too.

"Why don't you park your vehicle and climb in so we can talk," Clinton said. "It's colder'n hell out there and you're letting all the heat out." He nodded up at Kazakov's hand, still firmly holding the offending vehicle's door open.

Kazakov released the door and stepped back to the Perseus, wondering if Clinton was stupid enough to make a run for it. Of course, he wasn't. Clinton's vehicle chugged exhaust into the air as Kazakov pulled the Perseus over to the side of the road, parked, and climbed out, pocketing the keys. He climbed in the passenger side of Clinton's vehicle and settled into a comfortable, smooth-leather seat.

"Nice. American?" The name "Ford" was written on the dash and he'd never heard of it.

Clinton nodded. "What else? I had it brought over a month ago. I couldn't stand the clunky ride of the Ottoman vehicles and the Chinese ones just don't give the headroom." He shrugged.

"Krupin called me because he was concerned about you and your questions. They're similar to the ones I've been asking since Ivanov died. His special status with American business and the feeding frenzy that's started since his death has some of us suspicious. There's some suspicion that there might be someone in the embassy who's received a payoff to redirect Ivanov's monopoly."

Kazakov loosened his scarf in the heat pumping into the vehicle and inhaled the new car scent. He considered Clinton's words. "And that leads to following me?"

"It leads me to wonder why you're asking all these questions. We'd asked for the case to be quietly closed so that we could complete our investigation. Then I hear that a certain detective with a reputation of not letting go has taken on the investigation. I wanted to know what you were doing."

"You could have picked up the phone," Kazakov said into the now unpleasantly hot interior. Clinton seemed totally unaware of just how high he had the temperature. "Did you do the same to Chelomeyev? Follow him?"

Clinton shook his head. "Unfortunately, no. I knew the case had been closed, so I didn't bother."

So Clinton's pipeline into the police hadn't yet learned that they had another Kazakov on their hands in young Chelomeyev. If the young detective recovered. Of course, the other possibility was that they had followed Chelomeyev and beaten him when the young detective would not back down from the investigation. And had sent a warning to Kazakov now, too. Clinton had just overseen it.

"Chelomeyev was badly beaten, but then you would know that. I figure it had to do with a case he'd been investigating. Grigori Ivanov's murder seemed the highest profile and the one where people might have the most to lose. That's why I'm asking questions."

His gaze forward, through the windscreen, Clinton nodded. "Makes sense. I should have seen it. So who were the goons?" He lifted his chin down the street toward the graveyard.

Interesting. Kazakov studied Clinton's profile, but the man showed nothing beyond interest.

"A warning shot over the bow. They came to warn me off a case." Kazakov shook his head.

Clinton shot him a glance. "This case?"

"I wish I knew. They weren't exactly clear."

"Interesting."

"Thanks for the help, by the way." Kazakov said and was gratified to see Clinton squirm. "So while we're sharing information, why don't you share with me? Or isn't that the way American spies work?" Kazakov met Clinton's glare. At least the man didn't try to deny it.

Finally, Clinton shrugged. "Half the foreigners in Fergana are spies. The other half are their spouses." He grinned.

Kazakov simply waited.

"First off, we don't know who killed him or why, but we know that since his death over here there have been a number of troubling deaths in America. In Charleston alone, a tobacco mogul's son has been kidnapped and two major shipping companies have had executives die in mysterious circumstances. One was an unlikely vehicle accident and the other a drowning—when the female victim was deathly afraid of the water and never went near it. Over here, there was some immediate turmoil in the cigarette import side of things at the embassy. Too many business visa applications and applications to import—that sort of thing. But then most of the applications were withdrawn—all within the space of days. Two companies remain on the books and neither of them are the long-standing tobacco import companies." He looked over at Kazakov. "As you can see. There's nothing solid there, simply enough to make us suspicious."

"Makes me question who these upstarts are and how they came to be the last men standing. That's why you've been in contact with Krupin," Kazakov said. "Any names that I might be familiar with?"

Clinton sighed and shook his head. "Not on the face of it. That's the problem. The company principals are lily-white as far as I can tell and neither one has been in business before. There's no telling where they got the money, but both have presented business plans that your government has signed off on, even though Ivanov is barely in the ground. Someone clearly has friends in high places."

"The names?" Kazakov repeated.

"There's a fellow named Vladimir Kimkin who works for the government. He's a Deputy Minister of Communications so no one can claim conflict of interest over a tobacco contract. The other is a fellow named Constantine Bogomolov who manages the New Moscow library. Not exactly the kind of people you'd think would or could compete against the established tobacco industry, or the kind who would arrange murders." Clinton turned to Kazakov. "You see why we're concerned? These guys shouldn't be interested in tobacco. They certainly shouldn't be the last men standing in a competition to gain business permits with the American government. Not unless they got to someone."

"And then there's the body count," Kazakov said drily.

Clinton adjusted the heat in the car and the hellish temperature decreased to furnace level.

Clinton turned to him, worry lines between his brows. "You think the corporate man's kid is dead?"

Kazakov simply looked at him.

"Christ. They're like American royalty. One of the first families. Who here has a reach that long?"

Kazakov pondered the question. "To have a reach that long would mean they are far more powerful than any simple Ferganese business." But he could think of one man who might have such sway, a man whose presence was like tentacles spread through Ferganese society. "Enver Pasha?"

"The thought had crossed my mind," Clinton said quietly and checked the clock on the dashboard. He shifted in his seat. "Listen, I'll pull the tail off you if you agree to share information. What do you say?"

To get rid of the tail would be a relief. He only had to share what he wanted to, something he was sure Clinton would limit himself to.

"Deal." He slid the door open and stepped outside. Cold slammed into him, freezing sweat in his hair. He leaned down to peer back in to Clinton and gave him a business card. "You have a number or do I have to involve Khan?"

Clinton shook his head. "No. Just between you and me." He handed Kazakov a card he dug from a console between the vehicle's front seats. "My office number. Direct."

As if that should make Kazakov feel important.

He grunted at Clinton and pocketed the card, then let the door swing shut. He limped his way over to the Perseus, futilely sucking cold air through his teeth to quell the pain. It was ten to seven. Time to talk to the security-types.

———

The clouds closed in and the snow started to fall as he crossed the city. The snowflakes glistened in the streetlights and the streets were black ribbons until the snow began to stick to the pavement. Traffic decreased and soon the well-lit avenues and boulevards of the new city were behind him and vacant darkness filled the void beyond his windscreen. His headlights illuminated looming warehouses that materialized like ghosts out of the darkness and he wondered how many ghosts were out there wandering as a result of these cases. Ivanov, the murder victims in America, the kidnapped child probably, and even Chelomeyev wasn't out of the woods yet.

None of them had anyone to find their fallen arrow and plant it in the earth. Damn it, Chelomeyev did. He would find whoever had attacked the young detective.

He turned in at the ugly mockery of old city architecture and pulled in by the entrance to Transcontinental Security. The snow blanketed the parking lot and the few dim lights that were on over entry doors gleamed like eyes in the dark—all except the one over Transcontinental Security. The light there burned through the dark like a corona. He could only hope that the two officers he wanted to see could be so illuminating. Three company vehicles—two sedans in the sand color of the security company and a higher-centered utility vehicle similar to the Perseus were parked to one side of the door.

Kazakov climbed out into the falling snow. The huge flakes collected on his coat and clung to his shoulders. He crossed to the door and brushed the flakes off before pushing the door open and stepping inside.

A normal dry heat met him—not the sweltering heat of Eric Clinton's vehicle. Six men stood or were seated around the small office. Radulov, his oversized muscles threatening the seams on his sleeves, looked up from reading reports on his desk. "Good. You're here. I want to get these men on patrol. Elderov, Izotov, this is the detective I mentioned. The rest of you get out of here."

Kazakov checked them over as they headed out the door. All of them wore down-filled black nylon jackets that rustled when they moved and below their tan trousers they wore shiny black boots, but of a style different than the men in the graveyard. They were big men, too, and he felt them eyeing him as they passed to the door. He wondered if any of them were familiar with the old graveyard.

"You okay?" Radulov asked.

Kazakov looked at him, puzzled.

"You've got blood on your face." The big man touched his cheek and handed Kazakov a tissue. "On your coat, too."

Kazakov looked down at himself. Blood spattered his coat lapels. He was surprised Clinton hadn't said something. "Would you believe it's not mine?" He used the tissue on his cheek and left his coat alone. A tissue would be futile.

Finished, he turned back to the two remaining security guards and introduced himself. Constantine Elderov was in his late fifties with the squint of someone who had conducted too many surveillance operations. He stood taller than Kazakov by a good two inches and had the breadth of shoulder and chest to match, but he didn't use his bulk to intimidate. He had salt-and-pepper gray hair cropped close to the skull just like Kazakov usually preferred. Elderov nodded in greeting and shook Kazakov's hand congenially.

Sergei Izotov was another matter. Probably no more than in mid twenties, he stood against the wall with his arms over his chest and only stepped forward to shake Kazakov's hand when he'd left Kazakov's hand hanging for longer than needed. Slightly shorter than his partner, Izotov wore a curl of the lip that could easily turn into a sneer and used the handshake to try to prove that he was a stronger man. Kazakov had met his kind before—they'd applied for a career in policing but not been accepted. For Izotov, the blow to his ego was still new and tender. Radulov had probably partnered the kid with Elderov to try to smooth off the kid's rough edges.

"Thanks for waiting for me. I know you'd like to get out on the road, but I've a few questions about your patrol in the warehouse district four nights ago. Radulov let me read your reports and I note that you had to move along an undesirable. I was hoping to get a little more information."

"What's this about? Izotov asked.

"There was an attack in the old warehouse area, specifically in the gentrified section. We're not sure exactly when it occurred, only that it was sometime overnight. The victim was found in the morning in his apartment parking lot, beaten."

"So you can't give us anything better than that to go on?" Izotov's sneer was developing nicely, but Elderov gave him a look that shut the youngster up. Clearly, there was a certain respect there.

"Our report sets out anything of note," Elderov said. He looked thoughtful. "Our first pass through was a little early—seven thirty or thereabouts if I recall. The streets were quiet at that hour but we'd been hired to make sure they stayed that way. A year back there was a real problem with whores and drug dealers so we were hired by a group of building owners to roust 'em out and send them on their way." He cracked a knuckle and shrugged. "We did."

He glanced at Radulov, who leaned back in his chair. It creaked under him and he nodded at Elderov to continue.

"The last few months, we've kept running into drifters coming back into the area to do their business. So far we've run them off when they turn up and the apartment owners know to call us when they see something. Radulov radioed us that we'd got a call about someone hanging around on a street corner so we went to check it out. Turns out the call was right. There was a girl—a whore—plain as day by the clothes and the makeup. We told her to move along, but she wouldn't budge—said she was meeting someone."

Izotov jumped in. "We told her that was exactly what we were afraid of and to move her ass out of there or we'd call the police in.

Stupid bitch actually had the balls to try crying. As if we haven't seen that before."

Kazakov could count on one hand the number of whores he'd dealt with who cried. Most were street-hardened professionals.

"What'd the girl look like?" Kazakov held his revulsion for the young man in check. He might have once thought of whores that way, but he'd learned better. Maria had clinched it. Their life was no pleasure. Had he ever thought like Izotov?

"Young girl. Pretty enough except for a scar on her cheek. Redhead." Elderov said. "She was wearing one of those faux fur jackets and a too-short skirt. The kid looked cold."

"Or else she was coming down off a high. Or both," Izotov added.

It had to be the girl he'd seen down the street with the blonde named Raisa. She'd admitted seeing Chelomeyev.

"So what happened?" He looked from Elderov to Izotov.

The older man looked away a moment. Izotov rolled his shoulders.

"We helped her on her way, is what we did," Izotov said. "Why, did the bitch complain or something?"

Kazakov's stomach curdled. "What did you do?"

Izotov looked from Kazakov to Radulov to his partner, but even Elderov looked away. "She was waiting for a customer. I gave her a customer, okay? No harm done. Then I moved her down the street so the apartment owners wouldn't complain."

Radulov stood. His breadth of shoulders was matched by muscled thighs, but he had an unexpected grace as he came around his desk.

"Where the hell were you while this was going on?" he demanded of Elderov.

Elderov shook his head. "I'd gone inside one of the buildings to speak with the tenant association president. I wanted to make sure that there weren't any further issues."

"This was Nat Volkov?" Kazakov asked.

Elderov nodded, but a slight flush ran up his neck.

Kazakov sighed. "You left your partner with the girl so you could visit a girlfriend."

The older security officer shook his head. "He was just supposed to move her along, not fuck her."

Izotov shoved Elderov aside and glared defiance at Radulov. "He's supposed to be able to get his jollies but I'm not, is that it? He's been stopping for 'visits' ever since I've been partnered with him."

Hands up, Kazakov stepped between them. "You can deal with this later. What happened with the girl?"

"I left her down the street," Izotov said. He shrugged.

"And did you see anything that might indicate someone was coming to meet her?" He wasn't certain what it was, but there was something here. He just had to keep digging.

Another shrug from Izotov. "There were a few cars that passed by. Nothing notable. A couple of residents turned into the parking lot."

If he was meeting the young woman, he might pull into the parking lot rather than pull into the side of the road to avoid attracting as much attention, but what did that mean? Could the customer have roughed up the girl and Chelomeyev intervened? Maybe the girl came back after Izotov had left and met her customer. Maybe it was someone Chelomeyev shouldn't have seen and so he was beaten and left for dead. But if they were trying to kill him, surely there were easier ways…

Either way, he needed to find the girl again.

"The girl. When you came back later on patrol, did you see her again?"

The two security guards shook their heads.

"Did you see anything unusual around Nat Volkov's building? Anything at all?"

Izotov sullenly shook his head. Elderov looked like he was about to. Then he stopped.

"The car." He looked at his young partner. "Remember? The car? The model we hadn't seen before?"

Kazakov held his breath.

Elderov turned back to him. "We were driving away and noticed a car at the side of the road ahead of us. It pulled away just as we pulled even. It looked like it had one occupant, but in the darkness I couldn't see—the driver didn't turn on their head and dash lights until they were past us. The reason we even noticed it was because it was a make of car we hadn't seen before. Izotov, here, thought it was a make he'd read about—a lot like a Ziln in body style, but it's supposed to have superior speed and maneuvering."

"Let me guess. American. Ford." Why the hell was a spy like Clinton driving something so damn noticeable?

But then, unless you were a vehicle aficionado, would you even notice it wasn't a Ziln? And Clinton didn't exactly try to hide the fact he was a spy.

"That's right," Izotov said. "All the German manufacturers are out to copy them now. You'll be seeing a lot more like it on the roads. Word has it that they've done a deal with a Ferganese manufacturer to produce them here to sell into the Eurasian market." The young security guard's sneer had disappeared. He was like an eager child with the prospect of a new toy. "'Course, they'll probably make them too expensive for the average person." He sighed.

Kazakov felt wooden. He knew the car and most likely knew the driver, too. He'd sat in the damn vehicle and asked all the wrong questions. If Clinton had been watching Chelomeyev, had he seen what happened? Or had he been responsible?

He brought himself back to the present. "One last question." He turned to Izotov. "The girl. What was her name?"

The young security guard swallowed and his gaze skittered away. "I—I don't remember exactly. Mika, Mura. Something short like that." Nervously, he met Kazakov's gaze. "I wrote it down, though, when we first approached her." He dug in his pocket and produced a small black notebook similar to Kazakov's, but more tattered looking as if the user didn't comprehend the critical nature of its contents. The first time he was called to give evidence in court, his feelings would change.

He flipped through the pages. "Here it is," he said, finally triumphant. "Mura Stepanova."

"Does that help?" Radulov asked.

Feeling diminished by the man's huge stature, Kazakov nodded. "It just might. Thanks for your help. All of you."

"Can we go, then?" Elderov asked. "Our patrols are waiting."

Radulov only nodded at the bench along the wall and then turned to Kazakov, but his fleshy face was livid with barely-checked anger. "If there's any other way we can help, don't hesitate to call."

Kazakov nodded at the two patrol officers perched on the edge of the bench as he let himself out. A storm was brewing in Radulov and those two were about to bear the brunt. If they still had jobs at the end of the night was probably in question. A damn shame for Elderov.

Izotov?

Well, Kazakov couldn't say the same.

Outside, his breath steamed as he climbed into the Perseus. The night was silent under the muffling snow—all except the angry voice rising from inside the Transcontinental Security office.

Fighting his own anger and betrayal, he started the Perseus and left. Eric Clinton had helped him in the Yekaterina case. He'd thought the man was, if not a friend, at least a colleague.

He drove away wondering what else he'd got wrong in this case.

16

It was too late to confront Eric Clinton or to call Khan, given the challenges between them last time they had spoken. Instead, Kazakov set aside the throb of painfully bruised muscles from his side and stopped at a late-night supermarket to buy groceries for himself and Agafya Ryabkov, even though he knew the old woman would not thank him. With bags of milk, eggs, bread, and other staples, and two bottles of vodka piled in the back seat, he headed home, inhaling the scent of garlic sausage and apples as he drove through the snow that once more was masking New Moscow's sins.

The road was slushy from traffic through the city and the nearer suburbs, but once he reached the expansive tracts of faux dachas that were springing up on the lower slopes of the mountains, he was forced to slow. The snow fell too thick and visibility was down to barely two vehicle lengths. Thankfully, the Perseus chugged on as the houses fell behind and his headlights revealed darkness and the edges of undulating fields of snow to either side of the road.

When the trees sprang up to either side, he knew he was almost home. There was no hope of a plow coming this way at this hour, so he simply stopped the car at the entrance to Agafya's drive and climbed out carrying supplies for the old woman. Then he trudged through the two-foot-high snow up the slight slope of her almost hidden driveway. Under the eaves of the trees along the lane, the air smelled of pine. It was completely dark, but gradually his vision adjusted and he came out into her clearing as the snowfall slowed. Only a few flakes lazed through the sky onto the pristine snow that surrounded the slumbering dacha. A thread of pine-scented smoke twisted up from the dacha's chimney.

He thumped up the stairs to warn her someone was here and stopped outside the door. From inside came the sound of a radio. He knocked. "Agafya! It's me, Kazakov. I've just come from the grocery store and I bought too much. I was hoping you could help me out." It was a game that he'd played with her for the past four years, ever since her Russian husband had died leaving Agafya with almost nothing except the stone-walled dacha. He still wasn't sure how she survived.

"Go away, ghost!" came the old woman's ragged voice through the door. "I don't need your kind here."

"Agafya, it's me. Kazakov. Remember? We ate Christmas dinner together."

There was silence inside the dacha for a moment and then dragging footsteps approached.

"The detective?" Her old voice was muffled through the wood.

"Yes."

The stout wooden door pulled open a crack and, in the firelight loosed from the cabin, a bird-black eye peered out at him. She pulled the door farther open and peered beyond him. "There's ghosts. They're out there. They talk-talk-talk all the time. They won't let me sleep."

She peered up at him from her withered-apple face, her old felted skirt a circle around her black-stockinged legs. A short, felted, black jacket over a white, high-necked blouse completed her ensemble. It was her usual clothing. Traditional tribeswoman. He stomped the snow off his boots.

"You're lucky they didn't get you," she said as she shuffled aside to let him enter and then firmly shut and bolted the door behind him. "How did you get through?

"Actually, I didn't see anything," he said and plunked the bags of groceries on her plank table. As usual, the dacha was pristine with bundles of dried herbs in the rafters that gave the place a dusty sunshine scent like summer fields. The fireplace burned merrily, filling the space with light and warmth. He pulled the milk, eggs, and meat from one bag and the vodka from another.

"It would really help if you'd take this off my hands. As usual, I bought too much."

Agafya came to the table. "I didn't ask for this."

"No you didn't," he quickly agreed. "But you'd be helping me out by taking it off my hands. It'll go bad before I can use it."

She looked up at him suspiciously, as if she was going to argue that vodka didn't go bad, but her fingers had already strayed to the bottle. He knew she enjoyed a drink now and again.

Above the fireplace, the old transistor radio blared out music that then cut off and turned to a news report. The Ferganese announcer droned and Agafya closed her eyes and slumped against the table. "You see? They're always talking and more talking to me. I can't get them to stop."

He looked from her to the radio. Had she forgotten it was on? Was that all it was?

"Let me see what I can do." He crossed behind her and was about to switch the infernal machine off when the tone of the announcer changed. Breaking news, he said.

"Leonid Nikolaev's campaign has received a crushing blow with the revelation that the Ferganese People's Party has accepted contributions from Ottoman government coffers. The *New Moscow News* just broke the story that the Friendship Clothing Company, a primary donor to the People's Party, is a front for Ottoman government money laundering here in Fergana. There is evidence that, in addition to funding Nikolaev's campaign, the Friendship Corporation has also funded recent extremist operations in Fergana. There are calls for Nikolaev to withdraw from the campaign. This news shifts Boris Bure's Reformation Party into election contention and Bure is already capitalizing on the news."

The program cut to Bure's voice calling for Nikolaev's current government to step down in disgrace. He went on to talk about the historic value of independence that the current government's actions had placed in jeopardy and how the large parties were both too beholden to our ancient enemies, the Ottoman territories. He finished off with mention of the recent explosive attacks on Fergana and how they were clearly the result of the government's lax policies regarding foreign influence on Fergana's tribals. "Leonid Nikolaev and his government must be held responsible for the injuries to innocent people and the damages to any property. It is only through the grace of God that there have been so few deaths."

It was an explosive accusation—one that, if true, would bring a change in government.

Kazakov closed his eyes and felt his blood curdle at Bure's smooth-as-silk voice. The man was a mask. He just wondered what lay underneath.

The news program shifted to another story about treacherous road conditions in the mountains as Kazakov switched the radio off. Silence filled the dacha except for the fire crackling.

"Better?" he asked as he turned back to Agafya.

The old woman had opened the vodka bottle and poured two small glasses. She nodded and held a glass out to him. They knocked one back together.

"Better. The vodka always helps. Maybe I'll sleep tonight. I don't know." She pulled her jacket around her and shook her head. "I can feel the ghosts still gathering." She looked down at the groceries and regretfully shoved them across the table at him. "I can't pay you."

Always he'd accepted the few coins she found for him and then he'd found ways to leave them scattered around her dacha for her to find again. Pride was everything for the old woman and he would not take that from her.

"But you already did, remember? When I was here at Christmas, you fed me. This is a way to pay you back for the meal."

She looked confused for a moment, but her eyes strayed to the sausage and eggs. Her throat worked as if she could already taste them.

"I—I must have forgotten. Then thank you for bringing them to me." Her hands slid over the bounty and he smiled to himself.

It was worth the effort and the game they played to see her happy.

"I'd best be going," he said. "It's been a long day." He went to the door and Agafya met him there to unbolt the locks. Her old gnarled hand grasped his.

"You're a good boy, Detektiv. My husband always said so." She pulled the door open and peered out into the darkness.

He stepped past her, the cold air nipping at his chin and nose.

"Go swiftly," she said. "They're still out there and the darkness threatens."

Then she thumped the door shut behind him and he clumped down the snow-laden stairs. From his pocket he pulled some loose change and dropped it in the snow at the base of the stairs. It would be something for her to find in the spring. Behind, in the dacha, he thought he might have heard her humming an old tribal song. Something she knew better than the tale of the arrows of Ivan Mareson.

———

The next day dawned gray, with the cloud cover hanging low over the tops of the trees. Kazakov slept until seven o'clock and then floundered up thinking he'd overslept and groaned at the pain in his side and jaw. He'd obviously pulled and perhaps torn something in his side in the struggle in the graveyard last night, but at least no bones appeared to be broken. He pulled his t-shirt up. Purple and green bruising discolored his side.

"I might be getting too old for this," he said to Koshka, who had complained at his sudden movement but now burrowed into the warmth of the discarded covers.

He stood and swayed a moment and then staggered through the kitchen to the water closet. It hurt to piss and there was blood in his urine. When he was done, he stood at the kitchen sink leaning on the wood counter as he palmed cold water over his face. His beard felt too long, but the thought of shaving exhausted him.

When he was done running the ragged edge of his razor across his face, Koshka sat beside him, mewing plaintively as if she was going to fall over from starvation. He fed her and then swiftly dressed himself in a suit, white shirt, and tie. He cut himself a slab of bread and cheese and ate it leaning on the counter and pondering the business he had to accomplish.

He needed to phone Enver Pasha's office to confirm an appointment, and to arrange an appointment with Arthur Blackstone upon his return to find out more about Grigori Ivanov's competitors. He wanted to talk to Khalil Khan before he confronted Eric Clinton and he needed to find out more about the two men named as the principals in the last two companies standing to replace Ivanov's in the American tobacco trade.

And then there was Annuschka.

He hung his head, dreading the meeting. Dreading her assessing regard and how he never measured up to whatever her expectations were.

Derr'mo, she hadn't met his expectations, either. He often wondered what he'd ever seen in her. She was too sleek, too prissy and prim for his world. Everything had to be just so for Annuschka. Every movement. Every word.

Which was why, by the end of the marriage, she had made his skin crawl and he had spent all his time at the dacha to gain some freedom. It was also why he would not let her know he was coming. Keeping Annuschka on edge was the best way he knew to get the truth from her.

Koshka finished her wet food and plaintively meowed for more. He reached down and stroked her little round head. "That's all, little girl. That's all."

And that was all the time he had for dread and pondering. Straightening against the pain, he pulled on his boots, gun, and greatcoat. His hat he carried with him as he left the dacha, but he paused in the cold air to pull it on. A niggling feeling tickled his brain. Not ghosts like Agafya felt, though there were surely enough of them in his life.

No, this was something he felt when a case was close to solving.

It was a good sign.

By eight thirty he was headed down to New Moscow and decided to check in at his office to see whether there was any news on Chelomeyev and whether forensics had been able to match prints from the carnival with those at the explosives break-in. It was also a place to make his calls.

The drive in was uneventful. The wan winter light filled the fields and erased the shadows of the houses. Schoolyards were full of children, and mothers filed into busy supermarkets by the time he reached town. Yekaterina Square was still woefully empty of its statue and some joker had placed a snowman in the old tsarina's place. The snowman had sticks for arms positioned in the statue's pose. Instead of a cloak that swirled in the storm, the snowman wore a jaunty red scarf.

The snowman was clearly new because a newspaper reporter and cameraman were busy taking photos and interviewing passersby. The pedestrians who'd drifted in around the statue base seemed to see the humor in it. Kazakov couldn't help but smile. Now to see if the city fathers would allow it to remain there until spring. He somehow doubted it. He parked the Perseus and limped the short walk to the politseyshiyuchastok and up the broad front stairs.

He pushed inside to the reception concourse where a queue of citizens waited to speak to the lone harried officer on desk duty. Kazakov crossed the room to the door to the side and knocked once. The officer on guard checked through the window glass and let him in. Kazakov showed his ID and the uniformed officer nodded, but was not someone Kazakov knew—probably a good thing given a number of officers still resented his role in the deaths of two other detectives.

He rode the elevator up to the detective squad room. There was no one there, but as usual the stench of Ottoman cigarettes and wet wool filled the room. The sour reek of old tea provided counterpoint as he waded through the nine desks to his own. Two yellow message slips lay on the tea-stained wood. The top one said Rostoff wanted to see him as soon as he came in. The other one was a call from Enver Pasha's office wanting to set an appointment.

He grabbed the phone receiver from his desk and returned the phone call. The line barely brrred once in his ear before a smooth voice announced Transcontinental Corporation.

"How may I direct your call?" the smooth voice continued.

Kazakov could imagine the lovely girl in blue at the other end of the phone. "This is Detektiv Kazakov. A message was left me to call this number about an appointment."

"Aah, yes, Detektiv. I have the information right here. You are to come tomorrow at four o'clock. I trust that works with your schedule."

He thanked her and hung up and wondered how many people in a year might say that Enver Pasha's appointment time didn't work for them. He crumpled the Enver Pasha note into the wastebasket and made the call to Grigori Ivanov's company.

"Ivanov Tobacco Company," said a cheery voice at the end of the phone.

"Arthur Blackstone, please. This is Detektiv Alexander Kazakov from the New Moscow Police calling. I was told to call back for an appointment."

There was silence a moment.

"I'm sorry, Detektiv. Mr. Blackstone is still not here." The cheery voice was a little less cheery.

"Then I would like an appointment with him when he returns."

A little longer silence. "Detektiv Kazakov, I'm not exactly certain of his return date."

Not good news for his investigation. In fact, his absence was most convenient for whomever was behind the killing.

"Can you tell me when Mr. Blackstone left the country and his destination?"

"Let me see," the girl said, clearly wanting to be helpful. She left the phone for a moment and he heard a muffled conversation. She was probably checking whether it was permitted to provide such information. "Detektiv Kazakov. Mr. Blackstone left Fergana for America a week ago today. There were issues with the suppliers in America that needed to be dealt with."

Kazakov thought a moment. "To go to America on Mr. Ivanov's behalf—Arthur Blackstone must be very important in the company."

"He is, sir. He is Mr. Ivanov's right-hand man."

Odd that such an important person had not returned upon Ivanov's death. He said as much.

"Oh, he planned to return immediately, sir, but his business in America was very important."

"So something changed his mind for him," he stated and waited for whatever was forthcoming.

"I really couldn't say, sir."

Clearly the cheerful voice was rethinking her decision to share information.

"I'm sorry, sir. My other line is ringing. Shall I leave a note for Mr. Blackstone to call you when he returns to town?"

"Please." He gave her his information and hung up, wondering just what this meant. Why would Svetlana Ivanova give him this name if she'd known Blackstone was out of town? Was someone trying to keep the man from divulging information?

Pondering whether there was anything to his suspicions, he abandoned the squad room for the hallway. The place was distinctly quieter than the last time he had seen it. There were no stretchers and no blood on the floor. As usual, office doors were closed and no gusts of cordite-stained air streamed in from outside. How quickly things had been put back together. He wondered if memories of the fear were fading.

He knocked once and pushed open the door to Rostoff's reception area. Inside, a different female constable filled the receptionist's chair. She was pretty enough, with dark eyes and dark hair pulled back primly in a bun, but had none of the ethereal beauty of Constable Dabria Smirnova.

"Dabria?" he asked as he paused by her desk.

"At home. She says she will be to work next week. Apparently, once they cleaned the blood away, her wounds were not that deep." The brunette barely glanced up at him as she typed.

"Good. So it was not so bad, then. I was worried when I saw them carrying her out."

She looked up at him then. "It was bad enough. I went to visit

Dabria in the hospital. They have sewn her up, but…" She shook her head. "There will be scars, I think.."

He nodded, concerned for the constable, but asked, "Is he in?"

The brunette rolled her eyes. "And miserable as usual. See you don't rile him up. You can leave, but I have to deal with him." She turned back to her typing and Kazakov stood there, suitably chastened, before heading to the inner sanctum.

He knocked on Rostoff's office door and heard an oath and a grumble that he chose to interpret as permission to enter. When he pushed open the door, Rostoff looked up from whatever he was reading on his desk.

"What the hell do you want?"

Holding up the yellow memo like a token, Kazakov entered. "You left me a note to see you. I was hoping you might have gotten news from Forensics."

"Forensics!" Rostoff spit the word. "Those idiots wouldn't know their ass from hole in a snowbank. That's what I wanted to talk to you about."

"Did they check out both sites?" Kazakov approached Rostoff's desk, aware that he was taking liberties.

Rostoff shoved the papers he was reading aside. From in a desk drawer he pulled out a sheaf of paper and shoved it at Kazakov. "Imbeciles! They say there's no match."

Kazakov accepted the sheaf of papers and read. The prints of the sneakers and shoes he'd found at the carnival did not match any of the prints at the construction company.

Reading further, the forensics team had gone farther than Kazakov had suggested and had examined tracks elsewhere inside the carnival walls. There were copious prints but none that matched the heavy boot treads of the explosives storage shed.

"A dead end. I'm sorry. I thought we might find a match that would send us in the right direction." He looked back at the Forensic report. The prints at the construction site had been checked against employees and all the prints were accounted for except for one. The lone set of prints had a distinctive bar tread that the forensics team hadn't seen before. They were trying to identify the source.

"If they can find anything on the boots, perhaps it won't quite be a dead end."

"Pah!" Rostoff spat. He lunged up and stalked across to his window and looked out as if the destruction of the old statue was a personal assault. "Look at that! A snowman, and everyone laughs as if it is a joke! I won't have these—these heathens in my town! You know them better than any of my other detectives. The bosses are leaning on me from above and I need you here—not chasing around after whatever happened to Chelomeyev. Do you understand? I want you back at work and on this case today!"

For a moment Kazakov was amused that Rostoff actually thought his problem detective might be his savior. Rostoff had discounted and abused him too many times before for not being a team player. He shook his head.

"I'll help you, but not that way. I said I'd look into the explosions and whether they're connected to any of the old city tribesmen. I have. So far it's inconclusive. I'm spending time close to the old city on the Chelomeyev investigation. I'll keep my ears and eyes open and you informed if I learn anything. But I'm not walking away from the Chelomeyev case. There's something there and I'm getting close. Two thugs threatened me last night. There's something bigger going on— some connection between Chelomeyev's beating and the death of Grigori Ivanov. My investigation has revealed a number of motives and suspects. With Ivanov's death, it opens up a massive trade opportunity with America—a very lucrative one, and one his competitors were hungry for. I need time to look into their alibis."

Head bowed, Rostoff listened to his report, but the whole time Kazakov spoke he was shaking his head. When he looked up at Kazakov, his face was flushed. "You listen to me, Kazakov. You're overthinking things—looking for shadows where there aren't any. Murders like this, you have to look closer—the victim's inner circle. In my experience it's the wife—it's always the wife—or her lover. Have you found him yet? Have you satisfied yourself about her alibi? That's where I'd be looking. Proximity is always a precursor to murder. Why are you running around creating more work for yourself?"

Rostoff straightened and faced Kazakov, his ruddy complexion almost purpling. "Why, when there are far more serious cases to investigate? Close the Ivanov case quickly. Do what you must about Chelomeyev, but put your attention on these explosions. My God, Kazakov! There's enough explosive unaccounted for in the city to blow up Saint Basil's Cathedral! Or more!"

Kazakov sighed and nodded. Every other detective in the city was on the explosives case. How was he going to make a difference? "I haven't cleared the wife yet. I'm still looking."

"You've had almost a week. Two days. You have two days to finish off your damned enquiries and then you devote your time to the explosion investigation."

Kazakov raised his hand to protest.

"No!" said Rostoff. "No more. You will report for duty in two days or you have no job. Do you understand?"

His glare cut through Kazakov's protests. Finally, he nodded. "Two days."

"Then get out of my sight until then!" Rostoff turned back to the window, a figure of angry mourning.

Kazakov took his leave, well aware of Rostoff's secretary's glare, before he went out to the waiting Perseus. He'd been going to talk to Khan about Eric Clinton, but perhaps it would be better to speak to Annuschka instead. Get all of his least-favorite things over with. His hands made fists on the steering wheel as he swung the vehicle out into the road.

The communications section of the Ferganese government filled a portion of the basement of the parliament building that wore the façade of Empress Yekaterina's grand palace. Once, according to the legend, the façade of the original palace had guarded a place of gilt and golden glitter, opulent paintings on walls and ceilings, miles of hallways and ornate furniture. Now the palace façade could lay claim only to the miles of hallways connecting a warren of government offices that kept the country operating as well as—well—as well as a broken watch.

The lovely façade of white pillars and ornate carvings above windows and doors, guarded by gold-painted figures of cherubs and faux religious icons, had been built by the Ferganese government to honor the history of the Russian people. Unfortunately, what was left of the Russian people had only known the outside of the graceful building, so they placed the façade on a building of plain gray stone and set it on a piece of land where not a single tree grew. It wasn't even close to the river or situated to enjoy a view of the omnipresent mountains. No, the façade looked westward down over the sloping plains of Fergana toward the sprawling grandeur of the Ottoman Empire. Perhaps it was simply an oversight, but if so, it was a sobering one—a reminder of all that was lost and the Empire that hungered for them.

Given this, it was a wonder that the Ferganese parliament got anything accomplished at all.

The wind came off of the mountains again and brought the chill of China facing them over the mountains. At least the clouds had lifted while he was in speaking with Rostoff and now he could see the eastern Tian Shan and Ferganese mountains—at least their bases, for the peaks were lost in cloud. He walked down the curving street until he reached the front of the building.

The central stairs to the main entrance were roped off, preserved for state occasions. The workday entrances were at either end of the building. Kazakov climbed the narrow stairs at the northern end and entered the building. He found himself on a well-worn, workaday stairwell landing of gray concrete. He went down a flight and found himself in a huge open room with no windows and red tile floors. A ceiling of fluorescent lights turned the skin of the employees slightly green. A horseshoe-shaped counter corralled the small waiting area where Kazakov entered, with the remainder of the room filled with desks and ringing office phones. A well-lit hallway on the other side of the room presumably gave onto private offices. One closed door confirmed this because he could just make out the name: Vladimir Kimkin.

Of course. One of the men behind the remaining tobacco

companies vying for Grigori's monopoly. Interesting that Annuschka worked for him. Perhaps Kazakov could find out something.

Squaring his shoulders, he advanced to the counter, glad he'd shaved and worn his suit.

As soon as he touched the counter, a young woman at a nearby desk sprang up, her face and hair as perfectly made-up as an automaton at the carnival.

"Can I help you?" She rushed up to the counter, seemingly breathless, and beamed up at him.

"Annuschka Yevseyev, please. Official business." He flashed his badge at her and watched her gaze widen. This youngster with the glossy black hair pulled into a ponytail was far too young to have been here when he and Annuschka were married.

"I believe she is in a meeting, sir."

"Tell her Detektiv Kazakov must speak to her. Now."

The girl scuttled off and he inhaled the hot, dry air while watching the busy warren of workers. It was a wonder that communications from this usually closed-mouth government could keep so many people so busy, but what did he know of such things?

A short while later the girl scurried back. "I'm sorry, sir. She will be a few minutes. May I get you a tea? A magazine?"

He waved her offer away and stopped himself from pacing. Pacing always gave his nerves away to Annuschka and he did not want her reading him. How was he going to react to her? How was he going to read her when he could not recall being able to read her well before? He kept his head down, considering.

It was a long five minutes by the clock on the wall before he heard a familiar click of heels down the hall. He lifted his head and there Annuschka Yevseyev stood. His first thought was that she was still beautiful.

Annuschka was tall for a woman, about five foot nine, with smooth, pale skin and what he had always thought was a crowning glory of naturally red hair. Since he had last seen her, she had apparently thought better of that crown, for her thick hair was dyed almost white-blonde so that he was facing an ice queen. As if to emphasize the effect of her hair and regal bearing, she wore a cream-colored, single-breasted suit with a skirt that just grazed her shapely knees. Still lovely, still imposing, and still disapproving by the expression on her face.

"Kazakov. What can I do for you?" Though she had a low, throaty voice, the words couldn't hide the coldness of her tone, nor the ice in her gaze. She wasn't happy that he had interrupted whatever she was doing.

"Can we speak somewhere more private?"

"Why?"

Kazakov sighed. It was so like her. "I'm not here for a walk down memory lane, Annuschka. I'm here in an official capacity, conducting an investigation. The fact that I introduced myself as Detektiv Kazakov should have told you that."

She glanced away and nodded. "All right. I should have noticed."

She turned back to the dark-haired girl who was gazing up at Annuschka as if she was a goddess. "Tell Boris and the others that I'll be a few minutes."

Annuschka had been studying for her Masters of Communication while they'd been married. After the divorce she'd completed her doctorate at the University of Nanjing. He figured that, if anything, her obsessive analysis of every word would have gotten worse.

She let him through a gate in the counter and led him to the hallway and into the first room across from Kimkin's closed door. It was an office, obviously a communal one for occasions just like this. It had four bare walls and a desk and office chair along with a single, straight-backed guest chair, all in nondescript beige. In her cream suit, Annuschka seemed to fade into the background except for her piercing blue eyes that tracked his every move and her faint, spicy perfume.

"Now. You have quiet. What do you want?" She crossed her arms over her chest and didn't sit down.

He'd be damned if he'd sit when she didn't. Kazakov unbuttoned his greatcoat and pulled out his notebook and pen. He flipped it open. "I'm investigating the death of Grigori Ivanov and I understand you may have information pertinent to the case."

"Pertinent how?"

"Where were you over the dates of December twenty-eighth to January first?" He glanced from his notebook up at her.

Annuschka's gaze narrowed. "Why?"

"Because I asked you as part of an investigation. I am trying to independently determine your credibility as a witness to pertinent events." He knew a challenge to her credibility would rile her and was surprised that he took no pleasure in it. He simply wanted to challenge her to answer the questions. The tension he'd been feeling melted out of his body as he waited.

"If you must know, I was at our country home in the mountains. Nikolay and I went up for the holidays."

"I believe you are acquainted with Svetlana Ivanova and Olga Gruenwald."

Annuschka frowned. "Yes. Yes, I know both women. Svetlana is an old friend. Grigori was a good friend of Nikolay's. Such a shame about him." She shook her head.

"Tell me about them." Perhaps he could get her talking and learn more about the couple.

She gave him a pitying look. "Svetlana and Olga or Svetlana and Grigori?"

Derr'mo, he needed to be exact in his questions, because Annuschka would look for any way to make him sound and feel like a fool. "Start with Svetlana and Grigori."

Her shoulders worked. "They were a pleasant married couple. Happy. Grigori was busy with his polo and his business and Svetlana had her charity work."

"Happy because they each had their own interests and did not spend much time together?" Like their marriage had been, though he would never call it happy.

Annuschka simply looked at him. "There may be things you are unaware of about lasting marriages. People grow apart. They —accommodate."

"Educate me." He ignored her dig.

She crossed behind the desk and finally sank into the chair. Her faint perfume had bloomed into the air. Something he had asked had sent her body heat higher and she'd sought the protection of the desk between them. He smiled to himself. Annuschka might be good at reading the words, but he was good at reading people.

"It is very simple. One half of a couple becomes very busy so the other half seeks out their own interests. They still enjoy each other's successes and enjoy their time together, however limited." She spoke as if she had first-hand knowledge, so perhaps her current marriage wasn't complete paradise. The thought left him strangely saddened.

"These other interests of Svetlana's. Tell me about them."

Annuschka's hands fluttered across the bare desk as if seeking anything to land on. She noticed his regard and pulled them into her lap. "I told you. She has her charity work for the hospital. She is also very active in the art world."

The art world. He knew nothing of that, except for a news article he'd read about Enver Pasha where he'd given an award to a young girl. Then it came to him. The girl's name had been Kadija Bogomolova. Was she related to library manager Constantine Bogomolov who was now one of the principle candidates for the lucrative American tobacco license? He pulled himself back from the thought.

"Who were the people she worked with on these worthy causes?"

She looked up at him, clearly not happy that he stood over her and yet she refused to capitulate and move again.

"There were many people. Wives of diplomats and business moguls."

"You?"

She glared up at him. "Sometimes. If she needed communications assistance."

"Any men?"

Her glare intensified. She shrugged and Kazakov almost laughed at the uncharacteristic gesture. Annuschka never shrugged. It was always too inexact for her.

"Tell me about the men." he asked and rested his hip on the corner of the desk.

"She worked with gallery owners and physicians. I don't know all the names."

"But you know some of them. Perhaps one in particular? Someone she worked with often?"

"I know nothing for certain and I do not deal in rumors!" She stood and went to the door. "I really should get back to my meeting. I don't have any more time."

"When you were in the mountains, did you see Svetlana?"

"Yes. Yes, I did. Twice we spent time together and I saw her at the hill and in town."

"Tell me about that."

"Damnation, Kazakov, I don't have time. I have important business."

"And murder is not?" he asked mildly.

She closed her eyes just as she had done all the years they were together when she was barely holding herself together. "I saw her a number of times but we spoke twice. The first time Nikolay and I were having lunch at a restaurant and she and Olga came in. They joined us. It was very pleasant. I believe Svetlana had the pheasant in chanterelles." Her gaze flashed angrily. "The second time we held a party to celebrate the holidays. Svetlana came then, too. It was all evening and our driver gave her a ride home at the end. Okay? May I go now?"

Kazakov considered. "What were the dates that you saw the two women?"

She told him and it roughly concurred with what Svetlana had told him. There was more he could ask, but for now he had confirmed Svetlana's alibi and had strengthened his suspicions that there may be someone else in her life. There were other people he could talk to about it. Kasimir Krupin had mentioned that his wife might have information…

"Fine. We are done—for now."

Without a word, she opened the door.

"Annuschka."

She glanced back at him.

"How long has Vladimir Kimkin had an interest in the tobacco industry?"

Her smooth features creased in a frown. "What? He doesn't, of course. His business is communications." She shook her head and left, the click, click, click of her heels rapid on the tile floor as if she could not escape him quickly enough.

Interesting that such a promising business proposition was totally unknown to Kimkin's associates. He wasn't sure what it signified.

Once more outside, he breathed in deeply to cleanse his lungs of Annuschka's perfume, but a vehicle at the curb caught his attention. A low-slung Ziln limousine with a driver casually smoking a cigarette sat waiting at the end of the walkway that led to the communications entrance. Of course, the entrance also led to stairs that led upward in the building, but something told him that the occupant of the vehicle was currently meeting with Annuschka in the basement.

What had she said? *Tell Boris and the others I'll be a few minutes.* The cold air seemed to freeze in his lungs. Boris. Could there be another one who traveled in a Ziln limousine and was powerful enough that his vehicle could park in a no parking zone?

Buttoning his greatcoat against his sudden chill, he went down the stairs from the façade of the government building and strode out to the vehicle.

"You wouldn't happen to have a cigarette you could spare, would you?" he asked the driver.

The man nodded and hauled out a pack that he shook to offer Kazakov a smoke.

Kazakov accepted, but didn't light up. "Cold day to be waiting."

The man only nodded and offered a lit match.

Kazakov accepted again and drew in a long, sweet column of smoke. It had been a long time since he'd quit, but the craving was apparently never too distant. "So who's the VIP?"

"Candidate in the election," the man said, but the way his lips fell into a hard line, he wasn't going to say more.

Kazakov nodded at the cigarette. "Thanks. You saved a life."

He set off for the parking lot and his Perseus. It was only at the

Perseus that he ground out the cigarette—no one smoked in his vehicle, not even him. Then his hands started shaking. Boris Bure. Stepfather of the murder victim Yekaterina Weber and father of her unborn child. Also the candidate for the Reformation Party in the upcoming election. He was the slippery *mu'dak,* the asshole, who was somehow involved in his daughter's death, but Kazakov could never prove it. And now he was here meeting with Kazakov's ex-wife.

Maybe it was the knowledge, or maybe it was the cigarette, but he couldn't beat the heady feeling that beyond the information he'd gained on Svetlana Ivanova, he'd stumbled onto something more.

17

The noon hour sun glittered on the snowy tops of houses and the heaps of dirty snow pushed onto sidewalks by the plows. Pedestrians picked their way through the slushy brine on the streets and slipped and slid their way across patches of ice-covered sidewalks. The wind picked up the ends of women's hair and lifted the flags that flew above the door of the Grand Caravanserai Hotel, the latest Anglo-German enterprise to open in the city. There were hopes that it would lure foreign tourists to Fergana. Perhaps they would come to see what was left of an ancient city. More probably they would be lured by the lurid posters of Fergana's fabled mountains. They would want to ski and hike and see the tribal people and their flocks. There would be villages of people forced to wear their tribal clothes for photo opportunities, and for once, the people who had always lived on these lands would be given value.

If they weren't all arrested by the likes of Boris Bure.

Kazakov shook his head, disgusted at both his dismal visions of the future and wondering where he would fit. He turned down Suvarov Way to pull in across from the *New Moscow Now* newspaper building. The walkways along the frozen river in Potemkin Park were busy today with people trying to enjoy this respite of clear weather. The newspaper building's rough gray stone shone in the sun, the snow stuck to its sides from the recent snowfall like frosting. He waded through the slushy street and climbed the stairs—thankfully shoveled —and pushed inside the heavy wooden doors to the broad lobby.

He didn't bother with the receptionist, though she tried to stop him. Instead he caught the old brass elevator up the three floors to the newspaper's main room. As before, the place buzzed with activity. People typed. People rushed papers across the room. People filed out of meeting rooms. He spotted Kasimir Krupin among them at about the same time that Krupin spotted him. Krupin headed for his office, head down, shoulders rounded.

"May I help you?" A portly man with hungry eyes asked. "Do you have something to report?"

Kazakov waved him away and pushed through the sea of desks. He knocked once on Krupin's glass-topped door and pushed inside.

"I can't possibly speak to you right now." Krupin glanced up at him as he busily shoved papers into a briefcase. "My wife's ill and I need to go to her immediately."

If Krupin's gray hair had been wild before, it was manic now. All the hair stood on end and he was just as wild-eyed. He still wore the same sweater vest and appeared to be wearing the same woolen trousers as he had when Kazakov had interviewed him a few days before, though today his shirt was yellow.

Kazakov smiled. "Very good. I can drive you. I wished to speak to your wife, too."

The manic movements slowed. Krupin straightened. "What about?"

"What else? The weather? Svetlana Ivanova and her lover?"

"We don't know anything about that," Krupin said as he continued shoveling papers into his briefcase. When he tried to close it, it wouldn't close.

"Let me help you," Kazakov said and forced the thing shut so that the latches would reach. The sides of the case bulged, but the fasteners held. Kazakov picked the case up. "Shall we go? My vehicle is just outside. We can talk on the way."

"But my vehicle…,"Krupin protested.

"Can be picked up tomorrow, surely," Kazakov said.

Apparently shocked into silence, Krupin grabbed his coat and hat and allowed himself to be escorted through the desks and down the elevator. In the lobby he pulled his coat on and then followed Kazakov out the door.

"They know I've gone with you," he said. "If anything happens to me, they'll know who to blame."

Kazakov glanced at him and held the older man's elbow as they crossed the street. Things *had* happened to detainees of the New Moscow Police. But then, perhaps Krupin was concerned about something or someone far worse. Kazakov helped Krupin into the front seat of the Perseus and tossed the brief case on the rear seat.

"Your address?" he asked as he slid behind the wheel.

Krupin gave it to him and sat silently, peering out the window as Kazakov pulled out into traffic. "Why are you picking on us?" he finally said. "There are others who know far more than we do."

"Eric Clinton, perhaps?" He glanced over to see Krupin's reaction.

The newspaperman sighed. "You saw us, did you?"

"Hard not to when you led me right to him."

"He comes to me for information," Krupin said, which really meant that he sold information he thought would be useful to Clinton. Leaving Transcontinental must have left a sizeable hole in Krupin's pocketbook.

"What have you told him?"

Krupin looked at him, alarm on his face that he swiftly smoothed away. "Not much. That you were asking questions about the Ivanov murder. He has an interest, you know. American tobacco. They want it sold for the best price through government-controlled channels to ensure taxes are paid. Apparently, their government is very like Fergana in so many ways even if they are a very different people."

"One that looks to the future, not to the past." Kazakov said to gauge Krupin's reaction.

The newspaperman sighed. "Isn't that all Fergana is? A bit of the fluff off Yekaterina's cloak that was caught on a thorn in the wilderness. A last bit of evidence that Holy Mother Russia once existed."

The sentiment was so close to his own that Kazakov nearly pulled the Perseus over.

"Tell me what you know of Vladimir Kimkin and Constantine Bogomolov." Kazakov asked as he drove.

Krupin glanced at him. "One is a deputy minister responsible for government communications. The other manages the New Moscow library, but then you knew that."

"What else have you told Eric Clinton?" He thought a moment. "Or what haven't you told him?"

Outside the Perseus, a gust of wind caught the trees and sent ice crystals spraying off their branches.

"Each is the principal holder of one of the two remaining bids for the Ivanov tobacco rights."

Kazakov thought a moment. "It seems the vultures were circling even when Ivanov was alive for bids to be in place almost the moment he died."

"Business is built on contingencies and planning. Those two must have been at the right place at the right time."

"And had deep-pocketed backers, it would seem. I cannot see either man having the wherewithal to finance such a thing unless there is something I don't know. I just spoke with an intimate of Kimkin and they were totally unaware of him having an interest in the tobacco business. Did either Kimkin or Bogomolov come from money? Marry well?"

Krupin shook his head. "Just the opposite, it seems to me. Kimkin comes from a low income family and has a gambling problem. Bogomolov married a social climber and spends far beyond his manager wages. He has a brother, however, who owns a construction company."

The image of the Ziln limousine parked outside the government communications office and Annuschka's mention of "Boris" came to mind. "So someone such as Boris Bure could purchase Kimkin's services as a front man."

"I suppose." Krupin shrugged. "But there are others with deeper pockets who have more to gain or lose." He looked Kazakov squarely in the eye as if daring him to follow his thinking.

"Enver Pasha?" That didn't make sense when he'd seen Bure visit Kimkin's offices. Why would Bure, a vocal opponent to anything Ottoman, meet with Kimkin if he was bought and paid for by Enver Pasha—an Ottoman?

No. It just didn't quite make sense.

He pulled up at Krupin's address, a small home in an older part of the city that had neat houses with small lawns—all snow-covered—in fenced yards. A few homes sported established trees that loomed naked over the dwellings, but Krupin's address had only a snow-filled yard with a bungalow that showed weathered plaster that needed repainting. The places where paint had flaked off left the plaster to crack from the cold. A lone chimney streamed a thin trail of smoke that huddled above the house's covered front porch before being blown away by the wind.

When Kazakov turned off the engine, Krupin climbed out and looked further diminished and defeated by his surroundings. He stood looking up at the house as Kazakov joined him. "Once we lived in a grand house overlooking the river." He shook his head. "Look what I've brought us to."

He pushed open a creaking iron gate and led Kazakov up a neatly shoveled front walk to the stairs to the porch. By the look of the place, Krupin could use the money he received from Eric Clinton. Kazakov wondered how many other benefactors the newspaperman had and whether they paid him to write his articles. Or not write them.

Both of them stomped the snow off their boots and then Krupin unlocked the front door and let them in.

Heat, was Kazakov's first impression. His second was of an over-sweet, almost cloying scent.

Krupin shook his head and swept his hand at the house. "You'll have to pardon the house. My wife truly is unwell and I simply don't have the time."

The place had the same disheveled looks as Krupin. The entry's hardwood floors were thick with dust along the edges, dust covered the stair rail bannister, and crumpled clothing and books sat on the edge of each stair. To Kazakov's left was a parlor with books in stacks on the floor beside two chairs by a fireplace with an empty grate. One chair was covered in a tangle of blankets and yet had the air of disuse. To the right of the hall was a dining room that Krupin was obviously using as an office. The dark wooden table was covered in more books and papers. The chairs had been pulled away from the table and were stacked with still more books. The fireplace hearth had the signs of use though the fire was only embers.

Krupin followed his gaze. "Sorry about the mess. I've become rather immersed in a project. I'm writing the history of Fergana."

Interesting. "From whose perspective?"

Pausing from removing his coat, Krupin studied Kazakov as if he was a new species. "Now that is a question I would not have thought to hear from a policeman. Most histories are written by the victors, but we in Fergana did not win. So, I will tell a different story of the diaspora than the Ottomans." His eyes glinted in the shadowed hallway as he doffed his boots. Kazakov followed suit. Krupin pulled on flat-soled leather slippers that flapped as he led Kazakov down the hall.

"You should mention the people the Russians met when they arrived. In most histories, it's as if the tribal people simply disappeared and all their years of history here don't matter." Kazakov studied the old photos hung on the wall. They were of dour-looking men and women standing stiffly in old-fashioned clothes before a grand Ferganese house that overlooked the river, in Potemkin Park and at Yekaterina Mountain. Family photos that gave a sense of history, of the family's connection to this place. "What of Fergana before we arrived?"

Krupin stopped before a closed door and turned back to him. "It was not Fergana then, was it?" Then he smiled. "This way. My wife is resting. I'll ask you to keep this as short as possible."

Kazakov nodded. An entire people's history, if not erased, at least discounted as if it did not matter. Perhaps it was time for the Kyrgyz to write their own history. He should mention it to Khan next time he saw him. He swallowed back the bile that soured his throat. Krupin knocked once on the closed door and pushed it open.

"Margarete? I've brought company."

It was a bedroom—or what had become a bedroom. Once it had been a library, which explained the books piled around the house. Now most of the shelves were filled with feminine gewgaws, graceful figurines, colorful scarves, vases of plastic flowers, a crystal ball, sachets of pomander that filled the room with too much sweet. It was what Kazakov had smelled when he first stepped into the house. Two tall, narrow windows across from the door allowed daylight to flood the room and a roaring fireplace filled the room with heat.

Against one stack of shelves a bed had been placed, piled high with pillows that supported a wraith of a woman. She had large, luminous, dark eyes that spoke of underlying fever, and a dark green scarf wrapped tightly around her head that failed to totally hide a short bristle of hair. Though her face held fine age lines around the eyes and mouth, her form was child-like and petite. A bedside table bristled with pill bottles and against the wall stood a commode chair. Beside the bed stood a metal walker.

"Kasimir?" The woman's hands fluttered to the scarf and then to the top of her robe, the blue color of snow in shadows. Long, thin fingers decorated with seemingly overlarge wedding and engagement rings tugged the top more tightly around a thin, papery neck.

"I'm sorry, love. This is Detektiv Kazakov of the New Moscow police. He has questions for us about a case." He caught his wife's hand to stop its fluttering and kissed her palm. "Don't worry. You look beautiful. You always look beautiful."

She looked wryly at him. "And you were always a blind fool, Kasimir." But her gaze cleared as she looked up at Kazakov. "Pleased to meet you, Detektiv. I am Margarete Krupin." She freed her hand from Krupin and held it out to him for a brief handshake that surprised him with its force.

Here was a woman who had been a power, but illness had cut her down.

"You will have to pardon my indisposition, but it seems death has come knocking and we are having difficulty keeping him out the door." She touched Krupin's cheek affectionately. There was a luminosity to her that made her beautiful even though she was clearly very ill. "I have cancer and the treatments haven't worked. Thankfully, my good husband has brought me home to die. Now have a seat and tell me what we can do for you while I still have time?"

It was odd to see the way Krupin faded into the background in the force of Margarete's personality. Most often it was the woman who stepped back for the man, but he could not imagine this woman ever doing so. Those who assumed that her small size and fine features made her less of a threat would be mistaken. Kazakov did as asked and pulled a chair from beside the wall and sat by the bed. Krupin stayed where he was, perched on the bedside.

"I am most sorry to disturb you. Your husband said you were ill, but did not tell me of your condition. I am conducting an investigation and I believe that you may be able to help me."

She nodded after giving Krupin a reproving glance at his failure.

"I believe you know Grigori and Svetlana Ivanov?" he asked.

Her gaze grew curious. "Yes. Yes, we both do. They came to dinners at our house. I worked with Svetlana on hospital charities and for one or two benefits for the arts. We raised money for the new opera house, you know." She smiled as if they were happy memories and indeed the New Moscow opera house was one of the few modern buildings in the city Kazakov admired for its original architecture.

"What is this about?"

Kazakov glanced at Krupin. Clearly the man hadn't told his wife. "Grigori Ivanov was killed in his home. I was wondering what you could tell me about his and Svetlana's relationship."

"I told him that they always seemed a happy—" Krupin began until Kazakov held up his hand.

"Please. I'd like to hear your wife's thoughts."

A cautious light had come into Margarete's eyes. She thought a moment and then her gaze turned old and wise, as if the nearness of death had burned through her caution.

"Grigori Ivanov was a powerful man. No one was successful in circumventing his monopoly on American tobacco, though lord knows they tried."

She glanced affectionately as her husband as if he might have been party to such an unsuccessful attempt. Lately? When he worked at Transcontinental? Interesting.

"He controlled his company completely. I think that was in his nature. And with a company one has created, that is possible. Elsewhere in his life, who can say? Kasimir, didn't you once tell me that Grigori sold his entire polo string out of anger because two horses did not do what he wanted on the field?"

"That was years ago, Margarete." Kasimir waved away the story.

She cocked her head and held him with her gaze. "But it goes to show the nature of the man, just as Detektiv Kazakov's questioning shows that he knows the value of silence." She leaned forward on her bed, an impish expression on her face. "Let me tell you a little secret. Silence works wonders for weaseling out secrets and rumors, too." She laughed and started to cough. It caught hold until Krupin helped her with a sip of water.

She collapsed back onto her pillows, her eyes closed and what light there was in the room seemed to dim for a moment. Then she opened her eyes and smiled apologetically, her skin a little grayer. "It is unfortunate that laughter seems to be a foe. I have always liked to laugh. Now where was I?"

She knew perfectly well, but Kazakov humored her. "You were talking about Grigori Ivanov's need for control."

"Ah, yes. Well, companies and horses you can possibly control, but women are more difficult." She cocked a brow at him. "You know this, I think, from personal experience. You were married once, I know. Annuschka Kazakov was a friend of mine—before she began to fly in more rarified circles."

"Women are a different matter." It was all Kazakov would allow himself to say.

But Margarete nodded knowingly and thought a moment. "Svetlana Ivanova is a brilliant woman. She should have been a businesswoman on her own, but instead she married Grigori and became a trophy wife. Foolishness if you ask me, but no one did." She shook her head and closed her eyes again, clearly tiring even if she was enjoying the discussion.

"So what did this brilliant woman do with her controlling husband?" he asked and waited to let the silence sink in.

"She railed against it," Krupin said, surprising Kazakov.

"She would come to planning sessions for the benefits so filled with frustration it positively vibrated from her," Margarete said. "Then she would swallow it down and become the perfect planner. A perfect lady."

"So she just managed her feelings and kept on going? It did not affect the relationship with her husband?"

"I did not live with them, so how could I know?" Margarete said.

Kazakov had to smile. "My dear Mrs. Krupin, I believe that you know everything that goes on amongst your friends in the city. That is what you take your greatest pleasure in. Even here, now, I suspect your spies bring you information."

Her eyes widened in mock horror. "Detektiv! How could you have such a poor opinion of me? We have only just met!"

He laughed, seeing the pleasure the sparring gave her. Clearly, this had been a favorite part of her life. "I can see this tires you. Perhaps you could simply tell me what you know and what the rumors say, and then I will leave you to your kind husband."

"Only if you promise to visit again, Detektiv. I think I like you far more than I thought I might when I first saw you."

The thing was, he liked her, too. He nodded. "I'll come again."

"Good. What I know is limited. Svetlana came to all the usual charity meetings and swallowed down her feelings, but then something changed. I don't know what it was but she no longer seemed to carry so much anger. It was—as if she'd found something. A release."

"Or someone?" he asked.

"Or someone." She closed her eyes. "Someone who eased the anger from her."

"When was this?"

"About a year—no, fourteen months ago. I remember because I noticed it on a day when I was preoccupied." She opened her eyes to look at him. "I had just received my diagnosis. Incurable. It tends to make you more sensitive to know you are dying."

"Who was it? Who was the man? There must have been rumors?" he asked.

Her still gaze went deep, assessing him and somehow, he thought she found him wanting. Finally, she shook her head. "I'm sorry. Svetlana was very circumspect, for I never heard any man's name." She looked at Krupin.

"I'm sorry," Krupin said. "We must end it there. She's exhausted herself and I must ask you to leave."

Krupin stood and, reluctantly, Kazakov stood with him. "Thank you very much for your time. I will keep my promise and visit again."

Krupin showed him out of the room and closed the door behind them. "She was a beauty as a young woman. I could not keep my eyes off of her. Imagine my surprise when she said she could not keep her eyes off of me." There were tears in his eyes that he swallowed back. "If you are going to come again, make it soon. She hasn't a lot of time."

Then he showed Kazakov out into the afternoon sunshine. At the iron gate to the yard, Kazakov turned back to the house. The paint was worn, the real stucco showing through, but he couldn't escape the idea that with all that Margarete Krupin had told him, he had missed something.

He left Krupin's house pondering what he now knew. A lover could be a reason for Grigori Ivanov to be killed. It was a motivation he'd seen before. But who could it be? And how could he find out? At the moment he had no idea and he had other things to worry about. If it was simply a lovers' triangle that had led to Grigori Ivanov's death, how did that relate to Chelomeyev's beating?

Was Rostoff right that Ivanov's death was related to the wife? Were Ivanov's murder and Chelomeyev's beating not connected? But Chelomeyev's beating had to be related to one of his cases or something in his personal life.

Pondering this, he turned the Perseus toward Our Lady Yekaterina Hospital and Khan. He needed the truth about Eric Clinton.

Before he went to talk with Khan, he quickly checked in with the hospital about Chelomeyev. It was hard seeing the young detective still swathed in bandages alone in his room. The ward nurses said there had been no change in his condition, but the doctors still had hope. He was young and strong.

He was still alive.

Saddened by the sight, Kazakov retreated out of the hospital to the parking lot and the exterior stairs that led down to the morgue.

When he pushed inside the morgue's reception area, the scent of over-sweet body fluids and old death was a shock after the clean crisp air of outside. Not even the bite of cleaning fluid could cut through the nostril-cloying scent of rot. For some reason, today it seemed particularly pungent.

"Khalil Khan, please," he asked the young receptionist with the too-attentive gaze. She was pretty enough—as most young women were—with auburn hair worn long over a brick-red cardigan and primly buttoned blouse. Khan was certain that "they" had let the long-time receptionist go specifically to insert a government spy to spy on him. Whoever "they" were. Kazakov could only hazard a guess that Khan meant the government. At this juncture, Kazakov wasn't sure whether Khan was simply being paranoid.

"I'm afraid he is busy at the moment."

"He won't be too busy to see me."

The girl sighed. "He is conducting an autopsy. He asked not to be disturbed."

"Then tell him I'm here and I'm waiting for him." He planted his hands on the counter and leaned toward her until finally she slid her chair back and stood. She wore a modest black skirt and practical lace-up flat shoes totally unlike anything most young women wore, and then she had those watchful eyes. Perhaps Khan's assessment was more correct than Kazakov had believed.

She turned abruptly and left him for the hallway to the back and Kazakov stayed where he was. Five minutes passed and suddenly she reappeared silently from the hall. That was the purpose of the unattractive lace-up shoes. They were perfect for coming on people unaware. There was no telling the conversations she might overhear.

"He says he will be another few minutes." She thumped down in her chair and promptly ignored him, but he still didn't move. Better to prove himself an immovable object until he got what he wanted.

About five minutes later he heard the soft pad of Khan's light-footed tread. The man was slight and had always moved quietly. He opened the door to the waiting area and nodded Kazakov inside without a word, then led him down the hall to his office. Khan's white coat was pristine as usual, but his short, dark hair was tousled and he wore a weariness around his eyes that Kazakov had rarely seen.

With the office door shut behind them, Khan slipped behind his desk and sank into his chair with a sigh.

"You all right?" Kazakov asked and sat down onto the wooden guest chair facing the desk. Behind Khan were shelves of medical tomes, all neatly shelved. On the other walls were diagrams of the human body and a sheaf of government postings.

Khan shook his head. "The most recent Jane Doe. I'm finding it more difficult to do the young ones these days." He rubbed his eyes and smiled bleakly up at Kazakov. "I think it's the hazard of aging. They seem younger and younger."

"How young are we talking?"

Khan closed his eyes and worked his neck a moment. "Chronologically? Probably about sixteen or seventeen. In reality, she was probably going on a hundred. Girl was a prostitute and her body had the marks to prove it. She'd been beaten until she was almost unrecognizable. Her body was found by the river west of town. The river's mostly iced over, so the body must have been dumped there. A couple out for a walk found her."

Kazakov said nothing from his slump in the chair. Sometimes there was nothing that could be said. Their respective jobs were shit on occasion.

Khan sighed. "I think she was pretty once. Slim. She hadn't completely grown out of her baby fat yet. Long red hair. She was probably striking. How the hell did a girl like that end up walking the streets?"

Kazakov eased straighter. "Red hair?"

Khan nodded and worked his neck again.

"Derr'mo! I may know this girl."

"Really?" Khan cocked a brow at him.

"I interviewed her earlier this week on the Chelomeyev case. She was working the streets near where he was beaten."

"You have a name?"

Kazakov nodded. "Let me see the body. If it's her, then I can identify her until next of kin can be contacted."

Khan shoved back from his desk and stood, then led Kazakov from the room and down the hall toward the refrigerated autopsy rooms. The air turned cooler and Kazakov was glad for his coat.

The autopsy room gleamed of enamel and stainless steel, with a wall of body-sized stainless steel drawers along one wall and stainless steel examination tables in the center of the room above ugly square floor drains. A dripping hose sat coiled on one wall and cupboards of medical exam equipment filled the fourth wall.

Khan crossed the still-damp floor and pulled open a drawer. A draped figure lay inside and Khan stood aside to offer Kazakov a view.

The slim form under the sheet spoke of just how small the girl had been once she took off the impossibly high heeled boots she'd worn. Her length didn't fill the drawer she now inhabited and two of her could easily have fit side-by-side.

"You ready?" Khan asked.

Kazakov nodded and then wished he hadn't when Khan pulled the sheet back from the girl's face.

The nose was broken, the ears were smashed, and deep gashes filled the cheek and forehead where blows had ruptured the skin, but the fine features were there. So was the high forehead and the slight scar along one cheek.

He nodded and turned away while Khan covered the body and slid the drawer closed. "Who is she?"

"Name's Mura Stepanova. She worked the area near Chelomeyev's home. I wanted to interview her again. I think she might have known something." He shook his head, feeling like a bear coming out of hibernation, and suddenly knew he'd been wrong. He'd been so wrong. He'd been looking into the wrong case entirely. "Listen, I need to ask you some questions and you're not going to like them anymore than you liked them the last time we spoke."

A guarded expression came over Khan's face.

"It's—it's not about the challenges of the Kyrgyz people."

Khan's didn't look like he believed him.

Sighing, Kazakov shook his head. Khan wasn't going to like where Kazakov had been. "Look. The other day I visited Maria again." Not her grave. He couldn't call it that yet. "When I was leaving, two men attacked me and warned me off of the case, but they didn't say which one. When they were gone, I stepped into the street and found none other than Eric Clinton waiting. He'd been following me. I want to know what you know about the man."

He felt the little M.E. studying him. Maybe he didn't like what he saw, for he sighed and shook his head and led Kazakov out of the room. The door swung silently closed behind them, locking Mura and her secrets away in the cold dark of an autopsy room drawer. He fully expected Khan to lead him right out to the reception office and tell him to leave.

Instead Khan stopped at his office door and held it wide. When Kazakov entered, Khan closed the door and took his seat at his desk. "Have a seat," he said.

Kazakov did.

The fluorescent lights gleamed in Khan's dark hair, but tinged his darker skin a squeamish green. The little M.E. scanned the top of his desk as if searching for something. Perhaps it was where to begin. Finally, he looked up Kazakov.

"I consider you my friend, Alexander Kazakov, and yet I am not sure what I can tell you. What did Clinton say when you confronted him?"

"How do you know I confronted him?"

A slow smile bloomed on Khan's lips. "You forget. I've known you a long time. There is no question in my mind but that confronting is what you would do." He cocked a brow, waiting.

Sighing at his predictability, Kazakov nodded and leaned forward, his elbows on his knees, his coat heavy on his shoulders. "He said he was investigating irregularities in the American Embassy related to what happens to the lucrative American tobacco monopoly now that Grigori Ivanov is dead. At the time, it made sense. Now I'm not so sure. And the car he drives was spotted in the area the night Chelomeyev was beaten. I want to talk to him about it, but I want to know what I'm walking into. What can you tell me about the man? When you introduced him, you only said he knew about technology and data."

Khan looked thoughtful. "First of all, I have difficulty believing that he would have anything to do with your young detective's beating." He went silent, as if picking his words. "As you may have guessed, Clinton is—more than a technology and data man." He met Kazakov's gaze. "When we met, yes, we discussed data technology, but also other things—like my people and their position in Ferganese society. He was—interested. He was also interested in Fergana's position in the world. He expressed concern about the pressure the country is under from the two empires and wondered where the tribes stood on such matters."

Kazakov sat back in his chair and eyed Khan. "That's a little more political conversation than I thought you'd get involved in. What did you say?"

Khan smiled again. "I was careful. I told him that all I had were baseless opinions, but he said he thought I was better informed than that—that I must hear plenty in my community practice. It seems he knew all about me."

"And you know little about him. I suppose that is a typical arrangement—for a spy."

Kahn's wince was hard to watch. The M.E. looked like he waited for another blow to fall.

"So what has he done for you, or what does he have over you?"

Another shake of Khan's head. "Nothing."

"Nothing yet."

"Nothing at all and there will not be anything. I only share rumors that I might learn if I think it might help Clinton in the fight to keep Fergana neutral. That's all." He ran his fingers through his hair. "That's all." He sat with head bowed.

"And what happens if he asks for more, old friend? Now that he has the fact you've provided information to use like a weapon."

Khan only nodded. "I am aware of the risk. But I still don't see that he would have you attacked or have Chelomeyev beaten. He is a reasonable man."

"He's a spy! Set here to spy on us! And spies cause trouble, Khan. How can you think he gives a damn for your people?" Kazakov stood up to pace. "Why the hell is he following me? His story… it does not fully make sense or it is not the full story. No, there is some other reason. I just don't know what." He rubbed his chin with its midday stubble and turned back to Khan. "Any ideas? What information have you passed on to him?"

"Nothing recently, other than I told him what I told you. The explosions were not the work of my people."

Kazakov couldn't recall Khan making such a definitive statement before, but he was certainly definitive now. Kazakov nodded. "All right. Thank you for this discussion. It helps me—I think." He looked back at his friend. Still seated in his chair, Khan looked weary beyond belief and frayed as an old cuff. "I think this is my time to return your advice. Go home. Get some rest and look after yourself."

Khan graced him with an imperceptible nod and Kazakov left him.

Stepping out of the morgue was like bursting a bubble. Always he'd thought of Khan as a steady man who kept his life private. But Khan had talked to a foreign spy. He'd shared information with someone beyond Kazakov. It left him a little bereft for the special trust he'd thought was between them.

In the sunshine of mid afternoon, he turned back to the door to the morgue. Had Khan shared information about Kazakov?

A small pang of betrayal suggested he had.

18

Kazakov trudged up the concrete stairs from the morgue and across the hospital parking. The trees of the small park looked bedraggled and barren today, though in the spring they were a lovely green.

At the Perseus he stood inhaling the cold air and sorting through his feelings and what he knew. His feelings didn't matter. The evidence did. He let himself into the driver's seat and sat there pondering.

There had been the case of the beaten prostitute amongst Chelomeyev's files. Had he missed the connection? He'd given that file only a cursory inspection. Was Eric Clinton somehow involved? But why would a case like that lead to beating the assigned detective within an inch of his life?

Unless the case was the tip of the iceberg. He needed to get home and read the file more closely.

But first there was Eric Clinton to interview as well as the people at Chelomeyev's apartment building. And he needed to find out the name of Svetlana Ivanova's lover.

He started the Perseus and went to Chelomeyev's building, but found out little from the people who were at home. Most had been safely at home when the beating occurred.

Then he headed toward the American consulate. The area of New Moscow southwest of the city sat where the landscape was slowly rising toward the Pamir Alay Mountains. It was made up of long boulevards complete with mature trees and housed most of New Moscow's moneyed residents. As if in honor of their ongoing confrontation, the Ottoman and Chinese embassies faced each other like boxers across the treed boulevard that split the street. As opposed to the opulent tile-friezed mansion of the Ottoman Empire and the walled, multi-tiered, and dragon-carved compound of the Chinese, the American consulate was a modest brownstone house situated on a side street—a wonderful comment on America's place in the world. It sat behind a wrought iron fence and a postage-stamp-sized garden, like the others on its block. Only a small brass sign beside the iron gate told what was inside.

Kazakov parked at the curb and climbed out. The naked tree limbs etched against the blue sky and the wind was brisk, but not overly cold. He worked his shoulders and felt the ache in his side, now increased by the beating he'd taken last night. Clinton's men? He had to know. Were Clinton's actions sanctioned by his country?

Squaring his shoulders and trying to appear official but not overbearing, given he was dealing with a diplomat, he climbed the pale central stairs and used a flag-shaped knocker on the door. A young man in a gray military uniform and white gloves pulled the door open.

"Yes?" the young man asked. He had the fresh-faced, pink-cheeked look of an untried soldier, and yet there was something about the eyes that said there was more to this young foreigner.

Kazakov briefly bowed his head in polite greeting. "I am Detektiv Alexander Kazakov. I am hoping to speak to Eric Clinton. We have spoken before."

"Wait here." The young man shut the door in Kazakov's face and he turned to look out over the street. It was pretty under the snow. He imagined it would be lovely when the trees had leaves and the gardens were in bloom. The kind of place families aspired to but could never afford, like the crescent next to Yekaterina Park. A wealthy enclave. If he remembered rightly, Grigori Ivanov and his wife had their home somewhere nearby. He would have liked to have seen the crime scene, but the place had been released back to Svetlana when the case had technically been closed against Chelomeyev's will. And now the house stood empty because Svetlana could not bring herself to live where her husband had been killed.

The door clicked open behind him and Kazakov turned. Not Eric Clinton. In addition to the young soldier, an older man filled the doorway. He was shorter than Clinton, perhaps five foot ten, and distinguished with steel-gray hair combed straight back from a high brow. He had gray eyes set in a ruddy, outdoorsman's face much like Clinton's, but wore a well-cut gray suit that would have cost a month of Kazakov's wages. Maybe more.

"May I help you?" the gray-haired man asked in cultured Russian that still carried the slight twang of an American accent.

Kazakov repeated his introduction and request and the gray-haired man looked beyond him as if studying the street and its contents.

"Step inside, please."

The young military man held the door and Kazakov eased past him. The gray-haired man held out a manicured hand. "I am Thomas Edgar Hoover, the assistant to the Ambassador. What is this about our attaché, Mr. Clinton?" He scanned Kazakov's new great coat and apparently found it lacking.

"I was speaking with Eric Clinton yesterday regarding an investigation and I have a few follow-up questions."

Thomas Edgar Hoover shook his handsome head, his immaculate hair not moving an inch. "I'm afraid that is not possible. Mr. Clinton is —indisposed at the moment."

Kazakov stiffened. "What does that mean—indisposed?"

"It means that Mr. Clinton is unavailable for your questions."

"This is a matter of utmost importance. A detective was beaten and Clinton may have been a witness."

Thomas Edgar Hoover's gray eyes hardened as he shook his head. "I can't help you. I'm sorry."

"Clinton was working on his own investigation regarding the Grigori Ivanov murder. Had he found anything?"

"I am not at liberty to divulge anything to you, Detektiv. I think you have finished your enquiries here. And now I have other matters to attend to." Thomas Edgar inclined his head at the door.

There would be no information forthcoming here. Kazakov thanked him, went out to the Perseus, and climbed inside. He thumped his palm on the wheel and felt the impact right down his side.

This was no way to complete an investigation. He needed Clinton's information!

He hauled his phone out of his pocket and dialed the number Clinton had given him, but the number only rang and rang. Swearing, he hung up and rang Khan once more, praying the M.E. would take his call. When he was put through to Khan's line and heard the pick-up, he sighed in relief.

"Khan," came the M.E.'s guarded voice.

"Khan. It's Kazakov. Regarding the subject of our last discussion. Do you have an address for your friend and might you share it?"

"Why?" still guarded.

"I was just visiting his workplace and his employers say he'd indisposed—whatever that means. I need to talk to him about the young lady we were discussing." Why he was being so circumspect, he could only put down to the events that had happened and warnings from Maria and others that phone calls like this could be monitored. He suddenly didn't want anyone knowing what he was doing until after it was done.

Khan was silent and Kazakov could picture him considering, and the small frown that would form as he did. Kazakov allowed him the space.

"I will call him and see what I can learn. Let me call you back."

The line went dead and Kazakov looked up at the brownstone. He felt eyes looking down at him, so he started the vehicle and drove to another side street before parking. His phone buzzed and he picked up.

"Where are you?" Khan asked.

Kazakov read the address off the house he'd parked beside.

"Stay there." The phone hung up again and Kazakov scanned the street. The trees were slightly smaller here and grew crowded in front yards, their barren branches scratching at the sides of the houses. Down the road and over the rooftops stood the white crowns of the Pamir Alay Mountains, cold and cruel in the sunlight. The people who had lived here for eons were not so cruel, though they'd had despot rulers who were. The Russians had been fortunate to find their way to them and not be forced into those southern mountains. Or on to China. Who knows what would have happened then?

South to death in mountain passes. East to slow death as they were absorbed into the Chinese masses.

In the rearview mirror, the low-slung black Ford hunkered toward him and came to a stop beside him. The passenger side window slid down and Eric Clinton looked out at him. "I suggest you climb in."

Kazakov hugged his left arm over his gun and did as bid.

The smooth leather seat of the Ford cocooned around him as Clinton guided the car down the street.

"So? You came looking for me." Clinton said.

Kazakov studied him. Clinton looked like he'd been through his own wars. A cut was stitched above his left eye and the eye itself was almost swollen shut. Bruises swelled the side of his jaw.

"You look like shit," Kazakov said.

"Almost as good as you, last time we met." Clinton kept his eyes on the wheel.

"What the hell's going on, Clinton? You walk into a door? Or are you simply indisposed?"

Clinton snorted and then winced. "Talked to Hoover, have you?" He shook his head. "Doesn't know which way is up or who our friends are."

Friends. The glance Clinton threw at Kazakov seemed intended to ingratiate. Instead it put Kazakov on his guard.

"So what happened?" he repeated.

Clinton sighed. "Let's just say that certain people don't like my enquiries."

Kazakov eyed him as they cruised past the onion domes of the replica of Saint Basil's Cathedral. "What enquiries? And don't give me that shit about internal embassy issues." Even if they were real, he didn't think enquiries like that would lead to Chelomeyev's beating. And then there was the fact that he'd seen Clinton's Ford or its twin down by the old carnival site and near Mountain Construction. At the time he hadn't realized that he was being followed.

Clinton shook his head. "What is there beyond the Ivanov murder?"

"Don't play games with me, Clinton. I've half a mind to arrest you for obstructing justice. You've been looking into the explosions just like I have."

Clinton firmed his grip on the steering wheel. His eyes were on the road, his jaw set and firm as if he was considering what Kazakov had just said.

Deciding whether to respond or to kill him instead? It all depended on Clinton and the American's role in what was going on. Clinton pulled into a parking spot next to Potemkin Park—he had taken Kazakov on a cruise around the city. Gaze still facing forward, he sighed.

"I'm talking to you off the record. You can't use any information I give you. Agreed?" He turned to Kazakov for his answer.

Kazakov needed answers. He'd figure out how to get the evidence that he needed, but first he had to know what Clinton knew. He nodded. He'd decide whether to abide by his word later.

"You're right," Clinton said, once more gazing through the windscreen as if the traffic flowing past was of the utmost interest. The spray from the wheels gradually clouded the driver's side windows, and the heat from the heater and the interior's pungent new-leather scent became almost unpleasant. "As you know, the American Consulate has existed in Fergana for the past twenty years. About two years ago we began to hear some rumblings from our contacts in Fergana—and other places. It led us to believe that something was afoot in the region and the delicate balance might be changing. As a result, we opened the full Embassy here so that we could keep a closer eye on things. I was brought in as trade attaché." He glanced at Kazakov. "Yes, as a spy. In addition to my duties regarding trade, I was to cultivate other contacts."

"Like Khalil Khan."

Clinton nodded, not even shamefaced. "He knows people. He also feels that there is something wrong in Fergana. He says that you feel it, too."

"Trying to recruit me, too, are you?" Kazakov said.

"The thought had crossed my mind."

"Get on with your story. What does the opening of your embassy have to do with the explosions?"

Clinton glanced at him, then continued his study of the traffic. "First tell me whether the investigation into the explosions is anything other than what's been released in the news."

Frowning, Kazakov considered the question. He knew where Rostoff was pushing him.

"Officially? They're looking into terrorists from within the tribal communities. They claim that the unrest and protests over wages and opportunities were the precursors to the bombings. But all police work is objective. We let the evidence lead us."

"You really believe that?" Clinton asked, looking sideways at him.

Kazakov studied the park beyond his window. The sunlight glittered off the snow on the naked branches, limning everything in a hard, cold light. Breath puffed from the mouths of pedestrians who braved the paths along the river as if their souls escaped them. It was getting cold again. More snow would be coming. He sighed.

"No. It should be that way, but I can't deceive myself. My compatriots often have blinders to keep themselves focused on preferred suspects. The news fills with minor crimes by tribal citizens as apparent justification for the current mass arrests and yet..." He shook his head. "I've talked to trusted sources and I don't think our Kyrgyz citizens and their cousins are involved. Yet. Treatment like this may push them to it!"

When he looked up, he found Clinton nodding. "There are people worried that this will be used to foment unrest amongst the residents of the old city and their kin. Already the news is causing a backlash amongst the Russians. I hear whispers that the old city is in league with the Russians' old enemies, the Ottomans. People talk about dealing with the issue once and for all. I hear whispers of bulldozing the old city."

Derr'mo, who was he listening to? "Thankfully there are cooler heads in charge." He did not want to think about what could happen. Outside the car, the snow glistened in the park and a couple walked the promenade.

"For now," Clinton said.

Kazakov's attention snapped around, his rushing heart feeling like it would beat through his chest. "The election. Bure. He's been using these events against the current government."

Clinton nodded. "And his popularity is rising amongst Russians. People are listening to him and nodding. All it will take is another event and voters will flock to him."

There was no moisture in Kazakov's mouth. "There was more explosive stolen from the construction site."

"Shit." Clinton slumped in his seat. "We opened the embassy to try to draw Fergana into an Association of Independent States. We've been trying to open discussions with the government, but they keep putting us off. Another explosion could destabilize the whole region and put a whole other kind of government in power. Fergana is like the plug in the dike that holds back the water, though in this case it's a war. If Fergana acts against its tribal peoples—its Muslim peoples—it would be the perfect excuse for the Ottoman Empire to move in to protect its brethren. That would give the Chinese the excuse they need to attack to protect their interests. Whoever wins the war here—well, who could stop them if they turned their gaze on the rest of the world?"

It was a breathtaking analysis that was far above Kazakov's pay grade, but it made too much sense. "The Russian people live on the dreams of past greatness. Someone like Bure could play on that to turn the Russians against the non-Russian citizens. It could be as you said."

He felt sick at the thought. Was Bure so blind that he couldn't see the long-ranging repercussions of such actions? Fergana would be plucked like a scab off a wound and the fester of war would spread around the world "There is already a deep strain of prejudice. It would not be hard."

Clinton nodded, then smiled. "So, to answer your original question, I've been trying to track down who's behind it. Our government has a vested interest. We don't want to be drawn into a war, but if Fergana falls, we believe it's inevitable that the war will come to us."

So it was self-interest, but self-interest that might work to Fergana's benefit, too. On the other hand, it was very convenient that Clinton came up with this story right now. He was a spy and spies were notorious liars—or at least it made sense that they would be. Was Clinton simply spinning another yarn to keep Kazakov spinning his wheels?

"What were you doing five days ago at seven thirty in the evening?" Even if they both wished to stop whatever was happening to Fergana, Clinton still could have been party to Chelomeyev's beating. Had Chelomeyev somehow been implicated in the plot? He came from an important family…

Or was Clinton hiding something more?

Doubting Chelomeyev felt like a chasm opening beneath his feet. Pavel Chelomeyev was his reason for once more stepping out in the world. Had he been wrong? When he looked back to Clinton for the answer to the question, the man was frowning.

"Let me help you," Kazakov said "Your vehicle was spotted by two private security officers in an area they patrol. As soon as the car was spotted, it sped away. Your vehicle. And before you argue, one of the officers is a vehicle aficionado and knew what he saw. For a spy, you don't exactly drive an inconspicuous vehicle."

Clinton wearily blew a sigh up over his face. His forelock of hair trembled and he nodded. "All right. I was following two men. Russians. They'd been identified as instigators at some of the Kyrgyz rallies and as causing fights and property damage that had boiled over at recent protests. Over the past few days, something or someone had had them upset. They kept going back to that area as if searching." He shook his head. "Your informants were correct. When I knew I was spotted, I left; but I came back later to keep up surveillance."

"Not too good a surveillance in this very unique vehicle."

Clinton smiled sheepishly. "Sometimes hiding in plain sight is the best. If a vehicle, even an unusual one, is regularly in a location, it becomes part of the landscape. Besides, who would conduct surveillance while driving such a vehicle?"

"What did you see?" Kazakov forced himself to breathe evenly, to keep his body loose. He was close. He could feel it. And Clinton had the information—if he was telling the truth.

Clinton shook his head again. "I should have reported it. There was a girl, a prostitute if I'm any judge. She was standing around as if she was waiting for someone—a particular someone—not just any customer. Some guy I'd seen come home earlier comes out into his building parking lot and she comes running. Let's just say they know each other, shall we? Then a car drives up—the car I've been watching for. It comes screeching to the curb and my two guys scramble out. The guy with the girl tries to protect her and sends her running. My two guys go to take after her, but the guy stops them and they attack him. By the time they're done with the guy, the girl is long gone. Let me guess. The guy died and you're investigating the murder."

Did Clinton even realize what he'd said? That he'd sat there and rather than blow his cover, he'd let a man be beaten—perhaps to death? The overheated vehicle interior had gone so cold that Kazakov could no longer feel his fingers. He looked down at his hands. In the warmth of the Ford, he'd taken off his gloves and his fingers were fisted so tight they'd gone white. Clinton had seen it happening and done nothing.

"His name is *Detektiv* Pavel Chelomeyev and he is clinging to life in Yekaterina Hospital. I owe my life to him. The girl was—notice I say was—Mura Stepanova. She was found dead of a beating last night." And he could have saved her if he'd known. He closed his eyes a moment for all the deaths he could not stop. From what Clinton was saying, there were far more to come.

"Jeezus. I'm sorry. If I'd known…"

Kazakov's gaze snapped to Clinton but didn't believe the other man's apology for a minute. If he'd known, he likely would still have done nothing in the interest of his investigation. "If these men were after the girl that badly, there had to be a reason. You said they'd been searching the area. Looking for her, maybe?"

"Could be."

"Any idea why?"

"She knew something?" Clinton offered.

Kazakov straightened in his seat, a flush of heat running through his veins once more. "Chelomeyev had a file on a prostitute beating." He had barely given it a glance with the Ivanov case to deal with. But what if she told Pavel something? What if he put it in the file! It could be what he and Clinton were seeking.

He went to jump out of the Ford, then thought better of it. "Take me back to my vehicle."

His mind worked as Clinton peppered him with questions that he kept waving away. What if Mura Stepanova had somehow come into knowledge of who caused the explosions? That would make her a serious risk. If she'd been caught and beaten but somehow escaped, perhaps she'd told someone—a detective who she knew because he lived in the area she worked? Perhaps a detective who had shown her kindness and who had tried to help her? A detective that she had grown fond of and who had grown fond of her? That sounded like Chelomeyev. Perhaps a young detective who was fond of fairy tales found himself in the role of white knight rescuing the fallen princess? That sounded like Chelomeyev, too. And so did Clinton's story of the young detective trying to protect the girl.

At the Perseus, Clinton pulled in behind his vehicle and Kazakov leapt out.

"What the hell are you doing? What have you realized?" Clinton asked, scrambling out with him. "What do you know?"

The wind was brisk, stripping away the smothering heat of Clinton's Ford.

Kazakov shook his head. "I know nothing. I have only suspicions."

"Care to share them?"

Kazakov glanced at Clinton's vehicle and sniffed. "Like you share your information? In snippets and interspersed with fabrications and lies?"

Clinton had the grace to look away for a moment. "I really am sorry. I can see the beating victim meant something to you. I just couldn't afford to blow my cover. Learning what these guys wanted and having them lead me to whoever gives them orders was more important."

"You live in an ugly world, Clinton. One I don't want any part of." Kazakov trudged over to the Perseus.

"But where are you going?"

"Going home. Do some reading." He fumbled the Perseus's driver's door open and slid inside only to find Clinton sliding in the other side. "What the hell do you think you're doing?"

Clinton shook his head. "I know you don't trust me and you probably don't like me much either, but I've told you the truth. This case has implications for my country and I have to see it through. You clearly think you've got information, so if you think I'm not coming, you've got another thought coming."

Kazakov glanced down at the other man's pointy-toed, tooled, leather boots. He was pretty sure Clinton would follow him if Kazakov didn't allow him to come. Perhaps it would be better to keep the man close and learn what else he knew. Kazakov wouldn't have to reveal everything he knew. "You had best pray that we don't get stuck anywhere or have to walk because you'll get nowhere in those."

"They've done me fine so far."

The Perseus's engine turned over and he pulled out from the curb.

Down Suvarov Way gusts of wind rattled against the Perseus and tossed the naked branches of the trees in Yekaterina Park. Outside the city and beyond the suburban sprawl of tract homes, the wind showed its true strength, gusts slamming the Perseus sideways and lifting sheets of snow from the fields in glistening cyclones of ice that ate the visibility. Kazakov was forced to slow the Perseus to a crawl.

When they reached the trees, the wind lessened around the vehicle but lifted snow from the trees like sunlit, nascent clouds that rained silver and gold on the windshield. At least the plow had been through and the road was clear, but the road to Agafya's place was almost invisible with the drift of snow the plow had deposited. His own road was not much better.

He stopped to survey the drift and assess whether the Perseus could climb over without high centering. It would be close, but his side ached and there were Clinton's ridiculous boots and he didn't feel like shoveling. Beyond the drift, the driveway through the pines and leafless walnut trees was quite passable. He just needed to get there.

He backed up the Perseus, told Clinton to hold on, and revved the engine. When he dropped it into gear and stepped on the gas, the Perseus leapt forward, right into the four-foot pile of displaced snow. The snowbank exploded around them and for a moment the Perseus slid sideways, but then its front wheels locked in and it chugged up and over the pile of snow.

"Whoa!" Clinton said. "I wouldn't have wanted to try that in my Ford."

Then the windshield shattered and Clinton shuddered forward, a bloom of red forming on his chest.

19

The Perseus's cab echoed with the deafening thunder of the gunshot. Clinton slipped sideways against the passenger door. Kazakov dropped the Perseus in reverse, but the vehicle only slewed around, caught in too much snow. An explosion—another shot and the seat back exploded beside him. The Perseus's tires whined but got them nowhere. They were high centered.

"Down! Get down!" He grabbed Clinton and pulled him down across the console, throwing himself down beside him. The American's face was pale, his gaze glassy with shock. Thankfully the wound looked like it was too high on his chest to be immediately fatal.

"Shit. Shit. Shit." Clinton murmured.

More shots pinged into the Perseus as Kazakov struggled to loose his gun. The trouble was, just poking his head up to try to spot the shooters was just as likely to get him dead. Hung up as they were in the Perseus, they were sitting ducks. He yanked on the door handle to get the door open, but the snow held the door shut. He kicked the door. Again. Again. It shoved the snow back until the snowbank and the door offered some limited protection. He chanced a look over the steering wheel and two shots answered him, cutting the air where his head had just been. He crawled out and used the door as a shield, aimed for the places he thought the shots had come from. Someone yelled.

Kazakov ducked back down. "Clinton. Move your ass out of there or you're dead."

Clinton met his gaze and nodded, but the shock in his eyes spoke volumes. He used his legs and shoved himself toward Kazakov's door, but by the time he made it he was panting. Kazakov raised his head and took another shot. He had too few bullets to spend.

Then, bent over, he grabbed Clinton's shoulders and, apologizing for the pain he was about to cause, he pulled.

The two of them tumbled back over the snowbank and into the main road, Clinton landing on top of Kazakov. He shoved the injured man off of him and scrambled up using the high-centered Perseus and the plowed snowbank for shelter.

"Come on. We've got about two minutes before they come looking for us."

Clinton staggered up, and Kazakov grabbed his good arm. Keeping to the road and bent over to be less visible to whoever was shooting from the wooded hillside by his driveway, he led Clinton up the road.

The way wasn't steep, but Clinton was gasping as they rounded the curve of plowed road just uphill. As Kazakov had suspected, another vehicle was pulled in snug against the snowbank. The shooters had arrived and parked here where Kazakov wouldn't see the vehicle and had made their way on foot down to Kazakov's driveway and dacha. They'd believed that they could finish Kazakov off at his home and then return here to escape in their vehicle. It was a low-slung sedan and he supposed in poor light he might have mistaken it for Clinton's vehicle. Maybe. He tried the driver's side door and it opened.

"Get in. Get it going—a spy must have some sort of skills to start a vehicle—then head down the road to the city. I'll see what I can do to stop these bastards."

"You can't do it alone. There's more than one of them," Clinton said.

"You need medical attention and I need to catch these bastards. Now go, while you still can."

Finally, Clinton nodded. "I'll send help."

Kazakov slammed the door shut as Clinton reached under the steering wheel for wires. He just prayed Clinton's strength held until he was safe.

In front of the sedan, a set of deep tracks cut through the snowbank and led into the woods. At this hour of late afternoon, the tracks were stained blue-black. So were the shadows under the trees. Kazakov followed through the snow as from behind came the sound of a vehicle engine turning over. So Clinton had skills. Ahead, one clear track showed a heavy boot print that he would bet matched the tracks at Mountain Construction explosives shed. He kept going, the sweat from the adrenaline replaced by the effort of wading through the snow.

A barrage of gunfire sounded from the road. Clearly, the ambushers had tried to stop Clinton's escape. They'd be after Kazakov now unless they thought he had escaped with Clinton.

Unless Clinton hadn't managed to get past them.

He stopped for a moment to listen. In the wind it was hard to tell, but he thought he heard the roar of a vehicle engine farther down the hill. If his ears weren't deceiving him, then it suggested Clinton had gotten away. Good.

It was also good that he knew this area. That gave him an advantage. His dacha sat slightly downhill from where he stood. There was good cover amongst the trees. The track he followed led toward his dacha. They must have thought to catch him unawares at home, but the snowplow had caused a change of plan. They'd be after him now.

To conduct an assault like this, someone must be very worried. Bure? Did the man know about Kazakov's quiet research since he'd learned that Bure had been the father of his sixteen-year-old stepdaughter's unborn child? Was Bure prepared to conduct a frontal assault on his enemy? Clearly, someone was.

Around him, the wind hummed in the trees. The naked branches creaked. The half-frozen trunks groaned.

The odd thing was that he hadn't even been looking in this direction in his investigation. He'd been certain that Chelomeyev's beating was somehow connected to Ivanov's murder. There had to be some connection. He just didn't see it yet. But what had Kazakov done that had led to the decision to murder him and Clinton?

Ahead the hum and groan of the trees was broken by a human oath.

"*B'lyad'*!" Gutter Russian. "This fucking vehicle might as well be welded in place."

"Shut your face and keep shoveling. We need to get to out of here. That bastard took our vehicle and will be sending the police. It's this Perseus or walking."

Kazakov stopped. He recognized the voices from the graveyard. Whoever had sent the warning had gotten tired of Kazakov's investigation. And now they were here to stop him.

Bent low in the shadows, Kazakov crept forward. The sun was setting, sending a red glow over the sky that stained the shadows bloody. If he could capture these two, he just might be able to learn how the death of a prostitute related to the murder of a businessman.

Bure had to be the key, but he could not believe that Bure was foolish enough to directly order the death of anyone. No, it had to be Bure's backers. The Ottomans? But Bure was vocal in his dislike for all things Ottoman.

The Chinese? Bure had been friends with a man who had been a Chinese spy, but the man had turned double agent, which told Kazakov exactly nothing. And there had been those photographs of Bure and Enver Pasha in the newspaper. They had certainly seemed friendly.

If he could take these men alive, he could hopefully track them back to their master.

Ahead to his left was the clearing that held his dacha. The glow of the setting sun reflected off the open snow there. Above, the tops of the trees caught the light.

Keeping to shadows, he crept toward his driveway, careful of where he stepped. With the warmth today, there would be spots where the snow would crunch under his weight and that could alert his prey. Ahead, the men's oaths came from closer to the road.

He followed the sound.

The ruddy sunlight filled the trees and lit the scene at his driveway entrance. The two men labored with shovels that they had retrieved from the dacha. One dug around the doors of the Perseus. The other tried to clear the lump of snow that high-centered the vehicle. As Kazakov had thought, it was the bruiser from the graveyard and the smaller man who had told Kazakov to give up his investigation.

"I still don't see why we have to do this," bruiser said.

"You want to walk back to town?" the small man said. "They took the sedan, remember? Or maybe you'd like to wait for police—then you can admit that it was you who killed the little whore and beat their officer."

"I didn't know he was a cop. Neither did you!"

"That's right. And that's why I don't intend to be here when the cops come."

Kazakov stiffened. These were the men who had beaten Chelomeyev. No way were they leaving here. They also didn't seem to realize the police were already here.

Kazakov straightened under the trees, took aim, and steadied his gun.

The smaller man dislodged snow under the Perseus and the vehicle seemed to settle.

"New Moscow police," he called. "Hands up! On your knees."

Both men froze. Then both dove for cover—the bruiser behind the Perseus and the smaller man into the road beyond the snow bank. The bruiser lifted his head long enough to take a shot in Kazakov's general direction.

Kazakov leapt back behind the tree but didn't return fire. He had to husband his bullets and make each one count. He scanned the road. Where was the small man? Kazakov couldn't afford to have him come up behind just as Kazakov had.

Another wild shot into the woods momentarily kept Kazakov where he was. He shifted location closer to his driveway to gain a better shot of the big man. At this angle he could see the man's leg as he knelt in the snow behind the Perseus's cab. Kazakov took aim.

The soft crunch of snow spun Kazakov around. The smaller man stood spotlit in the trees, a weapon up and at the ready. Kazakov threw himself sideways, bringing his gun up at the same time. The man's weapon flashed as he shot in Kazakov's direction, or where he'd just stood.

He returned fire as he slid behind another tree and heard the man cry out. When he looked back, the man was down, clawing at his chest.

Kazakov scrambled up to his knees.

Where was the bruiser?

No longer by the Perseus.

A banshee yell came from the direction of Kazakov's driveway. The big man plunged through the snow, spraying Kazakov's location with bullets. Kazakov lunged sideways to the protection of a walnut trunk. Lunged again behind the shielding foliage of a pine. Bullets tore through the branches perilously close. He ducked and ran back from the pine to take cover behind another walnut. His breath steamed in the colder air—a sure giveaway to his location. He tried to suck the steam back and listen for his pursuer over the pounding of his heart.

There. The crunch of snow.

Crouched low, he poked his head and shoulders out beyond the tree and took a shot.

The big man screamed and Kazakov took a second look. The man was on his knees clutching his leg.

Kazakov scrambled up and rushed through the snow, weapon ready. "Down! Toss the weapon aside and get down in the snow!"

The bruiser brought his weapon up.

Kazakov fired, just as the bruiser did the same. The bruiser's bullet slammed a tree beside Kazakov, spraying him with splinters. Kazakov's bullet caught the bruiser dead center. The man fell backward into the snow.

Kazakov waded forward. The bruiser's empty gaze was trained skyward.

He checked for a pulse and went unrewarded. He hurried over to the smaller man, but the results were the same. If he'd wanted to make fingering Bure difficult, he couldn't have done any better.

.   .   .

He called Rostoff first and told him what had happened. Around Rostoff's angry yelling, Kazakov managed to get the Detektiv Chief Inspektor to agree to send an M.E. Then he tried to call Clinton's office to leave a message, but when another voice answered, he hung up.

For the moment, he was alone.

He retreated to the dacha to wait, but of course his two attackers had been there first. The place was trashed, Koshka nowhere to be found. The fire had been lit and Chelomeyev's files burned. The information he needed to connect the dots was gone.

Fatigue and pain flooded into him. All the physical effort had pulled muscles in his side that weren't ready to be pulled. He went back outside to the bodies to wait and a small mew brought his head around. Koshka picked her way through the snow and rubbed against his leg. He picked her up and she settled in his arms—an unusual action for the little cat who usually ordered him around. She head butted his face and purred ferociously as if she was happy to see him.

At least someone was.

When he heard vehicle engines on the road, he set Koshka down and shushed her toward the house, then he stepped out onto the road to flag them down. Along with the M.E.'s wagon came an unmarked police sedan and Kazakov sighed. It was years since anyone from Moscow Police had been welcomed to the place—beyond Chelomeyev.

20

─────────

Pogolin and Razin were there for two hours, wading past the bullet-riddled Perseus to invade the ransacked dacha with too many probing questions and too-prying eyes. After helping to free the Perseus from the snow, they left, following the M.E.'s wagon down the road toward New Moscow. By then it was dark outside and crime scene tape surrounded most of the forest in front of the dacha. They had told Kazakov they would take his full statement at the office tomorrow.

After parking the Perseus behind the dacha, he stood in the center of his dacha feeling exhausted and hungry. He righted his desk, table, and chairs. The sofa the intruders had left against the wall. He pulled the bedding off the bed and set it aside for washing. The two intruders had soiled it with Koshka's kitty litter. The soft flap-flap of Koshka's cat door heralded the return of the little cat after the police intrusion. He fed her an extra-large bowl of crunchies and soon the sound of a happy cat and the warmth of the woodstove drained away the worst of the day. He wanted to sleep, but his mind was too active. Too many things to sort through. Too much evidence to understand and none of it from the two bodies. Both men had, by their tattoos, clearly been Russian, but all labels had been removed from their clothing and neither man had identification. Perhaps their vehicle held something. At least the license plate should tell them something.

He called Clinton's number again, but this time no one picked up. Had Clinton died? Kazakov found himself hoping not. Was he in the hospital? Or had his embassy decided to hide him just when Kazakov needed him the most?

He set the phone down and pulled out a loaf of black bread. He sliced a piece off and buttered it, then put tea water on to boil.

It was as if every piece of evidence that might help him was being erased. The girl. Now Clinton and the attackers' car. Chelomeyev's file.

Chelomeyev.

Kazakov's hunger faded and he looked down at the heel of bread he held. Chelomeyev was the author of the file. He knew its contents. What if Chelomeyev hadn't been intended to live? The fact he had meant he still might wake up with the memory of what Mura Stepanova had told him. And that meant he was in danger from whoever had sent the two men to kill Kazakov. But the young detective had been in the hospital for days. Surely, they would have made an attempt on his life before now.

Unless they had left him alone until the girl was dealt with. They could have hoped that the girl would seek Chelomeyev in the hospital, or that he would recover and lead them to Mura—which suggested they knew of the feelings between the two young people. Now that the girl was gone, there was no reason to leave Chelomeyev alive.

"Derr'mo!" He grabbed the kettle off of the woodstove, added an extra log to the fire, and tamped the stove's vents almost closed to slow the burning. "Sorry, little girl. I have to go out again."

Koshka looked up at him with an indignant glare, but then resumed eating as he tried calling Rostoff's office. No answer. Rostoff and his fill-in secretary had likely both gone home. He pulled his boots back on and tugged on his greatcoat, hat, and gloves. He turned off the lantern and went outside. The chill air had flooded down off the mountains, but this time there was no snow. The air was crisp and froze his breath. In the darkness the cloudless night sky was awash with stars strung across the universe. Such views always left him breathless and diminished in the face of such vastness. In the face of such a view, it left him wondering why this case or even Fergana mattered.

But to someone, Fergana clearly did. What was it Clinton had said? Fergana was like the plug in the dike, the cork in the bottle. More like the lid of Pandora's box or a genie's bottle—if Fergana lost its neutrality and took the side of one or the other empire, it would spill war out upon the world.

A genie's bottle, and if Kazakov was any judge, it was Bure who wanted to pull the plug.

And the only way to prove it might rest in Chelomeyev's injured head.

When Kazakov climbed into the Perseus's bullet-riddled cabin, the cold followed him in through the shattered windshield. He turned the key and the engine turned over and roared to life. Then he buttoned the collar of his coat higher, pulled his hat down farther over his ears, and backed the Perseus out. He tried the detective office again, but there was no answer. He dialed dispatch and waited for the call to go through.

"New Moscow Police," a male voice said.

"This is Detektiv Kazakov. I am calling about Detektiv Pavel Chelomeyev. I have reason to believe he is in danger. A guard needs to be placed on him in Yekaterina Hospital."

There was silence at the end of the phone, then: "I will require someone of higher authority than you to provide authorization."

Kazakov closed his eyes and swore. "Get someone there. I will be there as soon as I can. If there are questions, have them talk to me."

He hung up and pointed the Perseus down the driveway and toward the city.

Frigid wind came through the space where the windshield had been. His nose and cheeks froze and he wished that he had brought a scarf and winter goggles. Instead he pulled his collar up around his face and kept going. Tears froze on his cheeks. He squinted against the freezing wind as he pushed the Perseus down the snowy roads. The passenger seat was dark with Clinton's frozen blood, and still the glorious stars shone pitilessly above.

He barely slowed when he came into the city's sprawl of subdivisions and wound his way down into the city to Suvarov Boulevard, barely slowing on the turn to Yekaterina Hospital. He skidded to a stop in the icy parking lot and leapt out of the Perseus, heedless of the tearing on his side. Up the front stairs and in the front doors. He crossed the lobby in a few quick strides and rode up to Chelomeyev's floor. He stepped out into the antiseptic smells and the beeps and hums of life-saving equipment. With Chelomeyev here, he might stand a chance if he was left to recover.

He hurried down the corridor to the nursing station.

"Chelomeyev?"

A nurse looked up at him from doing her charting, this one middle aged with frizzed red hair, pasty skin, and dark circles under pale blue eyes. Once she might have been pretty, but now she just looked tired. "Yes? What about him? Only family are allowed in to see him."

He flashed his badge. "When was the last time you checked him? Has he had any visitors?"

She shook her head. "No visitors and I last checked him fifteen minutes ago on rounds. Everything was normal considering his condition. His vitals have stabilized and there are hopeful signs that he is regaining consciousness. We plan to move him down to a medical ward tomorrow."

Kazakov exhaled and hadn't realized that he'd been holding his breath. "Good to hear. May I see him?"

Her lips pressed in a line as if she realized that he likely wouldn't leave until he was satisfied of the young detective's health. She stood up and hooked her head at him to follow and led him down the hall. Chelomeyev's room was dark, but the dials of the equipment around him showed where he was. As before, the three other beds in the room were empty.

Kazakov crossed to the bed. The covers rose and fell slowly over the young man's chest. As before, his head was swathed in bandages so

Kazakov could barely see his face. He nodded at the nurse and led her back to the doorway.

"Now you need to listen to me. There is a very good chance that there may be an attempt on this patient's life. I've requested a police guard, but I was hoping you could get security up here until they arrive."

Her gaze met his and must have read his concern. She gave a quick nod. "I can do that."

Relief washed through him. That was something.

"Okay. I'll be back in a little while, but first I need to check on someone else." He left her calling security from the nursing station and hurried to the elevators and back out to the night and the Perseus.

There was someone else who might know what Mura Stepanova had known. Someone who had no police guard or hospital staff to protect her.

Starting the vehicle, he turned the Perseus toward the warehouse district and Chelomeyev's home, then started a slow cruise down the darkened side streets. Mura Stepanova had been a youngster and clearly under the direction of Raisa, the blonde prostitute.

He spotted two women on a darkened corner and pulled up beside them. The two women gave his vehicle a once over and turned away.

"Hey!" he called. "Have you seen Raisa?"

One of the women, a dark-haired woman with leathery skin over bone dressed in skintight pants and a down jacket, open to show off overlarge breasts in a halter top, sashayed over to him.

"Raisa wouldn't want the business of one like you."

He held up his badge. "Someone's out to kill her. Now, have you seen her tonight?"

The leather-skinned woman looked to her friend, a blonde with big hair and an impossibly short mini skirt.

"She usually works a couple of blocks over. I haven't seen her tonight."

Kazakov paid the women for their time and headed to the identified streets. He was only a few blocks from Chelomeyev's apartment.

The street was dark. Few streetlights were in place and those that were had broken lights. The darkness bloomed darker in dark corners, but surely Raisa wouldn't be hiding. Unless someone had already come looking for her. If so, he suspected she would simply disappear until a body turned up somewhere.

He turned down the next block and spotted a lone, slim figure on the next corner. He accelerated down the block and caught the flash of blonde hair in his headlights. Raisa.

He pulled over and climbed out.

"What do you want?" From across the Perseus she faced him with her hands on her hips. "Haven't you caused enough problems? You scared Mura off."

"Mura's dead." He didn't bother softening the news. "Someone killed her for what she knew. There's a good chance they're coming for you, too."

"What the hell are you talking about?"

He rounded the Perseus and stepped up close enough that her cheap perfume caught his nose. "I'm saying that Mura's body is sitting in the morgue. She was beaten and killed. Her friend Chelomeyev was beaten and left for dead and two men tried for me today. I'm saying that anyone associated with this case has a target on their back. You were Mura's friend. She likely told you everything. At least that's what I think and I'm just a simple cop. The people who killed her aren't stupid. They'll come to the same conclusion."

She looked away to the deserted street, but from the street fronting Chelomeyev's apartment came the sound of a car engine. She shivered and wrapped her arms around herself.

"I don't know anything," she said softly.

"You keep saying that when they come for you."

Her jaded gaze jerked back to him. "Mura wasn't smart enough to keep her mouth shut. I am."

Kazakov sighed. "I don't think that matters anymore. Not to them. They're in clean-up mode and that means taking care of all the loose ends. You and I are still dangling."

She closed her eyes and in the starlight he could see that once she had been young and pretty, just as he had been young and hopeful once. Now, for both of them, the years had changed things.

"You know how these things work, Raisa. Girl causes a problem. Girl disappears. Mura's just the latest. Do you want to be added to the roll of unclaimed bodies?"

Her headshake was barely perceptible, but it was enough. He opened the passenger rear door for her. "Climb in and let's talk. You tell me what you know and we'll figure out some place safe for you to go."

She studied him for a moment and then shook her head. "White knights can end up dead, too, you know."

"Apparently. But so far I've had an aversion to dying."

She raised a brow at him, but ducked inside the Perseus and settled back on the seat where Mura herself had sat not too long ago.

Kazakov rounded the car and climbed in behind the wheel. He pulled away from the curb and aimed the Perseus toward downtown. "Tell me about Mura. What did she know that made her a risk?"

She swore. "It was what she didn't know that was the problem. The girl didn't understand that to stay alive and be useful she had to keep her eyes and her mouth shut." She shook her head, but when Kazakov glanced at her, there was pain in her eyes. "She was so young. She hadn't even given up hope yet."

"But she was on the street with you."

The cold air swirled around them as she nodded almost imperceptibly. "I was supposed to keep her safe—to teach her." Then she shook her head. "No. I will not feel sad for Mura. Perhaps it is what she wanted. She did not like this life." She looked him right in the eyes. "So what is it you want to know, Mr. Police Officer?"

She tried her best whore's come-on look. Kazakov looked back to the road, black and shiny between the snow-clad curbs.

"What did she know that made her so dangerous that she had to be killed?" Let Raisa determine what that might be. She wasn't stupid. Few of the women he'd met in this business were, and a survivor like Raisa certainly wasn't.

She sighed. "There was a party. A number of girls were invited.

Mura didn't stay where we were told to. She went looking for a bathroom. When she came back she was wide-eyed and scared. She said we had to leave, so we did. Our master wasn't happy when he heard. He beat both of us. But Mura didn't seem to care. It was like something had infected her brain. A few nights later, Mura had a bad date. Before I could stop her, she'd called the cops and a young detective came. He lived nearby. Tall, blond. Mura was smitten. She not only complained about the beating, but told him what she'd heard the few nights before. That was when I learned what had happened."

She pulled her faux fur jacket around her, but her teeth were chattering even though he had the Perseus's heaters on full. He needed to get her indoors and safe. The question was where. Clearly the dacha was compromised.

"She said that when she looked for the washroom, she found herself outside an office. Three men were inside who she didn't know, but she said they looked important because at least one was a Russian and wore a suit and tie, and his shoes were new and shiny. What caught her attention was the mention of bomb explosions. She thought they were talking about a war and stopped to listen instead of minding her own business. She said the men weren't talking about something that had already happened—they were talking about something in the future. A few small explosions using explosive that one of the men had arranged to have stolen from his business, and another larger explosion. They said that should get the people's attention and get the votes they needed."

Kazakov's hands tightened on the wheel. It was what Clinton had suspected was happening and it brought two of the cases and Chelomeyev's beating together.

He guided the Perseus farther into the city.

"Where are we going?" Raisa asked.

"The one place I can think of that you might be safe. The police station."

The back seat went silent, except for Raisa's rapid breathing, but at least she wasn't arguing the point.

He turned down the streets toward the center of the city and turned the Perseus into the police station garage.

"No," she said softly. In the rearview mirror she was shaking her head. "No!" More vehement. "Stop the vehicle! I'm not going there!"

Before he could brake, Raisa yanked the door handle and shoved it open. She tumbled out onto the wet pavement, then scrambled up and ran.

Kazakov swore and slammed on the brakes, then leapt out after her.

Raisa disappeared into the darkness beyond the garage ramp. Kazakov ran after, but by the time he reached the street, Raisa was nowhere to be seen.

Damnation! She was as good as dead out there. Didn't she understand that? And he needed her evidence for anyone to believe his allegations. Why couldn't she have trusted him?

Because even with her evidence, it was likely that people would doubt a prostitute's hearsay story. Not all the police in New Moscow could protect her from that. Telling her story wouldn't make her anymore a target than she already was, but surviving on her own was what she had always done. Police—no matter the risk—were always her enemy.

Panting, he shook his head and returned to the Perseus. He drove it down to a parking stall, then went into the building to the detective squad room. No one was there. He went down to Rostoff's office, but as he expected, both the reception area and Rostoff's office were dark.

Returning to the squad room, he phoned down to dispatch to ask about Chelomeyev.

"Dispatch," the voice said.

"Detektiv Kazakov here. I'm checking on the protection detail for Chelomeyev."

There was silence a moment and the sound of shuffling papers. "I don't have anything like that on the record. I just came on shift, though."

Kazakov slammed the phone down and ran for the elevator. Hospital security might help, but only as a stopgap measure. When he reached the Perseus he pulled out his phone, called dispatch back, and demanded Rostoff's home phone number. When they hesitated, he swore at them and asked for their supervisor. Another voice came over the phone.

"Who is this?" the voice demanded.

He told them. "There is an injured officer in Our Lady Yekaterina hospital and I have reason to believe his life is in jeopardy. Detektiv Inspector Rostoff is not in and your dispatch officer will not send a protective detail to the hospital."

"Proper protocol demands senior officer approval to pull men off the road on protective detail," said the voice.

"Listen, you contact Rostoff and ask him. Tell him the investigation that matters has gone another direction. Tell him Chelomeyev's a key witness. Tell him I'll be at the hospital protecting him."

"Shit. Rostoff's going to bite my head off," the supervisor said.

"Live dangerously!" Kazakov signed off and tossed the phone on the blood-stained seat beside him as he accelerated down the road. The night air froze his nose, and frost from his breath formed on his lashes. He was shivering by the time he slid into the parking lot by the hospital.

He left the Perseus cockeyed across two parking spaces and leapt up the stairs to the front door. Someone called his name as he burst inside and crossed to the elevator and up to Chelomeyev's floor.

The ward corridor was silent and his footfall sounded overloud, as did the beep-beep-beep of medical monitors. At the nurses' station there was no one around.

He swore and continued on to Chelomeyev's room.

The bed was empty.

It couldn't be. Chelomeyev had been here. He was sure of it. Still, he stepped outside and checked the rooms to either side. One held an elderly man whose slow sucking breath spoke of death hovering. The other room was empty, too.

He backed out to the hall.

"You shouldn't be here."

The voice spun him around and left him facing the same red-haired nurse he'd spoken with earlier.

"Where's Chelomeyev?"

She gave a small nod. "No longer here."

He almost grabbed her. "I can see that. Where is he?" Panic fluttered in his gut. If he had lost Chelomeyev…

"I discussed your warning with my supervisor. It was decided to move him downstairs immediately and not bother with security. I told that to the other officers. Perhaps the information could be shared…"

Other officers?

"Derr'mo! How long ago?"

The nurse frowned and checked her watch. "Perhaps fifteen minutes."

"Where?" Fifteen minutes and the men would have to assess Chelomeyev's situation before they moved. At least they would if they wanted to keep their attack clean.

She told him and he turned and bolted along the hall, found a stairwell, and bounded down a floor and in through the emergency exit. He stopped and breathed in the scent of antiseptic underscored with the scent of human feces and urine. The groans of the sick cut through the quiet. He looked left and right. If this floor was laid out the same as the unit upstairs, then Chelomeyev's room would be to his left.

He opened his coat and set out to the left, his hand on his concealed weapon. When he reached the nurses' station he knew that something was wrong. A slender leg was all he could see sticking out from a file table. He pulled out his gun and went past, fighting to keep his heavy boots silent on the linoleum.

At the door to Chelomeyev's room, he heard movement. Where the fuck was security? He chanced a peek around the doorframe. Two figures loomed over Chelomeyev's comatose figure—no one he knew from New Moscow Police. The one facing the door saw Kazakov.

Kazakov drew his weapon as the other man's gun hand came up. "Drop your weapons! Hands up! New Moscow Police!"

The other man's gun kept rising. The second man grabbed a pillow and smothered Chelomeyev's face.

"Drop your weapons!"

The attacker's gun steadied.

Kazakov fired. The gun's explosion echoed in the halls.

Kazakov's bullet hit the attacker high in the chest. The man staggered back, his shot burning past Kazakov into the corridor behind him. Screams came from one of the patient rooms as Kazakov took another shot at the man with the pillow.

He staggered, but kept on with his task. The man with the gun lurched upright and shot. Kazakov fell back behind the doorway, then leaned in low, aimed and pulled the trigger.

The bullet threw the shooter against the wall. He went down hard and didn't move, but the man with the pillow turned with a gun. Kazakov shot him dead center.

The man went down.

Kazakov pushed past the fallen men to Chelomeyev's bedside. He pulled the pillow from the young detective's face. Was he all right? Was he breathing?

Kazakov bent down and felt the faintest of breath against his cheek. He needed help and looked for his phone, then remembered that he'd left it in the Perseus. He ran back to the nurses' station and found two bodies. Young nurses with necks broken, their eyes like broken saucers. He looked past them and grabbed the phone, got the switchboard, and ordered them to call the police. "There's been a shooting. Two staff and two suspects dead." He demanded security attend Chelomeyev's ward.

When he hung up, the place ached around him. Silence punctuated by calls for help from frightened patients. He hurried back to Chelomeyev's room. Yes, the young man was still living. In fact his color was better than Kazakov had seen it. Some bandages had been removed from his face and though the bruises were hideous, it was still Chelomeyev.

Kazakov sagged against the bed in relief. From the ward he heard the ding of the elevator and heavy treads. He stepped out of Chelomeyev's room.

Two security officers faced him, guns ready.

Kazakov placed his weapon on the floor and raised his hands. "I'm Detektiv Kazakov. I called it in. You've got two nurses down in the station and two men in here." He nodded at the door behind him and backed a step away.

One man checked the ward station while the other held Kazakov in his sights.

"Two down. He's right," one guard said to the other.

They approached down the hall and went to collect Kazakov's weapon.

"Leave it. It will need to be examined by the police. There should be two more weapons in the room by the bodies. But I'm concerned that the patient needs help. They were trying to smother him."

The two guards looked into the room and then eyed him. "You took them down yourself?" one of them asked. The other used a radio to call for medical help.

Kazakov nodded. "There was no one else. Detektiv Chelomeyev is a witness in a difficult case. Someone didn't want his evidence coming out."

Two uniformed New Moscow PD officers arrived and took control of the scene. Kazakov found a chair and waited for the detectives to attend. Finally Razin and Pogolin arrived and the M.E.—a woman named Alyona Nickolaev—arrived from downstairs.

Pogolin took Kazakov aside. "Tell me again how you knew to come here," Pogolin asked, his stubble of silver-black hair like a fog around his skull. The odor of old, wet wool rose off his coat and his breath stank of the garlic and onions of his dinner.

Kazakov shook his head. "It is a case Rostoff asked me to look into. Actually, it is three cases and Chelomeyev turns out to be the key. Other than that, I cannot say until I make my report to Rostoff."

Pogolin's gaze clouded. "You expect me to tell Rostoff to simply wait for you to come in?"

Kazakov held his gaze. "Yes. Tell him what has happened. Tell him Chelomeyev is key to solving the case he is most concerned about. Tell him I had phone calls to make and will see him in the morning to provide a complete statement."

Before Pogolin could protest, he pushed past the detective for the elevator.

21

The night air had chilled further, and there was no protection when Kazakov climbed into the Perseus. The tree branches rattled in the small park across the parking lot. The sound of city traffic was much diminished here. It was eleven at night, and across New Moscow, people were settling in for the night; most probably didn't even appreciate the starlit heavens spread over them. But then the lights of the city diminished the stars just as Ferganese culture seemed to dim the Russian ability to see beyond their small city and country.

All except a few who were prepared to take advantage of the Ferganese failing. Of course, he'd suffered from blindness recently, too. He'd put the same blinders on that he'd thought limited other detectives, and he'd allowed them to misguide him into focusing on the Ivanov murder as the reason behind the attack on Chelomeyev. As if the people in the other cases were beneath his notice.

If he hadn't been so blind, Mura Stepanova might still be alive, Clinton might not have been shot, and the case of the explosions might have been solved instead of left hanging with too much explosive threatening the city. Actually, he wasn't sure whether the explosives were the biggest threat. The entire fabric of the city was unraveling under the influence of people like Bure—who suggested that Fergana's original tribal people were the source of all the country's problems—and, quite possibly, the influence of people like Enver Pasha on those same tribal people. They were creating a weakness in the weave of Fergana. It seemed like it would only take one tug and the whole thing might come undone.

So Bure's work and that of Enver Pasha might not be in concert, but would result in the same end. As Clinton feared, Fergana would leave its neutrality behind and the entire world would suffer for it.

At least Chelomeyev had the potential to give information that could deal with the threat of the explosives. And Kazakov had solved the question of Chelomeyev's beating, and Raisa's information pointed at the perpetrator of the thefts of the explosives. The owner of the company could also likely shed more light on the situation, as well.

That left the Ivanov murder to solve. Kazakov tapped the Perseus's steering wheel and let his breath wreathe around his face. Then he sighed and picked up the phone and dialed a number he didn't want to call. He should have made the call while he was still warm inside the hospital.

Annuschka picked up on the second ring. "Hello?"

Her cool voice sent a shiver down Kazakov's spine. "Thank you for taking my call."

"I was up."

He nodded to himself. "You always were a night owl."

"And you prefer the day. What can this night owl do for you at this hour?"

He could imagine her draped in the long, green, silk robe he had bought her, though it had been one of the things she'd left behind in the divorce. Proof once more that he didn't really know her.

"When we spoke, you said that you saw Svetlana Ivanova twice over the time the roads into the mountains were closed. Have I remembered rightly?" He had his notes, but he needed to check Annuschka's truthfulness and memory.

"That is correct. We met her and Olga Gruenwald on the street the day they arrived and had lunch together. Then a few nights later, we picked Svetlana up and had her over for dinner."

"And Olga as well? They were traveling together..." He let the question fall casually.

"Actually, no. It was just Svetlana. We had invited them both, but Olga had been taken ill—the flu or some such. She stuck close to their house for the rest of their trip and only emerged when the roads finally opened. Poor dear. She missed wonderful skiing."

"So you didn't see Olga the rest of your trip? Svetlana didn't reciprocate your dinner invitation?"

He heard her chuckle through the phone, the same throaty laugh that had always tightened his groin. This time it didn't work.

"Of course she did, you silly thing. Svetlana is the consummate hostess. She hosted a dinner when the roads were open and Enver Pasha arrived at his home in thanks for his hospitality in opening his home to her. I saw Olga then. Thankfully, she looked fully recovered."

"And what day was this party?"

There was silence a moment. Perhaps Annuschka checked her social calendar. He tapped his fingers on the frigid steering wheel and tried to turn up the Perseus's heater. It was already as high as it got and couldn't keep up with the cold streaming in the shattered windshield. He needed to get indoors because his nose was painful and his cheeks stung. Even his gloved fingers were tingling.

"It was January fourth, the day the road opened. That was how Enver was able to be there."

Kazakov brooded on the information. "In your time there, was Svetlana driving? You mentioned that you picked her up..."

"Actually, Svetlana doesn't like driving in snow, so when Olga took ill, we picked her up every day."

"Did you see her vehicle? Their vehicle?"

She was silent a moment. "Why all these questions, Alexander?"

"Just answer the question. It is for my investigation."

He heard her sigh and the clinking of ice cubes. A drink. Alcohol always mellowed her. "Enver Pasha has a garage, as do most of the rich in Biysk. He would not want his vehicle left out in the cold."

More like he wouldn't want anyone knowing his movements and when he was at home. Kazakov pondered that a moment.

"Thank you. You've been very helpful, Annuschka. It was good to see you today. You look like life is treating you well."

"Very well, in fact, thank you. You—you looked the same, Alexander. Always so driven regardless what the world does to you."

"That is me." He shrugged in the car. "I got the impression you've become involved in politics. Did I read that correctly?"

There was a pause that went on a little too long at the end of the phone. "I offer advice and expertise to friends, if that is what you mean."

"Ah. Non-partisan involvement, then, to anyone who comes asking. Your communications training must make you in demand. What was it you did your dissertation on?"

"Effective strategies in influencing the behavior of large populations." Her voice had changed and become more guarded.

"So interesting," he said. "Vladimir Kimkin must find you a particular asset."

There was silence a moment more. "We find common ground where we can."

"Ahh. And now I should let you go to spend your evening as you will. Thank you for your help. It has been nice talking to you again."

He hung up without waiting for her answering goodbye and sat shivering for a moment before leaving the hospital and taking the Perseus back to the New Moscow police station. He left his damaged vehicle there and claimed a replacement weapon and an unmarked sedan before going home again.

He knew what he had to do in the morning.

He woke the next morning from dreams of white flesh and an arrow quivering in the earth. Whether the arrow had just impaled itself or had been touched and then abandoned he didn't know, but in his heart he thought it was the latter. No one would come to the rescue because the impaled arrow said the arrow owner was okay.

He rolled over and felt the small, warm lump that was Koshka beside him. She mewed plaintively and then stood and stretched before walking over him and leaping down to the floor. Her next mew demanded food.

He pulled the covers up higher.

Another insistent mew and he opened one eye. The dacha's one room was filled with sunlight again. The plain wood walls gleamed golden and dust motes danced in the air, but his breath condensed in the air. He'd obviously slept long and hard and the fire had burned low. Koshka was seated by the kitchen cupboard where her crunchies lived. She mewed again.

He rolled over and threw off the covers, instantly regretting it in the cool air. He padded to the fireplace by the kitchen table and stirred the embers to life, then added kindling and another log. Soon the tick-tick-tick of the stove's heating metal joined the roar of air up the metal chimney. Then he filled Koshka's dish and washed his face in the sink. Tomorrow would be a bath day with all the challenges of heating water that such a thing entailed. Looking down at his bruised body, the challenges would be worth it.

He dressed in his suit and a clean white shirt, then enjoyed a quick meal of black bread toasted over the fire and slabs of sausage. Feeling mildly distrustful of his borrowed weapon, he pulled on boots and his coat and hat and headed out to the police sedan. The day was bright, the still air icy cold so that ice crystals placed a triple rainbow around the sun. He pulled down the ear flaps on his hat and hiked up his collar against the cold that tried to eat right through him.

The drive into town was uneventful, the roads surprisingly clear of traffic. The subdivisions were silent rows of houses, chimneys leaking smoke that puddled above the rooftops like bleak thoughts. The number of vehicles in driveways reminded him it was Saturday and he checked his watch. Nine o'clock.

He pulled out his phone and dialed a number.

"Hello," Kasimir Krupin's voice sounded old and tired.

"Hello. It is Detektiv Kazakov calling. I wondered whether it might be convenient for me to come and speak to your wife."

Krupin didn't answer, but Kazakov heard Margarete Krupin's voice demanding to know who was calling.

Krupin put his hand over the phone for their conversation was muffled.

Finally Krupin came back on and sighed. "My wife says to come, but I will tell you—against her wishes—that she has had a difficult night. I must ask that you not stay long."

Kazakov agreed and headed toward the Krupin residence, stopping once at a flower shop near Yekaterina Park for a bouquet of fresh flowers.

When he arrived at the weathered house with the rundown yard, he picked his way up the icy walk to the front porch. Krupin must have been waiting, for he answered immediately.

"I'm truly sorry to disturb your peace," Kazakov said as he wiped his boots and stepped inside.

Krupin shook his head, his mess of gray hair even more wild than usual. Large dark circles hollowed his eyes. "She would not have it any other way."

Though, clearly, he would.

Clutching his bouquet, Kazakov followed Krupin to Margarete's room in the made-over library. She sat up in her bed, but even in the short time since he'd last seen her, Margarete Krupin had moved closer to death's door. The skin of her face seemed to barely cover her skull and even a light touch of makeup and a bright blue turban couldn't hide her pallor. Her shrunken form seemed further diminished by the breadth of the bed, and her thin hands fidgeted on the bedcovers as if they could not stop for fear of never moving again.

"Detektiv," she said with a smile. "You could not stay away? Perhaps you have more questions for me?" There was a slight rise to her brow as if daring him. Then her gaze settled on the flowers and lit with pleasure. "For me? How thoughtful. Someone raised you properly, it seems."

She nodded at Kasimir to take them and he disappeared out the door with the flowers, for a vase and water most likely.

"Now what can I do for you?" Margarete asked.

Kazakov met her gaze. "Last time I was here we spoke of Svetlana Ivanova."

She nodded.

"You told me that she had a lover."

"Yes. There were all the signs to those who were looking."

"And yet you also told me that you didn't know the name of her lover."

Her gaze turned expectant. Her fidgeting stopped.

"No." Kazakov held up a hand. "Let me rephrase that. You said that you knew of no man's name. That was the truth, wasn't it? Because her lover was a woman."

Margarete dropped her gaze to her hands and nodded. "I wondered if you would realize. I—I did not want to spread rumors."

"Do you know who the woman was?"

Margarete sighed and smoothed the coverlet on her bed. "You know already, don't you?"

"I think so, but I would like you to say the name."

"Olga Gruenwald. The two of them became inseparable. She— Olga—is a strange one. A servant of Enver Pasha and yet something else again. There is a—an edge to the woman—a toughness. She hides it most of the time, but every now and again, you see a flash of ruthlessness. Like her employer, I suppose."

She settled her head back against her pillows, her eyes closed, and he could see death's fingers settle in the hollows of her face and clavicle. No matter that Kasimir Krupin wished to bring her back, there was no arrow to be found for Margarete Krupin.

"I'll leave you to get some rest. Thank you, Margarete, for all your help."

This time she didn't open her eyes, nor did she clasp his hand. Instead her lips curved in a slight smile. "I hope you'll come back. I hope there is time."

Kasimir Krupin returned with the flowers displayed in a vase. He settled them on a table where Margarete would see them as soon as she woke. Their perfume spread through the room, dispelling less pleasant scents. Then he urged Kazakov out of the room.

"Thank you for the flowers. She will enjoy them."

"Thank you for letting me see her. She's very weak."

Kasimir looked away. "Hopefully she will have a better day tomorrow."

"She is a great lady," Kazakov said at the door. "Please keep me informed as to how she is doing. I would like to come see her again. To bring her more flowers and make her smile."

Krupin nodded as Kazakov stepped outside. The door closed silently behind him.

The still air left him saddened, even though the day was bright. It was eleven in the morning and though Enver Pasha's office had set an appointment for the afternoon, he turned the police sedan toward the crescent that edged Potemkin Park and Enver Pasha's white-pillared house.

The paths of Yekaterina Park had been left uncleared so there were no walkers on this bright sunny day. Instead, the pines and aspens placed their slowly creeping, dark shadows across the snow as he pulled into the curb across from the tall windows of the Red Veil brothel. He climbed out of the vehicle and looked up at the brothel and then at Enver Pasha's house. It was like the two buildings loomed toward each other but never touched. They reminded him of the two brooding embassies he'd seen just yesterday.

Fitting, he supposed, given the brothel had housed a Chinese spy and he strongly suspected Enver Pasha spied for his Ottoman government.

He clumped across the street and up the stairs to Enver Pasha's house and knocked on the heavy wooden door. There came a flicker of lace curtain in the parlor window and then the door opened slightly. Olga Gruenwald stood there dressed immaculately in a pair of draped cream trousers and a simple blouse and cardigan to match.

"Detektiv? What are you doing here?" she asked through the four inches of space she allowed.

"I need to speak with Enver Pasha. Now."

He took her hesitation as confirmation that he was here and as permission to enter. He pushed inside and Olga fell back, though he was sure she could have put up a fight if she wanted. It was not his favorite way to work, but work it did. He stood in the broad foyer with its gleaming wood floors and bouquet of lilies on a table that put his meager bouquet for Margarete to shame.

"Well?" he asked, turning to hold her with his gaze.

She looked away before he did. "I—I will tell him you are here."

Her neat brown heels tapped on the floor as she left him to climb the broad mahogany stairs. He watched her cross the balcony above the foyer and then looked around. The soft sound of a radio from the back of the house suggested perhaps Svetlana was there. Not a surprise. These three—they were in this together. His task was to loosen the tongue of one of them.

A few minutes later, footfall came from above and Enver Pasha strode across the balcony to the stairs. He wore gray wool trousers and a soft gray wool polo shirt that looked as if it cost more than Kazakov's whole wardrobe.

"Detektiv. What brings about this pleasure?" Enver Pasha asked as he started down the stairs. Soft-soled black shoes covered his feet.

"I have a need to continue our conversation."

"And it could not wait until our appointment this afternoon? You caught me just out of the shower after a workout." Enver Pasha shook Kazakov's hand.

Indeed, the man's hair was damp and his skin held the healthy glow of exercise. The faint scent of incense came off of his clothes, or perhaps it was his skin. Kazakov really needed to get more exercise, too, but cases like this got in the way.

"It could not wait."

Enver Pasha cocked a brow in question, but Kazakov refused to say more until they were in private.

"My office is this way," Enver said with an incline of his head.

The door to the office was to the left off the hall to the rear of the house. The radio sounds were louder, a news program host clamoring about the need for a strong leader and a strong stance against the tribal terrorists. Enver Pasha ushered Kazakov past him into the office and then closed the door behind him with a shake of his head. The radio sounds cut off.

"Innocents are going to pay for this rhetoric," he said and crossed to his desk. He sank down in a high-backed leather chair and steepled his long-fingered hands. "Now how can I help you, Detektiv?"

As if Kazakov was the supplicant.

He supposed most of the men who faced Enver Pasha across this desk were just that. Just as at his business, Enver Pasha's home office was designed to reinforce that impression. Tall bookshelves filled the walls of the room that would have held three times the space of his dacha. Each shelf held the soft patina of gold embossed, leather-bound, regimentally ordered volumes. Probably expensive, and Enver Pasha gave the impression that he was the kind of man who would have read all of them. The wall behind the desk was bare of shelves, instead holding a magnificent abstract tile mosaic of vivid blues, reds, and golds that drew the eye from the edges toward the center where Enver Pasha's desk chair imposed on the view of the wall.

A perfect optical illusion to scare the hell out of the businessman seeking help. Even the position of the chair facing the desk appeared strategic to give the supplicant the full power of Enver Pasha's position. Enver Pasha casually shifted the chair and sat down, smiling.

"Actually, it is what I can do for you." Kazakov sat back in his chair. He thought a moment. He had rehearsed this scene on the drive into town, taking what he knew and adding what he suspected to his story. "As you know, I have been conducting an investigation into the death of Grigori Ivanov, an exclusive purveyor of American tobacco."

The sweet scent of incense seemed to fill the room as Enver Pasha sat waiting impassively. His dark eyes glittered in the light that came from the tall windows between the bookshelves on one wall and a single large wrought iron chandelier.

"In the course of my investigation, it became clear that there are a number of companies trying to fill the void left by the death. It has also come to my attention that Transcontinental is one of them and probably figures to benefit from its already well-established transport routes and expand those routes into the one area Transcontinental has been less successful in—routes into and across America. An exclusive deal with the United States of America would provide a stronger foothold on the continent. Am I right?"

Enver Pasha's expression had gone stony. He gave a sharp nod. "Transcontinental is always interested in expanding its network of services."

"How interested? I have friends who are investigating rumors of bribery within the American Embassy. And then there is Ivanov's death —that certainly worked to your benefit. But then I see that Transcontinental is not one of the finalists in the running for the monopoly." He shook his head. "It must be a great loss for you."

Enver Pasha abruptly stood up. "I will not have you come into my home and virtually accuse me of murder. Not when you yourself say that I have not benefited from Ivanov's death."

Kazakov stayed where he was and looked up mildly at his host. "I was not accusing anyone—yet." He looked down at his hands as if reading from a notebook. "You are a man who works very hard for your business. You put in long hours. It must take a terrible toll on you and your social life."

His host settled slowly back into his chair, the leather sighing under him.

"I have employees."

"Yes. Yes, you do. I met a few of your security officers. And then there is Olga. A most lovely and efficient woman, it seems." He motioned around the room. "Her work, I believe?"

A small frown line formed between Enver Pasha's brows.

"She introduced herself as your housekeeper. Your home is pristine."

Enver Pasha nodded.

"She must have worked for you for a very long time."

"A few years." Enver Pasha gripped the edge of his desk. "What does this have to do with Ivanov's death?"

Kazakov shook his head. "Bear with me. I am simply trying to get the facts clear in my head. Tell me, you are a very busy man, you have just confirmed this. Why did you drive up to the mountains to help out a woman who is only your housekeeper and her friend?"

Enver Pasha shrugged. "Simple, really. They needed a ride. The roads had just opened and they were scared to drive."

Kazakov held his gaze and waited. It was Enver Pasha who looked away first.

"But why not send an employee? I am trying to understand. Surely your time is more valuable than that. It is not many businessmen who are at their employee's beck and call."

Another shrug and a shake of the head. Kazakov smiled inwardly. He was getting to the man.

"It seemed like a good idea at the time. I needed a break and a drive into the mountains seemed the perfect thing."

"I see. It is a long trip to take alone."

Enver Pasha watched him warily.

"But then you were not alone, were you? Olga drove back up with you after she came into the city to kill Ivanov. She just hadn't figured on the snowstorm that would strand her in the city. So she and Svetlana concocted the story that she was sick and Svetlana kept up the ruse until you could come to 'rescue' them." He finger-painted the quotation marks.

Before Enver Pasha could respond, Kazakov continued. "No vehicle was seen in the mountains while Svetlana was on her own. In fact, she was picked up by friends and driven everywhere on the understanding that she does not like to drive in snow. And then there is the fact that Svetlana was known to be unhappy in her marriage, but then things changed when she took a lover—Olga. Her life changed then and she was happy again, but she had a problem. A husband who was very controlling. The business paid for expenses and they lived well enough, but it could not survive if she asked for a divorce and the business was split between the two of them. As a result, it was highly unlikely that she would get much if they separated. But there was one way to get the money that would allow her and Olga to enjoy her freedom—if the business and the rights to the American tobacco trade were sold."

He paused and simply looked at Enver Pasha. Neither man stirred and Kazakov could admire the strength inside Enver Pasha. Other men would squirm. Other men would ask questions. Other men would deny that Olga Gruenwald's actions had anything to do with them.

"The way I see it," Kazakov continued. "I have two choices. On the one hand I can produce the evidence that links Ivanov's death back to the person who might ultimately benefit the most from the death through two subsidiary companies that he has paid men to hold on his behalf. Or I can stop now and confine my evidence to the obvious— Svetlana and Olga were in love and Olga killed Ivanov to free Svetlana. All I need is evidence that she had returned to the city and then drove with you back to the mountains. Her alibi is gone then, and so is Svetlana's."

He felt the weight of Enver Pasha's regard. The man pursed his lips and steepled his hands, which must be his expression when assessing a deal. The nod, when it came, was almost imperceptible.

"Olga Gruenwald rode up to the mountains with me." He shoved up from his chair and went to the window. "I knew something wasn't right, but I couldn't put my finger on it. She asked me not to say anything…" He turned back to Kazakov, a mask of contrition on his face. "What can I say? Olga—she had an important place in my household. She was—very useful."

Kazakov could imagine. He had always known the woman was more than a housekeeper. Now his thoughts wandered wide to— assassin? Perhaps even paid to become Svetlana's lover? But now she was no longer an asset.

"I will need your statement."

Returning to his desk, Enver Pasha pulled out a pad of lined paper and a gold shafted fountain pen. "I will write one for you."

Kazakov sat back. He had Ivanov's killers, just not the man ultimately behind them.

22

———————

The hospital ward smelled of urine and antiseptic. The clear bag of yellow fluid hanging from Chelomeyev's bed explained the first. The small Kyrgyz cleaning woman with the gray hair and furtive gaze sweeping a damp mop across the floor explained the other. It had been three weeks since the young detective's beating and still there was no sign of recovery—at least to Kazakov's eye. The nurses said there were encouraging signs—Chelomeyev had begun to murmur in his sleep and open his eyes—but when Kazakov had been there on one such occasion, there had been no Pavel Chelomeyev in the young man's gaze.

Kazakov checked his watch because the curtains were drawn so the room was lit only by fluorescent bars across the ceiling. It was as if he sat in a tomb of kings, the four comatose patients in the room were so silent. Two of the patients on the four-person ward had changed, the previous occupants stolen away in the night. They had forgotten to loosen their arrows before they slept.

He caught Chelomeyev's hand and squeezed. "But you did not, young friend. You pulled your arrow loose when you came to me, only it took me this long to remember. You told me you had two cases to discuss, but I was too caught in myself to hear. I'm sorry. But I will be here for you and I will see the full investigation through to the end. I will find the bastards who paid those mu'dak who beat you. You wait. You and I will investigate together yet."

At least he would be here waiting when Chelomeyev woke. It was more than he could say about Eric Clinton. Neither Kazakov nor Khan had been able to gain any information about the health status of the American spy. Kazakov wasn't sure whether he hoped the man lived or died. Fergana didn't need more foreigners meddling in the country's future. Still… the man had provided Kazakov with a warning of what was at stake with the explosions and the upcoming election. The possibilities left him feeling sick for his country—and the future of the world.

A footstep in the corridor caused him to check the door. An unexpected heavyset shadow blocked the light from the doorway. The figure removed his hat and stepped into the room.

Detektiv Chief Inspektor Rostoff looked uncomfortable in his surroundings as he glanced around and then crossed to Kazakov. He nodded.

After the arrest of Olga Gruenwald and Svetlana Ivanova on the strength of Enver Pasha's statement, Kazakov had spent time briefing Rostoff on how he'd learned Chelomeyev's beating and the death of the young prostitute had been the work of the two men killed at his dacha. The evidence from the dead Russian girl, Mura, suggested it was Russians, not Kyrgyz behind the bombings.

At first Rostoff had been skeptical because the information was hearsay and therefore unreliable, but then Raisa had contacted Kazakov. She was frightened. She was alone and terrified that someone was following her. When she'd come in, she had told her story to the Detektiv Chief Inspektor. Now Rostoff was grudgingly willing to consider the possibility that Russians were involved in the bombings and Raisa was in protective custody in a safe house.

The challenge was that they needed the corroboration of her story from Chelomeyev. Hopefully the young detective could also tell them who Mura had seen engaged in the conversation regarding the plans for the explosives. Then they could move in on the perpetrators and hopefully work back to the people ultimately behind the explosions.

In the meantime, Kazakov was making very quiet enquiries.

"How is he doing?" Rostoff asked, nodding at Chelomeyev.

"It depends who you ask. The nurses tell me there is progress." Kazakov looked down at the bed and shook his head. The bandages had come off of Chelomeyev's head, but the discoloring lingered in a green pallor. Or it could just be the lighting. Either way, the only sign of life was the slow rise and fall of his chest and the slow, steady beep-beep-beep of his heart monitor.

"He was a good officer—one who showed much promise. His parents are devastated."

Kazakov nodded again, though he knew it wasn't true given his conversation with Chelomeyev senior. "I've run into his mother here a few times. She thanked me for coming, but I get the sense she'd rather I didn't come."

"To some, dying is a private thing," Rostoff said softly.

Kazakov stiffened. "He isn't dead yet. He might still wake."

Rostoff nodded. "Pray he does. We need his evidence if we're to have any hope of stopping whoever's behind this. The Raisa woman simply isn't a credible enough witness on her own."

Kazakov met his gaze.

That was the problem. There was so much that Kazakov knew or suspected and most of it he couldn't prove. The importance of the upcoming election in the fate of the world—at least as far as Clinton had been concerned. Enough to cause the American government to send in their spy. Enough for Enver Pasha to be here stirring the pot. Kazakov would have liked to charge the Ottoman at least with accessory to the murder for his role in transporting Olga Gruenwald back to Biysk and for supporting her alibi, but it seemed that having a solid case against the actual killers had been more important to Rostoff and the court system. However, there was still something niggling at Kazakov, something that didn't quite fit. The man had given up Svetlana and Olga too easily—as if he hoped giving up the women would stop Kazakov from asking more questions. Would he do that simply to consolidate his growing empire or was it something else?

Something to help the Ottoman Empire? Was Enver Pasha enough of a patriot or was he a man who only thought of himself? With a title like Pasha, the man had obviously proven himself. A patriot, then.

Looked through that lens, Kazakov had to reconsider the reasons behind the death of Grigori Ivanov. Not just for the money and tobacco monopoly. No, there was every possibility that the man had a connection to the Chinese. Derr'mo! With his Pan-Asia monopoly and his shipping practices, he could have been moving more than tobacco across the border.

Another suspicion about the Chinese for which he had no proof. Where else the Chinese were involved he didn't know, but he would bet they were also somehow supporting Bure's run for office. He needed proof of it and of Bure's involvement in backing the troublemakers who had caused the Kyrgyz demonstrations to turn violent. He'd started to use his contacts in the old city to get their version of what had happened at both events.

He glanced at Rostoff rocking on the balls of his feet as if he was counting off the seconds decency required him to remain in the hospital room. So far Kazakov had avoided mentioning Bure's name to his senior officer because he knew how Rostoff would react.

Kazakov needed evidence that clearly linked Bure to the rising unrest in the country as well as to the death of his stepdaughter. So far there wasn't enough to nail into the earth around the man—like arrow shafts—but one way or another, the time was coming. Kazakov's investigations were like that.

Maybe in a short time or maybe in a long time.

Inevitable.

Continue reading the first Chapter of *The Tsarina's Mask*, Book 3 in the Detektiv Kazakov Mysteries...

THE TSARINA'S MASK

Somewhere in holy mother Russia there lived a tsar who had a beautiful wife and a beautiful daughter who looked much like her mother. When his wife died, the tsar grieved deeply. Then he noticed how his daughter looked so much like his wife and determined to marry her. He came to his daughter and proposed marriage.

The princess was so upset that she went to her mother's grave and poured the story out. From beyond the grave the mother told her daughter to have a dress made covered with silver stars. The princess did as her mother bade, but when she wore the dress for her father, he proposed their marriage again.

Again, the princess went to her mother's grave and again poured out her story. Her mother told her to have a dress made with a silver moon on its back and the golden sun on its front. The princess did as bid and again her father told her that he loved her more than ever.

For a third time the princess went back to the graveyard to tell her tale. This time her mother told her to have a pig skin cloak made. The princess obeyed and this time her father was so incensed that he threw her out of the castle.

The princess wandered into the forest and when a young tsarevich *and his hunting party came by, the princess hid in the branches of a tree. The tsarevich's hunting dogs leapt at the tree and the tsarevich, being curious, sent his servant into the tree to see what had his dogs so upset.*

"What is it?" the tsarevich called to his servant.

"My Lord, there is some kind of beast in the tree—a marvelous wonder, a wonderful marvel."

"What manner of wonder are you?" the tsarevich demanded. "Can or can you not speak?"

"I am Pig Skin," the disguised princess replied.

"What a marvelous wonder! What a wonderful marvel!" the tsarevich said and brought her down from the tree and into his coach to take back to his palace to show his father and mother. He would keep the marvel there.

Voices outside the hospital room door interrupted Detektiv Alexander Kazakov's reading. He closed the book around his finger and inhaled the urine- and disinfectant-tanged air. The room was filled with shadow and lit only by a single spotlight that illuminated the page of the book of fairy tales he had been reading out loud to the comatose figure on the bed. Young, blond Detektiv Pavel Chelomeyev was still unconscious from a beating he had received a month ago.

The room contained three other beds, though they were thankfully now empty, their bedding pulled crisply across the mattresses, awaiting patients. Chelomeyev's bedding was pulled tight, too. Uncomfortably so for anyone who moved. It crossed the slow rise and fall of Chelomeyev's chest and tucked in around him as if he was a manikin or a children's life-size doll. On the other side of the bed the slow beep, beep, beep of the medical monitor was all that said that Chelomeyev still lived. Though the bandages that had swathed his head had been removed, the young detective was a shadow of his former self, his floppy head of pale hair shaved off and now growing out, the skin of his pale face seemingly pulled tight over bone and shadow. His lashes were dark crescents against the shadowed hollows of his eyes.

"There you are! Is this how you spend all your evenings? But then, don't tell me. I already know." Chief Detektiv Inspektor Valerian Rostoff filled the doorway just as his voice filled the room. An agitated nurse in white uniform stood behind him.

Kazakov stood—whether to greet his boss or to guard Chelomeyev from him, he wasn't certain.

Rostoff turned back to the nurse. "That is all. You can go. We have private matters to discuss." He waved her away and stepped into Chelomeyev's room.

Rostoff was a big man, a bear of a man in the old Russian style. Though he was only in his mid-forties like Kazakov, his ruddy face was marred by a bulbous nose veined like a drinker and deeply etched frown lines that dragged down his expression. He carried his fur hat, for the weather had changed for the better as the days lengthened in March, but he still wore his greatcoat. In the hospital heat it reeked of warm wool steeped with human sweat. He glanced over Kazakov's shoulder.

"Still unconscious, I see. A shame, really. The boy had promise. I hear his mother is most distraught."

Chelomeyev's father, a big man in the New Moscow Police Department, had done nothing to push the investigation into Chelomeyev's beating. Given what Kazakov had learned about the event, Chelomeyev Senior's inaction had filled Kazakov with concern —concern he had shared with Rostoff.

"Has promise," Kazakov corrected. "He is not dead and the doctors say there is no sign of brain damage. It is simply as if he has decided not to wake up."

"And so you spend your evenings here? Doing what?" Rostoff's gaze slid to the book in Kazakov's hand and yanked it loose. "Fairy tales? You read a detective fairy tales?"

"He studied literature in university and did his thesis on fairy tales. I thought they would bring him comfort," Kazakov said through gritted teeth. He, too, had always loved the old stories. "Now why are *you* here?"

Rostoff sniffed and dropped the book on the bedside. "There are better things to discuss over a man who cannot hear you." He shook his head again at Chelomeyev.

At least he was alive. That was the only blessing Kazakov could think of and the one he clung to. If he'd only listened to the young detective. If he'd only allowed him to finish his stories, there was every chance Chelomeyev would not be here. Kazakov sighed and looked back at Rostoff.

"What do you want? You wouldn't be here if you didn't want something."

Rostoff went to the door, checked the corridor and then pulled the door closed.

So something clearly had Rostoff spooked. The fact that he was here at all suggested that something was happening, though why he would come to Kazakov was a mystery. The two men had trained as police officers together, but beyond that they had nothing in common. Rostoff had used his connections and his propensity to be a 'fixer' to advance quickly, while Kazakov had become a detective with a nose for corruption and a high conviction rate, and that was where he wished to stay. He had refused to work with partners because few other detectives would put in the long hours that Kazakov would dedicate to his cases. Unfortunately, he made few friends of men like Rostoff who preferred to smooth over cases involving influential figures. By contrast, Kazakov was more concerned with truth.

"Have you been paying attention to the news?" Rostoff asked. He shifted uneasily to the room's lone window that looked out onto the parking lot and the dirty snow melting away in the park that fronted Our Lady Yekaterina Hospital.

"The news?" Kazakov pondered the question. "The election is only a month away." And all the polls said that the people of Fergana were most concerned about their security. Fergana was a small pimple of a country, caught between the superpowers of the Ottoman and Chinese empires. So far, that had worked to Fergana's advantage, because neither superpower dared to encroach on Fergana without rousing the ire of their great foe. But recent attacks in Fergana had raised the specter of domestic terrorism. The most recent had blown up the statue of beloved Tsarina Yekaterina. Her statue had stood in the central square of New Moscow as memorial for her leadership in the horrific diaspora of Russians after Moscow fell and holy mother Russia was lost. Their people had wandered through the Siberian wilderness until the kind tribal people of Fergana had taken them in.

In thanks, the Russians had gradually excluded the original people from the new Ferganese culture the Russians had built. Now some people were blaming the tribal people for the attacks and finding a solution had become an election hot potato.

"Is there some problem of Boris Bure's you now wish to solve?" asked Kazakov bitterly. Boris Bure was the current front runner in the election. He was also the stepfather of a recent sixteen-year-old murder victim and the father of her unborn child, but the evidence of this had been withheld—for now.

Rostoff turned back to him. "The man has power. We both know it. Better to remain on his good side, if a man wants a career."

Kazakov shook his head and felt sick to his stomach. He looked down at Chelomeyev. Was this what the New Moscow Police Department had come to? Chelomeyev had tried to do something more and look where it had got him.

But Rostoff shook his head. "It is not Bure. You may have heard about the murder of an old tribal woman in Biysk. It was on the news this morning."

The room ticked around them and the soft beeping of Chelomeyev's heart monitor ticked off the moments as Kazakov waited for Rostoff to explain himself. Biysk was a ski resort in the mountains enjoyed by Fergana's wealthy. The death of an elderly tribal woman should barely make the news at all.

When Kazakov didn't respond, Rostoff turned back to the window. Apparently, a slush-filled parking lot in the late afternoon's fading light was more interesting than Kazakov or Chelomeyev's room. Or perhaps safer.

"I received a call this afternoon from the Chief Inspector of the

Biysk Police Detachment. He has recently experienced a spate of retirements amongst his officers. He has no one with the experience to conduct a murder investigation and is seeking our assistance. You have something of a reputation for your interest in our tribal citizens and you did your part in the investigation into the explosions. I thought perhaps you would appreciate a lighter duty—given your recent injuries, of course."

Kazakov shifted where he stood. His side still ached from where he'd been shot four months ago. It had slowed him down, but he *was* recovering. He'd investigated Chelomeyev's beating last month and had chopped a cord of wood just this past weekend. Of course, now he paid the price in stiffness.

"And what of the investigation into the explosives? Who will pursue the source of the bombing plan? And what of the other missing explosives? They have not been found yet."

"I know. I know." Rostoff waved his questions away, his thick mop of hair shadowing his eyes. "But there are other detectives who can pursue this. You—you are a valuable commodity given how the tribals trust you."

The tribals. Therein lay the issue. He did not treat one Ferganese citizen differently from another. One might be a tall blonde Russian, the other a slight, darker skinned Kyrgyz descendent of ancient warriors or Sogdian Silk Road traders. They were all one and the same when it came to the law. Of course, not every detective saw it that way.

"Why this woman. Why now?"

"Kazakov, my old friend." Rostoff left his place by the window to cross to Chelomeyev's side. "You are entirely too suspicious. They asked and so I ask you. Will you help out our brethren in Biysk?"

And get his nose out of trouble in New Moscow. But that was left unsaid.

"And if I refuse?" Kazakov fingered the pages in the book of fairytales as he looked down at Chelomeyev. Let the young detective wake up. Let his mind be unimpaired.

Rostoff's gaze hardened. "There are those who say you should have retired after you were shot. So far I have denied them."

Kazakov sighed. Once he might have considered retirement, but at the moment there were undercurrents to his country that filled him with concern. He could not simply sit back in his dacha and allow ill things to happen. "Given the problems I cause you, I cannot see where sending me off to another department will enhance your reputation. At least not with that department." And Rostoff was all about enhancing people's views of himself.

Rostoff shook his head. "But you always tell me that you get results and that someone must take the side of victims even if they are tribal."

Kazakov rolled his gaze heavenward. It was unfortunately true. "All right. I'll leave first thing tomorrow, but on one condition. You must check on Chelomeyev regularly and keep me updated when I call."

Rostoff made grumbling noises but finally nodded. "Better if it was tonight. There are concerns that the entire tribal population could rise up and come down from the mountains. With the spring, the passes are opening."

"Tonight then." Kazakov glanced at Chelomeyev and nodded, though the chances of such an uprising were between slim and none in his estimation.

He touched Chelomeyev's hand. "It seems our reading sessions are to be interrupted old friend, but I will come back and finish the story of Pig Skin."

As if to prove he would uphold his end of the bargain, Rostoff snagged a chair and seated himself as if to assume Kazakov's role, but instead of reading to Chelomeyev he pulled a magazine from his coat's deep pockets and began scanning the pages. There was only so far the great Rostoff would go.

In silence, Kazakov turned away. There were many miles before him this night.

———

The village of Biysk lay southeast of New Moscow, deep inside the Alay Pamir Mountains. By the time Kazakov returned home to his dacha to pack and make arrangements with his neighbor Agafya Ryabokov to feed his cat, Koshka, it was full dark when the land lifted the road out of the fields and steppes that were the heartland of Fergana into the tall mountains that shielded that tender heart from the ravages of the Chinese Empire. It was well known that the Chinese had spread their fingers and spies into these mountains and there were rumors that they attempted to recruit the tribal people as their allies. Of course, there were also rumors that the Ottomans tried the same thing.

He had been driving five hours by the time he came over the pass that gave onto the village. To either side were the massive white peaks of the mountains hulking against the star-laden vastness of the sky. Ahead and below the road, a swath of electric lights pooled in the darkness along the edge of a river that he knew was likely still frozen as it bisected the valley floor. Contrary to the spring thaws that had occurred in the valley of Fergana, here heaped snow ran either side of the road and a thin layer of ice covered the pavement so that he had to slow the Perseus in the corners of the switchback turns that took him slowly down between the spruce trees that verged Biysk's valley.

Once the valley had been a pilgrim destination for Islamic true believers, for it was said that a saint had lived in the crags beyond the village. Others had said the epic hero, Manas, had stopped here to rest during his many battles against the Kipchaks and Mongols. With the advent of Russian Fergana, interest in the valley had waned, but the introduction of skiing from the Anglo-Germans had led to the development of the valley.

Kazakov slowed the Perseus to a crawl. He had brought his ex-wife, Annuschka, here for a holiday on their first anniversary and the lights had been a small huddle in the middle of the valley. Now they spread across its floor. Change had come to the valley.

He wondered what daylight would show.

He followed the switchbacks down to the valley floor, but a sudden abundance of roads turning off from the highway slowed him down. Signs advertised hot pools, hotels and resorts. The ski hill warranted its own broad avenue. Not where he planned to go.

Before leaving home, he had phoned ahead and made reservations at a small guesthouse that he remembered from long ago. It had been there that he had brought Annuschka—much to her displeasure, for the place held none of the amenities of home.

Following his own sense of direction, he wound through a maze of streets toward the river. Hotels and grand resorts grew up beside the road where once there had been fields of sheep and horses brought in from the hills. Before, the valley had been a patchwork of trees and fields. Now, in the darkness it seemed all that he could see were new structures and parking lots.

The road he followed dead-ended in a Y intersection by a thin line of naked trees. He stopped the vehicle and climbed out, sniffing the familiar scent of snow and pitchy woodsmoke. So not everything had changed. And over the purr of the Perseus's engine came the clear music of running water. There might still be deep snow on the ground, but the Biysk River's ice was breaking up. His breath steamed in the cold, but overhead the veil of stars was bound by a familiar crown of peaks.

That, at least, time had not changed.

Taking a guess as to the direction to turn, he took the eastward fork and found himself driving past behemoth resorts—some with bulbous rooflines reminiscent of New Moscow's false Saint Basil Cathedral— and all blazing with light as if they did not feel safe in their mountain surroundings. In daylight, hotel rooms would look out over the river and the mountains, but at night the drawn curtains apparently helped keep the frightening darkness at bay. Five minutes later, the resorts faded behind him and he found himself in an area that looked vaguely familiar.

Low, stone buildings stood back from a river that was known to flood in spring thaws. Chimneys uncoiled bluish smoke that rose half way to heaven and then spread across the valley. A few of the structures bore signs with expensive-sounding restaurant names, when they looked like the homesteads he remembered from before. Others still stood amid low stone walls with livestock loafing in the cold night air.

Kazakov sighed. He knew where he was now. He could spot a tribal ghetto a mile away. The original people of the valley had been locked away in a small enclave while the Russian well-to-do chipped at ghetto edges and bought up the rest of the valley. He kept going and found a cluster of small stone buildings close by the river and pulled over to the side of the road.

When he climbed out, all was silence except for the mutter of water and ice. Beyond the western peaks, a glow said where the moon had disappeared. He inhaled the cold night air and eased his shoulders. At least he felt whole and healed and ready to do what needed to be done.

His small valise in hand, he crunched down the side of the road until he spotted the long-remembered sign: *Guesthouse.* That was all it said. No reason to provide a fancy name to stand out when you were the only guesthouse in a small town.

He let himself through the cunningly-wrought stone wall by way of a wooden gate that squeaked in the night. A neatly shoveled flagstone walkway cut between four-foot snowbanks around the side of the house to a bright blue painted door under a single bare lightbulb.

Kazakov knocked once and listened to the stillness, soon broken from within the house by a hollow thump and then the quick thump-thump-thump of footfall.

The blue door pulled open revealing a crone of a woman with thick gray hair pulled into two loose braids, a nightdress and tattered felt robe were pulled around her wasted waist and sagging breasts.

"Yes?" She blinked owl eyes up at him from a rosy-cheeked face still very much as he remembered.

"Ayim Beshimov? Is it you?" He looked her up and down and it had to be, though there were ten years and countless lost pounds masking the diminutive woman he remembered. "It is Alexander Kazakov. I phoned about a room and we talked about the old days when I brought my wife to stay."

The owl expression wavered into something more akin to discomfort. "Yes. Yes, the detective. I remember now. Come in. Come in. Wood burns too quickly these days." She stepped aside to allow him to step past into the same immaculately scrubbed hallway he remembered.

Behind him, Ayim Beshimov clicked off the outside light and turned to face him. The hallway's stone and wood walls were scrubbed to shining. A single bulb swayed from a wire overhead, so light played across her face like a sea of expressions. Happy to see him? Sad?

Something about her suggested afraid.

He smiled at her. "When business brought me to Biysk again, I could not stay anywhere else but here."

Her wide gaze seemed to study him and then she nodded. "It is late. You must wish your room." As he removed his boots, she stepped past him and led him down the hall. "You asked for the room overlooking the river, but it is no longer available. My daughter lives there now with her family."

She led him to a door, swung it open and flicked on a light. Again, a single bulb hung from the ceiling of a ten-by-ten room. The comforting scent of burning wood came from a glowing fireplace against one wall. On top of the fireplace sat a kettle and warmth enveloped him. A single four-poster bed sat under the window set in the stone wall and a dresser sat against the unpainted wood wall beside the door. A clothing trunk was sandwiched between the foot of the bed and the door. Ayim Beshimov collected the kettle and poured hot water into a plain metal basin on top of the dresser.

"You wash here. There is tea, here. The washroom is down the hall as you likely recall." She motioned at a small wooden box above the dresser. "In the morning there is breakfast at seven-thirty. I will see you then."

With that, she backed from the room, pulling the door shut behind her. He stood there, listening to the shuffle of her feet down the hall, the opening and closing of another door and then silence enveloped him save for the sound of heat rushing up the metal chimney flue.

Sighing about the old saying that you could never go home again, he set his valise on the bed and began to unpack. He had to remind himself that it had been many years since he had been here and many things had obviously changed for both the valley and Ayim Beshimov.

He wasn't sure why he felt sad at the lack of welcome.

Watch for *The Tsarina's Mask* coming in March 2019.

TO MY READERS

1. Thank you for reading Mareson's Arrow. I hope you enjoyed it. If you did (and even if you didn't), it would be immensely helpful if you would leave a review. Reviews help other readers find this book.
2. Sign up for my Newsletter, and receive a free novel, a novella, and an award-nominated short story. To get your FREE eBOOKS, go to my website at www.karenlabrahamson.com.
3. While you're there, check out my website for information on my books, my adventures, and extra content.
4. For more links and offers, or to chat with me, check out Facebook at www.facebook.com/karenlabrahamson.

THE DETEKTIV KAZAKOV MYSTERY SERIES

Set in an alternate history Russia, the series introduces Detektiv Alexander Kazakov, a loner detective committed to finding the truth for the dead and murdered. The series takes place in a world where Catherine the Great's conquest of the Crimea woke the slumbering Ottoman Empire and brought the great Khans down upon Moscow. Two hundred years later the remains of the Russian population dream of Russia's past glories, while their new country of Fergana lays like the gristle in a joint between the rumblings of the Ottoman and Chinese Empires. The death of a young Russian girl sets Kazakov on a series of investigations that have implications for the entire world.

Books in the Series:
After Yekaterina
Mareson's Arrow
The Tsarina's Mask
Ivan's Wolf

ABOUT THE AUTHOR

Karen L. Abrahamson writes fantasy, romance, and mysteries as Karen L. Abrahamson and K.L. Abrahamson. Her best known books are the unique Cartographer series in which secret agents of the American Geological Survey use their powers to take on the purveyors of dark magic. Her romantic suspense and mysteries take readers on adventures to dangerous locations around the world.

Her short fiction has appeared in numerous magazines and anthologies; her short fantasy story "With One Shoe" was nominated for an Arthur Ellis Canadian Crime Fiction Award.

Karen's background includes time as a police officer, corrections officer, and probation/parole officer.

To find out more about her and her writing, visit www.karenlabrahamson.com

ALSO BY K.L. ABRAHAMSON

MYSTERY (WRITING AS **K.L.** ABRAHAMSON)

Phoebe Clay Mysteries

Through Dark Water

The Detektiv Kazakov Mysteries

After Yekaterina

Mareson's Arrow

The Tsarina's Mask

Ivan's Wolf

———

FANTASY MYSTERY (WRITING KAREN **L.** ABRAHAMSON)

The Aung and Yamin Mystery Series

Death By Effigy

A Death in Passing

Death in Umber

———

FANTASY (WRITING AS KAREN **L.** ABRAHAMSON)

The Cartographer Universe (in chronological order)

The Warden of Power

Impossible

The Cartographer's Daughter

The American Geological Survey Series:

Afterburn

Aftershock

Aftermath

Afterimage

Terra Incognita

Terra Infirma

Terra Nueva

Other Fantasy

Emberstone

Mutable Things

The Crystal Courtesan

Ice Dragon

ROMANCE, MYSTERY AND FANTASY
FROM TWISTED ROOT PUBLISHING

If you enjoyed this book, you might enjoy other titles available from
Karen L. Abrahamson in your local bookstore or wherever e-books are
sold or through
www.karenlabrahamson.com

*THROUGH DARK WATER: Eagles, Orcas and a killer stalk the
kayaking Mecca of Pirate's Cove, British Columbia. On a
holiday with her niece, school teacher Phoebe Clay has to solve
the case to protect herself and everything she loves. Find it at
http://www.karenlabrahamson.com/books/through-dark-water/*

AFTERBURN: Vallon Drake, agent of the American Geological Survey, the secret arm of Homeland Security that protects America from illicit changes to its landscapes, discovers her partner smothering in a wall. Now someone is rewriting the Seattle maps and killing AGS agents. Their actions threaten the safety of the entire Northwest and only rogue agent Vallon can stop it. Find it at http://www.karenlabrahamson.com/books/afterburn/

SHADOW PLAY: Star reporter Kaitlin Blackwood arrives in Cambodia and lands right in the case of her missing father. When men try to abduct her, the wrong man rescues her: B.J. McCallum, ex-man of her dreams, who comes with his own heap of trouble. The two must put aside their differences long enough to solve the case—and maybe save themselves in the process. Find it at http://www.karenlabrahamson.com/books/shadow-play/